Anna O...
Best Wishes
Lann C. Wright

Long Shot

A Katt and Mouse Mystery

By

L.C. Wright

Also by L.C. Wright

Castle Grey – A Katt and Mouse
Mystery

Monterey Madness – Mr. One Pocket

Publishers Note

To Melissa for her love and support.

In memory to my nephew, Joseph
Brandenburg. His family misses him dearly.

Prologue

With every job comes a challenge; every assignment a flaw. The shooter believed that this was one of those cases. The time of day was wrong—it was never good to scope into the sun. The target was too far away for the conditions—strong winds. Most important, he didn't have the time to plan as was necessary. It was all wrong.

Now it was too late.

He had made shots from this distance. Eight hundred yards, though considered extreme for everyone but the most skilled shooters, wasn't even half the distance he had used for his longest successful target—kill.

But this job was different. This time he would only have a few seconds to make two kill shots. At such a distance, the odds of success were damn near impossible.

The afternoon sun layered shadows across the steps of the courthouse. The autumn sun hung low in the sky, which offered no help in the form of clouds. The front of the building faced east as if giving homage to the powers in Washington from which the structure emulated. But unlike the grand erection of the Supreme Court, the Montgomery County Probate Courthouse in Dayton, Ohio was both smaller in size and under most circumstance held cases reflecting little of national import.

Dayton Salazar, attorney at law, so named by grateful immigrant parents, was conducting a trial that would be the exception to the rule. As lead counsel for the prosecution, he was smiling as he and his co-counsel exited the building. In very short order, he was confident that Boyd Weapons Manufacturers, LLC would not only be shut down once and for all for the crimes from which they had profited, but the president of the company, Jason Boyd, would also be convicted of murder and conspiracy to commit murder. It was a banner day because Salazar had just laid out the facts, and the facts unequivocally said…guilty. Seldom had weapons companies ever lost in court, but prosecuting attorney, Dayton Salazar, believed this case would be the one to put him in the record books.

When the 180 grain, 7.62mm round entered his head, Salazar was still smiling. The expression only changed a little by the time the man hit the ground.

The second member of the district attorney's team was Melissa Pound, daughter of retired military police officer and general, Robert Pound, and witness to the brutal slaying of her boss and close friend. She was also the beneficiary of having lived in a family that comprised of three generations of cops.

Had she been looking in the other direction, things would have been different.

But she was looking. She was looking directly at Salazar when circumstances changed her life forever.

Her eyes saw the immediate appearance of a hole in her boss and mentor's head. She felt the splatter of tiny droplets of blood—more like a red mist—as the bullet exited Salazar's brain and hit her face. And though her mind had a difficult time processing the information it was receiving, it wasn't the first time she had seen it.

Had the shooter chosen her as the first target, Melissa would have been just as dead as her friend. Because she had been selected second, maybe because she was younger or for any number of reasons, she was given enough time to realize what was going on and reflexively dropped before she knew why.

The second round was on target when the shooter pulled the trigger. What he couldn't do was change the trajectory once the bullet left the barrel. A lot can happen in the half a second it takes a projectile to leave the barrel of a rifle until it finishes its travels to the target. The mark was set. The outcome defined. Fortunately for Melissa Pound, the intended target, her head was no longer where it was supposed to be. The half a second was all the time needed to drop enough for the bullet to miss. It was close enough that the trajectory singed a hole through her closely cropped hair, just above the scalp.

Three steps above her feet, the explosion caused by the impact of copper and lead hitting concrete was followed by a ricochet that sent the projectile back to the defenseless young woman, entering her back and lodging painfully near her heart.

From that distance, the shooter once again reviewed his handiwork. Two rounds—two down. No one was moving. Both targets were bleeding. His job was complete. It was time to move on to the next job.

Two hours after the shooting at the courthouse, Joseph Brandenburg was at home cleaning his rifle. He had finished what his contemporaries would have considered a good day of hunting. It wasn't every day that a rifleman could go out and bag two moving targets so close together. It was a treat. He had been doing it for so long— killing—that it felt second nature. The difference now; he wasn't doing it for the government. He was doing the job for himself.

Of course, the money he was being paid more than kept him supplied with his modest needs.

Chapter 1

The tall blond strutted confidently into the book store knowing that she was about to make the deal she had been working on for the last three months. Her Ralph Lauren attire came straight from the Josephine collection featuring the dark chocolate pants and jacket that showed a hint of light tan stripes. The matching shoes, purse and even the hat she wore presented a woman of means.

The bookstore, Madison's, dealt in high-end, first edition books, and catered only to the most affluent clients. Douglas Ramsey, the proprietor, had met the blond, whom he had only known as Katherine on several occasions. He also knew that her visit had nothing to do with books. Ramsey also dealt in other commodities; items that someone of means— someone like Katherine—would be looking to acquire.

The smallish, weasel of a man smiled when he looked up from the magazine he was reading. As usual, he turned back to the counter behind him and lathered his hands with *Purell* so that any flesh-eating bacteria, of which he was so afraid, would be quickly killed. It was his ritual, and he was not ashamed to admit it.

He spoke to the tall blond as if their conversation was a continuation of something they had been discussing all along.

"I swear I don't understand why the government doesn't make the use of this product a law punishable by imprisonment for not using. Think of the savings we would have from unnecessary hospital visits alone."

"Douglas...how *are* you this fine day?" Katherine asked as she approached the proprietor and air-kissed each cheek.

"I'm doing well," he replied, knowing that he was about to make the biggest sale of his life. "I have a few items you might find interesting as a matter of fact; in addition to what we've already discussed. If you have a few moments, I would be honored if you would peruse them."

Katherine smiled at the man and said, "I would be honored."

Ramsey walked to the front of the building, pulled the shade, and locked the front door. The store was located on Francis Street in the old-town section of Annapolis, Maryland. Less than a block from where they stood was the historic State House, the oldest continuously used state capital building in the country. But even with such high visibility, the place seldom enjoyed much in the form of street traffic. When business *was* conducted, his secondary business, Ramsey wanted no distractions from the commoners that typically walked through his doors.

Ramsey then turned to Katherine and said, "Follow me," as he passed his beautiful new client and headed toward the rear of the building; never glancing back to see if she was there.

Pausing for only the few seconds it took to unlock the steel plated door to his private area, Ramsey turned and smiled. "I know you are a person used to enjoying the finest that life has to offer," he said. "However, I doubt that even you have been blessed with the sights I'm about to show you. I'm sure that asking you to use discretion once the item has been revealed is unnecessary. I simply like to make sure everyone is working from the same page…so to speak."

"Discretion has never been a problem for me, Mr. Ramsey," Katherine replied with a smile. "My concern is making sure that you haven't brought me back here as an effort to offer something other than what we've contracted for. If you are, I can assure you that your day would end a lot less comfortable than it began. Is that clear?"

Ramsey saw, maybe for the first time, that the cool lady had a streak of cruelty he had never seen before. It chilled him to the bone.

"I can assure *you*, ma'am, that is not the case. Your coins are here, and we will do the arrangement exactly as we discussed. I simply thought you might want to consider another purchase once you've seen what I recently acquired. As a matter of fact, it is because of you that I was willing to take a risk and procured the items in the first place. I hope I have not been too presumptuous."

"As long as we are of an understanding, then my time is yours." Katherine smiled again, only this time the threat in her eyes was obvious, and Ramsey flinched at the recognition.

Unlocking a drawer and then retrieving a dark, wooden box, Ramsey looked to the woman in hopes that he had made the right choice. He was then surprised when her phone buzzed, and without hesitation on her part, she answered. The flash of anger he showed was brief, and he hoped the tall blond hadn't seen it. For some reason, he knew something had gone terribly wrong.

Standing before him, the woman no longer seemed like the elegant, classy goddess he thought she was. Now she was something else—something terrible. Maybe it was the large, dark hole at the end of the gun she was holding, pointing directly at his face that gave him a sense of dread.

"What's the problem?" Katherine Katt of the FBI asked. Ramsey could only hear her side of the conversation, but he knew it wasn't good. "Now? I'm almost done here." Katt listened for several moments and then said, "If you mess this up, I'll shoot you myself." Then, "Okay…take care of it."

"It's really not necessary to point that at me," Ramsey stated, as the weasel slowly inched his raising hands. "I'm not a violent man."

"My day has just gotten a lot more congested, Mr. Ramsey. You said you had something to show me. How's about we get to that part…now!"

Ramsey jumped at the woman's harshness and opened the wooden box he still held. Inside the box was a red velvet bag with a rope-tie holding it together. Katt wondered what it was she had stumbled upon. Ramsey untied the bag and poured onto the table before him a single diamond, more beautiful than anything she had ever seen. It was so large, she wondered if it could actually be real. If so, it would be priceless.

Katt stepped closer to get a better look. "I'm going to assume for the moment that it's real, and you're under the impression that by showing it to me that I'll somehow want to make a deal for it."

"Have you ever heard of The Centenary Diamond that was discovered in 1986?" Ramsey asked.

"Hasn't everyone?" Katt replied. In fact, she had heard of it but knew very little about the discovery or the people involved.

"That stone was discovered in the Premier Mine, in Africa. The rough diamond weighed in at five-hundred ninety nine carats. It was then cut down to a flawless two-hundred seventy-three point eighty-five carats."

"That information may be useful at a social event or maybe if I ever get on the Jeopardy show; otherwise it's not of much use."

"What nobody knows is that when the Centenary was discovered…she had a brother called the Centurion. This stone and a half a dozen just like it, only slightly smaller, have recently been obtained for someone just like you to enjoy. Now…would you please put down your gun before it accidentally goes off?"

"If this goes off," Katt said, quickly glancing at her weapon, "it will never be because of an accident. Now…I take it that you have 'acquired' these stones at a considerable discount of which you will insist on passing along to me?" Katt questioned the sleazy proprietor.

"It just so happens that I've done exactly that," Ramsey smiled, though the sweat on his brow revealed that he was still not sure if the woman was going to shoot him.

"I'll tell you what," Katt said while returning to her persona of a rich and powerful buyer. She placed the handgun back into her purse and smiled at the weasel of a man. "Let's take care of the business at hand. My client, the reason for the call that just came in, is a bit antsy for the coins you promised. Assuming that everything is fine with them, I'll let you live long enough to make me a very good deal on the diamonds. As long as you do not try to cheat me, Mr. Ramsey, I think we could have a prosperous relationship."

"I take it you have the money we discussed?"

"Of course. Let me check out the merchandise, and then I will make the transfer like we agreed. Five hundred thousand dollars will be transferred to the accounts of your choice. The one hundred thousand dollars in cash you wanted will be brought to you by courier after I leave."

"I don't like that you didn't bring it with you," Ramsey frowned.

"Take heed, Mr. Ramsey, I didn't expect to leave here with you being alive. I thought you were lying to me. And the verdict still isn't finalized. I expected you to be lying, and then I would have shot you dead for disappointing me. Are you starting to realize how serious I am, Mr. Ramsey? I will make this deal with you. I will let you live. I will discuss with you what I can do for your diamonds. If you want to live through all of this, remember, never lie to me. Never cheat me. And above all else…never disappoint me."

Katt watched the droplet of sweat as it landed on the toe of the man's shoe and smiled.

Chapter 2

It had been months since Mickey James, the Sacramento detective and local hero, had returned to home from the adventure he shared with the beautiful and intelligent FBI Agent, Katherine Katt. In the short time they worked together, he had gone from hating the assignment to developing a curiosity about the agent, and then finally finding himself completely enamored by her. From the beginning, when she got right back in his face telling him about the history of his namesake, Mickey Mantle, he knew that she was different. When she saved his life, not once, but several times, he realized that he needed her to be a part of his world.

He didn't think it was love he felt. He didn't know what it was. What he did know is that if she asked him to do anything, he would jump without hesitation.

So what do you call that?

After she left and returned to the J. Edgar Hoover building in Washington, they had managed to stay in touch—frequently. As time went by, however, the calls became less and less frequent, and now it had been over a month since they last talked. James didn't understand what had happened, and the not knowing was driving him mad.

Along with the reduction of phone time, James' mood deteriorated at a rate even more severe. His cronies watched daily in anticipation of the decorated detective's call from the woman he now adored. As far as they were concerned, Katherine Katt of the FBI dictated just how good or bad their day would be.

"I feel like a fuckin' teenager," James spat to his new partner, Lenny Duncan. "I'm really beginning to think this whole thing with Katt was a huge mistake."

"So what're you gonna do about it?" Duncan asked. "The heart wants what the heart wants."

"Bullshit!" James replied. "You've been watching too much Dr. Phil crap. That kind of B.S. is what gives men a bad reputation. What I need to do is send her a 'thanks, but no thanks' e-mail and move on to greener pastures."

"Dumping a woman, especially a beautiful woman like Katt, by e-mail is all kinds of wrong."

"Who said anything about dumping her? Don't you actually have to be *with* someone, and I mean in the biblical sense, before you can dump someone. This would be more like a fond farewell."

James glanced around the corner of the abandoned hotel's hallway long enough to see the man they were chasing, aim to fire. He pulled back his head less than a second before the shot clipped the corner of the wall several inches from where he had been. Most men would have taken that as a sign to get their act together before they got themselves killed.

Not James.

"I mean, seriously, who the hell does she think she is?" James continued as he glanced again and realized that the shooter had moved on. James moved forward up the hallway and kept talking. "What does a guy have to do to convince a woman that she's important to someone like me?"

"Maybe she needs something more," Duncan replied. "Maybe you should consider moving to Washington. Long distant relationships seldom work out."

Another glance around the next corner, James saw that the man was cornered and dodged another shot. Talking to the criminal, James said, "Listen, asshole, you've got nowhere to run anymore. Drop your weapon now and you may live through the day. If you take one more shot at me, I'm going to get really pissed off."

There was no verbal reply, but the two consecutive shots followed by the click of an empty gun were all James needed to advance into the room. The man was in the process of reloading.

"Drop your weapon," James shouted, but the man kept working at his task. "Are you deaf or simply stupid?" James couldn't believe that the shooter was paying him no attention and finally managed to get the clip out of his pocket. When the clip slid into the grip and the slide was released, the man finally looked up and saw that he was facing down the barrels of the two cop's pistols. "I said drop it, asshole, and I won't tell you again."

James was a seasoned veteran. He knew when a perpetrator was thinking about what to do when his life was flashing before his eyes. It generally came down to one of two choices; live a life in prison or die. James also knew when the decision was made and didn't like what he saw.

James had never liked killing another human being. It wasn't as if he had never done it. He just didn't *like* doing it.

On the other hand, he didn't like the idea of getting shot either. He had recently been through that ordeal and had no intentions of going through it again. Beside, James needed the man alive. Scumbag or not, the man had information he needed.

How it happened, James could only speculate. The noise was deafening when Lenny Duncan pulled the trigger. The shooter was hit and spun like a top before hitting the floor. The entire event was slow in James' mind. He just could not believe that it had happened without being the one doing the shooting. That just wasn't like him.

Duncan walked over to the fallen criminal and kicked his gun away from where he had landed. James approached, expecting to see a dead criminal, and saw that the guy wasn't dead. As a matter of fact, he was writhing in pain from the very large bullet hole in the right shoulder—his shooting arm.

James looked at Duncan and asked, "Why did you shoot him in the shoulder? Procedure dictates the use of lethal force when confronted with a deadly situation."

"It seemed like the thing to do," Duncan shrugged his shoulder. "We need him to talk to us, and I figured he wouldn't be able to do that if he was dead."

"That's true," James countered, thinking about how it went down and why it was that he wasn't the one doing the shooting. A moment later, he added, "I screwed up. I should have taken the shot."

"Does it matter?" Duncan replied. "You? Me? What does it matter?"

"It matters because I took too long to think about what I needed to do. This shit with Katt is making me vulnerable. It's making me a bad partner. Maybe you should be looking for someone else to cover your back."

"Maybe you should take a trip to Washington and figure out where things stand."

"I don't…" James' cell phone rang. When he looked at the number, he smiled. It was Robert Pound, his uncle. "Hey Robert…long time no hear…"

"Melissa's been shot Mickey," his uncle interrupted. "I need you to come to Dayton."

"I'll be on the next flight," James replied. He then asked, "Is she going to make it?"

The Dayton International Airport was not actually located in Dayton. For the brave souls that choose to venture there, they would find that it was several miles north of Dayton just outside the town of Vandalia, Ohio. James knew that as well as knowing that to get from the airport to the Miami Valley Hospital, a cab ride would cost about as much as a rental. Knowing that he would be there for several days, he opted for renting. When he tried to squeeze into the small economy car they offered, he went back to the counter and changed to the much more expensive and much roomier town car. James could never be considered ostentatious, but the Caprice he wanted had already been rented out. Given the situation, he decided he could live with the flash.

James had a lot of vacation time saved up. He had considered his partner's idea of flying to Washington to visit Katt, but his cousin's situation took priority. Robert explained the circumstances of the shooting and that the locals had no idea who the perpetrator might be. James never hesitated to help his uncle out. He loved his cousin, Melissa, and the idea that she might not live through the injury was killing him inside.

After arriving, James picked up his service weapon that he had checked and then got in the rental and took the I-75 south. To him, the whole area looked like mid-America suburbia. Not knowing a quicker route, he exited east on I-35 before taking the South Main Street exit.

Miami Valley is a sprawling hospital and James had no history there. He relied on signage to get him through the parking maze, and was surprised that it had not been as difficult to circumnavigate the place as he expected.

James had taken the red-eye flight from Sacramento and was fortunate that most of the commuter traffic that morning was heading the other way. He was running on adrenaline because the last he had heard, his cousin was listed as critical, and the doctors told his uncle that making it through the night was little better than fifty-fifty. Those weren't the doctor's exact words. It was how Uncle Robert had translated them.

When he arrived in the ICU his uncle was sitting beside Melissa's bed, and James realized that the man was openly weeping. The hero cop thought he was too late.

Robert Pound was James' mother's brother. Robert had known James' father when they were in the military, and that's how his mother and father were introduced. It was a very short relationship—three months—when James' parents decided to get married. Most people thought they did it because she was pregnant. It wasn't. James wasn't born until three years later. They married because they didn't want to be apart, and the military had rules about the people you brought with you from post to post.

"I gave him time alone," the familiar voice of Katherine Katt said from behind. "It's been a long night for everybody."

"When did she die?" James asked in reply. His heart was aching as he turned to look into her deep blue eyes. He was too late to say goodbye, and the idea felt like someone was squeezing the air from his lungs. What he got in return was a look of confusion.

"She didn't," Katt said. "She isn't…dead. Mr. Pound is simply exhausted, and the doctor just told him that everything looks good. She's not totally out of the woods, that may take another day or so, but he says she should fully recover."

"Oh. My. God," James sighed. "When I saw him crying I just knew I was too late."

"It was nip and tuck for a while. The bullet did some damage. At first, they weren't sure if they were able to close down all of the bleeding. It was a ricochet. When it entered her body it had already been smashed to bits. The size of the wound was pretty big and hit her near several vital organs. They weren't sure what kind of damage went on in there and weren't sure if they were able to close everything. It looks like they did."

There were so many conflicting thoughts running through his mind, James wasn't sure what to say or what to do. He needed answers. Why was Katt at his cousin's bedside? Where had she been? Why hadn't she called him if she knew he would be there? Why hadn't she called him...period? Too many questions and yet none important enough to ask aloud.

Katt also had questions that needed answered. Why was James here in Dayton? When did he get here? Who are these people that would cause him to leave California? In time, she would ask. For the time being, she just wanted to spend some time with him. The questions could wait.

Katt moved in to give James a hug. She had missed him. Instead of accepting the offer, he turned his back to her and faced the room where Melissa slept and said, "I'm going to step in for a minute and talk to Robert. It's been a long night. I'll talk to you later."

Katt watched as James walked into the room; feeling the cold shoulder he offered. She knew that she hadn't called James in some time and believed he should understand the nature and long hours of undercover work. If the shoe was on the other foot, she would understand; maybe she wouldn't like it, but would understand.

Why was he being so cold?

Rather than be distracted with personal matters, Katt left the men to discuss whatever had drawn them together. She had her work to do. There was a killer on the loose, and he was carrying a very big gun.

Chapter 3

"I did as you requested," Katt said when her boss, Jonathan Blythe answered the phone. "I've seen the crime scene. I've talked to the locals pretending to be a reporter instead of an FBI agent; which got me nowhere, by the way. Maybe you can tell me what's going on now."

There was a long pause on the other end of the call before Blythe answered her questions.

"There's something going on, Katt," her boss started. "We've had shootings just like this in Atlanta, Chicago and Los Angeles. Until now, the victims have always been random. The shooter comes to town, picks a target, and then moves on to somewhere else. Not one of the targets has been anything more than your average Joe on the street."

"So what makes this shooting different?" Katt asked as she contemplated the man's words.

"This is the first time that the target has been a high priority person. The victim on this case is a government employee. He's never done that before. This time he actually tried to kill two at one time. He's never done that either."

"Is the bureau involved with those cases too?"

"Yes. We have a team doing what they can to break down each of those shootings and running with them."

"Then why am I here? You know what I was working on in Annapolis. I just hope I didn't blow my cover running out the way I did."

"It's a risk we'll have to take." Blythe replied. "It's a risk *I'll* have to take. I know what's at stake there. I think this is more important."

"What aren't you telling me?" Katt asked. She could sense the hesitation in his voice. As a forensics psychiatrist, she had been taught to read a person's voice just as well as that person's body language. Add to it that she had known her mentor since she was a child; she knew something was bothering him.

Again there was a long wait. Katt didn't interrupt his thought process.

"I'm not sure," Blythe finally said. "I'm sending you everything the other team has on the other shootings. What I need from you is perspective. I need you to tell me what they aren't picking up on. I want you to tell me if they've missed anything."

"And…" Katt coaxed.

"I want you to tell me if it's the same shooter."

"You think this one might be someone else?"

"I think we need to cover all the bases," he replied with what Katt could only take as a rehearsed line. "I need you to be ready for anything Katt. I also need you to be careful. Something's wrong with this case, and I want you to figure out what it is."

"I've never been involved with a sniper case, sir. I don't know if I'm the best person for this assignment."

"You know people, Katt. That's what I need more than anything. You'll figure out the rest."

Blythe didn't wait for Katt to answer before disconnecting the call. He sat back in his chair and stared out the window. He wasn't sure. He just hoped that he wasn't sending Katt to her death. The problem was…he simply didn't have a choice.

"I'm glad you're here," Robert said after James gave the man a big hug.

"I wasn't sure I was going to make it in time," James replied. "How did this happen?"

Robert told the detective what little he knew; Melissa was coming out of the courthouse, her friend was shot first, and it somehow missed her. The damage was done by a ricocheted bullet that lodged in her back near her heart. He told how the duo was working on a big case against a weapons manufacturer and thought they had the owner dead to rights. Now…he wasn't sure what would happen with the case.

"Do the cops know anything about the shooter?"

"Only that he made the shots from about five hundred yards in a relatively strong wind—maybe fifteen miles per hour."

James blew out a whistle. "That's a hell of a shot. Not many could make it. How did he miss Melissa?" James asked and yet was concerned how his uncle would take the bluntness of the question.

"Training," Robert replied as if he held a family secret.

James had been taught the same lessons when he was a child too.

He smiled knowingly.

Robert Pound was no stranger to violence. Having spent nearly thirty-five years in the U.S. Air Force's Security Force—their equivalent to the Army's Military Police—and retired as a Brigadier General, he had seen more violence than most.

Brigadier General Pound (retired) held one of the most prestigious positions in the Air Force when he took over command of the country's largest air force base—Wright Patterson AFB. Right after graduation from the academy, Pound was stationed at the base for six years before traveling the world and advancing up the chain of command. As a colonel, he requested to bring his family back to Ohio. He loved the area and decided that it was where he wanted to retire.

His daughter, Melissa, enjoyed the area and the schools she attended. Her mother, Juanita, did not want to be a world traveler and made her home at the base. Her fast rising husband was able to fly home frequently from wherever he was stationed and not disrupt their daughter's life.

After graduating Ohio State University with honors, Melissa then went to Harvard Law to get her degree. Never once did she think about practicing away from home. She merely wanted to get the best education she could get before saving the world.

The thirty-something woman made the law her passion and, like her father, was moving up the ladder to become something special in the Attorney General's Office.

"Why would someone want to do this?" Robert asked James. "It doesn't make sense."

"I don't need to answer that, do I?" James replied. "You've been around the block enough."

There are six dirt roads that bisect Blacksmith Hill Road near Ross Lake, Ohio and Joseph Brandenburg lived near the end of one of them. The reasons he had for wanting—needing—the seclusion were carefully hidden in a file known only to Brandenburg and the U. S. Government. He had spent thirteen years as their go-to guy when the problems they encountered seemed untenable. He was never good around crowds and loved the seclusion his job had given him. Now that he was out of the military, he enjoyed the freedom his little part of the world provided.

His home, located in the middle of a forty-five acre tract of land that butted up against the state forest, was small by most people's standards. The wood-framed home displayed what might once, a very long time ago, have been red-painted plank exterior walls. They now looked to be more like a mottled brick in color—where color still existed—and some sort of soft, brownish-colored, indistinct wood.

The less-than-lavish interior boasted two rooms, the first being a small lavatory with a sink and toilet, and the second room being everything else. The wood-plank floor was covered with a single, outdated piece of linoleum Brandenburg had found rolled up in a neighbor's barn. Its sole purpose was to discourage rodents and winter winds from entering without at least some effort. Seldom did the wind, or the rodents, pay it any heed. The home, if anyone could actually call it that had the benefit of electricity, but the man seldom used it. To him, the only things he needed, the land provided.

Brandenburg had few friends and even fewer visitors, so it was a surprise when he noticed the headlights of a car bouncing frantically up his drive.

"Where've you been, Joseph?" his sister Debbie asked excitedly as she exited the worn Chevy. "I was here yesterday, and you were gone."

"Hunting," Brandenburg replied without elaboration. The ex-SEAL had never been much of a talker. He loved his sister—in a fight-to-the-bitter-end-but-nobody-else-can sort of way. However, by his way of thinking, she talked too much. Then again, by his way of thinking, everyone else did too.

"Your truck was gone."

"It usually is when I go somewhere."

"You *never* take your truck anywhere."

"And your point?"

"The point is; you weren't here. Did anybody else see you?"

"Not if I can help it."

Debbie walked up to her brother, ignoring the Winchester 30-30 he held, and gave her brother a hug. Whispering in his ear, she said, "Tell me you didn't do it, Joseph. Tell me you didn't kill those people yesterday."

Joseph pushed Debbie to arm's length and said, "I didn't kill anyone yesterday. Why don't you come in and tell me what you're talking about?"

Debbie looked through the open door and noticed the other rifle resting easy against the rack where it belonged. She knew what her brother did for the government before he left. One night in a drunken rage he told her all about it—the killings. He never told her the details, but then she didn't want to know them either. However, she knew *it* was the gun responsible for over a hundred deaths. She would have been astounded if she ever found out the real total. It was the one she wanted more than anything for her brother to destroy. "It keeps me grounded," Brandenburg would say. "If it's here, it ain't out there somewhere killing someone else."

There was something else that bothered Debbie. Besides knowing how to look through a scope and pulling a trigger with the deadliest of accuracy, she also knew that her baby brother was an accomplished liar. The military taught him well; well enough to trick a lie detector. All she could do now was pray that this wasn't one of those times.

Chapter 4

Katt was confused by the way James had turned his back. At best he was dismissive—at worst derisive. Of course, they hadn't talked in a while, but that was the nature of the job. Sometimes, especially with undercover work, there would be long periods when either one of them would be out of contact. James would know that.

Maybe he's upset about something else.

Katt finished looking over the crime scenes— the courthouse steps where the victims were located when they were shot, and the church's bell tower where the shots had taken place. She left the hospital and from there drove straight to the Montgomery County Sheriff's Office, the department that had expressed vehemently from the beginning that they were the ones who would be in charge of the investigation. Katt had considered it surprising, considering that the crime had occurred within the city's boundaries, but figured it would be explained once she arrived.

"We didn't request the FBI," Sheriff Doug Martin said as he returned her ID, having given it a thorough look-see. "We are quite capable of handling our misfortunes without federal involvement."

Katt eyed the robust man trying to determine her best approach. She knew that the situation was about as political as it could get. The problem for her was that from all indications, the crime was similar to three other cases already being worked by the bureau, and her hope was to see if this one would be added to the list. If so, she would not need the surly man's permission. Unfortunately, there was enough dissimilarity to prevent her from doing that.

"I realize that, Sheriff," Katt replied. "I'm not here to interfere with the investigation or take it over. I'm strictly here for observation. The FBI is looking at this to see if it's a copy of other cases we're working on. For now, however, I, along with the bureau, would be happy to assist any way we can. I could maybe do a profile on the shooter if we eventually get enough information to warrant one. That's if you haven't caught the guy already." She smiled, hoping to disarm the local cop.

"That's mighty nice of you," the Sheriff drawled his words a little longer than necessary. Katt suspected that the man was attempting the 'good ol' boy' routine to give the appearance of ignorance. "Dumb like a fox" was Katt's immediate assessment, but kept the thought to herself. "If we get to the point where we're in need of the big guns…we'll let you know."

"Then maybe you can answer this for me, Sheriff. Why is the county taking jurisdiction of the case when the crime occurred in the city? Doesn't that seem strange?"

"Maybe it would in some places. But in Ohio, our rules work a little different than the places you've probably been. Here, the law states that jurisdiction goes to the presiding location of the crime. That would be Montgomery County."

"But isn't Dayton the overriding jurisdiction. Even though the city resides in the county, wouldn't the city be in charge?"

The sheriff looked at Katt as if she were an adolescent trying to figure out the workings of adulthood.

"That's a very good observation, young lady," the sheriff condescended. Katt got the feeling that the sheriff considered her a child. "However, the courthouse is owned by the county. Therefore, jurisdiction is ours."

"Except the actual shooting took place on city property," Katt observed.

"That's why we think it should be our crime scene," Katt turned around to see a not-so-tall, skinny man wearing a cowboy hat and looked like he had just dropped his date off at the local rodeo.

Standing next to him was an attractive six-foot gentleman wearing an expensive dark suit. His attire looked like it came from the FBI's clothing department store—except for the Bolo tie. Katt couldn't remember the last time she had actually seen anyone wearing one, other than her last trip to New Mexico.

"And who might you be?" Katt smiled at the intruders.

Cowboy hat introduced himself as William "Bill" Stetson and emphatically explained that somewhere along the line he was related to the folks who made the hats. Unfortunately, he had not been able to find the lineage to prove it.

Standing next to him, Mr. Bolo tie introduced himself as Mike Williams from the Ohio Bureau of Investigation. "BCI for short," Williams smiled as he shook Katt's hand. "I take it you're the FBI lady everyone's talking about?"

"Why would anyone be talking about me?" Katt asked. "I just got here a little while ago."

"Humble *and* cute," Stetson smiled. "I thought all FBI people were tiresome and humorless. I may have to rethink my position and send them an application."

"So then we'd have what…two waggish agents with good looks?"

"I'm not sure what waggish means," BCI Williams laughed, "but his tongue sure fit the bill when he saw you for the first…"

"That's enough gentlemen," the humorless sheriff interceded. "Agent Katt isn't here to join your little band of merriment. She's here to help us catch a killer. Does anybody object?"

"I sure don't mind," Stetson replied while looking at Katt from head to toe. It didn't seem to bother him that she stood as tall as he did. "Then again, I don't seem to have that right." Stetson turned and glared at the sheriff. Katt was surprised at how quick his temperament changed. "You've been pretty insistent that your department take charge of this case, and I don't agree. We have as much right to handle this as you."

"And that's why I'm here," Williams said. "The BCI will take charge. I've already talked to the A.G. and he knows that the two of you would never back down. Consider me a preemptive strike so the case doesn't get bogged down."

"Bullshit!" Martin yelled. "I would rather have the feebs run the show than you. All you guys are doing is taking credit for my case."

Katt watched the men spitting as they yelled at each other. It seemed unusual that there would be such hostility between them. She decided to intervene.

"Gentlemen!" Katt had to yell to get their attention. "What's the problem here?"

"The problem, little lady," Martin glared at Katt. "Is that it was my people shot out there, and they want to castrate my men before we even get a fighting chance to catch the son of a bitch who did it."

"Is that right, Mr. Williams?"

"It's Agent Williams, and no…there will be no castration involved. Look…here's the thing. As far as the attorney general is concerned, the victims are his people. He doesn't see them as county employees. He sees them as people he works with every day. Dayton Salazar was his friend." Williams paused to take a breath. "As for Michelle Pound…the entire office was—is—of the opinion that she will someday be sitting in the AG's office. They're a close group. And I, for one, do not want this case fucked up for political or power grandstanding."

"That's not what I was doing," Martin replied a little sheepishly after hearing what the BCI agent had to say. "I just want to catch the sumbitch. That's all."

"I think," Katt figured it was time to insert her capabilities a little. "This case has the potential of being explosive. Each of you has legitimate reasons for your position. As an outsider, may I offer an idea that might help?"

Each of them looked at the tall, blond agent, but none was willing to acquiesce. Finally, they all nodded.

"I'm not interested in this case from a bureau standpoint. It is, however, showing similarities to other cases we're working, but for now, unless things change, I will stay as an outsider yet available to offer what assistance the bureau and I can. As for who's in charge, it doesn't matter right now. Let's see where the evidence takes us. Let it determine who takes the lead. Until then, all that matters is the victims.

"After giving it some thought, I couldn't help but wonder how a case like this could be handled given the state's system for solving cases. Generally, I can see where the system would work—deal with what's on your turf and ask for help when you need it. That's okay, but whether by intent or default, this shooter's putting each organization under duress. By simply getting you all involved, he's created chaos that would take most systems days to work through, thereby buying more time to disappear. If he did it on purpose, the man is organized and highly intelligent. To catch him, we need the best each of us has to offer.

"Having said that, it seems to me that the BCI would be the logical choice to head the investigation. But like I said, right now it doesn't matter. I know I have no standing here. That's clear. But the longer you men stand around with your measuring sticks, arguing about who's in charge, the more time your killer has to get away with murder."

Katt took a step away from the men and gave them time to think about what they wanted to do.

With just the short time she'd had to cold read them, she hoped it was enough.

It wasn't.

"Well that was a real pretty speech, little lady" Martin said. "However, you don't know the way things are around here. And frankly, given that the AG has personal issues with the deceased, that's all the more reason that the BCI should not be handling the case."

"That's absurd!" Williams spat at the sheriff. "All you're interested in being the next election."

"I'm not interested in any elections," Stetson offered. "So with me taking the case, we can move forward without the emotional baggage or the politics getting in the way."

"Let me know what you gentlemen decide," Katt said as she left the room. "I'll be out there trying to catch your killer."

The men turned toward Katt and watched her leave the room.

"Women," Stetson said without mirth. "They can't handle a good debate."

Chapter 5

"You have to leave," Debbie told her brother. "They're gonna figure out that there're not that many people who could've made a shot like that. They'll come for you."

"Where would you have me go?" Brandenburg asked. "I can't hide forever. Hell I can't hide at all. There's no place I can run that they couldn't find me."

"You have to try."

"Why? I haven't done anything wrong. I'm sure they'll look at me and if they do…fine."

"It's not fine!" Debbie stood and shook her head. "You're a loner. A recluse. You don't have any witnesses to support where you were yesterday."

"I'm sure everything will be okay," Brandenburg stood and circled his arms around his sister. "They can't prove I did anything and they sure as hell can't convict me for something I didn't do."

"You're a fool, Joseph Brandenburg! They can and they will if they can't find anyone else. These were important people that got shot. If you think for a moment that your precious government won't hang you out to dry, you're a bigger fool than I thought."

"Just how big a fool did you think I was?"

Debbie looked at her brother, confused.

"I'm just trying to get an idea about how big a fool you think I am now. But to do that, I need an idea on where the marker starts."

The man smiled at his sister in an attempt to ease her fears. It didn't help.

"Don't make fun of me, mister. I don't want anything bad happening to you. Do you understand?"

"Of course. Now go home and stop worrying. There's nothing we can do now. If anything happens, I'll be sure to let you know."

Brandenburg watched as his sister headed down the long dirt drive. He didn't want her to worry about him. She had enough things to take care of without dealing with his issues. On the other hand, he knew she was right. They would come looking for him, and he wasn't about to go down without a fight. He had plans to make, and he suspected that the clock had already chewed up a lot of the time he had to prepare.

James and Robert Pound were leaving the hospital. The general needed a break. Melissa was still out from the surgery and didn't need anyone just then. There was nothing he could do anyway.

James was tired. He hadn't been able to sleep on the plane. It was because of something that happened when he was just a kid. An older couple who lived across the street from his family were coming home from a high school basketball game. Less than a quarter mile from home, some drunk with no brakes and no brain, ran a stop sign and hit the couple's car broadside. The woman died, never knowing what had happened. James vowed to never sleep in a moving vehicle, and that included airplanes. He had made up his mind that at very least, he wanted to have a fighting chance to survive. What measures he could take in an airplane he didn't know. Then again, fear is seldom a rational emotion.

"What do you want me to do?" James asked his uncle. "I can't imagine the locals will let me get involved with the case."

"You're a detective, Mickey," Pound said. "Surely they would let you help them." There was almost a pleading in the man's voice. James had never seen a crack in the man's facade before. He could hardly imagine the stress the man was under. Then again, after what he went through a few years earlier, he didn't need to imagine.

"I'm sure that if I called and asked, they would give me a brief on their current status. As far as actually working the case, there's no way. You know what it's like. Would you let an outsider walk in on one of your investigations? I don't think so."

"There's got to be something, Mickey."

"Actually there is something. There could be a couple of something's I can do. One I'll need your help with. The other requires nothing from you, but a little ass-kissing on my part."

"What do you need me to do?"

"I need you to get me in touch with the best officer in your old command that still has intel about military snipers. I don't know if the shooter was military. But I do know that if he was, the locals will have a harder time getting the information than you will."

"I can do that. I'll call you in an hour with the name. I'll even call first to make sure he knows it's coming directly from me. Now…about the second thing. Is there anything I can do to help you with it?"

"Unfortunately…no. I have to meet with someone who I really wasn't expecting to deal with here."

"Did it have anything to do with that tall, sexy FBI agent you were talking to outside the room?"

"You saw that, huh?"

"I see a lot of things, Mickey. What's the deal there?"

"You remember the case I had a few months back? The serial killer in Monterey."

"Sure. That even made the news back here. Of course, it would have been better if you were the one to tell me about it. I had to hear on the news that my only nephew had been shot taking down a killer and some mafia guys. Oh…wait…I remember now. The local cops got all the credit, but I called a buddy of mine who told me the real story. You and some FBI woman were the real brains behind that case. Are you telling me that *she* was the FBI agent?"

"I didn't tell you this…but, yes. She was the FBI agent I worked with. She's the one who saved my butt. She's the one who I've been sorta dating…long distance. And she's the one I just pissed off outside of Melissa's room."

"Then you lied to me. You'll have some *major* ass-kissing ahead of you."

Both men laughed. It was good to allow a little levity to enter what had been very emotional lives. James was glad to see his uncle, but the feelings were mutual. He was also feeling a twinge of guilt for laughing, knowing that just a few floors up from where they stood, his cousin was hanging on to life and would be devastated when she learned about the death of her friend.

James was playing catch-up. He decided to delay the much needed sleep he needed and took a trip to the crime scene. He managed to find a parking spot a block and a half from the courthouse and walked to where the victims had been shot.

The day was unseasonably warm. The sky was bright, and the cop from California was mildly surprised to see such a vividly blue sky. Unlike many of the cities of which he was familiar, Dayton didn't seem to be infected with the kind of pollutants that brought gray skies to beautiful days. He briefly wondered if smog was just a California thing.

The steps of the courthouse weren't difficult to find. The bright yellow "crime scene" tape cordoned the area so that no one would trample the steps where the victims fell. When he got closer, he saw that the blood had not been cleaned and hated the fact that so many people were stopping to take pictures to send to whomever one sends such a gory depiction of anarchy.

Above and below the tape stood two uniformed officers; inside was a forty something man and what looked like a large tackle-box. He was taking samples from the sight in hopes to find something that would lead them to the shooter.

"I'm afraid you can't come any closer," the lower-step uniformed guard told James as he approached.

James pulled his badge to show the cop and said, "I have an interest in what happened here. I'm just here to look."

"Your badge says, Sacramento PD. What's that have to do with here?" the same cop asked. "You're a little far from home."

"I'm related to one of the victims," James replied.

"All the more reason you shouldn't be here," the man with the tackle-box said. "Which one?"

"Melissa Pound, she's my cousin and just about the only living relative I have left."

"The name's Whalen Short," tackle-box guy said while extending his latex-covered hand. "I know Melissa. She's as good as they come."

"Mickey James," he replied, accepting the hand. "Look…I'm not here to step on toes. I just want to see what happened; see if I can get an idea why the SOB wanted to kill these people."

"Mickey James…I've heard of you. Melissa told me you've handled some pretty big fish over the years. You even had a run-in with a serial not too long ago."

"Yeah," James tried to hide his smile. He didn't like bragging, but knew that if the man knew who he was, he might be helpful. He was also surprised, if not a little proud, that Melissa had even mentioned his name. "We got the guy, but I took a slug for my efforts. I've only been back to work a few weeks. Then yesterday I got the call about this. Family first. At least that's the way it is for us."

"We're all family," Short said.

"You got that right," James smiled knowing that only one brother in arms could understand the code of what made men like cops stick together. Then taking a chance, asked, "Is that the tower he took the shots from? Pointing at the church down the street.

"Yeah," Short replied, following James' finger. "Hell of a shot, considering."

"Considering what?"

"Distance. Wind. Time of day. Hell, everything."

James was a fair shooter of long-guns when he was in the military, but never sniper qualified. He thought back through his time on the range and began to process the level of training and expertise it would take to accurately make those shots. The thought occurred to him that whoever did it was damn good.

"You'd have to be an expert to make that shot." James stated more as an observation than a question.

"Yes, but not necessarily the very best," Short replied. Looking around, he touched James' arm and walked him off to the side for some privacy. "Look," the scientist said, "if I tell you something, can you keep it to yourself? I mean really keep it to yourself. No bullshit."

"I'll take it to my grave if necessary. This is Melissa, and I want to know whatever I can to help find the SOB."

"Alright then," Short sucked in a lung full of air to calm his nerves. "I haven't even taken this to the detectives, but that's my next call. The shot didn't come from the church. I'm here because something didn't seem right when I went over the report and compared the ballistics to the autopsy. The angle was wrong. The kid who did the first report didn't take the angle of drag that gravity has on a shot like this. If the shooter was in the bell tower like he thought, the angle would have been six degrees lower. From the five hundred yards from the bell tower, there is hardly any drop in a slug of this size. In order for the shot to match the trajectory, the guy would have had to have been all the way over there." He pointed at an old building almost two city blocks farther away."

"That's an impossible shot," James replied in awe at the distance.

"There are maybe ten…no more than fifteen, men in the world who could do it," Short came back. "Whoever did it signed his death warrant."

"How do you mean?"

"I mean, all we need to do now is get a list of the ones who could have made the shot and get their alibis. The one that doesn't have one is going to go away for life." Short looked at the two uniforms that were watching the scene and back to James, "I've got to run. It seems we've got a new crime scene to check out. Give my best to Melissa, will you?"

"You bet," James replied. "Catch the son of a bitch."

"You bet."

Chapter 6

The rifleman seldom took multiple jobs in one city. The risk was high, and the rewards were seldom enough to justify the effort. This job was the exception.

While waiting for the next orders to come, he had checked and received confirmation that the money for the attorneys was in his account. Unfortunately, he was disappointed when he discovered that he had been paid for only one. It wasn't until he heard the news that he discovered that the second shot had actually missed and that her injuries were the result of a ricochet. Had she been the primary target, he would have had no choice but to finish the job up close and personal. However, Melissa Pound was not the primary target, and the shooter was instructed to let her live…for now. The news, to the man, was neither good nor bad. He simply didn't like leaving a job incomplete. More important, he hated missing.

Looking through the scope, he watched the science cop gathering particles of dirt and cement. He thought it was amazing that so much information could be gained from what the man did.

On the other hand, he was amused that the cops were still under the impression that the kill shots were taken from the bell tower. That had been his plan from the beginning. The opening in the tower had been a perfect diversion. The bell had been removed for maintenance and left a gap sufficient to both aim and accept the trajectory of the shot. Had the bell been hanging as it usually does, he would not have had that luxury.

As he watched, he saw a man he didn't recognize approach the scientist. It wasn't anyone he had seen before, but thought that whoever it was had to be a cop as well.

The men talked for a while, and the shooter was about ready to wrap up his vigil when the scientist turned and pointed directly at the shooter as if he were actually saying, "Go over there and catch him. He's waiting for you."

The shooter jerked back from the window and blinked his eyes. He wasn't in the same place where he took the shot, but rather he was a couple floors down and several rooms to the south. There was no way, he rationalized, that anyone could see him. He knew that wasn't the case. What he did realize was that it was time to move on. The scientist figured him out, and that was reason enough.

As for the other man he was pointing for, the shooter had no reason at the time to think of him again.

As was usually the case, Katt decided, it would be up to the woman to take the first step to resolve a conflict. It didn't make any difference what the relationship was. From her perspective, a man never apologizes; especially not first. She pulled out her cell phone and dialed.

"James," the detective answered brusquely.

"It's Katt," the FBI agent stated.

"I know whom it is. I have your name and number on speed-dial. Your name pops right up when you call. Of course, there were cobwebs trailing beside your name when I saw it appear."

"Very cute, Mouse. So am I supposed to apologize? I think you are being a little childish. But if that's what you need, I'll be happy to accommodate."

James had tried on many occasions to get her to stop calling him Mouse. He had told her from the beginning that his father was a huge Yankee fan and had named him after Mickey Mantle. Katt, however, took it upon herself to twist things around and said that his father was more likely to be a fan of Walt Disney. The more he tried, the more Katt insisted on using it. He got to the point that he stopped talking about it. He found it interesting that now, the only time she used it was when she was upset with him or wanted to make a point. He figured he could live with that.

"That kinda takes away the sincerity of an apology, don't you think?"

"That was the plan," Katt smiled, if only to her reflection. "If you're going to be a baby about things, then I misjudged who I thought was a strong, self-reliant, macho man. And if that's the case, well…"

"I get it," James felt trapped about his emotional state of mind. She was right. That was the kind of man she needed. She needed a strong person in her life that wouldn't put up with the kind of crap she was more than capable of dishing out. On the other hand, he hadn't cared so much for someone in a very long time. It was a tightrope act, and he didn't have a net.

Then again, he conceded, she was also a master manipulator. She was not only a woman, she was a woman who went to school to learn how to manipulate. He had known from the beginning that he was outclassed by the beautiful and highly intelligent, Katherine Katt.

"So what are you doing here?" James asked. "The last I heard you were on a secret mission somewhere in Virginia or Delaware or one of those other little, eastern states."

"I was…am…was on assignment. It's not over. I was pulled off of it because of the shooting and the politics that might rear its head. I take it that you know the girl in the hospital."

"She's my cousin," James replied. "I got the call yesterday and flew all night to get here. I didn't think she would make it."

"I'm sorry about that, Mickey. I didn't know, or I would have been the one that called you. Where are you?"

Katt hated the idea that James was in the same town, and they couldn't be together. Even though they had never been intimate, she liked the idea of being close to him. She thought many times about what it would be like to actually be close to someone again. She just wasn't sure if she could any more.

Katt wasn't a virgin. There was a time in her life when she thought life had robbed her of the best years of her life—her childhood. As a way of lashing out, she took it upon herself to act in a way that was unbecoming for a young lady. Her life was one that psychiatrists couldn't reach because Katt would never let them enter. She was smarter than they were, and both she and they knew it. It wasn't until she reached her late teens that she decided to settle down and get her life in order. Since then, men had never been a priority. Until James.

"I'm downtown at the site where they were shot." He didn't need to mention who 'they' were. "I decided to do a little looking around."

"You realize that the locals won't let you near this case…right? As a matter of fact, so far, they won't even let the bureau work with them."

"I take it you tried and they shut you down too?"

"It's purely observation only with them," Katt said. "Then again, I'm not sure they know who's going to be in charge of the investigation either. It seems they have a conflict about jurisdiction."

"I don't care about that," James replied coolly. "I don't plan to get them involved with what I need to do."

"Why don't we get together and talk about it," Katt suggested.

"Why? You've got enough on your plate without babysitting me."

"Are you going to stay mad at me? I wasn't avoiding you, Mouse. Things have been difficult."

"I understand difficult. I just think that for now, we need to do things our own way. We don't exactly see eye to eye on how to handle a case. Been there. Done that."

"Okay," Katt was surprised at how quickly the conversation deteriorated.

"Actually," James amended, "I do want to see you. For personal reasons, of course, but I also want to see if there was anything we can do together to find the shooter. You said that the locals weren't going to invite you to the party. I just figured that once we got our act together, we ended up working well together the last time…"

"We were a train wreck," Katt said. "We didn't work well together. We were at each other the whole time…until the end. What makes you think this would be any different?"

"Like I said," James finished. "That's what I was going to do. I can see that it was a bad idea."

James usually came around after a while. He didn't seem willing to do that this time. After she had hung up, Katt wondered exactly how much of that conversation was business and how much of it was personal. She also wondered if the relationship they had started was officially over. Whatever it was they had.

Joseph Brandenburg knew that sooner or later the cops or the FBI would come looking for him. That much was a given. He had the history, talent, and capacity to do the job at the courthouse from what his sister had told him. He then spent several hours trying to figure out what had happened and what to do. What he needed at that moment was to look at the site and see if it would give him an idea of the man behind the gun.

Every marksman was different in their approach to long shots. Some relied on camouflage in order to conceal their location. They used their surroundings to both infiltrate and extricate from the shoot site. They also had the ability to get closer to their target and seldom missed.

Another group was excellent from ranges exceeding a thousand yards. *The long shot record for a sniper kill exceeded three-thousand yards.* In the right conditions, and with the proper equipment, they could hit a target the size of a silver dollar consistently at fifteen-hundred yards. There was still the need for cover, but at those distances the need for cover wasn't nearly as important as the equipment used.

Brandenburg knew everything there was to know about shooting a long gun. He wasn't the official record holder for kills by an American soldier. That title belonged to the late Chief Petty Officer, Chris Kyle with a confirmed one hundred-sixty kill shots. Brandenburg's confirmed number was actually twenty-two less. Their difference was in the number of unconfirmed kills; numbers that would never be disclosed if the U.S. government wanted to maintain certain diplomatic ties.

However, none of that made any difference. Brandenburg never considered his job worthy of recordkeeping. For him, what he was more interested in were the lives he had saved by taking those shots. More importantly, he had to figure out who took the shots that had just turned his world upside down.

Dressed in dark gray—a color more suitable for hiding at night than black—Brandenburg drove north and east to Dayton. The sun had already settled below the horizon and the ghost of a figure—seen as a shadow more than anything else—moved like a wraith. He wasn't surprised that no one recognized his presence. That was how it had always been. The military had taught him well.

Using a monocular with night vision capabilities, he observed the courthouse steps and the cops standing guard. He wasn't concerned about where the victims fell. His interest lay at the location where the bullets began their journey. What he had seen on the evening news explained that the shots were taken from the bell tower—a distance of five hundred yards. Brandenburg didn't need a forensic scientist to tell him that the reporters were wrong. Looking over his shoulder, he figured that the shot had been taken close to four hundred yards further away. A tough shot, he thought. Too difficult a shot for anyone but one of the best out there.

It's you and me, my friend. They'll never find you, but I will.

Chapter 7

Leon Anderson had been a judge going on six years. At forty-two years of age, his appointment and ascent within the judicial ranks was considered unprecedented, but later considered a stroke of genius now that his peers had watched the man in action. Measured by both sides—prosecution and defense—as a modern-day hanging judge by many, he had been assigned to preside over the Boyd Weapons case. It was a bitter pill to swallow, and he was working late to decide if the case should move forward in order to comply with the "speedy trial" rules of law. The alternative would be a mistrial that could set the case back months if not years.

The tall, thin judge had spent the entire day reviewing precedence and had finally made up his mind. The trial would move forward as scheduled. The district attorney's office had agreed to assigning new council and told the judge that they would need only a few extra days to move forward.

"Mr. Silverman," the judge's clerk said with authority when the defense attorney answered his phone. "The judge has ruled that the case will move forward on Monday at nine-thirty. This is your notification. Also, the judge will expect to see you and the district attorney in his office at nine o'clock sharp."

"Did he tell you who the prosecutor would be?" Silverman asked. "It would be nice to know whom I'll be going up against."

"He said that you would be notified by Friday afternoon at the latest. That's all I can tell you."

"Very well," the red-faced, tweed-dressed, heavy-set man replied. "I will inform my client."

"Goodnight, sir," the clerk said.

Silverman didn't bother with a reply. Instead, he called his client and told them what needed to happen and hung up the phone. He wondered if his client had anything to do with the deaths of his previous opponent. *Of course they did* he mumbled quietly, and then looked around to see if anyone noticed.

He was alone.

Judge Anderson had been surprised when the district attorney told him that they had the capability of moving forward with the case. His expectation had been a lot of whining and complaining about the lack of fairness. In the end, he knew that he would have no choice but to declare a mistrial. Instead, the DA had completely surprised him by asking for a few days of prep time, and they would be able to continue. He was pleased. It was a trial that the judge had wanted very much to preside over.

His clerk had been instructed to contact all parties concerned, and the judge was relieved to be going home. It had been a long day, and he needed the rest; not to mention some one on one time with his wife.

Not encumbered with the notion of excess, Anderson pulled his gray Volvo into the driveway of his small single-story home and sat for several long moments to take a deep breath and wash away the law and the dirt that comes with the politics of his job. Never once had he brought his work home, and he had no desire to start now.

Anderson looked out the window of his simple—very safe—car and watched as Lucy, his wife stepped out the door to greet him. The smile on her face had brought joy to his boring life. And he couldn't believe he had been so fortunate as to marry the one woman in the world that he loved beyond life itself. Taking the three steps up to the porch, he held out his arms to embrace her. Lucy had been waiting for her husband with expectation and excitement.

The difference in years—he, forty-two and she, thirty-three—had made no difference to either of them. Their love was the one good thing of which they could always count on.

The evening air was cooling, and the leaves were turning. Had it not been for the lateness of the hour, he would have thought the moment perfect.

Roughly two hundred yards away, with the assistance of a 4X-Bushnell scope, the shooter painted the crosshairs, one inch above and one inch in front of the judges left ear. The shot would have been easy; almost unworthy of the five-hundred thousand dollars he would earn to pull the trigger.

This wasn't the time, however. Maybe tomorrow, the killer thought. It wasn't as though he needed the money; though one could never have too much money, he mused.

Deputy Director Jonathan Blyth had been expecting the call. "Blyth," he said as he picked up the phone.

"It's Katt, sir," she said to her boss. "I've got a preliminary for you if you have the time."

"Let's hear it," Blyth answered. The usually tough supervisor had known Katt since the day her family had been the victims of violence. Her parents had been shot and killed. Katt had lived, though he couldn't help but wonder at times during her youth if she wouldn't have been better off meeting the same fate as her parents. Just as quickly, the thought disappeared knowing the woman she had become.

It took years for Katt to get over that night. Two strangers dressed in black had entered the family's home and orchestrated one the most heinous of crimes. Not only did they kill the young girl's parents, but forced her to hold the weapon as the trigger was pulled. It seemed like forever to get Katt to understand that she wasn't the killer like they told her before they left. Rather she was just as much a victim as her parents had been. The only difference was the fact that their cruelty was more pronounced and lasted much longer.

"There's been a new development. The original thought was that the shot was from a distance of five hundred yards, give or take. That being the case, our guy could certainly have made the shot, but then again, so could a lot of others.

"I just discovered that the distance was more like eight-hundred yards and with the winds as strong as they were, it's likely that this shooting was from the same person."

"How sure are you about the new intel?"

"The local forensic guy just confirmed it. It seems that he shot *through* the bell tower opening to take them out instead of shooting from the bell tower."

"How the hell did he do that?"

"Apparently, the church is doing some renovations, and they've taken the bell down to do the repairs. Instead of an opening of less than a foot for the bullet to travel through, the opening was almost four feet wide and eight feet high."

"Pretty damn clever if you ask me. Made everyone waste a lot of time for nothing. Damn near twenty-four hours for the real scene to get discovered."

"That's what I was thinking. So what do you want me to do? I could go in with what we now know and take over. I think there's enough to make that happen."

"What do you think the locals will do?"

"As far as I'm concerned it doesn't matter. The last time I saw them they were still trying to figure out who was in charge. Maybe it would work better if I was."

"Then let's do that. I'll send a team for support if you need. Otherwise, they'll be on standby if you think the locals can do the job."

"They have a pretty good system here as far as I can see. The BCI has all the toys necessary to do the job. If there's anything we need that they don't have, I'll call for some help."

"I'll contact the governor and get the wheels spinning. We should have everything straightened out within the hour."

"There's something else, sir."

"Go on," Blyth hated the 'one more thing' comments because they were never good.

"Mickey James is here." The phone was silent long enough that Katt had to ask, "Are you still there, sir?"

"What the hell is James doing there?"

"The woman shot…the one that survived…she's James' cousin. I did some checking, and it seems that his uncle used to be a big shot general at Wright Patterson Air Force Base; now retired. James flew in overnight and I met him at the hospital."

"You met him?"

"Wrong choice of words, sir. I ran into him while I was there getting an update on the victim. He just showed up out of the blue."

"Is he going to be a problem?"

"I suspect he will be a complete pain, sir. I also suspect that if I play it right, he may also be helpful." Katt shook her head, not believing what she was saying. "If I use him properly, he could actually be an asset."

"You're playing with fire, Katt. If you'll remember, things almost got out of hand the last time you two played together. I don't want anyone killed because of this. We'll get the guy. It may take a little longer working it the way we are. On the other hand, I think there's less chance of getting our people, or anyone else, hurt. Keep James out of it. We can always bring him in later if necessary. But for now, don't tell him anything."

"Are you sure, Jonathan?" Katt asked in a familiar way. She was the only person working with Blyth that could get away with it. He also knew that she only did that when she was pulling a few strings of her own.

"Yes, Katherine, I'm very sure." Then added for clarity, "And don't pull any crap behind my back. I'll jerk you off this case in a heartbeat if I think you aren't doing this my way."

"Yes, sir," Katt said, and then hung up. She had thought about calling James right after talking to her boss. Now she couldn't do that. She had no doubt that she would be tempted to tell him what she knew if she met with James. That was a risk she simply couldn't take.

Chapter 8

James and his uncle, Robert Pound, had decided to meet at the Big Boy restaurant a few blocks from the hospital. The black-haired boy statue/sign had been a staple of the area for a long time, and anyone from the area giving directions would inevitably use it as a marker. The boy's smiling face reminded folks that the place was fun, and the hamburger looked too big for anyone; a testament of an appetite's impending doom.

The two men sat down and neither said a word until the waitress brought coffee and asked if they wanted to eat. Both men had things other than eating on their minds, but took advantage of the time and ordered burgers and fries. If nothing else, the military had taught them that there were two things you never missed out on; the chance to sleep or a meal. You learned early that in combat, both were a privilege, not a right and you never knew when you might have the pleasure of either again.

"What have you got?" Pound asked after the order was taken.

"I found out that they were wrong about where the shot was taken. I haven't gotten the exact location yet, but from what I saw, it had to have been seven—maybe eight-hundred yards. Too long for any amateur. Hell…too long for me."

"So you're thinking a pro did it."

"I'm thinking that the shooter has to be *real* good. He could be military or maybe a cop sharpshooter, but definitely well trained and one of the best."

"I made some calls. A buddy of mine got me a list of those that could have made a shot like that. Before you ask…no…I didn't know he was going to be that good. I took a chance of asking for the best because I knew that if just anyone could have made the shot, it wouldn't help us narrow the field. Now that you've confirmed what we're looking for, we have a better chance of finding the guy."

"And…?"

"And, the top fifteen are accounted for."

"Damn," James said more to himself than anyone.

"Except one," the general added with a smile. He saw the look on James' face and said, "Sorry. I didn't mean to draw it out like that. I just couldn't believe it could be so easy to narrow down the field. It's been a while since I've done the hands-on stuff. Computers nowadays are amazing."

"Yes they are," James was wondering if he had to drag the information out.

"There's a local man, ex-SEAL, ex-sniper, ex-stuff they wouldn't even tell me about, name is

Brandenburg, Joseph, mid-thirties and apparently as good as they get."

"What's he doing now?" James asked.

"Best I can tell...nothing."

"What do you mean?"

"I mean, they have no records of him doing anything. He lives off-the-grid somewhere over by Chillicothe on an old farm. He hunts and fishes and grows some vegetables, and that's all they know."

"Why was he discharged? If he's that good, it would seem to me that they wouldn't want to lose him."

"They didn't. He just decided one day that he'd had enough of the killing. He refused to go out on any more missions. They threatened to court-marshal and everything, but he didn't care. After a while, they just put him on a desk where he didn't have to do anything and just let him go. My guy inside told me that he's some kind of nut job. He also said he was the kind of nut job you didn't want to piss off."

"Just how good is he?"

"He's got the kind of record that puts him close to the top in every category of long weapon kills. They even have a file that no one south of the Secretary of the Navy can look at."

"Could he have made the shot?"

"My friend said that if he was the one doing the shooting, my daughter would not have been left alive. He wouldn't have missed. So...could he have made it? Yes. Did he make it? My guy doesn't think so. Brandenburg never misses...never."

"Then we aren't any better off than we were before," James sighed. "Where do we go from here?"

"We go to Chillicothe," Robert said. "We may not know who the shooter is, but chances are that Brandenburg does. If nothing else, maybe he can lead us in the right direction."

"He won't be leading *us* anywhere. You aren't going. I'll have a sit-down with him. You need to stay here with Melissa. When she wakes up, she'll need you to be there."

"I want to go. You know that, right?"

"I do. I also know that I'm right...and so do you. Don't worry. I'll keep you posted."

"When are you leaving?"

"First thing in the morning. I haven't slept in about thirty-six hours. I don't want to go out there half awake."

James managed to find a place that was close to the hospital and not very expensive. There was no budget for what he was doing, and on a cop's salary the expenses came directly out of his insignificant savings account.

"Call me afterward," the grizzled father said. "I need to know what's going on."

The two of them ate in silence. James wondered what Katt was doing and if they would ever find a way to be together.

Katt knew that there would be a degree of discourse once she went back to address the local cops. It was one thing to get invited onto a case. Even the most backwater towns hated having to admit they could not handle a crime. Cities were even worse.

To go into a place as equipped as Dayton, and then to take it over was nothing short of a slap in the face. After entering the station, Katt realized that her concerns were well-founded.

"This is bullshit, Agent Katt," Bill Stetson said as Katt entered the room. "You have no right to take over this case."

"I agree," Doug Martin, the county sheriff said. "We've all been around the block a time or two and know what we're doing. We didn't ask for and don't want you here."

"What about you, Agent Williams," Katt asked the BCI investigator. "Is the feeling unanimous?"

Katt was impressed when Williams didn't respond immediately. In her mind, hot tempers seldom came from successful investigators. Maybe she had been mistaken by the man's earlier demeanor.

"Agent Katt, the BCI is not unlike what the FBI deals with on a large percentage of cases. Like you, we are often asked to participate with the local authorities and have no jurisdiction until we are asked. However, there are times when asking is not an option. Under those conditions, we do what must be done, even to the extent of stepping on toes. However, in all circumstances, we attempt to work with the locals rather than exclude them. Before answering your question, I would like to know how you plan to move forward."

"Very well said, Agent Williams," Katt replied. "Less than an hour ago, I was told by my superiors that I would be taking over this investigation. I was given the choice of how I wanted to run it, which is unusual, by the way. The options presented to me were to either bring in our team or use yours. I elected to use the local talent because I believe you are good enough to get the job done.

"I've been given a short leash on this because the bureau chiefs are under the impression that nobody can do the job better than we can. I disagree. I know that's different than the company line, but I have my reasons. I am not a politician and believe that you folks are trained and motivated to solve this crime. I've worked with places a lot smaller than here, and we were still able to succeed. Unfortunately, I can't do my job without your help. So it's up to you."

"You're pretty good at speeches yourself, Agent Katt," Williams said to Katt. "The difference is that you want to take over. We don't have a choice."

"Everyone has a choice," Katt fired back. "You have the choice of us working together efficiently and effectively. I have the choice of accepting your help or calling in my own team. Either way, choices need to be made. I'll give you gentlemen thirty seconds to make up your mind. Then I'll make up mine."

It didn't take the full thirty seconds for Stetson to comment. "I'm with the little lady. She's cuter than you two."

"Thanks, Captain," Katt smiled. "I appreciate the vote of confidence. However, you call me 'little lady' again, you'll find my size eights firmly lodged somewhere that it would make it difficult for you to sit. You can call me Agent Katt, Katt, Katherine or even ma'am. I can live with any of them. Do we understand each other?"

"Yes, Ma'am," the captain replied humbly.

"Hell, if she can get Stetson to cooperate…count me in," Martin laughed. "I've never seen such a thing and want to see if…the agent…can make it work. Besides, I've got an election coming up and would love to have this feather in my cap before then. What about you, Williams? Is the BCI going to help out or are you guys going to hold your crime-solving-toys from us because the federal bureau is taking over?"

"I'm going to stay with it. I don't know about you gentlemen, but I don't have a problem taking orders from a woman. Hell...I'm married. I've been taking orders from a woman for years. How do you think I've managed to stay married?"

"You're a smart man, Agent Williams," Katt smiled. "Now, gentlemen, we have a lot of work to do. I need to get you up to speed on why this is happening; why the bureau is now in charge. We have a serial killer, and you're not going to like him one bit."

Katt spent the next hour bringing the heads of the local law enforcement agencies up to date.

Chapter 9

By midnight, the actual crime scene had been dusted for prints. The technicians had also searched for any additional evidence that might help them find the shooter.

They left empty handed.

Brandenburg waited another hour to see if anyone would be coming back and when they didn't, he decided it was time to check things out for himself.

The roof of the building had only one entrance, and it was being guarded by a uniformed officer. The man looked as bored as any seaman recruit Brandenburg could remember and decided that the jaded policeman wouldn't be much of an obstacle.

The ex-SEAL had learned his craft proficiently, and when the cop stepped past the shadow, in an instant, the shadow came alive.

The cop would have been easy to kill, but that wasn't the plan. At that moment, all he needed was a little time to look around and see what the killer had seen.

There are rules when it comes to sniping; rules that a hunter like Brandenburg would never break. That's why he got out of the military. It had nothing to do with his skills. The problem was that they—the military—the government—the people making the life and death decisions—didn't understand those rules.

A shootist, at least the man Brandenburg believed himself to be, would never kill an innocent. He would never take the life of a child unless that child was a direct threat to him or others. Like all rules, there were exceptions, but not without exhausting all other alternatives.

Brandenburg used to believe that he would never kill a child—period—until a child of eleven came strolling into a restaurant in Afghanistan and detonated a bomb that killed six of his friends. Brandenburg hadn't been there to see it happen. He was off on another of the secret missions the government liked him to do. It wasn't until he returned to his unit that he was told what had happened. It was at that moment that he amended his rules. Fortunately, he had never been tested to see if he could actually pull the trigger should he be called to do it.

The cop didn't know what was happening when Brandenburg slipped behind him and placed his arm around the man's neck. It was a move he had used on dozens of occasions. Only this time the outcome was different. This time, the victim lived.

Brandenburg took a chance. When he grabbed the cop, he whispered in the man's ear, "If you want to live…don't resist. I need time, not a life." For reasons he couldn't personally comprehend, the cop let go and allowed the would-be assassin to complete the choke hold and simply passed out. The ex-SEAL wasn't sure if he would have killed the man. He *was* glad that he didn't have to find out.

Once alone, Brandenburg stepped to the side of the building where the shots were taken. He didn't need a compass to get directions or a weathervane to check out the breeze. He knew in an instant the difficulty of the shot and listed the people in his mind that could have done it. After pulling his scope and finding the target, Brandenburg smiled. He didn't have to like what the killer did, but he did admire him for how it was done.

The morning sun was high enough to break the day, yet not high enough to climb over the surrounding mountain tops. James knew that if he was going to investigate the murder he would need transportation and was glad he decided to upgrade to a full-size vehicle.

The trip to Chillicothe was simple enough. All he had to do was get on Interstate 35 and head east. The trip took longer than he expected, but the landscape was nice and the timing for fall foliage could not have been better. What the locals called hills, James considered mountains and were covered with a kaleidoscope of colors. Reds, purples, gold and greens of multiple hues, reflected off the dew covered leaves. Had it been a vacation with Katt, James thought, it would have been a perfect opportunity to take hundreds of pictures. He also realized, in his old-fashioned mindset, the leaves would have been nothing more than a blurred background coloration with the pictures all focused on Katt.

He was fortunate that his car was equipped with GPS because once he got off the Interstate, the rest of the trip reminded him of a scene from the movie Deliverance.

Blacksmith Hill Road wasn't terribly difficult to find. The GPS got him there without incident. The problem from there was that the lady in the direction finder wasn't sure where James needed to turn off from there.

On his third try, James found the entrance he wanted and reluctantly capitulated to the ruts and stone covered dirt lane. He noticed the old pickup truck and suspected that Brandenburg was around somewhere, but had no idea where that might be. If he was in the house, a simple toot of the horn would get the man's attention. Hopefully he would avoid the man's ire.

Then, there was also the possibility that he wasn't home. Maybe he was out hunting or fishing. The tributary feeding Ross Lake was a little over a quarter-mile away and easy to get to on foot.

Of course, there was also the possibility that Brandenburg was lying in wait. According to the general, Brandenburg was not violent anymore. That was why he had left the military; he no longer had the taste for killing. He also told James that the man was nuts; which could lead to all kinds of trouble.

James blew the horn a couple times and waited in the car to see if he could get the man to come out without trouble—no luck. Finally, he got out of the car to take a look around the place; see if there was any sign of the sniper or anything that could help.

James expected to hear if anyone came toward him—but he didn't. He expected to have a sixth sense about danger when it presented itself—but not then. What he didn't expect was the feeling of a very large, very sharp blade touching his throat and no way to avoid the threat.

"You are not welcome here," Brandenburg hissed in James' ear.

"Believe it or not," James replied, "you didn't need to tell me that. I already got the message when I felt your knife on my neck."

"I didn't want you to get confused. Sometimes people are pretty stupid."

"I suspect you don't have to repeat yourself often."

"Never," Brandenburg said. "Now get off my property while you still have the capacity to breathe." He released James as quickly as he had caught him and stepped far enough away that James couldn't counter move.

James turned to face the thin, rugged, mountain of a man. "Can't do that," James said. "I need to talk to you and the only way I'm leaving is after having that conversation or in a body bag. You got the drop on me, and I respect that, Mr. Brandenburg. But you may discover I'm not as easy to beat as you might think."

"Maybe you *are* stupid," Brandenburg replied. "What's so important that you'd be willing to get dead over it?"

"My cousin, Melissa Pound. You know her?"

"Never heard of her. So the conversation is over."

James pushed forward. It was the first time in a very long while that he wasn't sure if he could beat someone straight up. "She's one of the people shot at the courthouse two days ago."

"Didn't do it. Have no reason to. And you're pushing my patience."

"I don't think you did it," James had no intentions of backing down. "I think someone you know did it."

"I don't know anything. Just leave me alone," Brandenburg glared, and then softened a bit. "And…sorry about your cousin."

"Thanks. But that's not helpful. I need your help finding the son of a bitch who shot her and you're the best chance I have of doing that."

Brandenburg stared at James for a long moment and then turned toward the house and walked away. James thought about pulling his weapon, but decided that the man probably had eyes in the back of his head and would still be able to kill him. He followed him to the house.

There were two rusty metal chairs on what might be considered a porch; though the deck barely rose six inches above the dirt. James noticed that close to half of the wooden boards that would be the decking were missing or broken. Brandenburg walked into the shack and left the door open. James decided that it would be unwise to follow the man. He was deadly enough in the open. He wasn't about to learn the extent of Brandenburg's capabilities in close quarters. James sat on the creaking chair he believed was the most stable.

Brandenburg returned with two bottles of Pabst Blue Ribbon Beer and handed one to James.

"It's a little early to be drinking, don't you think?"

"It's what I've got," Brandenburg replied. "The pump is broke on the well. What electricity I have from the generator I save for special occasions, of which you don't rate. And frankly, I need it. This shooting stuff has got me looking over my shoulders. I take it you're a cop?"

"I am," James replied and smiled as they clinked their bottles. "I'm just not a cop from around here. I work and live in Sacramento, California. I got the call that Melissa was shot and came running. Her father is Robert Pound, retired military. He's the one who told me you might be able to help."

"What makes you think I didn't do it?" Brandenburg turned to face James.

"I was told that you aren't in the business anymore."

"That's right."

"I was also told that if you were the one taking the shot, Melissa would be dead."

"You've got good intel."

"My uncle has friends all over the world. Some of them know people like you."

"They don't know anyone like me."

"I apologize for the slight," James was concerned he pissed off the man.

"It's okay. I don't mean to be hostile. My sister came up and told me about the shooting yesterday. I figured someone would be looking for me sooner or later. I'm surprised you got to me this early."

"You didn't seem that surprised to me. As a matter of fact, I would say that you were waiting for me when I drove up."

"I wasn't looking for you specifically. I just keep a close eye on what goes on around me."

"Like strange cars coming to the house."

"Something like that."

"So will you help me?"

"Why should I? I didn't do anything, and I don't want to get involved with it."

James pondered on how to approach the man. The ex-SEAL didn't seem angry or upset, but he needed the help. A fly landed on Brandenburg's face, but he did nothing to swat it away.

"I don't know," James replied honestly. "You've done more than your fair share for Uncle Sam. You've moved out here to BFE to get away from people like me—or anyone for that matter."

"Bum Fuck Egypt. Damn…you must be older than I thought."

"Sorry. It's an old phrase people used for out of the way places like this. I guess my roots are showing, and I couldn't come up with a more accurate description to use. Anyway…there's a reason why these people got shot and figuring it out is going to be hard enough without wondering if the next breath I took would be my last. It would help if I had a better understanding of the kind of person that I'm up against."

Brandenburg thought about it, then said, "I take it your being here isn't exactly sanctioned. So who's running the case?"

"I don't know for sure. Last I heard they were having some kind of pissing contest to see who would take lead. But my bet is that sooner or later it'll be someone not local."

"FBI?"

"She is," James smiled. "And she'll be a handful for whoever she works with."

Brandenburg looked at James and picked up a relationship from the past, but decided he wasn't going to ask.

"If she gets the case," James continued, "her name is Katherine Katt—that's Katt spelled with a K—and she's good people."

"I won't be working with the government. I can't trust them anymore."

"Then work with me. I'm not with the government. At least I'm not with the local government, and I'm sure as hell not with the Feds."

"You still haven't answered my question…why?"

"Because I want to catch the son of a bitch who shot my cousin and put the fucker in the ground."

"So revenge is your motive," Brandenburg said.

"Okay…yes. Maybe it helps that I stop him from killing anyone else. I'll grant you that. But, frankly, it's not very high on my list of priorities."

Brandenburg finished his bottle of Blue Ribbon and stood looking out over the land.

"I can live with that, mister…"

"James…Mickey James," he held out his hand to shake.

"Mister James. But, we'll need to talk about it later."

Brandenburg stepped into the house. James thought it was to get another beer. What he didn't know was that Brandenburg had already left out the back and was out of sight when the large, black SUV pulled up beside James' rental. Katt had arrived, and James had some explaining to do.

He couldn't wait.

Chapter 10

"What are you doing here?" Katt asked James who didn't bother standing. "I told you that you were not invited to participate in this investigation," she added.

"Funny you should ask," James smiled. "Since I'm not allowed to join your little group, I decided to do some fishing, got turned around and stopped here to get directions. The owner isn't home."

James could see the frustration building and was amused that Katt could do nothing about it.

"And so what...you decided to get a beer as a way to punish the homeowner for not being courteous enough to be here to help you?"

"Now, Katt...you know better than that. I'm not a vindictive person. I just happened to have one of those left over from last night. It was a little warm, but I was thirsty. What're you going to do?"

"Where is he?"

"Where's who?" James held his smile.

"Brandenburg. He's here somewhere. So talk to me. We need to talk to him."

James noticed that the three Chillicothe police officers Katt arrived with were coming back to the front of the house shaking their heads. "Not here, ma'am."

"So who're you looking for?" James asked. "I didn't get a look at the mailbox when I drove up."

"So you're sticking with that cockamamie story? Alright. His name is Joseph Brandenburg, Junior. He's ex-Navy SEAL. And he looks good for the shooting of Salazar and your cousin, Melissa."

"There are a lot of ex-SEALs, Katt. What makes this one unique?"

"His specialty just happens to be long range shooting. He's a sniper, Mouse…and a damn good one."

"Seems to me you've got this all wrapped up. I guess I'll be heading back to Dayton. Seems to be getting too late to get any good bites now anyway."

"Not so fast, mister," Katt said, standing firmly with hands on her hips. "You need to tell me what's going on."

James watched as the three men with Katt started surrounding him; impeding his path.

"What would you like to know, Agent Katt? Seems to me you've figured it all out. You had your crime, and now you've got your criminal. What could you possibly need from me?"

"You could start with the truth," Katt moved close enough for James to smell the faint scent of her perfume. "Why are you here?"

"I told you…"

"Yeah, yeah, you came here to do a little fishing."

"There you go," James smiled. "You *were* listening."

"What were you fishing for?" asked the unrelenting agent. "I'll put a hundred down that it had nothing to do with the slimy things that swim in water."

"I wish I could tell you more, Agent Katt. Unfortunately, it seems that for now, we're working things a little differently."

"I'm here looking for justice for your niece and Salazar. How's that so different?"

"You're looking for justice," James stepped even closer. "You may even be looking for a killer. I'm looking for a murderer, and you won't find one of those here."

"How do you know that?"

"Because you don't know what you're looking for."

"And you do?"

"I'll take that hundred dollar bet that I'm a lot closer to the truth than you are."

"It's against bureau policy to make wagers. But if you know something, you need to tell me, James. You know you do."

"What I know is that you have your agenda, and I have mine. I'll do my best to stay out of your way. Maybe it would be a good thing if you stayed out of mine."

Katt grabbed James by the arm and pulled him away from the three men who were taking in the conversation; confused why she didn't just arrest the man."

"What's going on with you?" Katt asked in a forced whisper. "I haven't done anything to get you this upset."

"Really?" James was incredulous. "Let me see…you haven't called me in over a month. You act like it's no big deal. You get a lead on a suspect, and you call me…oops…wait, you didn't call me. Even though you knew that it was my cousin lying in that bed. Why, Katt? Are we not on the same team?"

"This is a bureau case, Mickey. You're a civilian here. I can't just bring you in."

"Bullshit, Katt. You've got an agenda that I'm not a part of. It's that simple, and I get it. However, unless you intend on arresting me on some trumped-up, crap charge, I have some errands to run before going back to the hospital."

"You're acting like a child, Mouse, and you know it. You don't have to do things like this."

"I may be acting like a child, but at least you never have to wonder where I'm coming from. At least I'm honest." James was angry and wanted more than anything to just shut up and not say anything that would alienate himself from Katt. Unfortunately for him, that simply wasn't the way he was.

"I've been doing this job a lot longer than you, Agent Katt, and I've seen some pretty stupid mistakes by some pretty smart people, but this takes the cake. What do you know about Brandenburg? What do your files say about his character? What were the circumstances when he left the military? Do you know anything about the man?"

Katt was better at holding her temper, but James tested her every fiber.

"I don't know that he's our shooter, Mickey. We just need to talk to him and get his side of things."

"*What side?*" James raised his voice. "What if he doesn't have a side? What if he didn't have anything to do with your shootings? What then? You and I both know that your local-yokels will spread the rumors that they have a suspect; an ex-military guy that they think did the shooting. And as soon as that happens, you won't have any choice but to either hold him or watch him like a hawk. Either way, you're wasting your time."

"I work for the government, Mouse. They pay me to waste my time."

Katt could see that James was angry, but knew there was more to it. Somehow she'd managed to lose his cooperation, and that would not bode well for the days ahead. James was relentless and aggressive and when he wanted, could actually be disruptive, and she couldn't afford that."

"What do you want from me, Mickey?" Katt asked with a soft voice and then looked at the men watching them. "I have rules to follow…just like you. I can't bring you in on this case. I told you that. I have my orders, so what am I supposed to do?"

"Nothing," James' lips curled into a smile that Katt knew was fake. "I'll just go about fishing like I said earlier. I hope you catch the killer."

James didn't wait for a response. When the men questioned stopping James, she simply shook her head and allowed him to get in his rental car and drive away. Momentarily, she wondered if she would ever see the angry cop again, but immediately dismissed the idea. Of course she would. It may not ever again be friendly, but she knew for a fact that James would not be far from the action. The man was like a cockroach, she mused.

Chapter 11

Merlin Winslow Abernathy, III, finished his Cobb salad. He and two of his colleagues enjoyed the short meal, but then he excused himself due to pressing issues. The restaurant was only two blocks from the courthouse and afforded the man the time necessary to eat quickly and then walk to an area not far from the courthouse steps. The pressing issue was a ruse. What he wanted was to smoke one of his few pleasures in life; a 1964 Piramide Maduro cigar.

At close to sixteen dollars each, there were few cigars legally available in the U.S., which tasted as smooth and refined as those he enjoyed daily. The judge quietly blessed the day when he was introduced to the Nicaraguan stogie. It was the sole reason he believed that he didn't have ulcers like his contemporaries and vowed that as long as he lived, he would never deprive himself the pleasure.

The shooter had been given the intel about the judge's proclivity and decided that in order to make the job challenging, he needed to increase the distance by at least twice that of the previous targets. The judge would be stationary, and that made a difference when it came to bragging rights.

After all what's the value of a job, if you can't enjoy it.

Using a laser distance meter, the shooter decided that the distance of fourteen-hundred seventy-two yards would have to do. There was another building three blocks farther away, but from that distance, he would be reaching beyond the outer limits of his comfort zone and didn't want to risk the results. He understood that the job was more important than his own ego, but sometime down the road he would like to throw the job aside and see just how good he really was.

The shooter watched the judge clip the tip of the cigar, place the fragrant, phallic stick under his nose and inhale deeply. If the man remained true to his habits, he would take nearly twenty minutes to finish smoking and then calmly walk back to the courthouse.

There were two points the killer could use for this job: the first being where the judge sat on the bench. That would be the easiest and safest route to go. The second, and more difficult, would be on the courthouse steps. That target would be a little farther away only because the angle would change due to the lateral movement. On the other hand, it would be a more sporting shot. It would give the judge a chance to live, albeit a very small chance. There was also the added bonus of the man being on the move and that appealed to the sniper.

Judge Abernathy had been smoking less than ten minutes when his cell phone rang. The killer had no idea who was calling, but knew that his decision had been made for him. There would be no fun in this target. After taking one last glance at the tiny windsock he had set up the night before, he lined the shot in the crosshairs slowly pulled back on the trigger and felt the jump of the rifle as the explosion of the powder in the brass casing pushed the projectile from the end of the barrel at a speed of twenty-six hundred and forty feet per second. By the time it reached its target, the bullet would still be traveling at a speed of greater than twelve-hundred fps and would kill anything it hit.

Some people would consider bird droppings a bad omen. Others would be really grossed out, especially if you were a man of power and influence like that of a judge.

Judge Abernathy felt the splat on his shoe just after the Cardinal flew by screeching its hair-raising, high-pitched shriek. At the exact moment that Abernathy bent to wipe away the awful mess, a bullet passed by his head close enough to cause the judge to stop what he was doing and look around. It hit nothing but dirt and dug its way several inches below the surface. Something important had just occurred, but the man had no idea what it was. Shrugging his shoulders, he finished wiping up the mess and headed to the courthouse.

Duty called.

For a second time, his phone rang as he ascended the courthouse steps. Looking at the caller ID, the judge smiled. It was his granddaughter calling. He was sure that she had earned the part of the princess for the Christmas pageant and was about to congratulate her.

The shooter smiled. It was a bit of misfortune that something caused the judge to bend at the worst possible moment. It was a bit of luck that the shell hit nothing other than the ground which was soft enough to absorb the blow of the projectile with nothing more than a puff of dirt jumping into the air.

The next shot required nothing more than a lack of surprises.

The whole process of shooting a bullet was little more than math and a steady hand. The shell would go exactly where it was aimed; that was the steady hand part. However, the further away you were from the target, the more complicated the process became. With gravity pulling the bullet toward earth, wind pushing the object to the side and the density of the air resisting from the front, the bullet would eventually hit the ground; that's where the math comes in. If you know the constancies; speed, weight of the bullet, distance, barometric pressure and wind velocity, and then using a formula that has been tested and proven over the years, hitting a target is relatively easy.

Except for the steady hand thing again.

A close target measuring off by an eighth of an inch is merely off an eighth of an inch. At the distance of a mile away, that same eighth of an inch could miss by several feet.

Judge Abernathy never got to hear whether his granddaughter got the part. He never even got to say hello. The bullet ripped through his head and threw the man to the ground with such an impact that one person watching described the event as seeing an invisible two-by-four hit the judge in the back of the head.

The shooter wasn't about to wait around. There was no church tower to shoot through or anything that might aid with slowing the crime scene people. They would know quickly, and he had no desire to be there when they did.

One bullet, one kill. That was what he was taught. This time it took two bullets, but the judge was just as dead.

Katt had returned to Dayton. She was unable to make contact with Brandenburg and expected that it would take a court order to shake up that line of investigation. She had a feeling that Mickey James would be a problem; even more from a professional perspective than from a personal one. She was talking to the trio—Martin, Stetson and Williams—about her trip to see Brandenburg when the call came in.

Martin's and Stetson's phone began to ring almost simultaneously, and Williams said, "That can't be good."

"We have another one," Stetson said as Martin was hanging up. "This time it's a judge."

"Let's go," Katt said as she was moving toward the door. "Maybe this time we can get something that will help."

It took less than five minutes for Katt and the others to make it to the courthouse steps. The police cruisers already had the block cordoned off, and the uniformed officers seemed to know what they were doing by corralling everyone that might have seen something into a crowd of about twenty and standing about a hundred feet away. Katt thought the officers were doing an excellent job of containing the scene.

"What do we have?" Katt was about to ask, but Stetson was already ahead of her.

"GSW to the back of the head, judge named Abernathy, hit as he was heading up the steps. No one heard the shot, so I don't know what you want to make of that. I do have some theories, but that's why you guys make the big bucks...sir."

The officer thought he was talking to one of the detectives until he looked up and saw the stars on Stetson's shoulders.

"How many witnesses?" Stetson asked looking at the crowd.

"Seven that saw the judge hit the pavement," the cop replied. "Only one, a court reporter named Stephanie Brubaker, was actually looking at him when the round hit him in the head. They were passing each other, and the judge was answering a call. He said they were looking each other in the eye when his head exploded."

"That's how she described it? His head exploded?"

"Her exact words were," the officer said as he checked his notes, "quote 'the judge was smiling at me when his phone rang and then his face just disappeared,' unquote. We had to take her to the hospital because she was pretty shaken up. She was also wearing some of the judge on her and her clothes, and we wanted to make sure to get it before the evidence got compromised."

"Have any of them," Katt nodded to the group, "been interviewed?"

"No ma'am," the patrolman said. "I've left strict instructions that nobody say anything or call anyone. I even had their cell phones confiscated until the detectives get here. I figured it would be the best way to keep a lid on it."

"And no one gave you any lip about civil rights?" Stetson asked.

"I think they were all pretty shook up about it. I hope I didn't overstep my boundaries."

"Nothing that we can't fix," Katt smiled at the man. "I'll make sure it's okay."

"Thanks, ma'am. I appreciate that." The patrolman turned and walked back to the waiting crowd.

"That was pretty heads-up," Katt said to Stetson. "Taking the phones could be helpful if we can get them checked out quickly."

"I'll get some people on it right away."

Doug Martin was listening in and said, "Does anyone have any idea where the shot came from? We need to get some people over there and close that scene off as well."

"Right now," Stetson replied, "They have no idea where the shot came from. I wouldn't know where or from how far away it came."

"I do," two detectives came rushing up the courthouse steps. "We've had several 911 calls stating they heard shots over by McPherson and Floral Streets. We've sent patrol cars over there to see what's what."

"Detective Hershey, Detective Montclair, I would like to introduce you to FBI Special Agent, Katherine Katt. Go on detective."

The men nodded at Katt and then continued. "When the officers got there, the witnesses could only report that they heard the shots, but nobody could isolate where they came from. At first we thought it might have been a car backfiring. Then the calls started coming in about the judge here. Right now the best we can do is offer a general location." He told them where the calls came from.

"That can't be right," Stetson stated flatly. "That's damn near a mile away. Nobody's that good."

"Actually there is somebody that good," Katt returned his stare. "Remember our conversation about Joseph Brandenburg? He's that good…and then some."

Chapter 12

"Who's Joseph Brandenburg?" Hershey asked while looking around the group.

"He's an ex-SEAL and sniper with the Navy. Got out of the military a few years back and lives over around Chillicothe. I went to see him this morning to ask him about the shootings a couple days ago. The FBI did a search and his name came up."

"Well that's damn convenient, don't you think?"

"The brass in the military told us that they didn't think he would have had anything to do with it. I just wanted to ask him some things…some insight, if you will. Anyway, he wasn't there so I never got the chance."

"Maybe it was because he was here blowing out the judge's brains. Have you considered that?" Hershey continued. "It seems mighty coincidental that the man you were going to talk to, a man who you say could have made that shot, was missing at the time the judge was killed."

"I have considered it, Detective," Katt replied, looking the detective in the eye. "But right now he's still just a person of interest; someone we need to talk to. Maybe he had something to do with the shootings, or maybe he could lead us in the right direction. I don't know, but until we find out otherwise, we'll approach him as someone of interest only."

"Is that how you see it, Captain?" Hershey looked at Stetson.

"Until told otherwise, Detective…yes. Agent Katt is in charge of this investigation," Stetson replied. Katt picked up on the anger coming from the detective and the pacification being dished out from the captain.

Mickey James went back at the hospital. He wanted to see the general; not to mention check-in on his cousin. When he entered Melissa's room, he was shocked to see her sitting upright in her bed and talking to his uncle.

"Looks like I made a good call," James said, smiling at the two of them.

"What's that supposed to mean?" Melissa smiled at seeing James, but a little confused as she looked between the conspiring men.

"Oh…your father wanted to go traipsing around the countryside looking for the man everyone thinks put you in here and I wouldn't let him go. He needed to be here in case you woke from your beauty sleep." James leaned over and gave her a kiss on her forehead. "It's good to see you, cuz. However, it wasn't necessary to go to such extreme measures to get me to come visit."

"Really? Anything short of getting shot would barely make a blip on your radar. I'm glad you're here Mickey." Melissa smiled a sad smile. He suspected it was because of her friend's death. He was right. "Have you figured out anything yet?"

James looked between the two family members not knowing what he could or should discuss in front of her.

"It's alright, Mick," Pound said. "I've already told her everything we know up to this morning. Did you get a chance to talk to Brandenburg?"

"A little," James replied. "Then the FBI and Chillicothe cops showed up."

"Damn," Pound said. "If they've got him, we'll never figure this out."

"Don't worry about that," James smiled, reflecting on the sniper's disappearing act. "We were sitting on the porch, if you want to call it that. He said he needed another drink, and went back into the house. That's when the cops came, and he was gone like a Houdini disappearing act. I'm telling you I had no clue he had snuck out…just disappeared."

"So he got away?" Melissa asked, confused. "But we need him. If he shot Dayton, he needs to be stopped." She looked distraught and her heart monitor started wailing in response. The nurse came running in and shooed the men out of the room so she could help get the patient calmed.

The men were both worried that they had crossed a line. On one hand, they both knew that she was a strong and independent woman. They had seen it over her entire life. On the other hand, she had never had to cope with the kind of loss she was now facing.

"I guess I screwed that up," James said to the glass he was looking through, out to the parking lot. "I've never really been very good at stuff like this. I'm sorry."

"What are you talking about?" Pound replied. "You didn't do anything wrong. "She said she could take it and wanted to know what was going on. Maybe it's a little shock to the system for her, but she'll fight through it. I know her. She's tougher than you think."

"That's just it. I know how tough she is. I'm just not used to her being so vulnerable. I should have thought out my words before speaking."

"Stop it! You and I both know that there's no way to you can succeed in a mission by pussyfooting around. She knows it too. Now buck-up, son. And tell me what you didn't say in there."

James thought for a moment before responding.

"The man…Brandenburg…scares the shit out of me. That's what I didn't tell you and I'll call you a liar if you ever repeat it."

"I've never seen you scared of anyone, Mick. What the hell happened?"

James told him about getting caught unawares when he arrived, and the helplessness he felt with the blade firmly against his throat. "And then the way he disappeared when the cops showed up. The man's a friggin ghost, I'm telling ya. I've never seen anything like it."

"I tried to tell you," the general smiled. "They wouldn't tell me everything about him when I talked to my friends, but they did say that if he wanted you dead…you would be dead. Oh…they also said that you shouldn't piss him off. "

"I guess it's comforting to know that he didn't have me on his naughty list."

"Do you think he did it?" Pound asked in all seriousness.

"I can't say for sure," James replied, shaking his head still thinking about the morning visit. "If you were to ask me if I thought he *could* do it, I would give you a resounding yes. But if I were to have to make a choice…based on what I saw this morning…I don't think so. He doesn't seem like the kind of person who would make those kinds of mistakes."

"Like what?"

James looked over to Melissa's room. "Like…leaving anyone—Melissa included—alive for starters."

The men remained quiet for a time. James continued staring blankly out the window at the cars in the parking lot while his uncle found a seat and started flipping channels on the waiting room's flat screen.

Ten minutes later, Pound said, "Mickey…come look at this." He continued reading the flashing news bulletin as it ran across the bottom of the screen.

"ANOTHER SHOOTING ON COURTHOUSE STEPS."

"Have they said anything about who was shot?" James asked.

"There isn't anything but this bulletin so far. I'm sure the information will be coming through soon."

James turned from his uncle and pulled out his phone. "I'll be right back," he said as he turned the corner. He knew that Katt would know and didn't care where their relationship stood. His cousin was too important to let a petty disagreement stand in the way.

"Good morning, sir," the man on the other end of the phone said.

"It's not a good time to be calling me," was the reply. "I told you that I would be contacting you when I needed something."

"I suspect you've seen the news?" the sniper continued as if the reprimand had not been heard.

"Yes, I have. You managed to get this one right."

"You don't seem to be very gracious today."

"I'm sorry," the lawyer said. "I suspect I should give you a pat on the back to go with the money I've been sending. So...atta-boy."

"I'm going to let this attitude slide for now," the caller replied in an even voice that showed no sign of the irritation he was beginning to feel toward his employer. "However, I would like to know who it is that's trying to track me. I suspect that the FBI is now on the case. Is that so?"

"Yes. The FBI has one agent here for now. I suspect that will change as the body count rises."

"I suppose so. I'm not worried about it, but I need to get as much information about him as you can get me."

"We can start with the fact that he is a she. Her name is Special Agent Katherine Katt. She is some kind of profiler, but I don't know much more than that yet."

"That's the best they could do? One agent and a woman at that?"

"So far. How many were you looking for?"

"A lot more than that."

"Why?"

"My motives are my own. I guess I need to make an example of her and then maybe they'll take me a little more serious."

"We don't need any more cops here than what we have. And don't do anything stupid. I've spent too much on this project to let your ego get in the way."

"That's the second time you've insulted me. I suggest you consider carefully how you talk to me in the future."

"You work for me, mister. Not the other way around."

"Maybe. But then maybe you were nothing more than a means to an end for me. I have money. I have lots of money. I think from this day forward, you should consider us partners. I'm tired of the whole employer/employee thing."

"And why should I do that?"

"Because I don't clean mustard stains."

"What the hell does that mean?"

"Look at your shirt."

Less than an inch to the left of the man's tie was a tiny red dot about the size of a pin head. The laser was centered to a one inch mustard stain the man didn't know he had.

"This is a courtesy call, my friend. You may have a great career ahead of you and I may need you again down the road. Today I will allow you to live. I suggest you do what you need to do so that I don't change my mind tomorrow."

"What do you need…partner?" came a concerned reply.

"I need to know whatever you can find out about Agent Katt—where she's staying, what she's driving, everything. I'll call you tomorrow and get the information."

"I don't know how much digging I can do with the FBI. My access to their information doesn't get me to personnel. What do you suggest?"

"I suggest you get creative…and use soda water."

"Soda water?"

"To get the stain out of your shirt."

The caller hung up before the man could respond. He looked again at his shirt and saw that the tiny dot was gone. His first step was to go to the windows and close the blinds. The second was to go to the bathroom. It was as close as he had ever come to dying and he needed to clean up before his next meeting.

Chapter 13

"So you've decided to talk to me after all," Katt smiled, recognizing the caller. "I thought you were too busy fishing."

James didn't seem to notice the dig. "Who was it this time?" he asked Katt. "I just saw it on the news."

"Merlin Abernathy, judge, shot in the head as he was heading back to the courthouse." Katt could have told him more, but decided it was still best if she held back. "I really need to talk to your friend, Brandenburg."

"He's not any friend of mine, Katt. Besides, why do you think he did it?"

"I'm not saying he took the shot, Mouse, but there aren't too many people that can hit a target the size of a man's head from a mile away."

"How do you know that?"

"Because people were reporting shots fired from around that far away at the same time people were reporting the shooting of the judge. You met him, Mouse, and then he disappeared. Seems rather convenient don't you think. He goes into hiding and then people start ending up dead…again."

"I never took you for someone that would convict a person before they were found guilty, Agent

Katt. That's not the person I came to know not so long ago."

"There's a lot about me you don't know, Mouse. Besides, I'm simply trying to figure out what's going on. Maybe your friend could shed a little light on the subject for us."

"Still not my friend," James replied, a little miffed at her insistence to the contrary. "However, should this guy ever show up and I do get a chance to talk to him, I'll let him know that you're out looking for him. Maybe he'll just head right over and confess to you."

"It would sure save a lot of taxpayer money. Like I said, I'm not accusing him of doing anything wrong. I just want to talk to him."

"I'll be sure to pass the word if the opportunity arises. One more thing," James had paused a moment when he realized something Katt had said. "How many shots were reported?"

"Consensus said two shots were fired, but there was only one victim. Why?"

"Just working on a theory. I hope I'm right."

James hung up without saying goodbye. He didn't want Katt to realize how much she was getting to him. He trusted her with his life. He wondered if the same could be said in return.

"Was that the shooter calling to confess and offering to surrender?" Hershey asked Katt after she hung up the phone. "I figured that you might have this wrapped up in time for me to take my wife to dinner."

All of her career she'd had to deal with cocksure cops who didn't take her as anything other than a cute blond with considerably less intelligence than she possessed. Every new place, it was the same thing. There had never been outright hostility from them. Usually, the digs were subtle so that if she was to complain, the man—and it was always a man—could refute the claim and say it was just a misunderstanding. However, this time was different. The man wasn't so different. She was. This time, she was dealing with her emotions. This time, it angered her.

Doing everything she could to hold her building temper, Katt said, "I wish it was, Detective Hershey. Unfortunately, it was another detective who actually understands that being an ass doesn't qualify you as an intelligent human being." Then, smiling at the shocked cop, said, "Of course, he didn't understand it right away either. It wasn't until I saved his ass from getting killed…twice…that he finally came around. Let's hope it doesn't take you that long. I may not be there for you when my help is needed." Katt turned and left the man with his mouth open.

When Katt walked over to Hershey's captain, Stetson said, "That seemed a little harsh, Agent Katt."

"Not really," Katt replied, still trying to get her emotions under control. "I've worked with detectives and agents all over this country, and it never fails that at least one of them is more interested in the size of his…gun, than the case at hand. I'm sure your detective has a tough enough skin to get past my remark. More important, I hope it refocuses his attention to the case at hand."

"So where do we go from here?" Stetson asked. "Has your shooter had multiple targets in the same city before?"

"That's just it," Katt replied, looking toward the spot she imagined the shooter had taken the shot. "He hasn't. In the other cities, it was a one and done. He took the shot. Finished his job and then left. I expected to gather information and then try to predict where he would go next based on the intel from here. Had he remained true to his nature, I would have been out of your hair in just a few days. Things are different here."

"Then why is he staying?"

"I suspect that he's here because he has a job to do and whatever that job is, it isn't finished."

"That sounds a lot like you think there will be more victims."

"Based on everything I've come to understand about this guy, I can only pray that I'm wrong."

His uncle was waiting for James back in Melissa's room. He had been told in plain and concise terms that he was not to upset his daughter again. Doing so could be detrimental to her health. He made a promise he was all but certain he would eventually break.

"Judge Abernathy," was all James said when he joined the general and Melissa.

"What about him?" Melissa asked. "Has he done something wrong? Is he in trouble?" Then, looking at the men asked, "Has he been shot too?"

The general looked at his daughter trying to figure out a way to break the news.

"Yes," James said without preamble. He had always believed that the best way to remove a Band-Aid was quick. He applied the same philosophy to *almost* every other aspect of his life. "Less than an hour ago. However, that has nothing to do with you. I'm here for you."

"Why is this guy trying to kill us?" Melissa asked, showing sad eyes.

"That's why I'm here, Melissa," James replied. "What were you guys working on that could be so important to get killed over?"

"Right now we've only got one case we're working on. It's a huge case that could change the

Constitution and how guns are purchased or sold everywhere in America."

"Can you tell me any of the details?" James asked. "Just what you can, of course. I don't want you saying anything that could get you into trouble."

"You mean more trouble than getting killed?" Melissa responded sourly. "Or almost killed, in my case."

"Yeah," James replied. "I just need to get a handle on the basics for now. If that leads anywhere, then I may have to ask you for more details."

Melissa thought for a moment before beginning. "For the most part, the lawsuit is against the Boyd Weapons Manufacturer, LLC. Specifically, it's against Jason Boyd who has figured out a way to manufacture weapons here in the United States, sell them out of the country, and then get them shipped back here to be used in ways that are counterproductive to U. S. interests. In other words, a very high percentage of their weapons are used by drug cartels all the way down to street thugs.

"Jason Boyd has a lot of friends in low places—Mexican, Columbian cartels and several South American countries that he sells his weapons to for substantial discounts. His friends, in turn, find other ways to reward him for doing so.

"Up until recently, he had pretty much managed to stay under the radar until one of his high-ranking employees' kids got killed in a robbery used by one of Boyd's gun and he decided to turn state's evidence.

"We were about to expose it all. We had…have…everything we need to prosecute the son of a bitch. And unless the District Attorney, Jules Habersham, can figure out a way to keep the case going, it's all going to go by the wayside."

"Have you heard anything about what his plans are?" James asked.

"Not yet. I was told that he called to check up on me and is planning to stop by later today. Maybe I can find out from him then."

"What about the witness?" James asked. "What's his story?"

"What do you mean?"

"I mean, how sure are you that he'll testify? Do you think he had anything to do with you guys getting shot? Could he leak information out about where things stand?"

"Why would he? He came to us in the first place."

"What about his family? You say he lost a child. What's happening to the rest of his family? Could they be in danger from this Boyd guy?"

"We thought about that. We have the witness and his family secluded. They're safe from anybody that Boyd knows. Where are you going with this?"

"I'm just trying to get a feel for the dynamics of the case. I'm not drawing any conclusions. Remember, I'm sorta coming in blind right now. I'm trying to figure out why someone would hire a sharpshooter. I'm trying to figure out who could want to hire a shooter of that caliber to do something like this. You didn't mention Abernathy. Does he have something to do with the case?"

"No," Melissa said shaking her head. "I don't think anybody has even seen him around the case or talked to him about it. I know I haven't."

"It's one thing to kill the people trying the case," James took in a deep breath. Then almost to himself, said, "Then what's the purpose of killing Abernathy if he wasn't a part of it? What's the connection? Is he part of the reason you were shot? Or was he killed for something else altogether?"

The room went quiet. James didn't need anyone to tell him that there were a lot more questions than answers.

Chapter 14

Katt got the call with the location for where the sniper was perched for the Abernathy shooting. According to Stetson, the shot took place two blocks west of the art museum from the top of a building that was being renovated. The distance had been measured at just over fourteen hundred yards or approximately eight-tenths of a mile away. Katt caught a ride with Hershey and Montclair, figuring that the fewer vehicles around the crime scene the better.

"How does someone do that?" Katt looked with her naked eyes to the courthouse steps. "How long would a shot like that take just to get there?"

"At twenty-seven hundred feet per second," Montclair replied in a mechanical voice, "Just under two seconds. Maybe a second and a half would be more accurate."

"So," Katt continued as if talking to no one in particular, "the man was walking back to the courthouse. So he was a moving target. He was going up steps. So the shooter would have to take the angle into consideration. It wasn't very windy, but I would think that you would still have to account for it. What am I missing?"

"Temperature, angle of drop from here to there, humidity," Montclair spoke up again. Katt hadn't heard two words from the man before this. Now he was the encyclopedia of long distance shooting. "Then you have the weight of the bullet as well as the caliber. The powder behind the bullet—how fast it burns—or let's just say the speed of the bullet. The faster it burns, the less arch in the trajectory. That's about it as far as the weaponry is concerned. Of course, you still have to take the man into consideration."

"What about the man?" Katt was intrigued.

"The man as to be as cold as ice," Hershey interjected. "If the tip of the barrel were to move as little as a quarter of an inch at that distance, your shot would be off by as much as several feet at the point of impact."

"There can't be that many people who could have made that shot," Katt was still talking to herself, yet aloud.

"That's why we need to have a face to face with that Brandenburg fellow," Hershey said looking up from his notes. "If he could have made that shot like your people say he can, then we need to make sure he's not the one who actually took the shot."

"I'll get a warrant and go back there," Katt replied. She was still remembering what James had told her. Her head told her to do her job the way she was supposed to do it. Her gut told her that she had better slow down and walk it through before someone got hurt. She really wished James was there at that moment. Maybe he could help her work through this better than a couple of gung-ho cops. Unfortunately, James was somewhere else and wouldn't be there to save her if she got this one wrong.

From that distance, would I even hear the shot before the bullet went through my brain?

The day turned into night, and nothing new had been turned up. Katt had called her boss, Jonathan Blythe and updated the status of the case and got the warrants she needed for Brandenburg's shanty. She figured that her best opportunity to catch the man was just after daybreak.

The man had to be brought in. There was no question about that. What she wondered was, was she doing it right? As a rookie, she asked herself such questions, but never had she done so in years. There was something James had said to her that kept eating at her. She couldn't figure it out. Whatever it was, she hoped that once she brought the man in, he would be able to enlighten her.

By five-thirty the next morning, everyone was in place. Katt had organized the Chillicothe PD to supply the manpower necessary. The community was too small to have its own SWAT team. However, Katt had talked to Mike Williams of the BCI, and he had provided the men from their organization as well.

They would take point. All in all, there were twenty officers and agents surrounding the small cabin.

By six o'clock, there was still no stirring in the cabin, and Katt started wondering if maybe the man wasn't home or slept in late. His beater of a truck was parked in the front, so the expectation was that he was home. Waiting was no longer an option, so she decided that they needed to get Brandenburg's attention. Using a bullhorn provided by the local PD, Katt stood next to the car she drove up in and addressed the cabin.

"Joseph Brandenburg...this is FBI Special Agent Katherine Katt, and we have a warrant to inspect your building and bring you in for questioning. Please do not resist and come out with your hands in the air. You have one minute to comply."

Still there was no response and Katt began to get a bad feeling.

"What do you want to do?" Williams asked Katt as time ran out.

"I'm going to approach the door and see if there's anyone home. You stay here and cover me," Katt replied.

"Negative," Williams responded. "We'll go up together. There's enough firepower here to make sure we'll be okay. But, I'm not letting you go up there alone."

"Very well," Katt smiled at the man's chivalrous attitude and started for the cabin.

Once they approached the porch, Katt pointed to a folded piece of paper affixed to the front door. She pointed it out to Williams who shrugged his shoulders, and they both kept their weapons at the ready.

Looking from side to side, Katt had a feeling that she was being watched. The feeling always seemed to come when danger was present. Only, in this case, nothing seemed to be out of place. Danger wasn't anywhere to be seen.

Katt and Williams approached the porch— Katt on the left, Williams on the right. The one step it took to step up was no obstacle. Yet the creaking of the boards eliminated any opportunity of being stealth. They were exposed and hoped it wasn't anything to get killed over.

In order to get to the door, Katt took the precaution of ducking under what she suspected was the front window. She suspected it only because where the window opening had previously been located, all glass had been removed, and the opening was covered with a polyplastic of some sort that was stapled in place with the edges wrapped in a cardboard strip to keep the plastic from fraying in heavy winds. The material was translucent, but clear enough that she could recognize the shape of a human if he walked by. In her mind, there was no need to take any chances.

Katt and Williams reached the door at the same time without incident. Katt stood with her back to the left of the door frame and Williams mirrored her on the right. Williams pounded his fist against the door and called out to Brandenburg. There was still no answer.

They looked at each other and then at the paper hanging on the door and decided to check it out.

The paper wasn't folded as one might expect, but rather the top was secured with staples—the kind that were used on the quasi-window—and rolled from the bottom up near the top and held in place by a single pushpin.

Katt removed the pushpin, and the page fell into place.

On the page were two stick-figure drawings. One had the letters FBI printed above it and the other had the letters COP above it. They looked to be holding hands, only instead, each hand was holding a small star about the size of a half dollar.

There was no warning. There was no sound. There wasn't even a tickle of hair standing as a cautionary hint out of place. Katt noticed that there was more written below the stick figures and reached up to grab the note to see it better.

That's when the center of the paper just disappeared. Not the entire center, just the part of the star the stick people were holding. In the distance, a moment later—or maybe it was at the same time— came the rumbling of a sound that could have been mistaken for thunder echoing off the hillsides.

Katt moved before Williams had a chance to react. She jumped toward the man and hit him with all of her might and knocked him to the floor, screaming, "Move, Move, Move!" In the time it would have taken another bullet to strike, they were both off the porch running full speed to the cars.

"What the hell happened?" Williams yelled as they hunkered behind their vehicle.

Without thinking, Katt had managed to tear the paper off the door as she barreled into the state cop. "This," she said, holding the paper up for him to see.

They both read what was written at the bottom:

2,000 yards.
It could have been you.
It wasn't me.
Leave me alone before someone dies.

"Not very subtle," Williams said out loud, little more than a whisper. "Not very subtle at all. So what do you want to do now?" he asked.

"I suggest we drop back and regroup," Katt replied. "I think we might need a different approach."

"You don't have to tell me twice," Williams said as he grabbed his microphone.

Chapter 15

Katt had been in bad situations before. Most recently she had been involved with the serial killer in Monterey, California and was even kidnapped and placed in a position where she had little hope of getting away. Not to mention, during that same episode she had to save James' life because a cartel boss was intent on killing him and placed her in the line of fire. Then again, he had saved her life a time or two as well. So maybe she needed to call that episode a draw.

Those periods, as well as others, were a part of Katt's life—part of her norm. And yet, for the first time she found herself shaking. There was no warning. There was no way for her to protect herself or anyone else that she might care for. Every time she had been in a harrowing fight for her life, there was always hope. There was always a chance to survive. That man, Joseph Brandenburg, took away that hope, and it was bothering Katt beyond anything she could remember.

"How're you holding up?" Williams asked Katt when he walked up to her.

They had decided to stop in a Chillicothe downtown restaurant and try to figure out a game plan for bringing Brandenburg in.

"I consider myself a pretty good agent," Katt replied, staring into her cup of black coffee. "But I have to tell you that it kinda shook me up a little." She didn't need to explain what the "it" was. "Maybe a lot."

"Whew…thank God," Williams said. "Frankly, it scared the shit out of me." The two peace officers sat staring; Katt into her coffee and Williams out the window of the diner, wondering if he was out there somewhere taking aim. Williams continued. "I don't know if I can do this case. I've got a wife and kids to think about. I've been in some hairy situations, Agent Katt, but I've never been in one where I would have no idea that I was dead before it happened. Do you think the note was real?"

"You mean the distance? Or the rest of it?"

"The distance," Williams replied. "Hell…any of it. Is that really possible? That's damn near a mile and a half."

"Mile and a quarter," Katt looked up at her counterpart. "But what the heck? Anything over a mile is some pretty rootin, tootin, shootin." Katt intentionally used the slang and even drew it out a bit for levity. Williams smiled from her efforts. "The truth is, from what little I know about this guy, it wasn't even close to his record distance. He's one of a kind, and I'm not sure I can get to him."

"Then how do we do it? We sure as hell can't sneak up on him. He'd sit up somewhere and pick us off one at a time. Hell, with that kind of accuracy, we couldn't even bring in helicopters. He'd drop them out of the sky before we could get a bead on him. Anything short of nuclear would be a waste of time."

"Nuclear might be pushing the envelope," Katt smiled. "But I get the point."

"So what do we do?"

"Here's the problem as I see it," Katt studied the man's face. "There's a real good chance that he isn't the one doing our killing."

"Bullshit," Williams interjected. "There can't be two of them out here, can there? I mean, doesn't it seem just a little coincidental that impossible shots are being taken and there just happens to be the one guy who can make impossible shots, and he's innocent? Really? Does that even seem plausible?"

"I understand where you're coming from. Personally, I can't fathom shooting like that. On the other hand, he isn't the only one who could make that shot. There aren't a lot who could, but he's not the only one. I just need to figure out a way to get him to come to me."

"I'm not so sure *that's* a good idea."

"I'm open for suggestions," Katt looked at the man.

Brandenburg had no intention of causing harm to the FBI agent. He remembered the words from the California cop that she was a good person and figured that she simply needed to see that she had to be careful, or she could very well end up as a victim of the man who had been killing all of those people.

Once he heard that the judge had been killed, there was never a doubt in his mind that the blond agent would come looking for him. The only question was, when?

Brandenburg had scouted the area before returning home and knew that for the time being, the area was secure. He also suspected that it wouldn't be secure for long, so he cleared those belongings he cherished and hid them in the underground bunker he had prepared two years earlier—his military weapons, his Ghillie suit, camouflage, and enough supplies to last for several months in the worst conditions.

As the sky started turning to daylight, he spotted the vehicles driving slowly up his lane and knew who would be inside. At least he knew one of them; Agent Katt.

He had left a hand drawn note for them to look at and hoped that they would look at it carefully; giving him enough time to explain what he was capable of doing. For cases like this, mere words would never be enough. He believed a demonstration was the best way of making the point.

He had done research on the agent at an out of the way internet cafe and knew her to be both intelligent and diligent. What he needed at that moment was for the intelligent part to show through.

As he watched their approach to the cabin, he couldn't help but admire the lithe movements of an athlete. He recognized the caution she used going under what could have been a trap from the plastic covered window. Had he set a trap, he was sure she would have discovered it and was glad his only need for the time being was the demonstration.

By the time she had pulled the tack from the paper, he had already set himself for the shot. He was relaxed, sighted, and had already tightened his finger on the trigger. The time from shot to impact was less than two seconds, but a lot could happen in that time. One or the other of the two people standing at the door could have stepped in front of the target, and would be killed instantly. But he was pretty sure that with the two of them standing there, neither would step directly in front of the page—or the door—and block his shot.

The moment the page dropped, Brandenburg pulled the last fraction necessary to take the shot. Looking through the scope he could see that he was perfect and knew that it wouldn't take long for them to react. The FBI agent was the first to figure out what happened and Brandenburg was amazed at how fast her reaction was. She pushed the other cop to the ground and then they took off and hid behind one of the vehicles for several minutes.

Brandenburg had no intention of doing anyone harm. He wanted to make sure that they got the message and believed that they did. Now it was time to get some answers. He had no desire to be a part of whatever was going on. Unfortunately, it didn't seem as if he had any choice.

Chapter 16

James and the general knew that the shooter was long gone. Thinking about it, they figured that the best choice for the time being would be to try and narrow down the list of potential shooters. If the truth were to get out to the public that more than a dozen active duty men, at any one time, were trained to kill targets at distances up to a mile away, the military would have its hands full dealing with the public outcry about keeping those men on a short leash.

The general was able, through his military friends, to get files on over thirty sharpshooters—active and retired—that could have made the shots. With the judge getting killed, the military was certain that the FBI would come looking for help, and they would have to turn those records over. However, everyone up the chain of command agreed that it would be best if they didn't get in a hurry releasing information that could be potentially harmful to the military. It wasn't as if they didn't want the killer taken down. They just didn't want it to get out that they might have been the organization that had trained him.

After explaining that he had someone investigating that wasn't part of the usual chain of command, the government brass readily agreed to help. They all trusted that General Pound would do whatever it took to keep them out of the limelight.

James' phone rang, and he was both surprised and pleased to see who the caller was.

"I think he tried to kill me," Katt said in a voice barely above a whisper. She and BCI Agent Williams had driven back to Dayton with the understanding that they needed to put their heads on straight and get a plan together. Evening was approaching and as much as she hated to admit it, she was still feeling the effects of the shot that barely missed her head. She needed to talk to James. She didn't need him to save her. She simply needed a friend, and she realized a long time ago that she didn't have many.

"Did you say that he tried to kill you?" James asked. "Who? When? Why didn't you call me?"

The general's ears perked up when he overheard James' questions. "I'm with General Pound," James said. "I'm putting you on speaker."

Katt was about to complain, but realized it was too late.

"I think your buddy, Brandenburg, tried to kill me," her voice was flat. "I need to get him to come in, general. Can you get him to do that?"

Pound looked at James before speaking and shook his head. "I doubt it," he replied. "I don't personally know the man and even if I did, I doubt he would listen to me now that he's out."

"Why's that?" Katt asked. "I thought all you Army guys had some kind of bond or something."

"First, Agent Katt," the general scoffed, "I'm Air Force, not Army. Second, he had every chance to stay in the service and elected to get out. I seriously doubt he would take kindly to me trying to order him around now."

"Why did he leave, general?"

"That information is classified, Agent Katt," Pound replied. "So classified that the Secretary General of the United States won't even talk to me about it."

"Are you telling me that there's no way I can get that information? The military won't do anything to bring this guy in?"

"Do you actually have any evidence that he's done anything wrong?" James asked. "From everything I've seen so far, the only thing you have is suspicion that because he can do something, you think he's actually done it."

"You know me, James," Katt said, frustrated that James wasn't willing to help her. "I wouldn't ask for something if I didn't think it was worth the while."

"You said he tried to kill you?" James said. "How do you know it was him?"

"Because he signed the letter stating that it was him," Katt huffed. "Just before he blew a hole through it at two thousand yards, less than six inches from my face."

"He did what?" James almost yelled. "He took a shot at you? When?"

"This morning," Katt replied. "We went out there to talk to him; see if he would come in for a conversation. Apparently he suspected we would and set us up to take a shot at us."

"You went out there?" James was incredulous. "I thought you were smarter than that. That's got to be the dumbest thing I've ever heard."

"Why are you saying that?" Katt asked. "I knock on doors all the time."

"So you go knock on the door of a man you know to be able shoot the eye out of a gnat from over a mile away all the time? Someone who's been trained to be the best at what he does and is actually better than all of them? You do that?"

"When you put it like that…no. I just thought…"

"You didn't think, Katt, and that's the problem. I told you that you needed to let me in on this and that's why. You aren't chasing some lowlife whose kiting checks here. Joseph Brandenburg is a man far worse than anyone you, or any of your contemporaries, could ever imagine."

"I'm not a child, James, so stop acting like I am. I know how to do my damn job."

"Not this time you don't."

"Take us off speaker," Katt yelled.

She couldn't believe that she was letting James get to her. She had put up with his crap in Monterey when she not only held her own, but had actually saved his butt a few times. Now it was like starting all over again with him. In his mind, she was the demure little woman, and he was the rough and tough *man* that was put on this earth to protect her.

"I'm off speaker," she heard James say, though she was almost too far in thought to hear him.

"What is your problem?" Katt bristled. "I need you to help me figure this guy out, and your treat me like some rank amateur. I've paid my dues, buster, and I sure as hell don't need some lecture from you or anyone else."

James paused for a few moments before speaking. He knew she was pissed at him and to some extent, she was right. On the other hand, when it came to Brandenburg, she was wrong. He just didn't want her to be dead wrong.

"You're right," James replied in a conciliatory tone. "I sometimes forget that you've been around the block a time or two. You're young, and sometimes that's all I see. I forget that you're smarter than I am. Hell…you're smarter than everyone in any room you walk into. But Katt, this man is as smart as you and ten times, hell, a hundred times more deadly than us all put together. I've seen him up close, Katt. I've seen a smidge of what he can do. You don't want to go after him half-cocked."

"So you did see him yesterday?" she asked, confirming her notion that James was holding back.

"Of course I did," he smiled into the phone. "I thought I made that perfectly clear. But what I didn't tell you is that he had me dead to rights too. He came up from behind and…never mind. Look, Katherine," James almost never used her first name and she could tell he was serious, "we need to talk. You need to bring me in on this or people—more people—are going to get killed. This is one son of a bitch you don't want to piss off."

"I can't bring you in, James. Blythe won't let me. There's more going on than what's happening around here. I can't give you any details, but please trust me. I can't."

"I do trust you," James sighed. "I just thought you might have decided not to trust me. After all, you're the one keeping secrets."

"You're right. I am. So what do we do now? I can't tell you what I know."

"I guess we'll have to figure something out. In the meantime, stay the hell away from Brandenburg. I'm working on something and if I can help…I will."

James hung up the phone and just then remembered that the general was still in the room.

"Damn, son, you've got it bad," Pound laughed. "I would hate to be in your shoes. That woman is full of piss and vinegar."

"You have no idea, sir. You have no idea."

As Katt hung up the phone, she had no idea that the man she was really seeking was less than a hundred feet away looking through a scope, realizing just how simple it would be to finish off the woman once and for all. He smiled at the thought because soon, that was exactly what he planned to do.

Chapter 17

Brandenburg knew that for him to stop the killings, he would need information he no longer possessed. Had he still been in the military, he would be able to look up the details of any shooter on the planet, learn his techniques and then trap him. Over the years, he had done exactly that.

Being a civilian, on the other hand, gave him a certain flexibility that the military would never grant. What he needed more than anything was access to those records and knew that to get them he would have to break a few rules.

The cop seemed to be the best place to start, he figured.

The day before, when James left the cabin, Brandenburg had decided to follow him. He wanted to see if the cop was who he said he was. He expected James to be holed up in some hotel and was actually surprised when he arrived back in Dayton that he had actually gone straight to the hospital. He had expected that the bit about his cousin being one of the victims was a ruse to gain his sympathy.

When he left the hospital, James was spending a lot of time with some older guy that had a military presence. *Officer I bet*, Brandenburg thought. *He just has that look about him.*

Brandenburg couldn't spend a lot of time speculating about it because he had heard about the judge being shot and needed to introduce himself to the agent, but then he could come back soon enough to talk to James.

Now—a day later—he had a better idea. The officer might actually be the source he needed to get the information he needed. He would know someone, who knew someone that could get him what he wanted. That would be the approach. He didn't like doing things off the cuff, but couldn't see the downside of trying.

The old man drove home—a nice three-gabled home in an upscale neighborhood. The place set back off the street and was secluded, which Brandenburg figured was for privacy purposes. To Brandenburg, it was just the kind of place where someone could be attacked with little or no issues coming from the neighbors.

Parking his truck two blocks away on a side street, Brandenburg took notice that no one was watching him and found the darkness comforting. There were streetlights, but with all the trees and foliage, he had little trouble moving from shadow to shadow.

The old man seemed comfortable in his surroundings, Brandenburg surmised as he watched the old man for the better part of an hour. There was music playing—some old crooner stuff that Brandenburg didn't really care for, but was glad for the noise. It would help mask any sound he would make breaking in.

He was surprised that when he went to open the door, it was unlocked. It was too easy, he thought. It was something he hadn't expected, and anything out of the ordinary was something to stop and check out.

There was no trap, Brandenburg finally decided and thought the old man a fool for being so accessible. When he stepped into the kitchen and saw the man praying, he waited until he was done before making his presence known.

"It took you long enough, soldier," the old man said, completely surprising Brandenburg. "I would have expected to see you yesterday."

"I didn't know I was on a schedule," Brandenburg replied, stepping around so that he could see the man face to face. "Why were you expecting me?"

"You need answers," General Pound replied, "and so do I."

Brandenburg didn't move any closer. He could tell that something was going on and felt like he was way behind the man before him.

"You have me at a disadvantage. I didn't know until very recently that I would be coming here. I don't even know who you are."

"So why are you here then? It seems to me that you're taking an awful big risk coming here without the intel you need for a job."

"Things are little complicated. I figured it would be best to take advantage of a situation. You seemed alone and vulnerable. It was a gut decision."

"I see," the general smiled. "So how's that working out for you?"

"Not as well as I had expected. I take it the doors were left unlocked for a reason?"

"Didn't need you breaking any windows. Homes, nowadays, are expensive enough to maintain without having to go around replacing doors and windows."

"So why am I here?" Brandenburg asked.

The general thought it a strange question, considering that the man broke into his house without an invitation. On the other hand, maybe it wasn't so unusual for a man used to taking orders without hesitation. No matter how gruesome they might be.

"You have a job to do. You need something that you think I can give you."

"That's not what I mean, sir. You led me here. You knew I would be coming to you. That man, James, he came to me asking for help. I could have killed him without blinking an eye."

"Why didn't you?"

"Didn't seem right. Then he brought the feds to my door, and I don't take kindly to that."

"He didn't bring them to you. They went there on their own volition. James actually helped you by not telling them that you were there."

"Didn't know that."

"You wouldn't."

"So back to my question…why am I here? "

"Why don't you have a seat, son? This could take a little while and my food's getting cold."

The general didn't wait for Brandenburg to accept his offer. He stood and went to the stove to ladle out a bowl of homemade vegetable soup that had been simmering for a couple of hours.

"There's plenty if you'd like some," Pound offered. "I was expecting company and made extra."

"When's the company coming?" Brandenburg asked.

"He's already here. I was expecting you. I made extra food last night too."

For the first time, Brandenburg smiled.

"I guess it would be rude of me not to accept then."

The general reached for a second bowl and scooped out a large helping for his guest.

He went by the name Homer because that was what the children called him when he was young. Canadian born, his parents were U. S. citizens and moved back to Detroit when he was six years old. His older brother—two years his senior—David, took on the role of Snidely Whiplash of the old Dudley Do-Right cartoon series and, in turn, he embraced the role of Homer, his tuque wearing sidekick. After his brother died when he was thirteen, he put the Homer name away because it no longer felt right.

After his military stint, when business turned to him to do the things the military had trained him to do, he knew that he couldn't use his real name when contracting hits-for-hire. He remembered his old name; the name his brother gave him. Back then they just performed mischievous acts that were of no consequence. He wondered what his brother would think of him now.

Homer had been waiting for an opportunity to kill the FBI agent. He seldom acted on impulse, but his time in Dayton was getting short. His employer would have been upset had he known that Homer was actually doing these jobs for two reasons. The one involving the killing of lawyers almost seemed ironic. Over the years, he had heard virtually every lawyer joke there was and knew that few people respected them. It almost seemed an act of public service once he thought about it.

His other reason was more personally motivated. He wanted to make a statement and thought that by piggy-backing the two reasons he would be able to do the one job without compromising the other.

It seemed he had been wrong.

The FBI had only sent the one agent; deciding to let the locals ferret out the details of solving the crimes. That wasn't good enough. He needed a larger contingent of agents, and it seemed that the only way to make that happen was to raise the stakes. The solution seemed simple enough; kill one agent and they'll send a lot more.

Chapter 18

Brandenburg finished his soup and sat back; waiting for his host to speak.

"You've got trouble on the horizon," Pound said.

"Not the first time I've seen trouble."

"I imagine not. The government is looking for you."

"I've had whole countries looking for me before. I'll survive."

"The FBI wants you in a bad way; now that you've showed your hand."

"What hand have I shown?" Brandenburg replied, coyly.

"You're too smart to play games, Joseph. Is it okay for me to call you that?"

"My mother thought the name was good enough."

"Okay then, why did you shoot at Agent Katt?"

"I didn't."

"Seemed that way to her."

"How well do you know me, sir? I take it that you're military, or ex-military. And knowing what I suspect you already know, I would say pretty high up the ranks."

"Retired. General. Air Force," Pound replied. "I used to have some weight and found out that you were pretty good at your job."

Brandenburg smiled at the attempt the man made to downplay his record.

"Okay," Brandenburg replied. "Let's leave it at that for now. Anyway, if you've found out anything real about me, you would know that what happened this morning was nothing more than target practice for me. So your FBI agent can say whatever she wants to say, but the truth is the truth, I didn't try to kill her."

"Why did you take the shot? That's seemed a little grandiose, don't you think?"

"I've had the pleasure, and for the record I'm using that term loosely, to work with people who thought they were superior—FBI, CIA…generals—and do you know what they all have in common?"

"What?"

"They all have a tendency to underestimate their opponents. All the education in the world won't prepare you for what it's really like in the world. They all have degrees in all kinds of areas, and yet no one seems to get what it's like dealing with the scum of the world. Some of those so-called leaders even become the scum. I discovered after a while that the only way to get their attention is to give them a reason to look past that education and start thinking for themselves. And if you do that, do you know what happens?"

"You have my attention," the general sat back feigning at being relaxed.

"They will always do one of two things. One group will get thoroughly pissed off and then does everything in their power to hurt the person that forced them to be scared…or should I say, aware. The second group will actually heed the shock and take the time to evaluate the situation and appreciate the new information. I know what's going down, general. I checked out the scene where the first shooting took place—through the steeple. It was pretty damn good shooting if you ask me."

"How did you get to see…?"

"I have my ways," came the interrupting reply. "Now if you ask me, *that* was over the top; grandiose. I would have found a place that wouldn't have left so many issues to overcome. He took a risk—an unnecessary risk."

"Why do you think he did that?"

"Only two reasons I can think of," Brandenburg said. "He was either showing off, or he had been instructed to do it that way. Either way, he made a mistake."

"You mean killing only one of two?"

"No. Anyone could have done that. Anyone could have missed."

"You didn't."

Brandenburg picked up on the subtle comment. "You know more than you've led me to believe." He paused a moment. "I can live with that for now. I don't appreciate creating a wall through dishonesty, sir. Keep that in mind. I don't work for the government anymore."

Pound realized that the man before him was smarter than he had given credit. "I will be straight with you in the future. So what mistake did he make?"

"He gave me a clue as to who he is. Every one of us has a signature. We may take our shots at seemingly impossible distances, but the bottom line is that we all do things a little different. As he does more, he'll reveal himself. When he does that…I'll kill him."

"I don't do that anymore."

"You just said that you would kill him if you tracked him down."

"Then let me clarify," Brandenburg sat forward. "I don't kill innocents. Your shooter isn't an innocent. Him, I'll kill without remorse. I just can't— won't—kill innocents…anymore."

"I've seen a lot over my time," Pound said, looking in his cup of coffee, "but I can't imagine what you've had to do for the sake of your country, so I won't try. I won't pretend to know you by simply reading your file. I do know that you can't do this alone."

"That's how I work," Brandenburg replied. "Unless you know how to be a spotter, you can't help me."

"Then I'll ask again. Why did you come here?"

"Intel," Brandenburg replied. "I know a lot of the men the military has trained. I can even say that I know most of the shooters, but I don't them all well enough to narrow the field completely. I also know that we aren't the only game in town. Every country, or at least most of the countries, around the globe has a sniper corp. There's a good chance that this one is an import. I need information on them all."

"If their records are anything like yours, they won't tell you much."

"Nobody's jacket is like mine, general. Just get me what you can…please?"

"I'm sorry son. You've already done enough for your country. I already have someone working on it. You just keep your head down till we get things straightened out."

"You talking about that dude who came to see me yesterday? What was his name…James?"

"Yes. Mickey James. He's a good cop. He's my nephew, and he'll get to the bottom of this."

"He'll get killed. We—snipers—don't play by your rules. He won't see it coming. Just like your FBI lady didn't see it coming. He'll get killed without me stopping it."

"Then help us."

"I work alone, sir. I don't want to be responsible for anyone else getting hurt. I can't do that."

"Then we're at an impasse. I can help you get the information you want, but I won't; not without you letting us help you get there."

"I could force you to help."

"Son, this conversation is about to go someplace you'll regret going if you continue. There is no compromise here. You help us, and I'll help you. Take it or leave it."

After studying the matter, Brandenburg finally said, "Get me the information."

He didn't wait for the general to reply. He stood and left.

James was at the point where he'd had enough. Katt was as pigheaded as anyone he had ever met. She was strong, beautiful and as well trained as any cop he knew, but she wasn't invincible. At least she wasn't as much as she seemed to think.

James understood the moment that Brandenburg had slid the knife around his neck that he was dealing with someone better than himself at killing. James knew that he was pretty good at his job.

He even believed that given the right situation, he could take down just about any criminal that came his way.

Brandenburg was different. He was a ghost. He was beyond anything James had ever encountered.

The problem was that Katt was simply young enough, smart enough and successful enough to believe that she could get by with what she had already experienced. James recognized the problem and had to convince her to change her way of thinking; at least for this one case.

James knew where Katt was staying and decided to drop in on her unexpectedly. He could only hope that she would listen.

Chapter 19

Homer's employer wanted him to use the long gun to do the killings that were on his list. He wanted them to match as close as possible to the shootings that had already been done in other locations across the country. The boss didn't know who was doing the shootings and didn't care. He had his own agenda. The part that Homer found interesting was that the contractor had gathered enough inside knowledge to allow him to emulate those shots closely.

He didn't need to.

Homer had plans to make an impression on the FBI that would make them all stand up and take notice. He wanted to make a statement and to do that he needed to make a point; a very big point.

Katt was someone in which Homer had decided to get personal. She would make a great sacrifice. But then, there was no reason why he couldn't have a little fun at work.

In his youth, Homer and his brother liked to go hunting. Most of the locals hunted for the larger animals—elk, deer, bear, even moose. There were times when they did so because they needed the meat. Often, they just did it just for sport. But when it came to his passion, Homer preferred smaller game, like fox, weasel, and other beautiful creatures. What he liked the best was mink. They were beautiful, intelligent, and most important, rare. Agent Katt was Homer's mink of the two legged kind. And it was time to bag her.

Katt had decided that staying at hotels for any length of time got old very quick. She would stay at one if she thought the job would only be for a day or two. However, for cases that appeared to be much longer, she would find a bed and breakfast, or a quaint location, that would give her a degree of tranquility.

The Killymoon Bed & Breakfast started out as a small farm in the early nineteen hundreds on a forty acre tract of land east of Dayton. The original owners were of Irish decent and named the place after the castle near Cookstown in Northern Ireland.

After settling, the owners started making beer—a dark lager—and kept the place running for nearly thirty years. Unfortunately, the depression had taken its toll, and eventually the place was sold.

The original barn fell victim to fire, but the stables had survived. The only other remaining building was the homestead which had been restored and used in various business enterprises over the years.

In nineteen ninety-three, the place was bought by Sean and Maggie O'Leary and converted into a bed and breakfast. It had recently grown to become a popular resting place for those wealthy enough to afford a little peace from the hustle and bustle of everyday life.

Katt never considered herself to be wealthy. She had never lived extravagantly off the money she inherited when her parents died. To her, that would have been tantamount to profiting from their deaths. However, recently, she had come to the reality that finding her parent's killers would never happen, and thus it was in her best interest to move forward rather than constantly looking back. Mickey James had helped make that possible.

Most people preferred the convenience of staying in the large main house. They seemed to enjoy the companionship of the other guests, the home-style breakfasts, and the giant fireplace where Sean O'Leary served drinks and Maggie played the piano.

Katt had been told about the place by a friend. When she checked it out, she decided that she preferred the old stables where a part of it had been converted into one very large living space. It would have been more appropriate for several families staying together or one family with a passel of kids. Most of the time, it was used by small to medium companies as a retreat or convention. She preferred the seclusion and didn't mind making her own breakfast or paying the extra money to stay. They gave her a nice discount because of being in law enforcement, and because it was not the busy season.

Homer watched as the federal agent picked up an armload of birch logs for the fireplace and retreated back into the rustic residence. He had seen places like it when he was a child and thought they were attractive. He liked what the owners had done with the old place. He even considered doing something just like that when he retired from his job and decided to leave the killing to the younger crowd.

However, he wasn't there to do a story on the Home and Gardens network. He had work to do in order to earn some of the money necessary to afford such a place.

Taking as much time as necessary, Homer walked the parameter of the old stables to get a look around and determine the best vantage point for entry. He wasn't in a hurry because he thought it would be best to wait and make sure the woman was settled in for the evening.

An hour later, he observed an upstairs light go on and suspected because of the frosted windows, it was more than likely the bathroom. The lady agent was getting ready to take a shower, and the noise from the flowing water would be just the tool he needed to enter without being noticed.

It took less than a minute to disengage the better than average locks. Once he entered and closed the door, he made his way into the main part of the residence.

The running water made him smile as he realized that the agent had underestimated the danger she was in and would, in short order, regret not having taken more precautions.

Katt decided that she needed to get cleaned up from the long day. Her brush with a bullet zipping by her nose earlier in the day had shaken her then and still had her questioning her sanity. In her mind, she couldn't help but wonder if maybe James' insight might be something to seriously consider. She wasn't a fool and didn't believe that James considered her one. To her, he came across a little arrogant, and it upset her. But then she wondered if it was arrogance on his part, or something else; experience maybe? Or was it real concern?

Experience or not, she had been given instructions to keep James away from the case, and she wasn't about to go against her boss.

The shower was invigorating, and it felt good to get the sweat off her body. She never minded sweating for the most part. Her daily ritual included a rather extensive exercise regimen. This sweat was different. It came from fear; something she experienced seldom, and she needed to wash it away from her body. Washing it down the drain was the best feeling in the world.

After taking a few minutes to brush the tangles out of her shoulder length hair, Katt changed into a pair of Victoria Secret lounge pants and tank top. Her feet were bare as she made her way to the fireplace. It wasn't really that cold, but she thought the ambiance of the fire would work wonders to help her relax.

She had just finished lighting the fire when her phone rang. As she turned to see where she had left it, she saw a man completely dressed in black coming at her faster than she could move to get away. Then again, she had nowhere to go.

Instead of trying to run, Katt dropped low and charged her assailant, hitting his right leg just before it stepped to the floor, causing it to slide on the hardwood floor. The force of the man coming at her was dissipated, and he actually rolled over Katt's back.

Quick as a wild animal, the attacker rolled to his feet and faced Katt who had also managed to face the man head on.

She noticed that he was completely covered, including a ski mask that covered everything except two holes for his eyes and a small opening for his mouth. Katt wondered for moment as to where people actually went to buy such clothes.

The man was holding a Kalista knife by Blackhawk, and waved it menacingly at the tall woman. The blade was less than three and a half inches long, but nevertheless appeared quite menacing. She also noted that the man was several inches taller than her own five feet ten. He wasn't a heavyset man, but he wasn't thin either. Her calculation put him at a few inches over six feet tall and maybe 190 pounds.

"Why are you doing this?" Katt asked, trying to figure out a solution to her dilemma. "I've never done anything to hurt you."

The man was quite as he watched Katt move slowly toward an area from which she might be able escape.

"I need something from you," the man finally replied. Katt couldn't see it, but the man was actually smiling. "I need you to die."

"What will that accomplish? I'm a nobody."

"On the contrary," Homer stepped closer. "You're an FBI agent."

"I still don't see what difference that makes."

"The difference…," Homer moved quickly and slashed the knife at Katt. He was using the conversation to gain a couple of feet for the attack and almost accomplished his mission. Katt, on the other hand, had seen the move coming and countered.

Katt's instructor at the Academy had explained a basic principle in hand to hand combat, 'A miss by an inch is as good as a miss by a mile." The idea being that it wasn't necessary to have your opponent too far away. Otherwise, you had no way of answering the enemy's move with one of your own.

Homer thought Katt would move toward the door because that was the direction she had been moving. Katt on the other hand knew that if he was expecting her to go that way, then her best defense would be to change directions and head the other way. The advantage was the fireplace. Not the actual fireplace, rather the poker next to it. In a matter of three seconds, Katt went from being trapped to being armed with a weapon with length greater than that of her opponent.

The killer was beginning to realize that the attractive agent wasn't going to simply accept her fate and die. He knew that someone like her would be a little bit of a challenge, but wasn't sure she was worth the effort anymore. Standing out of her range of attack, he slowly moved the knife across his body and inserted its black blade into its sheath. A moment later, he reached behind his back and pulled a Heckler and Koch Mark 23 .45 caliber pistol and pointed it at Katt.

"If I had more time," Homer said, "we could dance all night. I like a feisty woman. Unfortunately, our dance isn't in the cards tonight. I have other people to do and things to see." He laughed at his own perverted humor.

"I would still like to know why you're doing this," Katt said, without showing the fear she felt. "If you're going to kill me, can't you at least do that much?"

"Drop the poker, Agent Katt. You know the routine."

"You know who I am? I don't get it."

"You don't need to get it. You need to drop the weapon before I shoot you where you are standing."

Katt was about to comply when someone knocked loudly on the door.

Homer turned out of reflex. Katt moved just as fast. The difference was the direction each moved. Katt turned in one fluid motion with the poker and threw it at the man standing before her. The man saw her movement and turned to shoot her while ducking away from the projectile. He missed Katt by several inches. The metal object soared over the man's head and hit the lamp behind him causing the light to shatter and make a ruckus that could be heard by anyone within shouting distance.

The front door was kicked open which caused Katt to glance that way. And when she looked back, the intruder was nowhere in sight.

Katt wanted more than anything to give chase, but realized that it would be foolish to do so. She would have to go get her weapon, and by then the phantom of a man would be long gone.

Katt stood for a second looking at the person who kicked in her door and then smiled. Her friend from California had once again saved the day.

"I take it that you'll be paying for those repairs," Katt said.

"Seems like the only reasonable thing to do," James smiled in return. He had no idea what had caused the lamp to explode. He didn't know that Katt had been in mortal danger and just by doing what he always did, managed to save her life. All he knew was that something had happened, and if Katt wasn't going to chase the problem, he wasn't about to leave her. "Got coffee?"

Chapter 20

"What's going on?" James asked as he pulled out a chair and plopped down with aplomb. He could see that Katt was upset, but had no intention of pushing her to talk. "I heard the crash and thought you might be hurt or something."

"I had a visit from your friend, Brandenburg," she replied without looking at James. "He was here to kill me. If you hadn't...."

"Wait...what? Brandenburg was here?"

"I didn't stutter, James. He was right here pointing a gun at me."

"You saw his face? You talked to him?"

"We talked, but his face was covered," Katt told him about the sequence of events.

"I don't think it was him," James said, though questioning his own conviction. "That just doesn't make any sense."

"He said he needed me to die."

"Why? You're not anyone special," James said the words before he could realize what he was saying. "I mean...you're just an FBI agent. I mean..."

"Why not stop while you're ahead."

"I didn't mean to be insulting. I'm just trying to get a handle on what's going on."

"So am I," Katt replied. She wasn't hurt because of what James had said. By her thinking, he was on the money. The bureau was holding her back, and it still bothered her. They were bringing her in on better cases than before, but she knew deep down that she would never get into the BAU like she wanted. "Look, Mouse, what are you doing here? I told you I couldn't bring you in on the case. My boss was adamant about it."

"Why's he being such a hard ass? You and I both know that we work well together."

"Do we?" Katt wasn't so sure. "If my memory serves me, we fight almost all the time. You're obstinate, abrasive, and you never listen to anyone but yourself."

"You forgot pigheaded," James smiled. "You also seem to forget that I'm always there when you need me."

Katt reflected on his words and couldn't deny his truthfulness. They had saved each other on more than one occasion. She just wasn't willing to go against her orders.

"I appreciate you coming here. Really...I do. Once again, you saved me. It's just not going to change my mind."

"Look...Katt...I came here because I don't think you really understand the type of guy you're dealing with. He's a trained killer. You need to let me help you with this. We won't even tell your boss man about it."

"I can't do that. I have orders, and there isn't anything I can do about it."

James looked at Katt and felt like something important between them was fading away. He didn't like the feeling. As a matter of fact, he hated it with all his being. He just wasn't going to sit there and argue about it. "Send me the bill for your door," he finally said and turned to walk away.

Katt knew that she was hurting him. The feelings he had for her hadn't gone unnoticed. She felt them too. She just couldn't come to terms with the conflict.

"James," Katt said right before he turned to corner.

James looked back at her. He did his best to show no emotion—good or bad. He just stared. Katt was about to invite him to come back. She thought they could at least relax and just talk. Anything was better than the way she was feeling at that moment. She had wanted it for a long time.

Back in Monterey they were close. They were within moments of being as close as two people could get. Then fate turned and took away the moment. All she had to do was say the words, she was sure. She believed that he would return if she asked him to.

History is a cruel mistress. All the tears she had shed. All the times she had refused to allow herself to get close to anyone. It all came back in a rush. Ultimately, she said nothing.

After a few moments of looking at her, James turned again and walked away. Katt figured it was for the last time. And it was her fault.

By the next morning, Melissa Pound had recovered enough that the doctors were thinking about releasing her from the hospital in a day or two. The doctors told her that her injuries were more of a close call than as life-threatening as they had originally believed. They also told her that if she were to take things cautiously and was very careful, there was no reason why she wouldn't be able to go back to work in the next week or so.

Jules Habersham, Melissa's boss—the District Attorney—was listening to the doctors and then waited for them to leave before saying anything.

The DA was more or less of average height and weight and didn't seem to have any distinguishing characteristics. On the other hand, he did have one quality that made him stand out anywhere he went: his personality. The man was colorful, charismatic, and highly intelligent. That was what he wanted the world to see anyway. He held the distinction of having the highest conviction rate the city of Dayton had ever encountered. Even cases that were based almost exclusively on circumstantial evidence were won by the man because the juries simply believed what he said and did what he asked of them.

"That's great news," Habersham said, grasping Melissa's hand. "I was hoping against hope that you would be alright."

"I was kinda wondering about that myself," Melissa smiled. "When I first came to…they told me that the bullet had hit real close to my heart. They weren't sure if it had done damage that maybe they couldn't see. I thought I would be out of commission for a long time."

"Well, you'll still need to rest up for a while. I'm going to assign the Boyd case to someone else. We have court coming up next week. There's no way you'll be ready for that."

"What do you mean? I thought we could get an extension given the circumstances."

"That option wasn't given to us. The judge wouldn't allow it. We either had to refile, which could take months, or do the trial now. I didn't think things would work out if we waited. Our witness is already squeamish. Once she heard what happened to you and the others, she was downright ready to jump ship. I didn't have any choice."

"Then you'll have to keep me on the team," Melissa said, staring her boss in the eyes. "We've already lost too much for me to sit on the sidelines."

"But the doctor...."

"I heard what the doctor said. You're going to get me someone to do the heavy lifting. I can show up for the trial in a damn wheelchair if I have to."

"The judge won't stand for that."

"The judge won't see it. I can travel that way. But I can sit on my butt as well as anyone. I know this case, Jules. No one alive knows it better than I do. I did the majority of the research on it, and I would be invaluable to the case. Who's taking point?"

"I am," the DA smiled. "I can't very well have a bullet-riddled employee showing me up, now, can I?"

"I'm not bullet-riddled anymore," Melissa smiled in return. "Besides, if you're smart, you'll allow me to make you look good."

"Your father, the general, isn't going to like it. He may have my head for allowing it. Are you sure you want to take that kind of grief?"

"Let me worry about the general. Besides, he isn't the one I'm concerned about." Melissa turned her head away for a moment in reflection.

"What do you mean? Who're you worried about? The shooter?"

"No...my cousin, Mickey. Once he hears what I'm going to do, he'll have my ass *and* your head.

How about we just keep this between the two of us for a day or so? At least until I can figure out what to do about him."

"I don't get it," Habersham said. "Why would your cousin be so difficult?"

Melissa laughed on the inside and smiled at her boss. "Mickey James was born in the wrong decade. Hell…he was born in the wrong century. Think Clint Eastwood and John Wayne combined, only for real. He's a force of nature. Tornados change flight plans when they discover he's in the neighborhood. And if he finds out that I'm going back to work before he brings down the shooter, he will be one very pissed off man."

"Is he dangerous?"

"Only to the people who piss him off. I might survive, but I can't promise *you* anything."

"I'll just have to keep my distance then."

"Jules," Melissa said, "I'm not joking here. Stay away from Mickey until I have a chance to talk to him."

"You seem to forget who you're talking to, young lady. I'm the DA in this town, and I have a little clout of my own."

"It won't matter to Mickey."

The DA left with a smile on his face. Mickey James may seem like the boogeyman to Melissa, but to Habersham, he was only a man.

The man wouldn't dare get in my way, the DA thought. This case is too important for some cowboy to mess up.

Chapter 21

"What the hell do you mean he almost got you?" Katt's boss, Jonathan Blythe asked.

Katt took the next several minutes necessary to describe in detail what had happened the night before. She knew that he would be upset and decided to wait until the morning to call. She also knew that he would be upset when he learned how she had gotten away.

"Mickey saved me again," Katt continued after a short hesitation. "He wasn't expected, and he hadn't called to tell me he was coming over. He just showed up. Had he not, I'm afraid someone else would have been making this call."

"Son of a bitch, Katt. That man is making you a walking, talking target. Everywhere he goes, people around him die."

"That's not exactly an accurate description, Jonathan. He's only here because the shooting hit someone in his family."

"Yes…and as soon as he got involved, the crazies all seem to find you to go after. Honestly, do you think the shooter came after you because you just happen to be there, or isn't it just possible that James did something to bring the guy to your doorstep?"

"I don't know," Katt sighed. "But I'm leaning toward the shooter's visit had nothing to do with James. But, it's still early."

"I've got agents in Cincinnati, Columbus and Cleveland that will be heading your way as soon as we're done. There's also a couple right there in Dayton that'll be at your disposal before the day is out."

"But…"

"Don't but me on this, Katt. You'll be in charge of the team. I'll get you the names within the hour."

"What about the locals?"

"I'll let you figure that out. This just went above their pay when this asshole came after you. As soon as they get there, I want you to put together a manhunt and track that son of a bitch down."

"James doesn't think Brandenburg had anything to do with it."

"I don't care what James thinks," Blythe stated and then hesitated. "Last night or any of it?"

"Any of it. He thinks it's someone else throwing Brandenburg under the bus."

"Do you think he's right?"

"I don't know. The guy who came after me seemed to be the right height and weight. I just couldn't tell because I never saw his face. I'm still leaning toward Brandenburg, but James is pretty damn sure of himself."

"So you're back to wanting to bring him in on this? The answer is still no, Katt. He doesn't belong around this case…in any way. Keep him out of it."

Katt hadn't thought anymore about bringing James on board. To her way of thinking, James wouldn't want to be around her all that much. She just hated the fact that her boss was so adamant about it. She understood his reasoning. At least she thought she did. She just couldn't get past the idea that he was trying to control her from his office. As much as they were talking business, it felt personal.

"You're the boss," was all that Katt could come up with. She didn't wait for his response and disconnected the call.

At one point in his life, Joseph Brandenburg had been what society would consider normal. He went to a small, backwater school in Arcanum, Ohio. He played sports, though not good enough to go anywhere. He was considered quiet by those who knew him best. All of that happened before the military.

In the Navy, he excelled in so many different areas the instructors weren't sure which MOS (military occupational specialty) suited him best. He loved to swim and shoot, which fit within the scope of a warrior. However, he also was quite adaptive with languages and the human anatomy.

His size and endurance gave him an edge in most hand to hand skills. The only drawback came into play when he was required to fold his large frame into small, confined spaces.

Living in the wilderness eliminated the worry about confined space, Brandenburg mused as he watched the police pulling into his drive. At first there was only one car that drove up. Soon after, there were several patrol cars and two unmarked cars crowding the front of his little getaway.

The advantage of being a sniper was that you were used to seeing things from a great distance. In a way, he was surprised that the cops were already coming back to the shack. He thought that after his demonstration the day before, they would either have an army of people looking for him yesterday or they would have left him alone. He hadn't expected them to wait an entire day to come looking for him, unless...

Fifty yards to his right he spotted the man coming his way. He moved slow and was quiet. Had Brandenburg been anyone else, there's a good chance the man would have been on top of him before he could have done anything to stop the intruder.

As it was, Brandenburg had the upper hand. The cop-sniper was good, but made a couple of mistakes; the first being that the cop was moving downwind. Brandenburg had learned the hard way that you never wanted to give your opponent the opportunity to smell you. Some snipers have only an average sense of smell. Brandenburg possessed a "super-sniffer" unlike many of his comrades. However, the cop's second mistake was that he had been wearing cologne that, though faint, was still strong enough for Brandenburg to get a whiff.

That caused Brandenburg to look in the right direction.

From there, it was simply a matter of memorizing the terrain and waiting to see if anything changed. It did.

The third mistake, and the most critical one, came as a result of a person who was more adapt to urban warfare than that of being in the country.

In urban conditions, there were few opportunities for a sniper to start from higher grounds and work his way downhill. In those conditions, you almost always had to climb steps to get to the higher ground.

In this case, the cop-sniper had arrived and had a general direction he wanted to stalk. Instead of going around the area and approaching from behind, he had either been told to go straight to the site or did it on his own to get into position just in case Brandenburg showed up. Either way was a mistake. The SEAL had been there all along.

It would have been no trouble for Brandenburg to take the cop out. He was close. He was vulnerable. And for his fourth mistake, the cop had his back to the apparition that could take him out.

Brandenburg took another look toward his dilapidated shanty. What he saw next didn't surprise him as much as he would have expected. Two large, black GMC SUVs raced up to where the cop cars were parked and slid to a stop.

Out of the first SUV stepped the agent to whom he had demonstrated his abilities, Agent Katt he remembered, and then smiled.

The Sacramento cop was telling the truth. She is tough.

Brandenburg had no desire to kill the approaching cop. He figured that it wouldn't necessarily be the case had the situation been reversed. On the other hand, it was important that he fix it so they wouldn't take him so lightly again. To do that, he needed to send a message—another message—that would give even the hardest cop something to think about the next time they came looking for him.

Chapter 22

Katt was upset when she heard that the Three Amigos—Stetson, Williams, and Martin—had collaborated with Chillicothe local and county police officers to raid Brandenburg's residence. She had all the intentions of doing that herself, but had decided to wait for her fellow agents to get into town before doing so.

She got word that they would be hitting Brandenburg's place around noon, and the last of the agents—those from Cleveland—were still hours away. Because of the time, she couldn't wait and took off with the ones she had.

The trip from Dayton took a little over an hour. When she and the other agents slid behind the Ohio Bureau of Criminal Investigation, Mike William's, sedan, she could see that he wasn't happy seeing the party crashers.

Katt sat for several moments trying to decide the best way to approach the state cop. The job of a profiler wasn't just designed to deal with criminals. Often, it was up to her to use her skills to reduce the conflicts that often arose when dealing with the local law enforcement personnel. She already had the authority to control the site and the job, but considered that it wouldn't be the best avenue to approach him. Then again, it seemed as if the only way to get their attention was by using a 2 x 4. She ultimately decided that being straight with the man was the best way to get through.

"What are you doing here, Agent Katt?" Williams asked with his hands on his hips. "I was under the impression that you had other plans for the day."

"How would you know what plans I had?" Katt asked, walking up to the Ohio agent. "It was my understanding that you wouldn't be acting on your own on this case. As a matter of fact, you specifically said that you would cooperate and understood that I am in charge here."

"That's true," the agent replied. "On the other hand, you also told me that the bureau would be keeping us in the loop. It seems that we've both been misled."

"What do you mean?"

"It means…why didn't you tell me that you'd been attacked last night? It means, why didn't you tell me that you were inviting some of your friends," he said looking over Katt's shoulder.

"I just found out about the reinforcements this morning. And, how did you find out about last night? I haven't told anyone about that," Katt wanted to know.

"Like you, Agent Katt, I know people too. Nothing goes on around here that I don't know about." Williams stuck his finger in the air and waved a circle then pointed at the house. It was his signal for his men to surround the building and then send in a team to check the place out.

"Maybe you do have your contacts, Agent Williams, but I'm still in charge."

"So what exactly do you want to do here? We've got a warrant to search the place and this time I have a man out there," Williams said while pointing into the distance, "who will be keeping an eye out for Brandenburg."

"Is it your plan to catch him or kill him?" Katt asked.

"Why, Agent Katt," Williams said, "I'm all about truth, justice, and the American way."

"I believe that about as much as your ability to leap tall buildings with a single bound. Why hesitate when I asked you the question?"

"I'm just covering my bases this time, Agent Katt. I'm not going to end up like things went yester…"

At that moment, they all heard a scream that sounded like nothing they had heard before. They knew that the sound was human. They also knew who had made the sound.

Everybody, that is, except the men and women of the FBI.

It took Brandenburg less than two minutes to sneak up behind the cop-sniper who had been sent to bring him in—or put him down. The effort was actually easier than the SEAL thought it might be.

It wasn't necessary to use force. The simple implication of force was all that was necessary; a gun to the back of the man's head was sufficient. It took another minute to tie the man spread between two trees with the help of the cop doing one arm at gun-point and Brandenburg doing the other.

The real difficulty came when Brandenburg explained his intentions to the cop who then started kicking violently. *Too little. Too late.* A sharp blow to his nose quieted the man's actions considerably. Blood ran from the man's nose and was one of the touches Brandenburg had in mind anyway. After tying the man's legs to the trees as well—spread eagle—he went about preparing for the exhibit that would give the cops pause.

Brandenburg had no intention of doing *real* harm to the cop. However, he needed to get everyone's attention. By using his razor sharp K-BAR knife, he cut the man's clothes off leaving him exposed to God and anyone else who might come along.

Brandenburg looked again through his scope and saw Katt and another cop face to face and decided now was as good of time as any.

Without preamble, the Navy man took the knife and dragged it slowly across and down the man's chest.

The cop screamed better than Brandenburg had hoped. He was a big man, yet had a high pitched voice when he was being cut. The laceration was barely enough to break the skin. He wanted shock and awe to get the all of the cop's attention and was getting plenty of that. Blood flowed freely down the man's chest. The area was quite vascular and would soak the guy's chest easily. He then did the same thing going the other way, so his chest revealed the letter X. Odds were in favor that the injuries would not leave a permanent scar. This was more about the blood than the actual damage.

Brandenburg was about to do the last cut along the man's stomach when something spat in his face. Looking at the cop, he noticed that something was missing; half of the man's head.

The cop was no longer the example Brandenburg had hoped. He was now the reason for the whole world to come after him in full force.

The killer had killed again. Only this time he'd managed to put Brandenburg right in the crosshairs. As far as the police were concerned,

Joseph Brandenburg had just graduated from a person of interest to public enemy number one.

Katt, Williams and the rest of the force reacted quickly. Katt understood the scream to be a call for help but didn't know who made it. Williams understood what the scream meant. The difference being that he also knew who was being tortured.

Brandenburg's home was approximately a quarter of a mile due west of Ross lake. The police had determined that the shot Brandenburg had taken the day before was somewhere due east of the lake on the ridge of the mountain that provided the valley that made up the lake. They didn't know exactly where the shot had come from, but were certain of the approximate area.

Katt and her agents along with Williams jumped into their respective vehicles and headed where they thought their man was located. A mile is a long way for sound to travel. Generally, most people don't realize that even soft sounds can travel long distances in the country when other noises are not a factor to drown them out. A quarter of a mile is no problem. A half mile would be difficult but not impossible. However, to make a sound travel a mile, even in the country, would take a huge effort on the part of the noise maker.

There was no direct route to the location where the cop should be. First they headed north and east on Blacksmith Hill Road and then turned east on Lick Run Road. Lick Run Road soon turned north again, so the group continued east and south on Musselman Mill Road. At the intersection, if you could call it that, where Lakewood Drive veered to the left, the group figured they were due east of the cabin and parked the cars.

At that point, they had to make a choice. A line of sight point could occur on either side of the road. The ridge closest to the lake would have been a considerably easier spot from where to shoot. The Ohio agent decided that he and his men would head up the hill to see if Brandenburg had used that area from which to shoot and or hide out.

Katt and her agents headed up the other side. She had spent a lot of time the night before looking at a topographical map of the area. Most people used the night to sleep, but not Katt. For her, nights were a reminder of the dreams that tormented her from her youth. Add to that her mask-clad visitor and Katt got very little rest; even less than normal.

Once she and her agents reached the top of the ridge, she wished she had been told to go the other way.

Chapter 23

Brandenburg never worried about dying. He had seen it too many times to let it bother him. He had caused it too many times to let it weigh him down.

As soon as he felt the blood hit his face, he dropped to the ground and rolled behind a tree just in case the man doing the shooting had a change of heart and decided to make him a target as well. He didn't expect it, but thought; why take the chance?

He had heard the shot and figured the weapon the killer used was silenced. However, he immediately knew the direction by how the cop's head had reacted. He knew that he should immediately run; reinforcements would be coming soon. He had intentionally posed the cop in a location that would be easy to find. And though he wasn't afraid of death, he didn't exactly wish for it to come sooner than God had intended.

Besides, whoever this asshole was, had messed with the wrong person. The first thing Brandenburg had to do was get away, and then he was going to make it his newfound goal in life to shut the bastard down...hard.

It had been a long time since Homer had tracked another killer—at least one as good as the one he was stalking. Brandenburg was something of a legend among the snipers of the world.

He remembered a conversation several years earlier when he had heard a rumor about an American who had waited over eight days for his kill shot to come along. That kind of patience was unheard of in his world. Sure, a day, maybe even a couple of days, could go by before a clean shot could take place. Anything longer than that could only be based on useless or inaccurate information.

However, in that case, the information was accurate. The problem from the beginning had to do with the paranoia associated with the target. Carlos Vander Gonzales—noted South American general, torturer, and all around scumbag—had made a lot of enemies and knew that somewhere, someone would try to kill him. As such, he took extreme precautions to make sure that anywhere he went an advance team would inspect the area rigorously a week or more before he would arrive.

The CIA had intelligence that the general would be flying in at some time to a small airfield and enjoy a weekend break with his new mistress.

According to the person telling the story, Brandenburg had no idea how long it would actually be before the man arrived. All he knew for sure was that he would get there sooner or later and had a green light to take him out when the opportunity presented itself.

Eight days later, the general showed up, and from a distance of over a mile away, Brandenburg took the one shot necessary to prevent the man from ever destroying another person's life.

That was the past. And though his handler adamantly objected to killing Brandenburg, Homer thought it was wrong to let the super-sniper live. The rationale was simple; if you don't kill him when you get the chance, it was quite possible—maybe probable—he will kill you later.

But that wasn't the plan.

The plan was simple yet eloquent. Do all the killings you need and then see to it that the police or FBI or whomever, discover, track down and kill the killer; in this case, Brandenburg. If you killed him, the boss explained, you left yourself subject to a manhunt that you could lose. With the technology of today, getting caught was more and more the likely outcome.

Homer had spent weeks watching Brandenburg from afar; always through a scope. So many times he had wanted to go to the man's decrepit habitat and check around the place. But, he refrained.

He had watched and discovered the man's habits. He noted, for instance, that Brandenburg liked a certain spot along the lake's bank to fish. He liked another spot along the very ridge they were standing on to hunt. He knew more about the ex-SEAL than he ever knew about any of his other targets and he wasn't even allowed to kill the man.

Homer was doing what he and Brandenburg had been trained to do. He loved the hunt and hated that he would not be able to finish the job. What he didn't expect was to be able to watch the master in action.

Step by agonizing step, he saw the precision that Brandenburg took in following the sniper-cop. Had he not had the advantage of an infrared scope to spot the man overnight, he would never have been able to spot him and more than likely moved on somewhere else.

After the debacle with Agent Katt, Homer found that he needed to get away from the city and decided to watch Brandenburg before heading back into town to finish off one more judge. It took several hours to get into place and was surprised that Brandenburg was already on the prowl. The ex-SEAL did not use the IR glasses that Homer used. He didn't seem to need them.

Then again, Homer thought, *if he'd have had them, he would have spotted me; just like I spotted him.*

Homer waited for Brandenburg to get into position and expected him to kill the cop—quietly. It never dawned on him that he would set himself up as if it had been the plan all along. Homer was ex-Marine Recon. He had been taught to observe, adapt, and improvise. Brandenburg had just given himself up to becoming the perfect patsy.

Katt saw the strung up and deformed body of the captured man and knew what had happened. He was an example, a message if you will, for anybody who might be stupid enough to come after Joseph Brandenburg.

After calling state agent Williams, she walked around the body and wondered how it was that Mickey James could have been so wrong about the man. Granted, what little she knew about Brandenburg indicated that he had left the military because of having his fill with killing. Then again, just how far would he go with his back against the wall?

"Jesus Christ!" Williams shouted when he met up with Katt and saw the destruction that used to be sniper Montclair—Detective Hershey's now deceased partner. "How the hell could someone do this? What kind of monsters does the Army churn out?" he finished.

Detective Montclair was also ex-military. He had been a sniper and tested very well after going into Dayton's HRT program. Every major city had their own version of hostage rescue and Montclair had volunteered to be a part of Dayton's unit. He had seldom been called into action, but jumped at the opportunity of going after the man they thought was out there killing their local people.

When Katt talked to the man the day before, when she had first met him, he seemed quiet and unassuming. She noticed quickly that he was well versed in the art of long weapon shooting. What she didn't know was that he would be the one Williams asked to try and protect her and everyone else attempting to get ahold of Brandenburg.

"Navy," Katt replied quietly.

"What?"

"He was Navy," Katt clarified. "Not Army."

"I don't give a flying fuck what he was," Williams shouted. "He killed a good man. That's what I know. Montclair was married and had three kids, all under the age of ten. Do you really care what color uniform he wore?"

"I'm sorry, Agent Williams. I meant no disrespect. But in answer to your question, the military—all military—turn out some of the most ruthless fighters the world has ever seen. Just keep this in mind, I'm not standing up for him in any way. But, those same ruthless men are the ones that protect us. Don't go categorizing him with all military men. I don't know what happened here yet. On the surface, it seems that Brandenburg killed him after torturing him to make a point of some kind. At least that's my assessment. I'm just saying to keep it together, sir. We have a lot of work to do before making any decisions."

"How open minded do you want me to be when I have to go tell his wife that her husband won't be coming home to dinner? How calm do you want me to be when we sit down with his children and try to explain that their daddy was tortured and then shot through the head because some asshole decided to make a point and used their father's brains as a magic marker?"

Katt replied in a soft voice; barely above a whisper. "I've had enough of those conversations to know what you have to do. You've been around long enough to've made them yourself. It's never a pleasant thing to have to deal with. However, right now, we need to focus on what is right here in front of us. Brandenburg is still in these woods. He only has a ten minute head start. We have enough people here to start tracking him down. Have them spread out and cover the area. They're your people, sir, and they need you to be their leader."

Williams wrestled his eyes from the ground in front of him and with a great deal of effort, focused them on Katt. He then chanced a glance at his men and saw their eyes focused on him and decided Katt was right. There would be time later for remorse and maybe even a few tears. At that moment, however, they had a job to do; find the son of a bitch that killed his friend.

Chapter 24

Brandenburg knew that he was now, officially, at the head of the FBI's most wanted list. Whoever killed the cop-sniper would never let him leave the body until the last second. He had to stay put and wait to get arrested or find another way out of the mess he was in. Running wasn't an option for another reason; there was nowhere to run. Sure he could get a few miles in the woods, but as soon as the police brought in the dogs to track him down, he was finished.

There was always the possibility of fighting. He could take out the dogs if he wanted to. They would be easy targets and then go from there. But to him, that route was unacceptable. Killing a dog that was merely doing its job would never be a viable option unless they too were killers. He could live with kill or be killed. He just wouldn't kill a tracking dog.

He made the decision. He knew that his choice was a big risk. Chances were that what he was planning would not succeed. He had little time, and of all the possibilities, it was the only option that might work. He just wasn't sure.

The work of a cop is never as glamorous as what you see on TV; especially that of a detective.

Most of the time a cop is sifting through reports, files, bank statements, phone records, and any other document that might garner a little insight on the bad guy.

In the case of Joseph Brandenburg, the available information did little in the form of direction that James was hoping to find. There was his early military career, in which the man performed like nothing he had ever seen. His proficiencies in weapons were beyond belief. What made it even more amazing was the fact that, as far as James could find, Brandenburg had never fired a weapon before joining the service. Add to that all of the other skills he had accomplished, it was a wonder that the Navy was willing to let him go.

After that, his records got murky. He was sent here and there for various clandestine jobs that were either not mentioned or redacted. There were entire timelines that had no information at all.

After he got out of the service, which was relatively uneventful, Brandenburg moved back to Ohio. He bought the small tract of land where he currently resided, and that was about it. There were no credit cards on file. There was an old truck that he owned with a listed address at a Chillicothe P.O. Box, and that was it. He didn't even have a utility bill to track.

James' uncle, General Pound, had brought over several files on potential snipers that he somehow managed to acquire and left them for the Sacramento detective to peruse. It was easy to get the names, Pound had told him. But to get the files was damn near impossible. Pound told James that Melissa was being released from the hospital early, and he needed to go pick her up.

After going through the files once, James was about to start through them again when his phone rang.

"Agent Katt," James said as a way answering the call, "I was under the impression that we had said our goodbyes already."

"So did I," Katt replied, a little hurt. "However, circumstances have changed since we last spoke."

"What? You called to apologize? I can't believe it."

"No, Mouse. Not those circumstances. There's been another kill. This time it was a cop...a city cop."

James had no response. He felt foolish for his comment. He felt worse for the cop's family.

"What can I do?"

"Help me bring him in," Katt's voice was firm...professional even.

"Who? Brandenburg? I think you're off base about him, Katt. I don't think he's the one doing this."

"The cop was killed out near his place, James. We were going in to do a search of his home. They sent a sniper out in the direction where he shot the note to me from across the lake. From a mile away, we could hear the screams where Brandenburg tortured the man to get our attention. He then put a bullet in his brain to finish the job."

"How do you know it was Brandenburg? Maybe it's someone trying to set him up."

"Why are you so sure it's not him?" Katt asked, frustrated.

"Because he offered to help find the man who is the killer."

"What are you talking about? When?"

"Last night, while you were being attacked, Brandenburg was at the general's place trying to talk the man into getting some information that will exonerate him and, just maybe, help catch the shooter."

"Why didn't you tell me this before? Damn it James, you could have kept a cop from getting killed."

"Don't pull that shit on me," James bellowed. "I wasn't the one with my panties in a wad and intent on bringing him in. I told you that I didn't think he was the shooter, and you wouldn't let me in on the case to help anyway. You want the glory of taking down a sniper. Then you have to live with the consequences of failure. Maybe you should call your boss to bitch to him about it. He seems to be the one pulling your strings these days. Maybe he can help with the grief."

Katt was quiet for what seemed like a long time. In truth, she did blame herself for what happened. Granted, she didn't even know what Williams had planned. Maybe, if she were going to throw out blame it should go there. But no matter who was to blame, it wasn't James.

"When did you hear about it; about Brandenburg visiting your uncle?"

"About a half hour ago," James replied quietly. "I don't know why the general decided to wait to tell me. He just showed up here, dropped off some boxes, told me that Melissa was getting out of the hospital, and then what seemed like an afterthought, told me about Brandenburg. He seemed distracted. It was only just a few minutes ago that I put two and two together about last night." He paused a moment and then said, "I would have called you, you know. I just didn't know what you guys were going to be doing this morning."

"I know," Katt sighed into the phone. "I know."

The whole conversation slowed even more. Then Katt said, "He still could be the one from this morning, you know. Maybe things just got out of hand and…"

"No way," James interrupted. "You don't understand the man you're dealing with. He doesn't let things get out of hand. Whatever happened this morning had nothing to do with Joseph Brandenburg. I would bet my badge on it."

"I'm not sure it'll make any difference. The locals are going to track him down, James. And I don't think he'll make it back for the trial."

"If they go after this man, Katt, there'll be a lot more body bags. You have to stop them."

"It's too late. They already have the hounds and are going after him. I can't stop anything here."

Homer waited until the last minute to leave Brandenburg next to the body. He was surprised that the man didn't try to run for it sooner. He wouldn't have shot him, but he would have put the fear of God in him with a close shot; maybe even one that wounded him.

Instead, Brandenburg didn't even try to leave the area. Maybe he expected Homer to go for a kill shot. He didn't know for sure who was shooting at him, but if he had read the papers or watched a little television, he must have seen how good the sniper was.

Homer heard the cars as they raced up the road and figured he had just enough time to make his escape. He also figured that if Brandenburg had any chance of escape, he would have to move immediately. Give the guy a fighting chance.

Chapter 25

There was no way, and Brandenburg knew it, that he could outrun the police. There were a lot of them. And even though he was still in good physical condition, the cops would easily be able to circle any possible escape routes.

Instead, he decided that the best way to help his chance of escape would be to hide in plain sight.

The Ghillie suit was something he wore anytime he was on the hunt, or in need to be a fly on the wall. He knew that sooner or later, most likely sooner, the cops would be calling in the dogs to track him. He also knew that they would know his scent from where the cop had been killed and would track from there.

The local terrain was hilly and thick with brush. There were only so many trails and the cops would follow any of them where the scent was present. Brandenburg also knew that his scent would be on two of them that led from the murder site.

Less than thirty feet, closer to twenty, from the dead cop's body there was a thicket of wild raspberries. Brandenburg knew that, as well as all of the other brush in the surrounding woods. The beauty of a top-of-the-line suit was that if you needed to blend in, you would take some of that very brush and strategically add it in order to add credibility to the disguise.

Brandenburg had already accomplished the task overnight and didn't have to waste the time doing so right then. The suit was thick, carried the appropriate blend of green and browns, including the raspberries stems, and most important, close enough to the sight that when the dogs started sniffing around him, the handlers, he hoped, would pull the dogs away from the thick, thorny brush and keep them on the trails.

Katt hung up the phone with James and turned back to face Williams who had just hung up from talking to Stetson. Montclair was his man, and it was only right that Stetson was called first. When Williams asked if he could contact the man's wife, Stetson refused the request, saying that he would take care of it and that Williams needed to catch the SOB who murdered his detective.

Williams hated the fact that he actually felt relieved that he didn't have to make that call. There was already enough guilt. Talking to the man's wife was going to be brutal.

"What did your friend have to say when you told him that his buddy was now a cop killer," Williams asked Katt.

Katt explained enough to Williams about Mickey James and their connection that he knew she and James had been discussing Brandenburg at length. The question didn't surprise Katt even a little.

"He still thinks that Brandenburg is being set up," Katt replied, putting her phone away. "He thinks there's more going on here than meets the eye."

"I thought you said he was a good cop," Williams said. "Sounds to me like he's got a little bromance going on with Brandenburg."

"He *is* a good cop," Katt stated, maybe a little too emphatically, while placing her fists firmly on her hips. She didn't know why she felt like it was her duty to defend Mickey James, but she did, and would. "As good a cop as you've ever seen. He doesn't get taken in so easy. Maybe that's been my problem with this case. I'm seeing what the killer wants me to see."

"Maybe you've got a little bromance—or would that be romance—going on there too, Agent Katt?"

"You don't get it do you," Katt said walking up to look Williams eye to eye. "Everything we know so far is because the killer wants us to see it. He's managed to do things that, in theory, only one person could have done. And like any good detective, or FBI agent, we applied Occam's razor to the scenario and voila, everyone, including me, comes to the conclusion that Brandenburg is the villain. Mickey

James doesn't work that way. He's the exception here. He sees everything that is presented and then asks what's missing and why?"

"I can't work that way, Agent Katt. I can only work with what I know. I may get it wrong every once in a while. And if I do, I start over until I get it right. What the facts are telling me is that Brandenburg is up to his ass in this mess, and I'm going to bring him in."

"I hope your definition of bringing him in actually means bringing him in. I would hate to put cuffs on you for stepping over the line, Agent Williams."

"I'm not the one you need to worry about, Agent Katt. I won't be the one to put him down unless I have to. I can't say the same thing about some of the others."

"Then let's hope we find him first," Katt said.

Brandenburg was lying close enough to the agents to hear every word they spoke. He had only used the ploy once in Bogotá, Columbia. The plan worked well, but they didn't use hound dogs.

In theory, the plan should work. Stay close to where they know you've been, blend in with the scenery so they can't readily see you, and they will start the search in the direction where they think you went. They already knew his scent would be around the victim so they wouldn't be looking there. Once they start fanning out, the cops wouldn't have a reason to stay on-site other than a crime scene tech would snoop around a bit.

The dogs can't tell if a person was moving left to right or right to left. They only knew that the spores and skin cells you left behind would be on the ground and ready for the hound's nose to pick them up.

Brandenburg listened to the conversation and decided that he liked agent Katt. He had no illusions that she would arrest him if she ever found him. He just liked the idea that she was willing to accept the possibility that someone else could be doing the deeds. That would have to be enough for the time being.

For now, all he could do now was wait until nightfall and hope that whoever was guarding the scene would get lazy enough for him to slip away.

Sheriff Doug Martin was beginning to feel left out from the investigation. The FBI had brought in a team of their own. The BCI was able to go wherever they wanted in the state and Stetson had enough specialized men to phase the Sheriff's Department out.

Truth be told, the department had enough of their own work to keep them busy, but it wasn't right that his people had been shot and killed, and there wasn't anything he could do about it.

Martin was rereading everything that had come through and noticed a detail that, to that point, had been ignored. The people downtown who reported hearing gunshots stated that they had heard two shots spaced some time apart. After Abernathy had been killed, everyone focused on locating where the shots came from and sealing the scene of the crime—the steps.

He figured that it was the second shot that killed the judge. What nobody had bothered to check out was what happened to the first shot.

After calling a couple of the witnesses for a better description of the events, he picked up the phone again and made another call. He was going to find that other bullet. He knew it was the worst kind of needle in the haystack scenario. He also knew that smaller things than a bullet had been used to put a killer away for life. And since Ohio was a death penalty state, he also knew that if he could find that bullet, maybe it could be used to fry the man responsible for killing his friends.

"Blythe," Katt's boss said when his phone rang. He hadn't even bothered to look at the caller ID to see who it was. As soon as the caller announced himself, he wished he had.

"Do you actually think you're doing her any favors by setting her up to get killed?" James stated firmly into the phone. "I've been trying hard to figure out what you're trying to do here, and the only thing I can come up with is that you want Katt dead. That's the only thing that makes any sense."

"Detective James," Blythe replied stoically. "Why am I not surprised by this call?"

"Cut the crap, Blythe, and answer my question."

"My answer is…you are delusional. There is no way I would ever put Katt in harm's way; at least no more than any other agent."

"I don't believe you, Blythe. For some reason, you've put her in a situation where the best she can do is survive. To do that, she has to fail. Because if she does succeed in getting close to this maniac, she'll be dead before anyone can stop it."

"She managed to do alright last night, and that was pretty close. I think it's you who has the death wish for agent Katt, Detective James. It seems anytime you get near her, someone tries to kill her. Is that simply a coincidence?"

"You're twisting everything around and you know it, Blythe."

"What do you want, Detective James? Or am I supposed to guess?"

"I want in," James replied. "I want to be able to protect Katt from the S.O.B. who's going around and killing people…including a cop."

"What cop?" Blythe asked, surprised. "I've not heard anything about a cop getting killed."

"It just happened. I guess Katt hasn't had time to tell you about it. Now she's out chasing this mad man around out in the woods. Is that what you had in mind? Last I heard, a combat trained sniper is a hell of a difficult target to catch, especially when you're in his backyard doing the looking. She and a lot of good people are going to get killed out there if you don't do something smart…and soon."

"And you think you have a better chance of catching him than the FBI team that's after him? I don't think so."

"Then let me explain it another way, in case you don't realize just how serious I am here. If Katt gets hurts, I'll fry your ass. If she gets killed, I'll…let's just say I am a firm believer in the Old Testament; eye for an eye and all that."

"Are you making threats to a deputy director of the FBI, Detective James? Because if you are, you could have a few problems of your own."

"I'll gladly pay for my sins, Mister Deputy Director. I hope the hell you're willing to pay for yours."

James wished he had one of those old rotary phones that were heavy and solid so he could slam down the receiver. Modern technology didn't account for that aspect of personal gratification and James hated the state of what man now had to endure.

Chapter 26

The body had been removed from the mountainside. Men and dogs had left to find the man who had killed one of their own. The only people left at the scene of the crime were two rookie Chillicothe uniforms. Neither had ever seen a sight so gruesome, and neither had any idea how close they were to a man so capable of killing them.

Katt had followed the first dog and the man who controlled it to the south. The trail wasn't flat, but the terrain wasn't nearly as difficult as she expected. The most bothersome aspect of the hillside was that the shrubs were thicker than she had hoped. Truth be told, without the dogs, Katt expected that Brandenburg could have hidden in any one of a dozen places. With the dogs, she believed that they would finally track him down.

Her phone chirped for the third time—Blythe. She didn't want to talk to her boss at that moment, but she knew she couldn't put it off forever. She knew that if she didn't answer now, he would call one of her new team and that wouldn't go over well.

"Katt," she answered in a put-off tone.

"I see you're still keeping unwanted company, Agent Katt," Blythe said.

"If you mean the group of agents you sent me, then I guess you wouldn't be far off. Or did you mean the guy who just killed a local cop just because he was in the wrong place at the wrong time?"

"I mean Mickey James," Blythe cut her off.

"I have no idea what you're talking about," Katt replied, confused. "Mickey James isn't anywhere around here."

"Then how did he happen to find out that the local cop was killed before I did?"

"I called him," Katt replied stiffly. She hadn't even thought about calling her boss. She called James because she wanted to know if he could help her find the killer. After he angered her, her mind went to the job at hand. She figured she would take care of everything else when the time was right. "We had another killing here, and I called him to see if he or his uncle had any idea where I could go next with the investigation. I planned on calling you, but the situation was delicate and I put my focus there. How did you find out about it?"

"Your boyfriend called me to give me the what for. That's how. He seems to think you can't do this job without him."

"I'm sorry," Katt's face was red. "I didn't know that. He shouldn't…"

"Your damn right he shouldn't," Blythe bellowed. "Listen here, Agent Katt. I've cut you a lot of slack when it comes to your job. I've given you the kind of latitude I would never give anyone else. But, this thing with James is getting out of hand. Get it under control or you'll be assigned somewhere he won't be able to track you down."

Katt had no idea how to respond to her boss. This wasn't like him. She knew that he was right. James could get under anyone's skin. Her feelings for James were something she needed to separate from her job. The thing that bothered her most, however, was that when Blythe said that her boyfriend had called, she didn't mind the allegation. As a matter of fact, she kind of liked it.

What did that mean?

Katt was taken aback by the man's anger and didn't understand why he was so upset. On the other hand, he was crossing a line.

"Jonathan," Kat started then paused. "Let me start over. Deputy Director Blythe, I don't understand what's going on here. I also know that you are my boss, and it's my duty to do my job in the most efficient manner within the guidelines you establish. Maybe it's the pressure from above. Maybe it's something else. Whatever's going on, I apologize if you think I've not done my duty. And should you decide that someone else is better qualified to lead this investigation, I'll step aside and be a good team player. But…and it's a big but…you don't get to tell me how to handle my personal life. You've earned my respect as a boss. You have even become a dear friend. However, with regards to whom I date, spend time with or even sleep with, that is my business alone. Is *that* understood? If you want to send me somewhere else just let me know, and I'll pack my bags. But if you want to catch the son of a bitch whose killing people around here, then let me do my job the way I see fit."

Blythe wasn't surprised by Katt's response. He was more surprised it took her so long to get there. Blythe had wanted Katt to move on and get a life of her own. She needed someone to care about, but couldn't pressure her into doing something about it. He was aware that Katt liked James and had been doing everything in his power to force her to make a decision about her feelings toward the man. On the other end of the line, he smiled.

"How exactly do you see fit to do it?" Blythe said without comment concerning Katt's tirade. "Let me guess, you think James can do the job better than us all."

"No, I don't," Katt retorted. "But if I can honest, sir."

"Please…be honest. Why stop now?"

"I think it's narrow minded to ignore the kind of help and experience that someone like James has to offer. If you don't want him on the case, I understand and will abide by your ruling. But we could use a little insight on the shooter that he might be able to bring to the table."

"He'll put you in harm's way," Blythe said.

"I'm already in harm's way! Can't you see that? If anything, James will see something that I don't. I don't know what it is about this case that's so different than the others, but to be honest, I think I could use a little of his wisdom. I don't care about who gets the credit. I'm tired of people getting killed because I can't see through it. James can bring perspective that I need."

"What about the other things we discussed...the other cities?"

"I won't bring him in on those. We have enough information from what's happened here to get by without it."

"Then it's your call. Just keep me posted...before you call anyone else."

Blythe hung up, and Katt heard the sounds of a braying hound. The problem was they were coming from somewhere else.

The sky had turned black, and what started as light rain swiftly turn into a downpour. Brandenburg maintained his stealth-like silence and knew that whatever the police were hoping to find was quickly washing into the lake.

More than anything he could imagine, the ex-SEAL wanted to get up and run away. He knew that it would be foolish, and he knew he wouldn't do it, but the urge was almost rabid.

Even though the sky had darkened considerably, there was still enough light for the two cops to see him if he tried to move. The beauty of how he was hiding was also the biggest problem. The raspberry bushes were similar to a rose bush; they were covered in thorns. The thorns would cling to anything they came in contact with and should they release, would move like a whip and cause a sound or eye movement at the very least. In other words, they would spot him.

Instead, Brandenburg lay silent and readied for nightfall. Then he would go find a certain retired general and get those files one way or the other. The game got personal, and he would be damned if he would go to jail for the crimes he didn't comment.

If he had to go to jail, it would be because they caught him killing the bastard that set him up.

Katt was sure she would be hearing from the other team and that they had hit the scent or maybe even caught the shooter. Then again, she had never been around hunting dogs and didn't know that the other one had hit the strong scent of a fox and brayed for a little bit until the trainer got it back under control.

When the rain started, the dog she was following continued moving in the same direction that it had been going all along. When the deluge struck, the dog stopped where it was standing and then lay down looking back at its master.

"We're done, Agent Katt," the trainer said. "There's no way she can work in this," he finished while holding his palms in the air.

"We can't lose him," the Katt replied; frustrated.

"We've already lost him. The only kind of dog who could get him now are the kind that hunt by sight; Dobermans maybe. My babies hunt by smell and the rains washed all of that away."

Katt was about to reply when her phone rang. It was Agent Williams.

"I take it you're being shut down too," Katt said.

"Like a virgin holding a dime firmly between her knees," the man said. "Sorry, ma'am. My daddy was from Kentucky, and they called that a hillbilly's birth control. I know that came across wrong, but if I don't make a joke, even a lousy excuse for one, I think I'll go crazy."

"That's okay," Katt responded. She was drenched to the core, tired and could actually appreciate the man's coping mechanism. "I guess we're done here too. If we don't drown, I guess we'll meet up later. I don't think there's anything else we can do out here now."

"This sucks, Agent Katt. We lost a good man today, and we aren't any closer to solving this case than when it first started. And I'm starting to run out of ideas."

"I know what you mean. But I still have one more thing I can do. It might not help, but desperate times sometimes mean desperate measures. How about if we meet tomorrow morning at say…eight o'clock at the station. I'll let you know if it'll be of any use or not by then."

"I'll see you in the morning," the agent replied. "Stay upright."

Katt had heard the remark a few times before. It meant don't get yourself killed. She wondered if there was anything she could do to make sure she survived.

Chapter 27

Mickey James was frustrated by being held out of the investigation. He thought that maybe it was time to go home. Katt didn't seem to care for him being around. Blythe sure as hell didn't want him there. If it wasn't for Melissa, he would have caught the next flight.

When he entered the general's home, he was completely surprised to see Melissa sitting on the living room couch looking frail, yet smiling.

"Hey, cuz," Melissa said. "Wasn't sure you would get here before I had to lie down."

James quickly walked to the woman and gave her a bear of a hug.

"Easy, Mickey. I'm still a little sore," the woman grunted. "You need to get control of those vise-like arms of yours."

"Sorry," Mickey backed away. "I'm just really happy to see you. I guess I got carried away." He looked around the room and then saw his uncle. "Why didn't you tell me she was here? I would have gotten here sooner."

"We needed to talk for a little while," Pound replied. "I knew you would get here sooner or later."

"Well I'm glad I got here when I did." James looked back to Melissa. "I thought you weren't getting out for another day or two. What changed?"

"I've got the Pound DNA, I guess," Melissa replied, smiling. "Can't keep us down."

"That's a good thing," James returned the smile and reached over and grabbed her hand. "I was really worried about you."

"I know," she squeezed Mickey's hand. Then changing the subject, asked, "So what have you been up to? Is there anything new on the case?"

"There was another shooting," James let go of Melissa's hand, stood and turned his back to her. "It was a cop."

"I know. It was on the news. Have they made any progress?"

"I don't know. I'm sort of out of the loop right now. My contact with the FBI has made it clear that I can't get involved. Her boss is kind of pissed at me too."

"You called her boss?" Pound asked. "Why?"

"He was putting her in danger. He's sending her out to face someone she can't bring in, and it's going to get her killed."

"So you thought you would do the honorable thing and tell him just how dumb that was, I suppose?" the retired general said with a tilt of the head.

"Someone needed to," James growled.

"Would either of your two like to fill me in on whom we're talking about?" Melissa asked. "Remember, I've been out of commission for a bit."

Pound could tell by the way James was acting that he wasn't about to volunteer the information and decided to do the honors.

"Do you remember the case in California that Mickey completed not too long ago and got shot?" Melissa nodded. "Well he worked that case with an FBI agent by the name of Katherine Katt. And he has a crush on her."

"Damn it, General," James jumped in. "It's not like that."

"Well what's it like, cuz?" Melissa asked. "Are you two an item or not?"

"How the hell do I know?" James replied, getting angry. "I can't seem to get through that thick head of hers. Now it doesn't look like I ever will."

"Wow," Melissa shook her head. "You've got it bad." She looked at her father. "So what does this have to do with the case?"

"She's running the case," Pound said. "Apparently, she and Mickey aren't exactly seeing eye to eye about how to run it. And in this case…she's the boss."

"Does she know how you feel about her?" Melissa asked.

"She knows," James replied. "I think she knows."

"Let me restate the question. Have you told you how you feel, Mickey James? Have you actually said the words?"

"Not exactly," James shrugged his shoulders. "That's not how I operate."

"I know how you operate; somewhere between the clicks of a beetle and the grunts of a mole. Damn it, Mickey, if you really like this woman you need to grow a pair and talk to her."

"I tried. She just keeps distracting me…and I keep pissing her off."

"Then have her call me. I'll straighten her out," Melissa said. Then shaking her head, said, "You're worthless."

"No way are you going to talk to her," James said. "If you do you'll be wanting to talk about wedding bells and baby showers. No thanks."

The darkness of night had settled on the hills near Chillicothe. The rain had stopped almost as suddenly as it had started. The air smelled clean and fresh and even though most of the forensic clues to the cop's murder had been washed away, Williams had requested two Dayton police officers to stay the night with replacements due to arrive around two a.m. to relieve them.

By nine o'clock, the countryside was alive with the sounds of nature that neither of the men had ever spent time with before. The men had spent their whole lives in the city and knew Dayton's every street. But as a team, they couldn't tell the difference between a cicada's chirp and a grasshopper rubbing its hind legs. To the cops, the noises were just something they had to listen to.

Another sound they didn't recognize was the slithering sound of a man sliding on his belly as he attempted to get free from the men watching the secluded location.

It took the better part of an hour for Brandenburg to move fifty feet, and by then he was far enough away that they could not hear his steps as he slunk down the hill. He knew that time was running out. Sooner, rather than later, the cops would trap him and there wasn't much he could do about it. He would never kill anyone in order to protect himself. He just didn't want to go to prison.

When he returned near the location where he had left his truck, Brandenburg was surprised to find that it was still right where he left it. It seemed strange. It was off the road almost two miles from where the cop had been killed, but it wasn't exactly hidden.

He expected that the cops would have made a complete sweep of the Ross Lake area. Anyone with half a brain would have spotted it right away. So Brandenburg did what he does best—he waited.

It took less than ten minutes for him to spot the trap that had been set. It took another thirty for him to see it all.

The truck was parked about thirty feet off the road in a lane that curved away from the main road almost immediately when you entered. To the casual passerby, it looked more like a turnout than a lane. The only people who know about it were local.

Brandenburg suspected that the police were getting the assistance from some of the people who lived in the area; either Chillicothe police or some of the neighbors. Most of the people around the area knew Brandenburg as a quiet, unassuming ex-military man who had seen combat. Because of a smart-ass rookie cop, it didn't take long for everyone to know that he had killed before. He didn't figure it would take much convincing to get them to believe he was a cold-blooded killer.

Hiding in a scrub of bushes about thirty feet from the truck was a cop named Billy Jo Westbrook. Brandenburg knew the kid and wasn't surprised that the young man would have volunteered for the assignment. Brandenburg and Westbrook had stood toe to toe back in the spring when Westbrook decided that he needed to demonstrate his newfound authority. The confrontation ended when his training supervisor intervened and told Brandenburg to just move along. No harm. No foul. Brandenburg suspected that the smart-ass cop was trying to get even.

On the other side of the truck was another man Brandenburg knew. His name was William Beaumont, known locally as Billy Bose, who was also with the Chillicothe PD. He had been in the navy many years earlier as a bosun (or boatswain), and his friends used that for a play on his name. Brandenburg had nothing against Billy Bose and had no desire to hurt the man. As far as Westbrook was concerned, he didn't care one way or the other.

Either way, he needed to get to his truck. He knew that he would be taking a risk driving the old beater around, especially if they were looking out for him. On the other hand, he didn't have many choices. He could steal a car, but that would just add to the charges he was already accumulating. His choices were limited. Considering the obstacles the killer placed before him, he didn't see too much of a risk to neutralize the two cops and then be on his way.

Chapter 28

Homer had been listening to the police scanner for nearly three hours and was curious that there hadn't been any chatter about the cop killer, Joseph Brandenburg. He had done everything in his power to make sure that they were close before leaving the scene. Had he waited any longer, they might have spotted him, as well. He was surprised that Brandenburg had not tried to run away after hiding behind the tree. There wasn't anything on the news other than what had been said earlier—Joseph Brandenburg was still at large.

When his phone rang, it had been expected. His employer would want an update.

"Am I hearing the news right?" the caller asked without preamble.

"I don't know what news you've been listening to, so I can't say," Homer replied. He loved playing with words. After joining the military, he had come across the book, *The Tyranny of Words*, by Stewart Chase (a book about semantics and communication) and made a commitment to use the concept of brevity and proper speaking when possible. He also liked to use it to piss people off.

The man didn't seem to appreciate the slight—or recognize it—as he continued talking. "They're going after Brandenburg? They seem to be confident that he's the one doing the shooting."

"That's the same thing I heard. It was always the way I planned for it to go down."

"Then we're just about finished, aren't we?"

"It would seem that way," Homer replied. "According to our contract, I only have one more job to do. Do I have the green light?"

"Not yet. I still need him to do one more thing before it can be finished."

"I don't like waiting," Homer said in order to put on some pressure. "You have twenty-four hours or the price goes up."

"We had a deal, damn it."

"I will keep my end," Homer smiled into the phone. "But if you intend to drag this out, you just have to pay for the inconvenience. I could go somewhere else and get paid more than you'll add to my wait."

"How much more?" the boss asked. "And don't be greedy."

"I was going to say a hundred K for making me wait. You just convinced me to make it two-fifty instead."

"Bullshit! You aren't worth that much." He had already forgotten the earlier conversation the two had about the mustard on his shirt. When it came to money, the man seemed afflicted with selective amnesia. It would eventually prove to be the worst decision of his life.

Brandenburg knew that the most expedient solution to the problem was to kill both cops and then just go about his business. That was what the military had taught him so many years ago. But, the men before him were not a threat to national security. They were simply in his way—an inconvenience—not worth killing.

In order to take them out, he needed to use a stealth approach and hope that they had been given orders to maintain radio silence. Otherwise, killing them might be the only alternative.

Billy Jo Westbrook was the closest cop. Brandenburg slowly made his way to where the rookie cop was hiding. More than anything Brandenburg wanted to put the hurt to the cocky kid. His youth and arrogance were the ingredients for a future bad cop. A little scare just might be in order.

As quiet as humanly possible, the ex-SEAL moved behind the young cop and was about to spring on him when he heard the vibration of a silenced cell phone. Westbrook quickly looked at the caller ID and answered the phone. Brandenburg could only hear the one side.

"I can't talk right now, baby," Westbrook whispered. "I'm on a stakeout trying to catch that fuckin Brandenburg guy who killed a cop out here." There was a pause as Westbrook listened for a few moments. "Don't you go worrying your pretty little head, sweetheart. I could take that guy with a blindfold on. If he comes by here, I'll put him down like the rabid dog he is. Then we'll bring his corpse in for questioning. Now I gotta go. I love you."

No sooner had Westbrook hung up his phone he felt a large hand wrap roughly across his mouth and then felt the cold steel of a knife against his throat. Brandenburg knew better than to speak to the young, arrogant cop. He had been trained to never give the enemy a chance. The difference was, the kid needed a lesson. He needed to know what being a combatant was all about. He needed to respect—fear even—what the men and women of the military did for people like him. It may not have been a great time for dispensing out lessons, but Brandenburg wasn't sure he would ever get another chance.

"I hope you really love that little woman of yours," Brandenburg whispered into the man's ear. "At least she'll know that before you died that you actually had a heart. But then again, I suspect that you have another one hiding in the wings somewhere that you dabble with on the side. Am I right? Feel free to shake your head if you agree."

Westbrook vigorously shook his head up and down. Brandenburg had no idea whether the cop was telling the truth or simply agreeing because he thought that it was what the man with the knife wanted.

"Here's the deal," Brandenburg continued. "I have the choice, right now, to let you live or to kill you. I heard what you said to your girlfriend, and it seems to me that you've already made up your mind that I'm guilty. So...it seems to me that killing you would be nothing more than eliminating someone who planned on killing me anyway. Self-defense is the way I see it. So I would be doing myself a favor by killing you. Don't you agree?"

Westbrook shook his head in disagreement.

Ignoring the denial, Brandenburg said, "On the other hand, if I let you live, I might be trying to trick you into thinking that I'm innocent when I'm guilty. If you did, then that would make you gullible. Are you gullible, Officer Westbrook?"

The head shaking continued.

"Then I'm at a loss of what to do. Killing you would really help me out right about now. Not because of anything I did or didn't do with those shootings. I didn't kill anyone, and you guys are going after the wrong man. It's as simple as that. However, I don't like you. You're an arrogant prick with a badge, and you've pissed me off. Now I have to do your job and find the son of a bitch who's out here killing people. When I do, maybe others like you will think twice about jumping to conclusions."

Brandenburg didn't waste any more time discussing the issues He knew that the cop was significantly scared. The smell of urine told him that. As quick as lightening, Brandenburg put the young cop in a choke hold and before long, Westbrook was out.

When Westbrook's phone buzzed again, Brandenburg knew that he had taken too much time and that the mistake could cost him dearly.

Katt had already cleaned up and needed to get in touch with James. It was time for them to lay everything out on the table and hopefully mend what she hoped wasn't irreparably broken. The word that came to mind was rollercoaster. It seemed to her that she and James were in and out and up and down when it came to what they meant to each other. More than anything, she hoped that somehow they could figure things out.

James was trying his best to keep his uncle and cousin from jumping to the wrong conclusions. He had explained about the case in Monterey and how things there ended. He then went on to tell them about how the two of them had been distant and that he was about to fly to Virginia to have a one on one with her when he got the call about Melissa. When he ran into her at the hospital, he was sure that the reason came down to fate, but when she refused to talk to him he was no longer sure. To him the whole thing was no longer in his control and that he was seriously considering going back to California. There wasn't much he could do here anymore.

Just then his phone rang. It was Katt.

"Were your ears burning?" James asked when he answered the phone.

"No," Katt replied. "Why, were you talking about me?"

"As a matter of fact I was."

"I hope it was complimentary. I would hate for people to get the wrong impression of me."

"I only spoke the truth," James said, attempting to remain aloof.

"I need to see you, Mouse." Katt had picked up on the distance and figured she would have to work past it. There was too much at stake for their personal differences to get in the way. "Where are you?"

"Visiting my relatives. They let Melissa come home today. We've been catching up."

"Can we meet somewhere?" Katt asked, hopeful. "It's important."

"Why don't you come here? I'd like to introduce you to the family."

"This is about the case," Katt replied.

"Then by all means come here," James said. "I'm sure they would like to get an update on your search for the man who almost killed my cousin."

"I'm bringing you in, James," Katt almost blurted. "This is important."

"Then come here," James was unrelenting. "I'm tired of the FBI's idea of protocol. It's either that or you can wave goodbye as I catch my flight out of here. I'm not playing games anymore."

"Help me out here, Mickey."

"I tried that…remember?" James paused and then asked, "Are you still going after Brandenburg?"

"You know we are. He's the primary suspect. Even if he didn't do it, he's got some things to answer for."

"You mean that stunt he pulled with the shot he took? Bullshit. They want to fry his ass, and you plan to help them do it."

"I plan on getting to the bottom of this," Katt raised her voice. "And if you know anything about me, you know that I'm telling the truth."

James didn't respond right away. He knew that Katt was an honest person and would never go after blood. The problem was that she wasn't the only person out there looking. He also knew that without any credible alternative, she had no other choice.

"Come here," James' voice was softer. "We have some information that you might be able to use—something that could help."

"I'll be there soon."
The line went dead.

Chapter 29

Billy Bose hung up when Westbrook didn't answer his phone. He thought he heard a noise across the way, but didn't want to give up his position. Brandenburg would pick up his movement in a heartbeat if he was in the area.

Then again, if Westbrook was in trouble, he didn't have a choice in the matter. He would have to break cover and hoped it wasn't because the rookie cop had done something stupid; because if he screwed it up, there would be hell to pay.

As quietly as he could, the veteran cop moved parallel to the truck into the woods. He thought that if he did that he would be able to clear the area and see more. He also thought it would be less conspicuous and retain his cover until he knew what was going on.

He made the diagonal cut across the back of the truck and realized that Westbrook wasn't where he was supposed to be. Now concern was creeping in and replacing the anger he felt. *Westbrook is a pain in the ass, but he's never left his post.*

Moving closer, Billy saw what looked like feet sticking out from under the brush and reached for his radio. Something was amiss, and he didn't think it would be wise to ignore the fact that the man they were hunting was a cold, hard killer.

Brandenburg knew that there was no way he could let the man radio for help. He was fifteen feet away—plenty of time for the cop to react if he heard him coming. The decision was simple—stop him as quickly as possible.

Brandenburg was as quiet as a cat, but even cats make noise when they move fast. Billy Bose heard the noise before he saw the man coming at him. There was little time for reacting.

When Billy Bose expected trouble, the first thing he always did was draw his service weapon. The Glock-17 was the standard weapon for the Chillicothe Police Department and used the nine-millimeter Parabellum rounds. It was an older version in the Glock family of firearms and still used the seventeen-round clip. Billy Bose used to tell his friends that if a bad guy can move faster than thirteen hundred feet per second, he'd give the bastard seventeen chances to get away. What he didn't expect was for someone to travel that fast *toward* him.

Brandenburg was on the cop in less than two seconds, but in the world of ballistics, two seconds were a huge amount of time. Billy Bose turned toward Brandenburg and was prepared to fire when he saw what could only be a cross between the Swamp Thing and The Creature from the Black Lagoon. The ex-SEAL hit him, and the blast from the gun could be heard at night for several miles. The blood and flesh that the bullet carried with it was of far greater concern to the two men.

The time of the attack, from start to finish, lasted less than five precious seconds. The gun lay immobile on the ground next to the fallen cop. Billy Bose, though still breathing, wouldn't be going anywhere for some time. Brandenburg leaned down and whispered in the man's ear, "I didn't want to hurt you, but you left me no choice."

Brandenburg stood and looked at the piece of crap truck and retrieved the keys—his purpose for causing the damage to begin with. Turning back to the cops, he bent down and grabbed the cop's portable radio. He had no intentions of killing the men and decided to contact the police department once he was far enough away. Brandenburg figured that by the time anyone arrived, he would be long gone.

After grabbing the radio, Brandenburg stood to leave. He never looked back at the men on the ground and didn't bother with the blood that had spread on the man's clothes—his blood.

It took less than the allotted ten minutes for Katt to get where she needed to go. Instead of getting out of her car and meeting with James, she needed to stop for a moment and figure out how she wanted to handle the situation. Katt was a thinker. The problem was, for the first time in her life she was having difficulty dealing with emotions—her emotions.

Katt knew that she was smarter than most people. It wasn't a boast on her part. It's just the way things were. She was young. She understood the concept of experience being a great teacher and took nothing from those who had it. But, she figured that she gained from everyone's experience by reading and studying the files on just about every case she could get her hands on.

The problem here was, there weren't that many sniper killings on record that she could draw from, and most of those cases didn't involve professional shooters. She was running blind, and she knew it. It was the reason she needed help and she hated herself for it. She felt weak.

James saw Katt's car when she drove up to the house and wondered what was keeping her from coming in. He too had doubts about how to handle the rift that had formed between them.

Unlike Katt, James didn't look at the case as something special. For the most part, it was like every other case he had worked on. Time and experience had shown him that people didn't have a lot of reasons to kill another person. Greed was generally at the top of the list of reasons with jealousy and lust close behind. James knew there were other reasons, of course, but when you bring a professional killer into the mix, it was *always* about money.

As such, James reckoned if he could get Katt to listen to him without the two of them getting into an argument, he could convince her to approach the case from a different perspective. That was the plan anyway. But given their recent history, he wasn't about to hold his breath.

James watched Katt get out of the car and when she got to the house, opened the door for her. Her smile melted something inside. He wished, without success, she couldn't touch him in those ways, but couldn't help what he felt.

Homer had been waiting for a call from one of his many sources. There was work that needed done, and with or without Agent Katt's demise, he needed to know that he was still moving forward.

Katt had proven to be something of a challenge. He expected her to fight for her life. On the other hand, he didn't count on her being as adapt to the martial arts as she was, and he certainly didn't expect for her friend to come crashing through the door.

The news was good…great even.

The FBI had sent reinforcement to help the lady agent. If he played his cards right, they would feel his wrath as he was sure she would.

The killer, like most of those who followed a path of destruction, had not always been filled with malice and hatred. There was even a time when he was happy—full of hope. He believed that his was a perfect family. He had a hard-working father who loved his wife and played hockey with his boys. Their mother was the center of the boy's daily life; the disciplinarian when necessary, a teacher always, and the nurse that mended his many youthful bumps and bruises.

It all changed when his brother died. It was a freak accident, really. No one expected that a trip to the grocery store would be the end of the family as they knew it. A drunk ran a stoplight as mom and the boys were heading home. Maybe she should have seen the car coming and could have done something to avoid it.

The mother never got over the fact that she was the one driving. His father took the brunt because he was working late. It was the curse of being a cop. Had he been the one going to the store, Homer's brother might still be alive. His mother might not have drove his father away to build another life; a life without him.

It no longer mattered. His father had made his choices.

Homer would make his own.

Joseph Brandenburg had been shot before. It came with the territory. Fortunately, the wound was of the lesser variety. Sure, it hurt like hell. They always do. But fortunately, this time, the bullet grazed his chest and literally ricocheted off one of his ribs. Bullets don't cut in nice clean lines as would a knife. In this case, the bullet tore away several inches of flesh and the wound bled profusely.

Before he lost too much blood, he took out the First Aid kit he kept in the truck and quickly applied pressure with a large, sterile gauze pad. After the blood stopped flowing, he pulled out a second pad and applied and taped it down with several large strips of duct tape. It wasn't fancy, but from a practical perspective, it worked.

It would have been best to have the wound treated properly; a few stitches and maybe a little Lidocaine to ease the pain. But hospitals had a thing about gunshot wounds. It was policy that they were reported, and Brandenburg didn't have time to get the kind of help he needed. He also didn't have the time the cops wanted to give him for a crime he didn't commit.

Time is running out. I've got to find the bastard who's doing this.

Chapter 30

"I was surprised to hear from you," James said as Katt entered the home.

"I was surprised to get a call from Director Blythe telling me that you were…less than gentle in expressing your concerns for how the case was being run."

"He never could take a joke," James smiled, remembering how pissed off her boss seemed. He considered it a victory that the man even answered his call in the first place. "Besides, he needed to hear it from someone, so I volunteered."

"He's really angry with you, Mouse," Katt took a step closer. "I could have got in a lot of hot water over that stunt." She wasn't angry any more.

"You getting killed seemed worse. I did what I had to do and won't apologize. Good or bad, I protect the people I care about."

"I know that."

"So where do we go from here?"

Katt and James were standing in the doorway and hadn't even bothered to close the door. They were intensely looking into the other's eyes; looking for a clue that would give them a tomorrow to look forward to.

"You could start," the general butted in, "by introducing the young lady to the rest of us. I'm too old to chase you around and Melissa's too crippled. Now get your butts in here."

James extended his hand as a gesture to let Katt take the lead. When she turned to enter the living room, she saw a normal home without a lot of the frills she expected from someone who had been so highly decorated. Most of the generals she had met before were staunch and tried to impress. General Pound (retired) appeared nothing like that.

Pound stood and offered his hand to Katt, which she gladly accepted. She then turned slightly and went directly to Melissa who didn't get up but gladly accepted the gesture as readily.

"You look a lot better than when I first saw you," Katt hung on to Melissa's hand a few extra moments. "Like everyone else, I didn't know if you would make it through surgery. I apologize if that's coming across a little blunt. I'm just amazed that you are doing so well."

Melissa smiled at Katt and said, "I've been told that more than once. I'm just grateful that things weren't as bad as the doctors first thought. It looks like I'll be okay in a week or two."

"That's fast. When do you think you'll be able to get back to work," Katt inquired.

Melissa's face flushed. She hadn't expected to have to deal with that question just yet. Then again, someone as strong as Agent Katt was just the kind of person who would want to get back to work as soon as possible. She should have expected it.

"Next week," Melissa replied sheepishly.

"Bullshit!" James exploded. "There's no way you'll be ready by then."

"Calm down, Mickey," Melissa responded in a soft but firm voice. "I don't really have a choice. The judge won't extend the trial date beyond Monday, or we'll have to start over. We'll lose the witness…if we haven't already."

"Habersham put you up to this, didn't he?" Melissa's dad said just as surprised as James.

"He didn't put me up to anything. I volunteered. Nobody knows this case better than I do; at least now." Melissa hung her head. The movement caught James by surprise, and he backed down.

"We'll talk about this later," James said and meant it. "You'll be lucky if I let you out of this house until we catch the son of a bitch who's been shooting everyone."

"We still have a few days to make that happen," Katt interjected. "That's why I'm here. I need your help."

Everybody looked at Katt expectantly.

"I thought you said I was out of the loop. Blythe was pretty emphatic about that when he hung up on me as a matter of fact."

"Things have changed since then," Katt replied. "Apparently, your conversation with him didn't fall on deaf ears."

"What kind of help are you looking for?" James asked. "I only ask because the last couple of times we talked, you were convinced that Brandenburg was your man and all you needed to do was catch him. Is that what you want...for us to help you catch him?"

Katt felt, more than heard, the animosity coming from James. He had been correct with the statement, and she knew that she had to approach the matter differently.

Katt said, "I know I've been very focused on Brandenburg being the shooter. Frankly, I'm still of a mind that he still could be. However, I know you well enough to know that when you set your mind to something that you usually have a reason. I don't want anyone else to die, and I'm not sure how to move forward."

"You still haven't told me what you expect me to do," James said. "If you aren't willing to accept the possibility that it's someone else, then I don't think there's anything I can do to help you."

Katt was flummoxed by the remark. She had come to them, willing to bring him in on the case, and now he was backing away. It didn't make sense.

"What do you want, Mickey? Brandenburg is out there. He's the most likely person to be involved.

You know…walk like a duck, talk like a duck. That sort of thing. Why are you so sure he's not the one?"

"How many people do you think could have made those shots?" the general asked. Katt was so focused on James she almost forgot the others were in the room.

"I don't know," Katt paused to gather her thoughts on the question. "Maybe a half dozen…a dozen tops."

"Would you believe close to fifty?" the general smiled, condescending. "My nephew is right about one thing, Agent Katt. The person responsible for those shootings is not Joseph Brandenburg."

"How can you be so sure?"

The general paused for a moment to decide how much he was willing to say. He looked at James who nodded his assent, so the general continued.

"Because he told me so," Pound replied. He continued by telling her about his late night visitor and the bowl of soup they shared. He also explained that the meeting happened at almost the exact same time she had been accosted at the place she was staying. When he finished, Katt sat down on the large wingback chair that was next to her.

"And you're sure about the timing?" Katt asked the general.

"I wasn't until Mickey told me what had happened and when. By then it was too late. But then the hospital called, and I got distracted. You know how it is for us old folks?" Pound smiled.

"Why didn't you tell me this?" Katt accused James.

"What he knew and what he told me weren't the same timeline. Like he said, he got that call. It wasn't until just before you called me today that I knew what happened," James shrugged his shoulders. "Besides, I've tried several times to get you to stop long enough to listen and you just kept going on about Brandenburg this and Brandenburg that. We haven't worked together enough for me to know for sure, but I never expected you to be so blinded in a case. Frankly I'm disappointed."

Katt took offense to the accusation and was about to counter, but then realized that James was right. She had never before been so sure of herself. It was true. She told herself that she was open-minded, but the truth was, she wasn't; at least not this time. Her face grew flush from embarrassment.

"Why are you so sure about Brandenburg?" James continued.

Katt had to think hard about the question. It wasn't like her to jump to conclusions. There was something different about Joseph Brandenburg. Then it dawned on her.

"Because he scares the hell out of me," Katt finally replied. "I think I took this case for granted. Another dirtbag, another case. They all seem to be the same sometimes. I just had to outsmart him and bring him to justice. Then he demonstrated what he could do with a rifle. My god, people, how is that possible?"

"It's possible because that's how we train them," the general replied. "You haven't even seen him at his best."

"What do you mean?" Katt asked.

"What I mean is we've only looked at people who could have made the shots in this case. When we looked into Brandenburg, what we found out was that he was much more lethal than anything we've seen. I haven't said anything to Mickey yet because I just found it out a little while ago. Joseph Brandenburg is and was the very best that's ever slung a rifle. But even that doesn't give you the whole picture." Everyone listened to the man's every word. "Do you remember the movie, Rambo?"

"Everyone knows that movie," Katt said.

The general smiled. "Compared to Joseph Brandenburg, Rambo is a pussy. Forgive my bluntness, but I shit you not. He is the only rifleman to have over four hundred kills, and he never missed. I'll rephrase. Until the shot you witnessed, the one that hit the target but not you, he never missed what he was aiming for. That little show was for you, Agent Katt. He didn't miss…he simply missed you.

"You asked how we know that Joseph Brandenburg is not the killer you're looking for." He sat down next to Melissa and said, "Because my daughter is sitting here, able to breathe and will maybe, someday, be able to smile once again. That's how I know. Had Brandenburg been the one shooting, I wouldn't be able to say that."

No one said anything for quite a while. The implications of what the general had said weighed heavy on their minds.

Katt then asked, "So what do we do now?"

"Now that we've got your attention," James replied, "I'm glad you asked."

Chapter 31

"You have a go," the contractor said to Homer when he picked up the phone. "When can you get it done?"

"So what? Before you were putting me off. Now you want to rush me?"

"I decided that we've gone too far to change the plan. It's time to finish this."

"Then I will agree to our original terms," Homer said. "It'll be done tomorrow. I will see if I can do it in the morning. If not…tomorrow night at the latest. His morning schedule fluctuates. His evening schedule is more like clockwork."

"Don't screw this up. I've come too far to not finish it now."

"Then let me remind you…don't be late with my payment. We'll all live longer that way."

After they had hung up, Homer opened the folder his contact had sent to him. The FBI was in town. He had the list of who was important and the how to finish the lot of them. The exception, Homer decided, was the beautiful Katherine Katt. He wanted more from her than to just die. He wanted her to know that she wasn't as good as she thought. He wanted her to *feel* what it was like to die. And if time permitted, he wanted to enjoy some private time with her as well. That was the plan, and now he simply needed to execute.

Execute…one of my favorite words.

Katt's phone rang just as James was about to go into his idea of how to handle the case.

"Katt," the agent answered.

"You pal has done it again," said BCI Agent Williams. "Brandenburg has taken out two more men."

"Damn it," Katt replied. "Are they dead?"

"Not this time,' came the intense reply. "It seems he didn't want to make matters worse by killing any more cops. So this time he just knocked them out. And get this, he says he's innocent. Can you believe that horse shit?"

"How do you know? Did one of them talk to the guy? Are they sure it was actually Brandenburg?"

"One of the officers, Billy Bose, was knocked unconscious. The other, Billy Jo Westbrook, was put in a strangle hold and choked out. Before he did it, though, he told Westbrook that he was innocent and that we were forcing him to find the killer on his own."

"How did you find them?"

"Brandenburg called it in. And yes…according to Westbrook, it was a positive ID. Apparently they had a little brush-up several months ago. Westbrook didn't get a look at the man's face, but said he recognized his voice; even though it was just a whisper."

Katt wanted to ask more, but first she needed to check on the men. "How are they doing?"

"They'll be okay. Both are embarrassed about getting the crap beat out of them, but the strange thing is what Billy Bose said."

"What?"

"He said that he was attacked by someone who looked like a monster of some kind. Craziest thing he ever saw."

"What kind of monster?" Katt asked, curious. She never took anything for granted and often times believed that what people call monsters are sometimes just your mind playing tricks.

"He said it was big, hairy and growled like a wolf. It doesn't make any sense if you ask me. If that information ever got out, I don't think we can use his testimony. I'm sure it was Brandenburg. Like I said, Westbrook recognized the voice. He just didn't get a look at him. He came up from behind."

"Let me talk to someone, and I'll call you back." Katt hung up the phone before Williams could protest.

Homer had placed a tracking device on Katt's car. He wanted to know where she was at all times.

From the first moment he saw her, he realized that she would be his when the time was right. Tonight was that time.

Less than a block away, Katt was visiting with some old retired general and was surprised to see the attorney he had shot—the one who got away. To him, it was extremely fortuitous.

As the evening progressed, Homer realized that it could be difficult to kill them all at once. He also recognized another problem to his desires. The man he saw standing on the courthouse steps—the agent's friend—was with the small group. He was big and looked strong. Homer considered that he would be a formidable opponent one on one. For him to attempt to kill Katt and the rest would be challenging enough; he didn't need to take on someone with a hero complex.

He would have to wait. Divide and conquer and all that. Time was on his side, the killer knew. Sooner or later, each would go their own way. When they separated, that was when he would strike. The night was young.

Katt told the rest of the group what had transpired on the call. That he was positively identified and had hurt the two cops.

"He didn't kill them though…right?" James said.

"Not this time," Katt replied. "But it does confirm that he was out there when the other cop was killed. Listen, James, it doesn't look good for the man. I know you have your theory about what's going on, but one way or the other, Brandenburg will have to stand accountable for his actions. He hurt those two cops. They're witnesses."

"So he would have been better off killing them," James replied sarcastically. "At least then he wouldn't have left a witness."

"That's not a nice thing to say, Mickey," Melissa stepped into the conversation. "Look, Agent Katt, I don't know who shot me and my friends. You think it's this Brandenburg guy, and Mickey and Dad think it's someone else. It seems to me that you should be considering all options instead of focusing on just the one person."

"You're right Melissa. I should. But you haven't had a bullet whiz by your…. Oh crap. I'm sorry. I misspoke." Katt was flustered and wasn't used to it. That wasn't like her. "I don't know if you were told, but Brandenburg did a little target practice next to my head and it still has me a little shaken up. But you're right. I need to start working on this the way I've been trained. And now I have to figure out why one of the cops tonight is screwing up the case by saying he saw a monster. Just those words alone will keep me from using him as a witness."

James and the general looked at each other. "What about a monster?" James asked.

"Both men were rendered unconscious. The one that identified Brandenburg was choked from behind, but said that Brandenburg spoke to him. He recognized his voice. The other—the one who was knocked unconscious, said that just before he blacked out he saw some kind of monster coming at him."

"What kind of monster?" the general asked.

"He said it was big, hairy and growled like a wolf," Katt replied. "Or something like that."

The general got up from his seat and walked into the dining room. A few moments later appeared and handed Katt a couple of photos. "Could it have been this?" the general asked.

Katt hadn't seen or even thought about a Ghillie suit in over ten years. She had done her combat training, but it was basic and consisted more of urban combat than anything else. What she was looking at made all the sense in the world.

"You're right, general. I would bet that was exactly what the cop saw."

"In that case, with someone like Brandenburg, you could have walked right past him and never seen him. No wonder he got away."

"Impossible," was Katt's retort. "We had dogs chasing his scent. "They would have found him. As a matter of fact, we were hot on his trail until it started raining."

"Wouldn't have mattered in most cases," Pound said. "You were going the wrong way."

"How do you know?" Melissa asked. The ex-military cop had everybody's full attention.

"Because you were leaving the site of where the young man was killed right?"

"That's because he was there," Katt stood her ground. "We looked everywhere around the body. We would have seen him."

"No…you wouldn't have. Brandenburg, or whoever killed that cop, was within spitting distance…literally. The only way to defend against dogs is know how they work. The man's scent was all around the kill site. Of course, you would expect the dogs to get the scent there. So what you did was take the dogs away from the site and get them headed in a direction away from the site. They'll pick up the scent because, unless they are specifically trained to do so, dogs can't tell direction. They'll follow that scent for miles if necessary. And all the while, your killer is hiding at the starting point. My suspicion is that you used locals dogs—hunting dogs and not dogs trained regarding time and directions. Those dogs are hard to come by."

"Son of a bitch," Katt swore. "Here we had him and walked the other way. How are we supposed to beat someone like him?"

"You're still focused on Brandenburg being the killer," James smiled. "The solution is in the question. We let a killer find the killer. That's how you do it."

A light turned on in Katt's brain. For the first time since the case started, she finally realized that she should have been working with James all along. She knew she would never make that mistake again.

Chapter 32

Mary Margaret Koch—known to her friends as Maggie—lived in the split level home three doors down and across the street from where the general lived. Every night, at exactly ten o'clock, the sixty-five year old woman went for a walk around the block regardless of the weather. By her own words, she was more predictable than the new high-speed European rail trains and saw more inclement weather than a mailman.

The neighborhood was anything but dangerous. Her and her husband, Russ, who stayed at home and watched the local news, had lived in the old house for nearly three decades. Not once had an ambulance driven on the street for anything other than when poor Mr. Snider had a heart attack and Lucie Sullivan fell and broke her collarbone at the age of six years old. The last time was over twenty years ago.

Maggie had the personality of a fighter. Though retired, she used to work for the Dayton Police Department. After thirty years there, she retired with full benefits and from that time until eight months earlier, she had spent four days a week working in a shelter for battered women and two days a week volunteering at various other shelters for the indigent. Maggie Koch was not afraid of the dark.

Of course, it didn't hurt that when she took her walks, a friend joined her.

The friend's name was Bear. That's it, just plain Bear; a six year old *Dogue de Bordeaux*. The breed is also known as a French Mastiff and became popular with the old Tom Hanks movie, *Turner and Hooch*.

Maggie liked her nightly walks. As far as she was concerned, she would take them even if Bear wasn't with her. But the woman wasn't stupid. She understood that things had changed over the last twenty years. Crimes had escalated, and they often poured out and into the nicer communities. As such, she enjoyed the fact that with Bear walking with her, she had the luxury of being able to relax.

Nothing bothered Bear. Dogs in the neighborhood, as well as most of the neighbors, gave the one hundred-sixty pound brute a wide berth when they saw him coming. His brown silky fur was interspersed with black. Not enough for spots, but enough to give the dog a perpetual look of needing a bath. The ugliness of its face looked cute when he was a pup. As he grew older, he looked just plain mean. The constant drool dripping from his jowls made you wonder if he had just finished a hearty meal or if you might be next on the menu.

It was ten o'clock exactly when Mary's door opened, and she and Bear walked down the driveway in the direction of the Pound residence. It wasn't planned that way. It was simply a matter of circumstance. The night before the two friends had gone the other direction, and this was Maggie's way of diversifying her excursions.

Russ and Maggie had known the general and his wife for years. They became friends soon after Melissa turned five. As Maggie walked by the house, she felt a sense of nostalgia; missing the general's wife—her old friend—and wondered how Melissa was getting along. Maggie knew about the shooting, but didn't know that Melissa was sitting inside, just a few feet from where the old woman and Bear were taking their stroll.

A few houses past the Pound's residence, Bear stopped and stuck his nose in the air. That alone was nothing unusual. Bear, like most dogs, wanted to know what odors are attacking his senses. What was unusual was the low, almost guttural sound that was coming from somewhere deep inside.

The hackles rose high, and the dog refused to move. No matter how much Maggie prodded Bear, all he did was stare at the gap between two of the houses that, like the Pound's residence, were sitting back from the street. For the first time that Maggie could remember, she was scared.

It took nearly ten minutes for Bear to finally take a step. Whatever danger the dog had sensed had moved along. The two buddies continued their walk around the block and nothing more happened. It was something Maggie could not forget, and she knew that when she got home she would tell her husband.

Homer seldom rushed a job. So far his interest was to scout the house where the FBI agent was visiting and then determine the best way to kill her. He wasn't the sentimental type. He did what he did for the money, and by his way of thinking, it was just a job that had to be done.

There were occasions, however, that gave the killer a certain thrill. Like tasting ice cream for the first time was the best way he could describe it. Agent Katt fit that description to a T.

He held his spot in the shadows for nearly an hour when he noticed a woman approach with some kind of huge, horse of a dog. Generally, he considered those occurrences nothing more than a distraction.

This time it was different.

Homer knelt behind a small shrub that flanked both sides of a sidewalk, angling forty-five degrees from the house he was watching and across the street. He had a great view and wasn't likely to be bothered by anyone. He was all but invisible.

When the old woman's dog stopped, the killer couldn't remember seeing a more spectacular beast.

He then heard a rumble that seemed to come from a faraway place and sounded like distant thunder. After a few moments, he realized it came from the very core of the beast and didn't like it one bit.

The problem was twofold: First, he could not run. The dog would catch him and his cover would be blown. The second problem was just as bad. He couldn't stay where he was either. If the dog decided to sniff him out, Homer knew that he wouldn't stand a chance against the massive hunk of flesh and muscle.

His only alternative was to try and move away slowly. He had to stay in the shadows. The old woman was watching in his direction like a hawk. Homer was sure she couldn't see him. He knew how to conceal his position. However, if the woman saw his shadow or any part of him move, he felt sure the woman would release the hound on him.

It took nearly ten minutes to slink into the night, at which time he decided that it was best if he stayed away for a while. Should Agent Katt leave, he could still follow her. The tracker would not allow her to hide.

Chapter 33

James told Katt about the files the general had acquired for him. He explained that he had gone through them a couple of times and with her help could whittle the total down to a manageable number.

"How many have you got it down to so far?" Katt asked.

"About a dozen or so," James replied. "However, I'm pretty sure I could get it down to five or six with one more look."

"Where are the files?"

"At my hotel," James said, and then grinned. "I wasn't expecting to see you tonight."

"You were expecting to go over them with the general weren't you?"

"Tomorrow," James said. "I came to spend a little time with my cousin," he lied, "and then go back to work."

"Then that's what we'll do," Katt stated firmly—still a take-charge FBI agent.

James was about to reply to Katt's command when Melissa jumped in to save the man from himself.

"Mickey," Melissa said, "Don't be a cad. Why don't you offer the woman a drink?"

"Because that's my job," the general replied. "What would you like, dear? We have iced tea, coffee, juice…"

"Juice would be great," Katt replied, appreciating the gesture.

"So," Katt looked back to James, "How do we get in touch with Mr. Brandenburg? I would expect him to be half way to Montana by now."

"Why Montana?" Melissa asked.

"I don't know. It's just one of those remote areas you read about. It could be Mexico for all I know about the guy."

"You really don't know these guys, do you?" James said. "Their entire life has been about being able to control everything around them. They spend hundreds…thousands of hours just learning how to control their breathing, how to read weather patterns, or anything else they need in order to be the best at their craft. They learn how to push fear away from their being and remain calm no matter what's going on around them.

"Now, for the purpose of this discussion, let's assume that Brandenburg is innocent of these murders." Katt was about to jump in, but James held up his hand to quiet her. "I said let's assume for this discussion. If that were the case, then someone is out there stealing everything he ever stood for. And not only is he doing that…he's also bringing shame to the man's family and name. No one with the character and fortitude like Joseph Brandenburg would ever allow that to happen. He would die first, and I'm not being grandiose when I say that. If anything I'm minimizing it. Death to these men is about honor and doing what's right."

"How can a man who's killed over a hundred people know about honor?" Melissa asked, looking directly at James.

"Over four hundred," a voice said as the group looked at the general walking in carrying a tray of drinks. Behind him was Joseph Brandenburg holding a semi-automatic pistol to the general's ear. "It was over four hundred men and women I killed, and every one of them was done with honor."

Katt pulled her service weapon in the blink of an eye, but she had no target. Brandenburg was very careful to keep a hand on Pound's shirt collar, so the man had no chance to move away. The intruder, though several inches taller than his captive, was crouched behind and completely hidden.

"Drop your weapon!" Katt yelled. "Drop it now!"

"Or what?" Brandenburg asked with humor. "Do you have me surrounded?"

"It will go a long way in helping your cause," Katt replied.

"I have no cause, Agent Katt," Brandenburg replied. "From the intel I've managed to gather over the last couple of hours, I'm dead already. I just haven't quite got to the stinking part. So why don't you do everyone a favor and put your weapon away before you accidently shoot someone."

"If anyone gets shot," Katt stood a little taller, "it won't be by accident."

Brandenburg looked at James, and said, "I see what you mean. She's a handful."

"You have no idea," James replied. "Katt, why don't you put the gun down and listen to what the man has to say. Based on my assessment, he has the upper hand."

"Seems rather even to me," Katt said, not willing to relinquish her sidearm.

"One against one isn't always equal," James said. "He's covered and you're exposed…and I mean that in a purely professional way." James smiled. "He's a professional…"

"And I'm not?" Katt blurted.

"…with apparently over four hundred bodies to his name, I was going to say. Look, Katt, if he wanted us dead, we'd be dead by now. He's not big on talking to the people he intends to kill. Just holster the weapon…please!"

Katt looked at James and then back at Brandenburg. As her mind raced for a possible way to get the upper hand, she drew a blank. Slowly, she lowered her gun and waited for her life to end. She didn't know why, especially since everyone else seemed intent on praising the killer before her.

"I won't relinquish my weapon," Katt glared at Brandenburg. "You'll just have to kill me first."

"You don't like me, do you?" Brandenburg smiled. "I can tell. Does this have to do with my demonstration the other day?"

"Demonstration? You almost killed me, you arrogant prick," Katt replied. As scared as she felt, she made up her mind not to show it.

"Katt," James said. "Let's hear what the man has to say…okay?"

"He's going to say that he didn't do it. He'll say that he didn't have any motive or he'll tell us the same crap every other criminal says to tug our heartstrings. That's what he's going to say."

"I have no intentions of telling you that," Brandenburg said. "It wouldn't matter if I did. You wouldn't believe me. So I won't waste either of our time."

The comment came as a surprise to everyone.

"Then why?" James asked.

"You told me what was going on and that I could trust that Agent Katt is an honorable person, detective. Honorable or not, she has no choice but to go where the leads take her. Based on what happened today, I now know that I'm in a crap-load of trouble."

"What happened today?" Katt asked. "Did you kill the wrong cop?"

"I didn't kill the cop," Brandenburg said.

"I thought you weren't going to say that you were innocent."

"I didn't say I was innocent," Brandenburg stared at Katt. "I said I didn't kill him. I was there when it happened, but I wasn't the one who shot him."

"Then who did?" James asked. "It would be a lot easier all the way around for you...for everyone, if you told us who the shooter is."

Brandenburg paused briefly before starting again.

"I suspected," Brandenburg said, looking at Katt, "that you—or someone—would be visiting this morning. I figured you would send someone out to the location where I demonstrated my abilities earlier. That seemed like the logical choice. After that, I waited. I'm good at waiting, you know. According to the government, it's one of my special skills. Anyway, I was right. Your man came by to set up; thinking I was a late riser, I guess. He waited for me to come along and," another long pause, "was going to take me out."

"Take you out or bring you in?" Katt asked.

"According to the brief conversation I had with the man, it was the former. He had no desire to bring me to justice; at least not the kind you get in a courtroom."

"Did he say why?" James asked. "Would you mind if the general set the drinks down? I'm starting to get thirsty."

"I will not give a second warning. If anyone goes for their weapon, I will shoot to kill. Understood?"

Everyone nodded. No one spoke.

Brandenburg let go of the general.

"We didn't exactly have an in depth discussion. It was about that time that I saw you drive up, Agent Katt. The rest of them had been at the house for a while before you got there. I guess they were waiting to hear from their sniper friend. When you arrived, I decided that the lessons needed to step up a notch. I just wanted you to leave me alone."

"What did you do, son?" the general asked in a soft voice.

"I cut the man," Brandenburg replied. "I knew that at that time of day, his voice would carry. I knew that they needed a reason to be afraid of coming after me."

"You cut him?" James inquired. "What does that mean? The news never said anything about that." James looked at Katt. She recognized the questions he must want answers to.

"Yeah," Brandenburg said without the appearance of remorse. "They needed to see blood. It seems to be the only thing that gets their attention.

They needed to know that if they come after me with orders to kill, they would have a fight on their hands."

"Then why did you shoot him?" Melissa asked. "It seems to me that you would have been able to get further without doing that?"

"You're the one who lived," Brandenburg stated, matter of fact. "Congrats. Everything I've heard is that you're a decent person…for a lawyer."

"Considering the circumstances, I'm going to take that as a compliment, but that doesn't answer my question."

James smiled at the tenacity of his cousin.

"You're right," Brandenburg said. "But I didn't say I didn't kill the man because I told Agent Katt that I wouldn't plead innocent. My objective is to state the facts. I hung the cop to display him and cut him superficially; to first draw blood, and second to get him to scream. I was going for the shock value. As I was about to make the third cut across his belly, there was a shot, and then the man's head exploded in from of me.

"Agent Katt, there will be two things you can do to prove my story. When the ME tests for gunshot residue, he will tell you that there won't be any like what would appear if I would have shot him. Second, he will have a cut approximately an inch and a half on the right side of his abdomen. It occurred when I started to make the belly cut, and the bullet hit its target. I immediately hit the ground and rolled to safety. Had I been able to finish the job, he would have been sliced all the way across."

"Let me get this right," Melissa interjected. "You want the world to know that you are guilty of torture, but not murder. Is that right? As a prosecutor, I would have a field day with that."

"I don't expect any of you to understand what happened. None of you know what it's like to be hunted like some wild animal. When you do…we'll talk then. In the meantime, you have a real shooter out there that's going to keep killing unless you do something to stop him. I think I can help you find him."

"So who is it?" Katt asked. "If what you say is true…and I'm not saying it is or isn't, who's out there killing these people?"

Brandenburg hesitated. He knew that he didn't have that answer; only suspicions.

"Ask yourself this," Brandenburg said. "Forget about the shooter for a minute. Who's paying the shooter…and why? A man like this isn't killing for a political cause. He's getting paid by someone who wants something. You need to figure out what."

"Okay," James said. "What else?"

"The shooter isn't active duty…at least not any more. I know all of the ones still in. He's not one of them. You need to look outside—retired, maybe, but more than likely removed. Figure out what kind of person would be willing to kill on American soil and not bat an eye."

Everyone looked surprised at the intelligent man before them. It seemed that the group expected Brandenburg to be something else—something less. Maybe they wanted him to be someone they could easily decipher.

No one expected the doorbell to ring.

Chapter 34

Startled, everybody glanced at the door.

Katt didn't want the uninvited guest to get hurt. James was concerned that Brandenburg would get violent; not because he was a bad person, but because he was caught in a web not of his making.

When they glanced back to get a reading on the man with the gun, Brandenburg was gone. He hadn't made a sound. It was like a wraith passing by. You were never really sure it had even been there. The chill left in his wake was enough to catch your breath.

Who was this guy?

The general was the first to recover when the doorbell chimed a second time and went to answer the door. Russ and Maggie stood on the stoop smiling and Maggie was holding a plate of cookies. The general opened the door.

"You're up past your bedtime," Pound smiled at the unexpected guests when he opened the glass encased storm door."

"Robert," Maggie gushed, "Russ just heard on the news that Melissa had come home from the hospital, and we wanted to say hello if it's not too late for her."

"Your timing is impeccable as always, Maggie. Our company was just leaving and then we were going to have a nightcap before retiring for the night."

"Oh, good," Maggie said, giving Pound a hug. "We won't stay long. Here," she said handing over the plate of cookies. "You'll have to forgive me. I would have baked a fresh batch if I had known she was coming home today."

The general walked them into the living room and made introductions all around. The only person missing was James, who had stepped out the back door to see if he could figure out where the sniper had gone. Katt had stayed put to hopefully protect those still inside.

As James entered the common area, Pound said, "I believe you met Mickey a while back. He came running as soon as he heard what happened."

Russ reached out to shake James' hand when Maggie pushed past her husband and wrapped her arms around the startled cop.

"I am so glad you're here," Maggie said. "They need you here until this whole mess is finished. I'm worried that my old friends are in over their heads on this one. And I'm pretty sure the FBI people they brought in aren't going to be much help either."

"What do you mean?" James asked, then winked at Katt. "Melissa is going to be fine."

Maggie looked at her husband, and then back to James. "Look, Mickey," the woman said, "I've been out of the police business for a little while. You know, in my time, I was a pretty good cop."

"I know that, Maggie. What's going on?"

"Do you know Bear?" Maggie asked.

"I think I saw him when he was less than a year old."

"Well, he's grown up a bit since then."

"Harrumph!" Russ grunted. "He's a damn horse that eats meat."

"Hush," Maggie reprimanded while the rest of them smiled. "He…Bear's not afraid of anything."

"Why should he be?" Russ butted in again. He then looked at the group, and asked, "Do you know what Bear calls a Cocker Spaniel? An appetizer. He thinks the mailman would make a great lunch."

"*Anyway*!" Maggie was getting frustrated with her husband. "I think Bear saw something tonight that scared him. Or worried him. I can't tell the difference. I've never seen him like that, and I got to thinking that maybe someone might be out sneaking around. And then I thought about Melissa and couldn't help myself. I just had to come down here and tell you about it."

"And I told her that she needed to mind her own business," Russ added.

What little color Melissa had regained from surgery had disappeared. Katt noticed, as did Melissa's concerned father.

When the introductions were made, Katt's title as an FBI agent had been omitted because it seemed the thing to do at the time. She rectified the oversight.

"Ma'am," Katt said, "I'm an FBI agent on assignment with the case. And even though the shooter has been unpredictable up until now, I think it's just a matter of time until he makes a mistake. And when he does, we'll be there to take him down."

"I don't mean to be rude, Agent Katt. The things I said earlier? I'm sure they came across as harsh, and I'm not usually that way."

"It's not a problem. People say things they don't mean all the time."

"Oh…I wasn't apologizing," Maggie said. "I meant every word of it. I've still got friends on the force, and they tell me that this man you're going after is one, cold-blooded son of a bitch. Brandenburg…right? Anyway, when Bear got worried tonight, I was afraid that he might be out there skulking around, and I just wanted you folks to know that if you need for Bear to come stay awhile, I would be happy to bring him here. I'll take care of the feeding and everything. He'll just be here to keep you company…and to bite the leg off any unwelcome visitors."

"That's sweet of you," Melissa said. "I love Bear. He's such a cutie. But, I couldn't ask you to do that."

"You didn't ask," Maggie replied. "Remember, I offered him to you as a guard."

"But he's your dog, and if anything were to happen to him, I could never forgive myself. But thanks anyway."

Maggie seemed disappointed. "The offer stands until this guy is caught. I just want you to know that."

"Thank you."

Maggie and Russ bid their goodbyes and the general closed the door.

"What do you think got Bear worked up?" Melissa asked, concerned. "Do you think he's out there looking for me? To finish the job?"

"No," the general replied without conviction. "You're not on his radar anymore."

"How could you know that?" Melissa asked.

"It just makes sense," the general replied. "He's had plenty of chances to do something if he was going to."

"What chance?" Melissa asked, startled by her father's callous remark.

"I'm sorry, I didn't mean it that way. I'm just saying that if you were the primary target, he wouldn't have waited to shoot you… damn this isn't coming out the way it's supposed to."

"Let me see if I can clear it up for you," James said. "He didn't kill you because you weren't the primary target. If you were, he would have shot you first. If he was desperate, he would have come after you in the hospital. But he didn't. There's no reason for him to kill you now."

"Way to soft-shoe that explanation, Mouse," Katt said, looking at the pale woman.

"Look," James interjected, "there's no soft approach to talking about this. Melissa's been around long enough to know that if she's in danger, then she damn well needs to know about it up front. Rip the damn Band-Aid off. That's the best thing to do."

"He's right," Melissa said. "I don't like it, but he's right. And the way, Brandenburg just waltzing in here tonight doesn't make me feel any better. Besides, if Bear saw or smelled anyone, it probably was Brandenburg. We know he was out there."

The group stayed quiet while thinking over the evening's events.

"Alright," Katt huffed. "You know your cousin better than I do." There was a pause. "So what just happened here? How the hell did Brandenburg get the drop on us?"

"He did what he had to do," James replied. "The good news is that he didn't come in here with guns blazing. He knows he's in deep shit and he wants a way out of it. I think he knows that he can't do it alone, but I don't think he knows how to play well with others."

"So can we use him?" Pound asked. "Can we trust him?"

"I don't know if we can trust him or not," James said. "I do think we can use him though."

"How?" Katt asked. "We don't even know how to reach him to ask."

"We follow the lead he's already given us," James stated with a crooked smile; holding a coin for everyone to see. "It's a direction that might just give us a heads-up on where to look for the one who's truly responsible."

They all looked at the coin and wondered what he meant.

Chapter 35

Homer had driven directly to the bed and breakfast where Katt was staying. The dog had drawn too much attention. It also wouldn't help for him to get to the FBI agent with such a large crowd around her. Sooner or later, she would have to leave, and he knew that the most likely scenario was that she would come back to her room for the night.

He checked the tracking device every fifteen minutes and her car hadn't moved.

With time on his hands, Homer wondered how Brandenburg had managed to get away from the cops. He knew that he hadn't given the ex-SEAL a lot of time to make a run for it and out in the country there just weren't that many places to hide. Once again, the hero had accomplished the impossible, but he was now a wanted man. Sooner or later, the FBI would hunt him down. The plan was perfect.

After his brother died, Homer's father poured all of his time into work. After a year or so, the distance between the man and his wife became insurmountable. They each blamed the other and the only one who had nowhere to turn was Homer. In time his isolation would be the driving force that would take him away from the fun loving child to being a cold-blooded killer. He had his reasons for revenge. This was simply the first time he could put his plan into action.

Checking the tracker again, Homer realized that, finally, Katt's car was on the move. He knew from experience that the trip was less than fifteen minutes away. The problem was that Katt's car wasn't heading to the Bed and Breakfast. It was going in the opposite direction. Homer started his car and took off after her.

After a while, the little red dot that represented Katt's car stopped. Twenty minutes later, Homer had pulled alongside the curb in front of a Holiday Inn just a couple of blocks off Interstate 75, south of downtown Dayton. He wasn't sure why it was there. He just saw the car. He had to figure out why.

It didn't take much effort to discover that the man at the front desk liked having a little extra cash in his pocket. And thanks to his employer, the fake ID of the shooter being a cop helped too.

The clerk had seen the car park out front and noticed the beautiful blond woman. He was reluctant at first, but finally divulged that she was, in reality, visiting an out of state cop. Money or no money, he was surprised that the clerk wouldn't give up the out of state cop's name. They were located at the far end of the building on the first floor, Room 138. If Homer wanted the guy's name, he would have to make the introductions in person.

Homer decided that he could kill the cop and take Katt for himself. It seemed the logical thing to do. Unfortunately, he had made it a rule to never take on someone without knowing his opponent. He remembered a friend of his doing that very thing when he was stationed in Okinawa. His friend was a brute of a man who had a bad temper and a need to punish someone—anyone—for the Dear John letter he had received earlier that day. The little man he attacked should have been nothing more than a warm-up for the night's activities. Instead, the small man happened to be the reigning champion in the country as a master of Shotokan karate. It took several weeks for his friend to recover.

The man inside the room may be a cop, but Homer wasn't about to find out what more he brought to a fight without checking him out first.

Three hours later, when the light flicked off, the killer knew that Katt was in for the night.

James had suggested that the general and Melissa to get some rest because he and Katt had a lot of research to do. Everyone was still running on adrenaline, but Pound relinquished for the sake of his daughter. She needed her rest and wouldn't even consider stopping until her dad offered to do the same.

The next day was going to be a big one for her. Her boss, Jules Habersham, would be coming around ten in the morning to review the case, She needed to be alert if she was going to keep him from changing his mind about allowing her on the case.

Katt followed James back to his hotel and wondered if they had finally managed to get past the problems of the last several days. In her heart, she knew that James cared about her. She just questioned whether it would be enough for her to get around her past.

For nearly three hours, they poured through the files that the general had given him. What they were looking for they weren't sure. They only knew that the Canadian twenty-five cent piece meant something to Brandenburg or else why would he have left it behind?

By two o'clock in the morning, it didn't matter how much coffee Katt drank, she was tired to the bone and needed to get some rest.

"I think I need to leave," Katt said. "I can hardly hold my eyes open."

"I thought you told me last time that you hardly slept," James replied.

"I don't usually have two days in a row where I'm either being shot at or chasing a killer through the woods. I hardly slept last night…damn, was that last night?" Katt asked. "It seems so long ago."

"I know what you mean," James smiled a sad smile. He didn't want her to leave. They had finally been together for a few hours without fighting and he didn't want the time to end. "Look, Katt, we'll just have to start up again in the morning. You can lie down on the bed and get some rest. In a few hours we'll get going again. I'll just rest on the sofa. That way you don't lose the drive time. There's got to be something there."

"Can you call down for a wake-up call?" Katt asked. "I have a meeting with the sheriff in the morning. Maybe we can get a few hours rest and then have another couple hours before I have to leave. That's the best I can do."

James would have preferred different accommodations than the one proposed, but he wasn't going to be greedy. Any way he could spend the night with Katt was good enough for him. At least it was for now. Maybe in the near future, they could come up with a better arrangement.

The sun was high enough to remove the darkness of night, but not yet elevated to the point to clearing the mountain peaks or clearing the morning dew.

Homer had set aside his frustration about his chance to kill the FBI agent. He decided that it was good that she had one last night of bliss with the man she visited. If he had his way, it would be her last.

It was time to get back to the job at hand.

Judge Leon Anderson would be the last of the judges to die. Homer didn't know the plan of the man who had paid him to do it. He just knew that he would get a fat paycheck, and that was all that mattered.

The distance was only sixty yards; mere child's play for a sniper of his caliber. But like all shots, even the close ones had their intrinsic problems.

A shot from long range was more difficult. There were so many factors involved; it was no wonder that there were only a handful of people in the world who could make those shots. But up close, another problem was built right in; it was always difficult to get away.

The sound of a high-powered rifle is quite distinctive. It is loud and will startle the most seasoned hunter. Unfortunately, it usually doesn't take a person very long to overcome the shock and start looking around; especially in the direction of the gun fire.

Then again, mornings were always worse than evening shots. With any sniper, the time necessary to get away is important. If you kill someone in the morning, the police have an entire day of daylight to track you down. The shooter has few shadows in which to hide. At night, the world is blanketed with dark, and the dark is a shooter's best friend.

The judge had already completed his exercise by using his treadmill for thirty minutes and then using the balance of his hour routine on free-weights. Sometimes he would vary the routine, but he had a busy schedule and didn't want to do anything he had to think about. The workout freed his mind to think about his job. He was ready to go.

His shower was finished and his wife, being the good wife that he loved, had made his breakfast and brought the day's paper for him to peruse. He never once asked her to do those things. It's how he knew that she did it out of love.

The judge was a fortunate man.

Homer checked his watch and knew that even though Anderson was timely in most ways, sometimes he would deviate his routine, and if he did that this morning, the shooter would have to wait. Realistically, he would have preferred to wait. However, if the conditions were right, Homer intended to finish the job early. You could never tell what the evening would bring.

Anderson opened the door at exactly seven-fifteen; right on schedule. He turned and kissed his bride goodbye; taking a few extra moments to hold her, appreciating the woman he was so fortunate to have in his life. He knew that he was a fortunate man and never wanted to be that guy who would take advantage of the woman he loved. After releasing her, he spoke the words I love you, and quickly turned his back and walked to the car.

Homer could see no reason to wait. He knew that his best shot would be when the judge stopped to get in the car. Homer heard the high-pitched chirp of the Volvo and readied his aim. The judge entered the scope's field of vision, and the sniper placed his finger firmly on the trigger. The life of one more judge was about to end.

As the judge stopped to open the door, Homer tightened his finger to a point where only a fraction of an ounce remained. The judge was about to enter the vehicle when he suddenly stopped and waved his arm to someone out of Homer's field of vision. Moments later, a dog came bounding over to the judge who bent down and petted the Beagle's floppy ears. After a few more seconds, a neighbor stopped by to talk.

And just like that, Homer's chance of a payday was delayed for another time—later that night. He wouldn't risk losing his freedom in order to expedite a few dollars.

Chapter 36

Katt walked into the conference room filled to the brim with other law enforcement people. Williamson and Martin were guests in Stetson's building, but both had been there often enough to feel right at home. Also present was Habersham, the District Attorney, as well as Detective Hershey who was now assigned as the lead police investigator to the case. The FBI was present with only one additional agent, Special Agent Wesley Walker. Katt nodded quickly to the man with whom she had met for the first time the day before. This was the new taskforce and they had been waiting for Katt.

Following Katt was an unexpected visitor—Detective Mickey James from the Sacramento Police Department.

"Who are you and what are you doing here?" Stetson, the impromptu leader of the group, asked.

James was about to answer when Katt intervened.

"Gentlemen," Katt said. Other than he, the group consisted exclusively of men. "This is Detective Mickey James of the Sacramento, California Police Department and he's here at my behest."

"With all due respect, Agent Katt," Stetson said, "we already have a quorum for this taskforce, and it wouldn't be appropriate to have any outsiders muddying up the waters."

"I appreciate your concern, Captain Stetson," Katt replied with a smile. "But if you are using the word quorum correctly, it means that you have the minimum number of folks necessary to get the job done. It doesn't mean you have the maximum as you might have thought you meant. And if you think that his input isn't necessary, then you might be right to exclude him." Turning to James, Katt continued. "Mickey, you might as well leave. I don't think your conversation with Joseph Brandenburg is relevant to our discussion and I will call you later."

Katt turned back to the group and waited for someone to understand the meaning of what she just said.

Williamson, as usual, was Jonny-on-the-spot. James was almost out the door.

"When did you speak to Brandenburg?"

James, not one to miss a great entrance said, "Which time?"

There was a flurry of murmuring around the room as James closed the door behind him and stepped closer to the audience of enraptured listeners.

"How about you start from the beginning, Mr. James," Stetson caught up. "How do you know Brandenburg?"

"It's detective," James said. "I may not have jurisdiction in your fine city, but I will respect your titles if you respect mine. And to answer your question…I don't."

"Then how is it that you came to speak with the fugitive? And why are you even here?"

"Melissa Pound is his cousin," Habersham offered. "She told me about the notorious detective from California. She spoke highly of him as a matter of fact. Then again, she also mentioned that he might be someone to keep an eye on. It seems he has a reputation as a rabble-rouser."

"Did she use the term notorious?" Sheriff Martin asked. "It doesn't sound so complimentary to me."

"She more or less gave the man the highest regards, with a caveat of something in the form of 'loose cannon', if my memory is accurate. I did a little checking and discovered that he has one of the best closing records of any law enforcement officer in the state. He also has a sort of 'lone wolf' mentality to go with it. I suspect that he's been doing a little investigating without going through proper channels."

The group looked at James with discontent. James didn't care.

"Is that true, *Detective* James," Williamson asked. "Have you been swimming in the wrong pool?"

Katt could tell that the meeting was heading in the wrong direction and James's purpose for being there was getting pushed aside because the local officers were too concerned with themselves than for getting to the job.

Katt was about to speak. She couldn't afford to have the meeting turn against her. It would get back to Washington, and that would get James knocked out before he even had a chance. James decided that he would be the one to respond and jumped in before Katt could get started.

"I have no intention of answering that question. You want to hang me out to dry to save face for the shitty job you've done so far…more power to you. My cousin was shot in your city. Four people are dead because you're so worried about your crappy little fiefdoms that you can't see the bigger picture. If you want to catch the son of a bitch whose killing your people, then I suggest you get your heads out of each other's asses and forget about what toes I may or may not've stepped on and start figuring out a plan to catch him. If you want the information I have, then shut up and focus on the job at hand, and stop worrying about how you got the information and be happy about the fact that you have it."

James took a breath and was about to continue when Katt stepped up.

"Gentlemen, as Detective James so eloquently said, the information is more important than the means it was acquired."

"Not if he's harboring a fugitive," Habersham said.

"I can assure you that he is not," Katt continued. "If you'll listen to the man, maybe we can move forward with catching the man responsible for killing your citizens."

"You mean Brandenburg," Stetson said.

"I didn't stutter, Captain. I mean whoever the shooter is," Katt replied with her eyes staring straight at the captain. "Right now we don't know who the shooter is. All of the evidence points to Brandenburg. I will agree with that. However, since last night, some things have come to light that may prove beneficial for us to keep an open mind to the possibility that the sniper may be someone else."

"He killed Detective Montclair," Stetson said as if it was a proven fact. "He was a good man...a good cop...and a father. Brandenburg needs to be brought to justice. Period!"

"How do you know it was Brandenburg?" James asked. "Do you have any evidence, other than that it was close to his home, that supports that fact?"

"He took out two of my officers later that night. He was positively identified."

"I suppose he also confessed to the crime?" James baited the captain. He already knew the answer.

"Of course he denied it. They always do. I suppose all of your criminals confess out there in LaLa Land."

"Nope," James smiled. "They're just as crafty as the ones you have here. They will tell all kinds of stupid stories. However, I'm just wondering something. Those other two officers…did he kill them too?"

Stetson hesitated before answering; seeing the trap. "No."

"Hmm," James said. "It would seem to me that if he had killed the first officer, there wouldn't be a lot of incentive to let the other two live. After all, like you said, they positively identified him. It seems to me that if he would have killed them there wouldn't have been a positive ID, therefore eliminating the possibility that he would be convicted by that means."

"Whoever said that criminals are smart?" Habersham voiced. "More times than not, they're pretty stupid."

"Are you of the opinion that Joseph Brandenburg is stupid? Let me rephrase, are you of the opinion that our shooter is stupid? Because if you are, you'll never catch the guy."

"So what exactly are you saying?" Williamson asked. "I take it you don't think Brandenburg did the shootings? Then who did?"

"That my friend is what we're here to figure out."

Chapter 37

Brandenburg was a wanted man, and he knew it. Somewhere out there, someone was attempting to take away his life. What the killer didn't know was that, in spite of his efforts, he had identified himself to the one man who could stop him.

The military teaches their men and women many things. One of the most important things you learn is the art of war. Not like the book; real war with real lives on the line—theirs *and* yours. There was one underlying rule that all soldiers who lived long enough to serve his time and get out alive learned; your opponent.

Brandenburg believed in that rule. He believed that if he spent enough time getting to know the person he was intent to kill, he would figure out how to get the job done and live another day. But he took it further. As a student of history, Brandenburg had also figured out that sometimes in war, if the circumstances warranted it, your friends could become your enemies and your enemies could become your friends.

Brandenburg studied his friends as hard as any enemy. He knew that someday one of them could turn on him. He just didn't know who. Now he knew. At least he was pretty sure and had to act on that knowledge.

Agent Katt and the cop from California—James—seemed to be the kind of people he could trust, though he never really trusted anyone in such a degree that he would be willing to turn himself in for. However, he did trust them enough that he could use them to get what he needed. They just didn't know that he was using them so that he could finish the war his new enemy had started.

He needed information. He needed to get the kind of facts that only people on the inside of the investigation could get. If he was going to kill his opponent he needed to know who the next target would be, and for that he needed help. It was something he wasn't used to.

Only time would tell if they were as smart as he hoped they would be. For now, he had no choice but to wait.

The taskforce listened intently as James explained his encounters with Joseph Brandenburg. He and Katt had decided beforehand to leave her out of the story. There would be questions to answer that she didn't want the room to get distracted by. Besides, she thought it would give James more credence if he could say he met with and talked to Brandenburg twice and lived to tell about it.

"So why did you get to live and not Montclair?" Detective Hershey asked.

James didn't want to say anything to upset the detective any more than he already was. The two men had been partners for years and he, as much as anyone in the room, understood the pain he was dealing with.

"I think, when the forensics come in, you'll know the answer to that question, detective," James replied. "I know that everything points to Brandenburg killing your partner. He so much as admitted that he was the one who made the cuts on him. But, he also pointed out that he wasn't the one to do the shooting that killed him. He said to check for stippling around the entry site, and you wouldn't find any. If he was going to kill the man, his weapon, as close as he was to Montclair, would have left residue."

"That could simply mean that he has a partner," Habersham said. "It doesn't clear him of anything."

"Let me tell you what I know," James replied. "I know the pain of losing a partner. I know that when we lose someone close that sometimes our realities get distorted. I also know that you don't know shit about how someone like Brandenburg works. He's a loner. The only person that he would ever allow in his life would be a spotter."

"Don't spotters also shoot?" Stetson asked. "I know they did when I was in the service."

"They do," James replied. "The problem is…Brandenburg's spotter is dead. That's one of the reasons he left the Navy. That and having to work with folks like you," James muttered.

"I beg your pardon?" Habersham asked. "I think we've been more than generous with the time we've allotted you this morning."

"That's just the thing," James barked back at the puffed up District Attorney. "You've allowed me the opportunity to tell you some things about Brandenburg and never once asked what we can do to find the killer. You people are so concerned about getting your victory that you've completely forgotten about justice. There are many possibilities about what happened out there. Brandenburg could be the sniper, but he didn't kill your man, Captain. He may be guilty of multiple sins, but you don't seem to care about finding the truth. If you want to do what is right, then get your heads out of your asses and start thinking about how to solve this before someone else gets killed."

With those words, James turned and left the room. He had already made up his mind that the group sitting in that room was too stupid to catch the killer. He had no choice but to go after the shooter himself.

He wondered if Katt would ever forgive him if he got killed.

James heard the conference room door open and close again as he was walking away. The funny thing, he thought, was that he wasn't even angry. He had spent enough time around arrogant politicians that the people he just left didn't rate high enough on his piss-O-meter to warrant a heavy sigh. He turned to see who was walking quickly up to him. It was Katt.

"Stop right there, mister," Katt hissed. "I had to jump through too damn many hoops for you to walk out of here."

"Listen, Katt," James started but didn't get far.

"Shut up for a second and listen." Katt pointed to a couple of chairs lining the wall. "I want you to sit here and wait for me. This isn't over, and I'll be damned if I'm going to risk another victim because you can't play with others."

"I could play with you if we weren't constantly being interrupted," James tried being funny.

"Sit! Shut up and wait!"

Katt turned and walked away before James could say another word.

When Katt arrived back in the conference room, there was a buzzing from the other members in the room.

"Alright everybody," Katt said. "Take your seats and come to order."

For the first time in a long time, Katherine Katt was angry. People were dying, and nobody seemed to want to do what needed to be done to stop the shooter, and she was tired of it.

"Are you people out of your minds or just plain stupid," Katt said, allowing the roar in her head to do the talking.

"Now wait just a gosh darn minute, little lady," Stetson replied. "I think…"

"I don't care what you think," Katt said, staring down the man. "For reasons I can't comprehend, the lot of you are more interested in politics than the people you claim to care about. It stops now. I have worked with the man who just walked out. I know him to be a pain in the ass, an arrogant prick and the most frustrating cop who has ever strapped on a gun. He's also the best cop I've ever had the pleasure to work with, and I would trust my life to him ahead of any one of you. I can say that because I have. He's saved my life more than once and that was on the same case.

"All you can see is someone coming in here that isn't on your force and automatically discount anything he might bring to the table. But let's be clear here, Detective James, without any of your help, has made more progress on this case than all of you combined.

"He isn't in it for the glory. He doesn't care which of you gets the credit. He wants to protect his family. That's the only motivation pushing him. What is motivating you? Can you answer that honestly and say it's as pure?

"We have a choice to make. Better still, I have a choice to make. Let him assist in the case and get it solved, or shut each of you down and the FBI will take over completely. I have already been asked how I want to handle it. I told my superiors that I could work with you and together we could solve the case. Now I don't know. From what I just witnessed, I'm beginning to lean toward doing this without your petty issues."

Katt stopped to let her words sink in. Seldom did she use such brash tones with high-ranking local officials. Frankly, she had never had to. But, for the first time in her career, she was dealing with a group that seemed to have a built in set of rules that was prime for what the killer was using to take advantage of. There were too many jurisdictions; too many built-in problems for this group to get a hold of. It was time to be tough.

"He's too much of a loose cannon," Habersham said. "He has no respect for the uniform."

"I agree," said Stetson. "I've never had a detective, mine or anyone else's, who treated my office with such disrespect. We can solve this without him."

"How?" Katt asked. "What have you or your people brought to the table that's brought you one step closer to solving it? By the time you get to the point of solving anything, the shooter will be in another country for all we know. We have a rare opportunity to stop this guy, but can't make any progress because of all your bickering. Without James, where will you go? What will you do next?"

The room was quiet. Nobody was willing to use the information James had brought them as a starting point, and there was very little else to go on.

"So what would you have us do, Agent Katt?" Williamson asked.

"I would like to invite Detective James back and get some ideas from him," Katt replied. "He's ex-military. He has a unique understanding of the kind of man we're up against. He seems to have the ability to get information we don't have."

"What kind of information?" Williamson asked. "You hadn't mentioned anything about other resources."

"I was leaving that to James," Katt said. "If you don't know by now, Melissa Pound's father is a retired general—military police. He has the ability to get information from the military that we can't get because of national security and…"

"National Security my ass," Habersham said.

"Granted," Katt acknowledged. "They may be clinging a little tight to that catchall excuse, but whether it's real or fabricated, it works. He…and James…know Brandenburg at a level we'll never get access to. They also know, not just suspect, that Brandenburg is innocent. They can't discuss some of the details with us because, again, of national security. But they can use the information to lead us in a better direction."

"Surely you can get that information, Agent Katt," Sheriff Martin said. "I thought the FBI could get anything."

"You've been watching too many T.V. shows, Sheriff. What I'm talking about is overseas information that the FBI can only get if the military or CIA deems us worthy. Joseph Brandenburg is someone very special to those people. He's done things for this country that could be a huge embarrassment if it were ever found out." Katt wasn't sure about that part, but thought it sounded like something she could use to help the cause.

"The thing is…Brandenburg, if he's guilty, will take his punishment for any crimes he's committed. However, the government is not going to assist in this case without the help of General Pound and his nephew, Detective Mickey James. The military trusts these men. I should think that's good enough for us to do likewise."

Chapter 38

James had no idea what Katt was doing. He knew she was pissed off and he actually thought she looked hot when she was mad. On the other hand, he didn't want to ever again be on the back end of that anger. Had it been anyone else, he would have already left the building. For Katt, he would wait until next week.

James hadn't heard the footsteps until they were right on him. His mind was drifting to places he would like to take Katt. When he looked up, the agent was standing before him with her hands firmly on her hips, as if she was about to scold him for being tardy to class.

"Come with me," Katt said. "And this time, you better be on you best behavior."

Katt turned and Mickey followed.

I wonder what she would look like with her hair in a bun and she wore those old black-rimmed glasses?

James smiled at the image of the school teacher fantasy that passed before his eyes.

It was seldom good form for any criminal to do his deed in broad daylight. Unfortunately, for Homer, time was no longer on his side. He had made a commitment and things weren't exactly coming together as planned.

Melissa Pound was feeling better each day and believed that she would be fine by the time the trial came around. Then again, her doctor told her that she needed to be cognizant of doing any exertion that might jeopardize her recovery.

The general had told Melissa that he had some errands to run. Being alone for the first time since the shooting was something she wasn't looking forward to. When her father asked if she would be okay for an hour, she quickly rejected the notion that he had anything to worry about. Once he was gone, however, every sound the old house made caused her to be anxious.

It was going on ten-thirty when Melissa entered the kitchen for a cup of tea. She would have preferred coffee, but was again following the advice of her physician.

Staring out the kitchen window, waiting for the water to come to a boil, Melissa looked at the sugar maple and how the leaves were starting to turn. Given another week, those leaves would be a beautiful shade of gold. With her back to the basement door, she had not heard the silent steps of the man as he approached her from behind. It was only when the knife touched her throat, and a hand clasped her mouth that she knew her days as a prosecutor were finished. She only wished she had done everything she had planned.

The task force had listened to what James had to say about his interactions with Brandenburg. And though they no longer shared outward signs of hostilities, it was still evident that they hadn't embraced him as one of the gang.

Katt observed the group and wanted to scream at the men with whom the community had placed their faith, but she couldn't. She had to let James fight his way into the group and earn their respect. That was the key to moving forward. She had done all that she could.

"So, Mister…er, Detective James," Williamson said, "How do you propose we move forward from here?"

James didn't react negatively to the question. He felt the contempt of being an outsider and understood where they were coming from. Had the situation been reversed, he wanted to believe that he would be more open minded than this group, but truthfully knew that he would be pretty much the same.

"Look guys, I've done something here I want to apologize for. I've crashed your party and had no business doing that. I had no intention of stepping on toes or placing my agenda above anyone else's. I'm here to protect my cousin, Melissa, and got caught up in the whole thing. When I went to see Brandenburg that first time, I thought he would be like every other crackpot I've ever run up against. But I was wrong. Very wrong.

"What I discovered was a man who could kill any one of us anytime he wanted and never work up a sweat. I have been face to face with cold-blooded killers in my career and stared them down. I've been up against some of the most ruthless S.O.B.'s this country has ever grown, and they never bothered me. This man—Brandenburg—knows more about the concepts of killing than all of them put together. But there's something else. I could also see that this man is also someone who's had enough of killing and doesn't want any more of it, but that's just this man's opinion.

"The problem is…whoever's out there doing this, screwed the pooch. He got Brandenburg involved.

"Right now, Brandenburg has turned into the hunter. I've held one last piece of information from you that I need to show you." James reached into his pocket and pull out the coin. "When Brandenburg left the house last night, he was in a hurry because he didn't know who was at the door. He also knew that he didn't get a chance to review the files I told you about or give us the information we need to contact him. He left this Canadian twenty-five cent piece as a clue."

"What's it supposed to mean?" Martin asked. "Call someone who gives a damn?"

"Actually," James replied, "I believe he thinks the shooter is Canadian. Brandenburg knows these men. He knows their profiles. He also knows their signatures. Something's got him thinking that the shooter he wants us to look for is from north of the border. I don't know if that means he's a Canadian military person or simply someone who came from there."

"It could mean that or any of a dozen other things," Habersham retorted. "We need to stick to the facts at hand and not go off on some wild goose chase."

"And what facts do we have that will lead you on a chase of any kind…wild or otherwise," Katt asked. "As best as I can tell, we don't have anything that could actually lead us anywhere. The shooter is really good at long distances, which means he's probably either military or ex-military. However, I looked on Google and found that there are long distance shooters from around the world. We know the type of bullet he shoots but not the gun. We know that he has an agenda, but we don't know what it is. Care to add to the list, gentlemen because I've pretty much run out of facts that we know."

"We know the victims," Williamson added. "Maybe that's something."

"I'm glad you brought that up," James said. "Because, in answering your question of what I think we should do next, my answer is to divide and conquer."

"What do you mean" Williamson asked.

"I mean…so far we've…you've focused your attention on the shooter," James continued. "For the record, that made sense given what information was available. However, I also think that we need to consider the victims. Why would he kill these people? What's the motive for them as opposed to someone else? Is there a connection between these victims that means something we hadn't already considered? I think we need to split this group into two parts; one focusing on the shooter and the other on the victims. Maybe if we come at it from both ends, we'll figure out how to meet in the middle."

"I don't see how focusing on the victims is going to help," Habersham said. "It seems to me that the best way to stop the shooter is to find the shooter."

"Generally, I would agree," James said. "When all you have is a single victim, you can oftentimes focus on the killer; physical profile, method, intelligence, etcetera. In cases like that, the information about the victim will assist the case and may indeed lead to motive, but it's the killer whom we focus our attention. The victim is important, but to find the killer, looking at the motive, i.e. the victim, will give us a lot of information that will help lead us there."

"To be more specific," Katt added, "Victimology is an integral part of how the FBI goes after a killer. We use a blend of profiling, both the victim and the killer, to see if a pattern or other clue, develops."

"Sorry, Agent Katt," James said, "I was focusing my information for the one person here that doesn't hunt criminals for a living." James smiled and gave Katt a wink. It was his way of telling Habersham that he should leave the hunting to the hunters. Katt did not return the smile, but noticed that the district attorney's face turned a slightly warmer shade of pink.

Message received.

I've been taken to a place where you cannot find me. I'm told that if you do exactly what you are told, I will remain safe. Do not call the police. Don't even call Mickey. You will be contacted in a few hours. – Love, Melissa

Chapter 39

The general read the note completely three times before laying it down on the counter. A tear trickled down his cheek, but he hadn't noticed. His baby had been taken and there was nothing he could do about it. Just five short sentences and he covered all contingencies. Mickey wasn't a cop from around here, so the kidnapper had to know about him being a cop somewhere else. Why else would he have specified not to call him? Did he know before or did he force Melissa to tell?

Oh...sweet Jesus!

He'd only been gone for about fifty minutes; not even the hour he had said he would be gone. How could he have been so stupid to leave her here? She had been a damn target, for Christ's sake. She was unfinished business. He couldn't believe it was happening to his baby—his daughter.

The general decided to wait...for a while, anyway. It was almost eleven. He would give the son of a bitch until two o'clock. After that, all bets were off.

"I agree with Detective James," Katt said. "I think we should divide the group into two. James seems versed on Brandenburg so he should definitely be on the shooter team."

"Please forgive the intrusion," James butted in, "but I don't think I should be leading anyone. I'm more of a follower." He was offering the barb at being humorous. It didn't work.

"I had no intentions of placing you in charge," Katt replied and smirked. "That honor…or curse…belongs to Agent Williamson. He's had a lot of experience and his position gives him more latitude in the state than the others. I will head up the victims' team. I would appreciate DA Habersham to join me. Since most of the victims were a part of the court system, I believe he would be able to offer valuable insight."

"I would be honored," the DA said. "No offense gentlemen, but the lady seems to have taste."

There were smiles around the room with a guffaw from James. Katt was glad to get the two headstrong men separated. She knew things would work better that way.

"What about the FBI?" Sheriff Martin asked. "I saw that you had a contingent with you yesterday. Are they sticking around?"

"Yes," Katt replied. "Some of them will be assigned to the two teams. The rest of my people will have other duties to attend. Right now we are going to take a short break and meet back here in fifteen minutes. I have a couple of calls to make and then we'll get set to find the person shooting up your fair city."

The men rose and for the first time seemed to have direction. Katt looked at James and nodded her head to indicate that she needed to talk to him. James followed her until they got out the door. A short trip down a corridor, another short left and the two of them were alone.

Katt stared into James' eyes for a long moment before speaking.

"How much do you trust Brandenburg?" Katt asked as if inquiring for the first time. "I'm having a feeling that something bad is about to happen and can't shake it."

"To be honest," James replied. "I don't trust him any farther than I could throw the guy. He's an unknown. I can't get a handle on him. My thinking that he's not the shooter is about as far as I can go."

"Thanks," Katt said.

"For what?"

"Being honest with me," Katt replied. "I wasn't sure if you were so caught up in your cause that you couldn't see past it. I should have known better."

"Not to worry," James smiled. "People underestimate me all the time."

"I hardly believe that. Do you think you can catch this guy before he kills anyone else?"

"Sticking with the truth…I don't know. I'd like to think I could, but it all depends on when that next shot is due to take place."

"Do you think he's done?"

"Nope. I think what we've seen so far has been done for a reason. I don't think these shootings are the real target."

"Why do you think that?"

"Just a guess," James said, looking uncomfortable in his shoes.

"Well," Katt said, "Paraphrasing what Doctor McCoy told Spock, '*I trust your guesses more than I trust most people's facts.*' So, I'll take it."

"He's taken her," the general said when James answered his phone. He had waited a total of fifteen minutes deciding whether to call his nephew, the cops, or simply to wait as instructed. Waiting wasn't an option, and the general trusted James more than any cop he knew. "I wasn't supposed to call you or the cops," he continued, "but I don't trust the son of a bitch to tell the truth."

James was trying to catch up with his uncle, but hadn't quite made the connection.

"What are you saying?" James asked. "Who's taken whom? Melissa?"

"Yes, damn it. The son of a bitch has taken my daughter. You need to get back here. Now!"

"Let me talk to Katt. She can help."

"No, Mickey. You can't do that. The orders were specific. No cops. And no you."

"He mentioned me by name?"

"He didn't write the note. He made Melissa write it. Can you stop talking and get over here, son. I need you to do that right now."

"I'm on my way."

The general had never worked with Katt. And even though she was an officer of the law—an FBI agent—she could also do the right thing. He couldn't just leave without tell her.

Katt had told the group to reassemble and was waiting outside the room when James raced up the hallway. She could tell it was bad news.

"I need a promise," James said without preamble. "What I'm about to tell you, you can't repeat until I say that it's okay. Can you promise me that?"

"What's wrong, Mickey."

"Promise me you'll speak to no one…please."

"I promise," Katt was reluctant, but James knew she would never break her word. He told her what happened. "Go! I'll cover for you."

James barely heard the last part as he slammed through the doors.

"Let's get started," Katt said to the group as they reconvened. She decided to play the low-key card and hope nobody would notice. It didn't work.

"Where's your friend, Agent Katt?" Agent Williamson asked. "I thought he was now an integral part of this investigation."

"He is, Agent Williamson. I sent him on an errand. He needed to get me some material that could assist the group. We'll discuss the nature of that information once he returns. In the meantime, I think we should focus on the victims for now. It seems that there hasn't been a lot of discussion up to this point and that needs to be rectified."

"I'm not sure that's going to help," Habersham said. "However, in the spirit of the taskforce, maybe I should be the person to start."

"That was going to be my suggestion," Katt replied. "You knew these people as well as anyone…right?"

"I wouldn't say that," Habersham replied. "I knew them from their public, or should I say their working lives. I didn't really know any of them that well personally."

"Do we have a breakdown of their personal lives?" Stetson asked. "I would like to have that information available as well."

"I will see to it that everyone gets a copy of their personal histories as well as the interviews conducted by the police with their friends and family since they were killed," Katt said. "However, it's currently the working theory that the shooter is doing these under a contract. As such, the personal issues won't be disregarded, but I think for now we'll push forward with the business side. If it had been just one person, the personal aspect of their lives might make more sense. But with a contract shooter involved, as I'm starting to believe, as well as multiple victims, it just makes more sense that it's either political or greed motivated.

"With that in mind, let's look first at the first victim—Dayton Salazar. What do we know about him?"

"Male in his fifties, married, two children," started Habersham, "who was embarking on a very public case—Boyd Weapons. If he were to actually win that case, it would change the landscape on how weapons of any kind were bought and sold in this country. It would, in essence, change the fourth amendment of the Constitution of the United States."

"That seems like motive to me," Doug Martin, the sheriff, said. "There is certainly enough money available to pay for a hit. Hell, there's enough money for several hits to be made."

"Then does that also include the shootings of Melissa Pound?" Katt asked.

"Salazar was lead chair in the case," Habersham said. "However, Pound was—is—more than capable of continuing the case without Salazar. As a matter of fact, I haven't told anyone this yet, other than the judge and the defense attorney, but with Melissa's help, I intend to prosecute the case anyway. The trial was given a short delay, but as it stands now, we'll be starting early next week."

"Then if stopping the case was the motivation," Katt allowed, "then that would put you and Melissa right in the crosshairs. Maybe we should consider keeping the two of you in protective custody." Her comment was more of a thought than anything else, but it would need serious consideration before the day was done."

"But that doesn't account for the Abernathy shooting," Williamson said, focusing on Habersham. "What does he have to do with the Boyd gun case?"

"Nothing," replied Habersham. "I've been kept abreast of this case since Salazar started it and Abernathy's name was never brought up."

"Then maybe it was something different that Abernathy was working on. Two separate motives for two separate cases."

Katt shook her head and said, "I don't buy it. What's the likelihood that two different people hired the same shooter—or two different shooters—to commit the same kind of crime at the same time? That's beyond coincidence."

"But the Boyd case makes the most sense," Martin said. "A gun case interrupted by a gun seems almost poetic."

"I understand, Longfellow," Katt smiled, "but the truth still exists that the two crimes have to be related. There's no way that they can't be somehow. There's got to be something else—some other motivation."

"Like what?" Habersham asked. "What do the two shootings have in common; besides the rifle?"

Katt thought about the question as did everyone else. They couldn't see the connection.

"My mentor told me once, a long time ago, that sometimes it isn't what you see that's important. Sometimes, the important thing is what you don't see. Tell me about the positions they held." Katt said, looking at the DA.

"You already know about Salazar," Habersham said. "He was an assistant district attorney. He was sharp and had the potential of doing great things during his career."

"What about Abernathy? What did he do?"

"He was an Appellate Court Judge. Actually, to be technical, he was a judge of the Supreme Court for District Two of Ohio. His position was pretty high up the ladder. He pretty much ran the show. If a court ruled on something, they would take it to the appellate courts. If that didn't work, it went to the

Supreme Court of Ohio. Around here that's district two. If it doesn't finish there, the only alternative is the Supreme Court of the United States. You can't get a lot higher around these parts."

"So who takes over with him being gone?" Katt asked.

"It's an elected position and goes for six years. However, if a spot needs to be filled between elections, then the appointment will be made by the governor of Ohio."

"Who would be the most likely candidate to replace him?" Katt asked.

Habersham thought for a moment. "There have been rumors flying around that the most likely person to replace him would be Judge Anderson. He seems to be near the top of the list anyway."

"Is there anybody else?" Katt asked. "Who else would benefit from Abernathy dying?"

"There could be others," Habersham said. "I can get you a list of the judges that would benefit most directly. However, I must warn you, Agent Katt, these are powerful men here in Ohio. None of them are going to appreciate you accusing them of murder."

"I have no intentions of accusing them of anything, Mr. Habersham. Right now, I'm simply trying to figure out the void left behind. If things keep going this way, I may talk to them for some insight."

The DA looked at Katt and slowly shook his head. He wondered if the woman from Washington had any clue the firestorm she was considering.

Chapter 40

Melissa woke in a haze. Her hands and feet were hogtied behind her back. A gag was held firmly in place, along with a blindfold. She lay on her right side and began to wonder why she was still alive.

She tried for several minutes to free the binds, without success. Then a man's voice whispered in her ear.

"Can I trust you not to scream?" She knew the man's lips were next to her ear, yet it seemed distant somehow. The whispered voice came as a hiss and yet it seemed familiar in a way. "Things are quite sensitive for the moment. Screaming might cause a problem for me that I would just as soon avoid. So…can I trust you?"

Melissa paused for only a moment before shaking her head in assent. The man gently removed the gag from her mouth, yet was ready to replace it at a moment's notice.

True to her word, the shaken woman knew that she wasn't in the kind of shape necessary to defend herself. The best she could hope would be for Mickey to come and rescue her. She also knew that the odds of that were slim.

"I can remove the blindfold if you desire. As it stands, since you haven't seen my face, there's a chance that if things work out, I won't have to kill you if I leave it on. However, once you see my face, there won't be any turning back."

"You're going to kill me anyway," Melissa said. "So what difference does it make?"

"Actually, I haven't made up my mind who I will kill before this is over. You and your father have placed me in a very difficult position. A position…"

"What have we done to you? I don't even know who you are."

"I'm the person that gets to decide if you live or die. I'm the person that's being hunted by your father and your cousin." He took off the blindfold. "I'm Joseph Brandenburg and at the moment, I'm pissed."

James ran from his car and into the house. The general was waiting in the kitchen. Without saying a word, Pound handed the note to James and waited for him to finish. He saw the man's shoulders drop and knew that James now understood just how serious things had gotten.

"I'm sorry, Mickey. I don't know what I was thinking. Nobody bothered her at the hospital. I thought that she was out of harm's way."

"I asked you to stay with her. What was so important that you had to leave her alone?"

Mickey looked at the terror in the man's face and immediately regretted his words.

"I'm sorry," James said. "I had no right to say that. What can I do?"

"You can find her, Mickey. Find my little girl."

"I need help," James replied. "I can't do this without help."

"The note said to leave the police out of it. He's going to know they're involved."

"Not unless someone tells him."

"That's the point," Pound replied. "I've been thinking about this case for some time. I know you guys have been thinking about it too, but since I've been pretty much out of the loop, I've been trying to put this together myself and can't see how the shooter's been able to do what he does without someone helping him along the way."

"So talk to me. Start at the beginning."

"Look...you've been in the military. You know how we operate. Nothing gets done without a crap-load of planning. For a sniper, it's maybe even more so. A sniper needs intel. He can't just set up shop and hope for the best. He needs to know where the target's going to be. He needs to know everything there is to know before taking the shot. There's just too much information that needs gathered to pull off a shot like that."

Pound took a breath before continuing. "Go on," James said.

"Then he killed Abernathy. How did he know he would be there at that exact moment? How did he know from where to shoot? There are too many variables for an outsider to get on his own. And then there's something else…Katt. How did he know where to go to get after her? She doesn't even live around here. She didn't go to a traditional hotel to stay. Yet somehow he managed to find her and attack her without as much as a pause in the action. There has to be help on the inside; someone who knows everything that's going on."

"You came up with this all by yourself?" James asked, amazed.

"I've done police work a lot longer than you, son. There was a time when I was pretty damn good at it too."

"I'm beginning to think you might still be pretty damn good," James placed a kind hand on his uncle's shoulder. "So what do you want me to do? I still can't do this alone."

"Do you still trust your lady agent?" Pound asked. "Maybe she has some resources that we could use."

James was somewhat embarrassed. "I've already told her," he said. "I'm sorry. I had no choice.

But she won't say anything to anyone before I get back to her. I promise you that."

"Then you need to go back and get her alone. Explain what's going on. Maybe this guy will call soon. I'll follow up with you if he does. If not, then you'll still be ahead of whatever timetable he had planned."

"You promise not to do anything stupid?" James asked.

"Absolutely not," Pound smiled as the men shook hands. "But, I will do everything in my power not to do anything that will screw things up. For now, I'll just wait here until I hear from someone—you or him."

James turned and left. There wasn't much he could do from the house. Katt would have a way to help. At least that's what he hoped.

James returned to the precinct with stares coming from the cops as well as the FBI that were present. Katt halted the meeting so that James could bring her up to speed. After explaining the note and the kidnapping, he also explained the general's perspective regarding the person who might be assisting the killer.

"It makes sense," Katt said after James had finished. "I wish I would have thought along those same lines."

"That's why I mentioned it to you," James said. "I hadn't thought of it either. The problem is, I have no idea who that inside person might be and don't feel comfortable telling everyone just yet."

"The news will get out," Katt replied.

"I know. I would just like to hold off on telling everyone as long as possible. We need some people to work on this that we can trust, and I'm all out of ideas on where to get them. I need you to put a team together that will work on it without compromising the shootings."

"Hang on a second," Katt said and dialed a number. "Lester...I need you at the police station right away." Katt listened for a few seconds and then hung up. "Lester Henderson will be here in a minute. He'll head up the team."

"Do you trust him?" James asked.

"He's an FBI agent,' Katt replied as if the answer should be enough. James didn't agree.

"I don't care if he's the Pope. Have you worked with him? Do you know him well enough to know that he can't be compromised?"

"Of all the people Blythe sent me, he's the only one that I have worked with before. I know he's familiar with several of the others and can trust him to not take anything for granted. And for the record, James, I'm offended that you would question me about this."

"I'm not questioning you or your integrity, Katt. I'm questioning the rest of them. There's something big going on here and I'll be damned if I can figure it out. My thinking is that whoever's behind it has got to have a hell of a lot of pull to put it together. I just can't take any chances."

Agent Henderson strolled up to Katt, and she introduced him to James. The two men eyed each other like the combatants they were and then shook hands. Katt explained the situation and told him that he was personally responsible for the team he gathered.

Katt also explained the possible leak within the ranks.

"How long has she been gone?" Henderson asked.

"Less than two hours," James replied. "She was taken from their home in broad daylight. I don't know if he's that good or if it was an act of desperation. Either way, it sucks for the good guys."

Katt turned to James and felt sorry for what he was going through. She knew that everything was coming to a head. It was time to turn things around.

"Come with me," Katt said. "We've got a killer to catch."

James was about to object and tell Katt that Melissa had to be the priority. After a moment's thought, he realized that everything that was happening had to do with the killer. If they could find him, he could find his cousin. Nothing else mattered.

Deputy Director Blythe used to tell Katt, "It's hard to concentrate on draining the swamp when you're up to your ass in alligators." Katt wondered if the situation she now faced would fall into that category.

"Blythe," the boss man said in a chipped voice. "Tell me you've figured out what the hell's going on and will be coming home soon."

"I wish I could, sir," Katt replied. "I'm calling to tell you that things have gotten worse. Melissa Pound has been taken by a person or persons unknown. We now believe that there is a security breach that has been giving the shooter inside information. Other than that, we think we are getting a grasp of the situation, but don't know that as a fact."

Blythe didn't respond right away. It had only been twelve hours or so since Katt last updated him. At that time, he was feeling somewhat positive that his star agent would figure things out and close the case soon. Now, he wasn't so sure.

"One at a time, Agent Katt, tell me about everything."

Katt started with Melissa Pound. She told him about the note left behind and that she had assigned Agent Henderson to lead that investigation.

"Agent Henderson is a good man," Blythe said. "He's handled several kidnapping for ransom cases over the years. You chose well."

Finally, she explained the team's belief that the shooter was getting help from within. That information was something the Deputy Director didn't want to hear. Katt was sure that he would like it even less if he realized that the idea and the very small circle of those on the team consisted of James and now Henderson.

"You've got a right fine mess on your hands if that's true," Blythe said. Katt could hear the anger in his voice, but never got the impression that the anger was aimed at her. "So how do you plan on solving this?"

Katt hesitated. She knew what she was about to ask might be considered a weakness, but was not about to let her ambitions stop her from doing her job.

"I need help," she replied. "I need some people from Langley; people that you know personally or that can be trusted at a higher standard than normal."

"Do you hear what you're saying?" Blythe asked. "You're telling me that you don't trust the people you're working with within our organization. You're telling me that you think the FBI has a mole and is committing an act of treason."

"Actually, sir, I'm not," Katt replied much calmer than how she felt. "I'm asking for people to be brought in so that I can use them to eliminate the FBI and then focus on the people that are really the target. If I'm going to do this, time is of the essence. I don't think the shooter is done and I need to find the leak before someone else gets killed. With more time, I could do it with the people I have. I don't have that kind of time, sir."

"How do you know that? How do you know that he isn't done killing? How do you know that there is a leak…for sure? How much of this is coming from you and how much is coming from your buddy, Detective James? You didn't think I had forgotten about him did you? This is a mess, Katherine. And I don't know if what you're asking is in the bureau's best interest."

"I don't know what it is between you and Detective James, sir. What I do know is that he has done more at getting useful information than the entire police department and the bureau combined. James isn't the problem here and I don't mean to be disrespectful, but I need some help to be sent here. If not, then I need to get back to figuring this out before someone else dies."

"Then I will get them on their way," Blythe said. "Look…I just wanted to make sure that your compassion for the man wasn't the driving force behind your decisions. He can be quite persuasive. But, he's also a loose cannon that could cost you your job if you aren't careful. Your men will be there in about three hours."

"Thank you, sir."

Katt knew that Blythe was more of a mentor than a boss. She just wished sometimes that he would learn to trust her when it came to her heart. As soon as she thought the words, she knew the answer.

Because I'm a wreck when it comes to my heart.

"One more thing, Katherine," Blythe said. "If you find this guy—this killer—bring him in alive."

"Sir?" Katt didn't understand the request.

"I want you to bring him in alive…if possible. He could be a good source of intel."

"Yes, sir," Katt replied. "If at all possible."

Chapter 41

The task force had been waiting for Katt's return. The room was small and bland, and there wasn't enough room to walk about when everyone was standing. Agent Williamson was on a call when Katt entered, and Captain Stetson was conversing with Montgomery County Sheriff Doug Martin. James was standing with his back to the group; staring out the window. Katt felt for the man. She knew that he was in turmoil about Melissa, and there was nothing she could say or do that would make things better for him.

"Let's get back to it everybody. We need some answers and time has just run out."

"What's going on?" Stetson asked.

Katt wanted more than anything to answer the man. She was concerned that she had misspoken and threw out a hint about Melissa that could come back to haunt them. Instead, she said, "I just spoke to my boss and he's of the opinion that things aren't finished here yet." She was hoping that her lie would cause the group to question where he was coming from.

"Did he get any new information?" Stetson asked.

"No," Katt replied. "He just thinks that we are on the right track and his gut's telling him to push harder, if at all possible. He too thinks that things aren't done here. That's all."

James wanted more than anything to tell the group about his cousin. He knew that collectively, they had a better chance of finding her than he, or the FBI, had. He couldn't take the chance though. He had no idea what was going, but he did know that someone was getting information to the killer and was not about to give them anything more than what they already had.

"I've been thinking," James said. "I don't think the Boyd Gun case is the reason behind all of this."

"Why?" Katt asked, voicing what everyone was thinking.

"It's too easy," James replied. "It's the red herring to throw us off track. Look at it this way; the best lies told, whether by a con artist, a politician, or anyone else are always filled with enough truth to be believable. If the mark is even a little smart, he'll need to know that whatever he's buying has a modicum of identifiable truth.

"Then let's look at the case. Boyd manufacturing would make the most sense. Guns are being used to kill the people involved in a gun case. It's a no-brainer, right?

"The problem comes from Judge Abernathy; a man who has absolutely nothing to do with that case. If we look at them separately, there would be no possible link. However, if you look at them together, it blows the gun case out of the water. The killer screwed up. He would have been much better off to stab him or use a hand gun…anything but a rifle."

"So where does that leave us," Stetson asked. "I still don't see the connection."

"Look at it as a straight line," James replied. He walked up to the head of the room and picked up a dry-erase pen. "If we consider who's died so far, then the judge would be here." James wrote the judge's name on the top left of the chalkboard. He then wrote the names of the attorneys that had been shot on the top right of the board. Finally, he drew a straight line between the names leaving a gap in the middle of the chalkboard. "What we need to do is figure out the commonalities between these attorneys and Judge Abernathy. If we can find a common denominator, I think we can figure out who will be the next target."

Katt found it interesting that James was able to disassociate himself from "the attorneys" considering that his cousin was one of them.

"Let's say we can figure that out," Katt said, liking where James was taking the group. "How does that help us catch the killer?"

"It might not," James stated honestly. "The problem is that with a long shot artist, he could kill from just about anywhere. On the other hand, if we can figure it out, maybe we can put that person—the next potential target—in police custody and protect him or her until we get a better handle on what's going down."

The group looked at James for a moment and then turned to the board. Collectively, and without prompting, they started talking about the victims and what they had in common. It took the better part of two hours for the group to narrow the possible targets to two people—Judge Beatrice Ross and Judge Leon Anderson. Of the two, Anderson was the one that made the most sense.

Katt looked at James and smiled a sad, tired smile. Somehow, out of chaos he had managed to find clarity.

James saw the smile and returned the gesture, but there was nothing there that would allow him to see the good until Melissa was returned home safe. Until then, he needed to find the man holding her before something bad happened.

He hoped more than anything that nothing bad had happened already.

Homer had always considered himself to be a patient man. All snipers were if you asked anyone in the military who actually knew them. However, looking at the home he had planned to infiltrate being covered by FBI agents was taxing his patience to the core. It wouldn't have made him any difference whether he took the girl or her father—the man he now understood to be a retired general. Either would have been satisfactory to set things up the way he planned.

That option was no longer viable.

His contact had let him down and he was getting angry. It compromised his plans drastically. A good soldier knew that the difference between life and death almost always came down to the quality of the information you could get to perform your duty. His intel was now flawed. He didn't care if he was able to kill the last target. That was simply for money. But, to kill the FBI agents—more than anything—was the thing he needed. Now, he was no longer confident that he could accomplish his job if he couldn't trust the man or the information he received.

Katt was driving as she and James left the courthouse.

"I want to go by the house and see how the general's doing," James said.

"I was going to suggest the same thing," Katt replied after hanging up from Sheriff Martin.

James was about to call his uncle when his cell phone rang. He didn't recognize the number but put the call on speaker anyway.

"What would be the odds of you and I sitting down and having a conversation," the voice at the other end asked.

"Somewhere between when hell freezes over and never," James replied.

"That's what I expected," Brandenburg said. "Would the chances increase if I were to tell you that I have your cousin and that she is fine?"

"You son of a bitch," James spat in the phone. "If you lay one…"

"Please don't threaten me, Mr. James. I saved your cousin. You should be grateful."

"Then bring her home," James said. "If what you're telling me is true, then you no longer need her."

"Actually, I do need her. She's the reason you'll come see me…alone. I will not harm her, Mr. James; whether you see me or not. But then, there's enough of a threat that you won't take the chance that I'm lying."

"I'm not alone right now," James said looking at Katt.

"I see. You are with the beautiful agent friend of yours…Agent Katt."

"Yes. We were going over to see if we could help in the investigation of Melissa's disappearance."

"Then I guess my timing was fortuitous. You can save yourself a trip. Anyway, I still need to see you. We have work to do, and I can't do it if I'm being hunted like an animal."

"What did you expect? You kidnapped the daughter of a retired general and the cousin of a cop. We police don't take kindly to that sort of thing. So how do I know you have her and that she's okay?"

"Listen to this," Brandenburg said and put a recorder to the phone.

"Mickey…this is Melissa. I wish I could tell you what's going on. Frankly, I'm pretty damn confused by it all. I thought Joseph Brandenburg was the killer, but now I'm not so sure. As a matter of fact, I don't think he's the killer at all. I'm okay, Mickey. He hasn't harmed me in any way. Now I know that you're the kind of person that won't take this message as proof of anything, so I need to tell you something…Sunbird. Did you get that…Sunbird? That should tell you everything you need to know about what's going on. I love you Mickey. Please call dad and tell him that I'm okay and that I'll be seeing him soon."

There was silence for several moments before anyone said anything.

"She wouldn't tell me what Sunbird meant," Brandenburg said. "I can only hope it was something that will convince you that I'm telling the truth. Time is running out, and I can't do this alone."

"What do you want?" James asked. "I'm not going anywhere without Agent Katt. She's too valuable if we're going to try working together. She can get information I can't reach. You can trust her."

"Can I trust *you* is the question?" Brandenburg replied.

"I'm not too keen on walking into a trap. Are you close to Melissa? If so, tell her Waterloo. She'll explain it to you. We can meet whenever and wherever you want. Call me back after she confirms my position."

James didn't need to keep the sniper on the line. He didn't want to waste any more time and hanging up was the best way to get them to come together.

"What was all of that?" Katt asked, as she looked over at James while driving. "Sunbird…Waterloo…what are you people, secret agents or something?"

James laughed for the first time in what seemed like days. He had the best news he could hope for, and that made everything seem good to him.

"You need to understand the way things were for us growing up," James offered. "We were the kids of both military and cops. We had to exist in a world unlike what most kids considered normal. My father discussed IEDs and military tactics while Melissa's father discussed crimes and shootouts. That's what it was like for us.

"As we grew older, she and I use to play these games. We would create a scenario that involved some kind of police action and see which one of us could figure it out. We actually stole pictures from crime scenes that I don't think were ever missed, just to make it seem more real.

"Anyway, we decided that if either of us were ever kidnapped, we needed to be able to let the other know if the situation was safe should there ever be a need for a drop off, pickup, or anything that could possibly harm the other. She always loved the story about the Phoenix. You know the one that flies to the sun, get burned up and then falls back to earth only to be reborn.

"The thing is, she could never remember the name Phoenix. When she tried to remember, she kept saying, 'you know…that sun bird.' After a while, we decided that if she were in trouble, she would say the word Phoenix. She would tell some elaborate tale about it and use the word Phoenix. However, if she used the word 'Sunbird,' that meant everything was good. It's just the game of a child that stuck with us."

"And Waterloo?" Katt asked.

"Same kind of thing for me. I used to read a lot of history books about famous military men. For me, if I said, Patton, things were bad."

"Why Patton?"

"I thought he was a real badass," James smiled. "If Patton was around, I was in deep shit. That's how my mind worked."

"And Waterloo?"

"Again, a kid's way of thinking. Napoleon lost the battle at Waterloo. The fight was over," James said, extending his hands, palms up. "I figured that if the fight was over, there was peace. Anyway, that's what it means. If she tells him that we have an accord because of something we came up with as children, maybe he wouldn't be so paranoid."

"Do you think he'll drop his guard?" Katt asked, hopeful.

"Not in a million years," James replied. "He won't trust either of us until this is over. Even then he'll keep up his guard. What it does mean, is that he'll give us a chance to earn that trust so that we can do what needs done. For me, that's good enough."

"Then let's call the general," Katt said. "He could use some good news."

Chapter 42

He suspected that somewhere along the line that Special Agent Katt would start putting some of the pieces together. To that end, Homer had left enough bread crumbs to lead her people where he wanted them to go.

It wouldn't be enough to merely kill one or two of the fabled agency; he needed to kill at least a dozen of them. Anything less would be considered a failure.

The killer knew that the FBI would be setting up a perimeter at the judge's home. He knew that the judge would be under heavy guard and that was exactly what he needed. The more the merrier.

This one final target would be more than enough to get the required number of agents to come and to miss was not something he was willing to accept.

What he didn't know—and time would tell—was the timing of his final shot. That was why he had planned things the way he had. One way or the other, he was going to win this battle. He expected it to be later in the night or maybe tomorrow, but like Brandenburg, he was ready for the long wait.

The general had taken the call from James while Katt called the team responsible for finding Melissa Pound. She didn't know why Brandenburg had made the moves he made, but thought that it had something to do with the shooter. Hopefully she would soon find out.

"We'll know more in a little while," James said to his uncle. "As soon as we have her back, I'll call you and let you know."

James ended the call and turned to Katt.

"He's really pissed," James said. "I think he would kill Brandenburg if he could get his hands on the man."

"Do you think he was being honest when he said he did it to protect her?" Katt asked.

James pondered the question before answering. "I think he has an agenda for everything he does. One possible scenario is that he took her because he thought she was in danger. I can also see where he did it as a way to leverage his situation should he get captured. There might also be a dozen other reasons why he did it. He told us what he thinks we want to hear. That's what I think."

They pulled into the secluded spot where Brandenburg had told them to go. It was off the beaten path, flat and easy to spot from a distance; the perfect place for a sniper's ambush.

Katt was driving while James scouted the surroundings as they drove to the place and said, "I don't like this. We're too exposed."

Katt turned off the motor, leaned forward to check out the area as best she could through the windshield.

"I take it he chose the spot for that very reason. He'll know if we changed our minds and tried to set a trap."

James' phone rang.

"Hello," James answered.

"It seems you've decided not to test me," Brandenburg said. "I appreciate that."

"Right now, all I care about is getting Melissa back safely," James replied then put the phone on speaker.

"I see you brought Agent Katt along. I hope she's as good as you say she is, Mr. James. A lot is riding on what we do next."

"We're here. So what do you want us to do now?"

There was a pause before anyone spoke.

"Mickey?" It was Melissa.

"Hey, kiddo," James sighed at the sound of her voice. "Good to hear from you. Where are you?"

"I don't know," she replied. "He brought me out into the boondocks. I know a lot about the area, but I don't know this place."

"Are you okay? Has he hurt you?"

"No. He's actually been quite the gentleman. You wouldn't expect him to be a cold-blooded killer the way he's treated me." Melissa paused for a moment, and then said, "Look, Mickey, you need to meet with him and work with him. I can't come back to the house just yet. I'm safe and out of harm's way here…wherever here is. He's explained some details about what's going on, and I think he can help you guys. He's just a little cautious. Just be straight with him and I think everything will be okay."

"You're sure you want to stay there? Your dad's concerned. Hell…I'm concerned. I don't want you to get hurt."

"I'm safe here, Mickey. I told him about the Phoenix like we planned a long time ago. I meant it."

"Can you get away? Is he restraining you in any way?"

"No. I've got complete freedom here. The front door isn't even locked. He wanted me to feel safe and I do. Just take care of business and get this over with. Tell dad that I'm fine and safe. He just needs to be careful too. The killer might come after him since he couldn't get to me."

"I already thought of that, and we have agents at the house already," James said. "But we need to find him and shut him down. Let me talk to Brandenburg."

Melissa didn't say goodbye.

"Yes, sir," Brandenburg said.

""We'll do this," James said. "You want us to be straight with you. Then you have to be straight with us. Tell me where Melissa is staying. I can get someone there to protect her while we're doing what we need to do. That's the deal."

James could hear Brandenburg cover the phone while he did something—supposedly talk to Melissa.

"Okay," Brandenburg said. "Just make sure that the people you bring are trustworthy and bulletproof. If he finds this place, he'll kill them all."

Brandenburg told them the location and then where he wanted to meet Katt and James. They were miles apart.

"We'll be there in fifteen minutes," James said. "If you're sure she'll be safe, we'll get some agents on location in less than thirty."

"Deal," was all Brandenburg said before hanging up. He then turned to Melissa. "You go to that spot I showed you and don't come out until you hear the words, 'olly olly oxen free.' That's your signal that you're safe."

Melissa smiled at the handsome man standing before her. Another place, another time, she might want to get to know him a little better—maybe a lot better.

"Be careful," Melissa said. "I don't want anyone else hurt because of me."

Brandenburg smiled and touched her shoulder.

"Nobody has been killed because of you, Melissa. They've been killed by some greedy people who thought you were in the way. Now go. I can't stay here any longer and neither can you. It's not safe."

He turned and walked out the door. Melissa looked around, sighed and did the same.

Katt and James pulled into the parking structure just as Brandenburg instructed. Neither of them knew when the ex-SEAL would get there, but the hope was soon. As far as they knew, Judge Anderson was still a target. Time was running away from them and they had so few clues as to where to go that it seemed ridiculous.

They got out of the car and waited.

"If you promise not to shoot me, I will come out now," Brandenburg said. "I have a weapon, but I have no intention of using it; at least not on you two."

Katt and James both turned around where the voice was coming from. James was about to draw his weapon when Katt held his arm. She looked at him and shook her head lightly.

"Move slowly," James said, keeping his hand at rest on the Glock. "I won't shoot you if you give us the same courtesy."

Brandenburg stepped out of the shadows with his hands raised to shoulder height—palms facing out. He walked slowly towards the two expectant officers never once taking his eyes off James.

"I didn't think you were going to show," James said. "You have some issues that you need to account for."

"I understand that," Brandenburg said. "I'm here as I told you I would be. However, you taking me in isn't what we need to discuss, my friend. There's a killer out there that we need to stop."

"Leave that to the cops. We'll get him."

Brandenburg laughed. "You don't have a clue who you're dealing with, Mr. James. And if I'm right, you'll be hearing about other deaths soon...unless we stop him."

"So you know who he is?" Katt asked, reading between the lines.

"I do," Brandenburg said. "He's a contract shooter, and he's one of the best. You'll never get close to him."

"But you think you can?" James asked. "How?"

"By being better than him," Brandenburg replied without a hint of pretentiousness. "I've studied him at length. I know his habits."

"Couldn't he say the same about you? After all, according to you, he killed Detective Montclair right under your nose. Seems to me, that makes him better than you."

"It put him in the right place at the right time. I didn't know I was being hunted, Mr. James. Until then, I only knew that people were being killed by a sniper. I was concerned that it could come back on me. That's why I did a little demonstration, Agent Katt. However, I wasn't aware that I was anything more than an ex-Navy man looking to stay out of trouble. When he killed that officer, he made it clear what he intended to do with me; kill me or have me arrested for his crimes. Neither of those options fit well in my plans."

"What makes you think you can catch him?" James asked again.

"There's a good chance he knows about me. I have a reputation among our little group. But that's where we differ. He knows *about* me. But like I said, I've *studied* him. I know his moves. I know his habits. I know everything there is to know that will give me the edge I need." He paused for a moment and then said, "But, just so we're clear. I have no intentions of capturing him. I intend to kill him."

Katt and James looked at the man facing them and then at each other. What they saw was a killer—cold, calculating, determined.

Chapter 43

"So who is he?" Katt asked Brandenburg again.

"And this time we don't want a cryptic answer," James added. "We need a real name to work with."

"His real name won't help you," Brandenburg replied. "He hasn't used it in years. He now goes by the name, Homer. He's originally from Canada, but has lived in the U.S. since his teens. He was bumped out of the military after only a few years and has been doing contract work ever since."

"How do you know that?" Katt asked. "I've checked with my people and the name Homer has never come up...ever."

"That's because the military doesn't want you to know about him," Brandenburg said. "He was a prodigy. He understood ballistics as well as anyone. At one time, he was on the same track as me."

"What happened?" James asked.

"The government screwed up on the psych eval. It took them a little while to realize that the same tools necessary to be a great shooter, could also be a detriment if there was no governor on it to control his actions. He never got it that people have value. The people we were assigned to kill were bad. They were out there destroying civilization. Our job was to reign in those that were doing harm. I knew that—know that. Homer never got the message. Or if he did, it didn't sink in. The mistakes started mounting when he would take out targets that weren't on the kill list. He would actually use people for target practice from varied distances just to see if he could hit them. When they tried to court-martial him, he got away and has been missing ever since."

"How do you know it's him?" Katt wondered.

"Like I said, I know him. I know how he works."

"Can you really stop him?"

"If I have an idea where he'll be next, then yes, I can take him out."

"We might know whom that will be," Katt said. "We think that he'll either go after one of two judges."

"I can't protect them both," Brandenburg said. Is there any way you can narrow it down to just the one."

"I think we already have," Katt replied. "One of the judges has been placed in protective custody. The other, the lesser target, has agreed to being watched around the clock until we catch the bastard."

"Then we don't have much time," Brandenburg said. "Take me to the location."

"Why?" Katt asked. "The place is crawling with police and the FBI. He can't get anywhere near the judge."

"You don't get it," Brandenburg said. "He doesn't have to get close. Homer takes these cases as a challenge. The harder the target, the more he enjoys his job."

"How can he expect to hit a target when he doesn't even know where we're keeping the man?" James wanted to know. "He's not a magician, is he? A mind reader, maybe?"

"He's neither of those," Brandenburg smiled. "He's got someone on the inside who has probably already told him where the judge is being kept. And unless you have walls that are over a foot thick *and* steel plated, he'll kill your judge."

"How's that possible?" Katt asked. "I've never heard of such a thing; even if he does know where the judge is being held."

Katt and James looked at each other. They both had seen some interesting situations in their time. They both seemed to want to believe that this man before them was full of hot air.

"I know it's possible," Brandenburg said, because I've done it myself. With technology, infrared lenses that can detect body heat, hell…with the right equipment, he can practically read the book your judge is holding. Now…I would really like to continue our little conversation, but if you want me to stop Homer from killing anyone else, we'll need to get a move on. Time is running out."

"You'll have to go with us," Katt said. "You're wanted for the murder of a police officer and several other not-so-minor charges. I just can't let you...."

Quicker than anything Katt or James had ever seen, Brandenburg held a pistol at their faces; slowly moving the barrel from side to side.

"I was afraid you might say that," Brandenburg said. "Like I said, you have no idea what you're up against. Now, Agent Katt, I don't know you very well. You seem like a nice, upstanding officer of the law, and I would hate to have to hurt you. Detective James, you on the other hand don't seem so upstanding, but I do respect you. You came to my home and even with a knife at your throat stood your ground. There aren't many people I know that would do that.

"So here's the deal, you are going to tell me where the judge is being held, and I'm going to go there and try to stop Homer from killing him. You can go see your cousin if you want. Or you can do whatever you normally do to protect the good citizens from bad people. Either way, my going to jail isn't an option."

"Like I said," Katt replied, "You're going to have to atone for your actions."

"I understand that," Brandenburg said. "I give you my word…if I manage to live through what I have to do, I will turn myself in and make sure you even get the credit. However, right now, we're wasting time. I promise you that I am on your side."

"Facing down the barrel of a gun doesn't lend itself to making me believe you," James said. "We came here with the understanding that we were working on mutual trust."

"That kinda went out the window when she insisted on taking me in…don't you think?"

"I see your point," James replied.

"Hey!" Katt exclaimed. "Whose side are you on?"

"The man has a point," James smiled. "I can't say I wouldn't't'a done the same thing if the shoe was on the other foot."

Katt looked at James and realized that it didn't matter that she was on the side of right. The only thing that mattered moving forward was stopping the killer from doing any more damage.

"Alright," Katt relented and gave Brandenburg the address where Judge Anderson was being sequestered. "I have a strong feeling that this is going to come back and bite me in the butt."

"It won't if he can stop the shooter," James said. "If he does that, you'll be the golden child of the FBI."

"I'll call you when I have news," Brandenburg said, looking at James. "Melissa gave me your number."

Katt and James were driving back to Dayton. James had talked again with Melissa and was assured by her that she was fine and in good condition. Katt told Henderson, the agent in charge, to take her home and to stand guard with those that were already there.

When James disconnected the call, Katt said, "I have to call this in to my boss. He's going to need an update and to know that we met up with Brandenburg."

"If you do that, he'll be pissed."

"He's going to be pissed anyway. It's just a matter of when."

James didn't reply; there weren't any words that would make things any easier for her.

Chapter 44

"Why didn't you tell me about this sooner?" Homer asked the man paying him. "You've all but guaranteed a failure on my part."

"It's that God-damn cop from California that's to blame," the man said. "He doesn't think like the rest of them. Once he had all of the information, it took him less than an hour to put the pieces together."

"What the hell are they doing letting an outsider in on this?" Homer asked. "You were supposed to have these imbeciles under control."

"That, you can blame on your friend, Agent Katt. Apparently, she and the cop had worked together back in California, and they seem to have something of a connection. It was totally unforeseeable."

"What part?"

"What do you mean?"

"I mean...what part was unforeseeable? The part where they worked together? The part where he would be given a written invitation to join the party because you wanted his cousin eliminated? Those parts? But...forgetting all of that...once you knew about these conditions, why didn't you put this together so I could do something about? I could kill the cop. I could kill the FB…,"

"You already tried to kill the agent. How did that work out for you?"

"You are really starting to piss me off," Homer hiss into the phone. Maybe I should just take my money and do some of the other jobs that have been offered."

"Wait!" the moneyman said. "We're too close to not finish now. Look…I'm sorry about the comments. There have been unforeseen circumstances that we need to get past. I've given you the information you need for the judge. So finish this job and we'll be done. Okay?"

"How sure are you of the intel this time?"

"It's spot on. If you go to that address I gave you and wait, they'll bring the judge right to where you need to take that shot. After that…you can do whatever you want."

Homer waited several moments before replying. "Your life will depend on it," he spoke slow and clear wanting to make sure the listener heard what he meant.

Homer disconnected before the man could reply.

"You've really made a mess of this, Agent Katt," Deputy Director Blythe said in a professional tone. For the total of their relationship, the DD had never talked to Katt in such a way that she had ever felt so small—so much a failure. "You've managed to not only allow your key suspect to get away, you've given him the information he needs to now kill the person you believe to be his next target. Have I got the gist of the report accurate?"

"Yes, sir," Katt replied. "The killer has been a step ahead of us the whole way and…."

"Which killer are you referring to, Agent Katt? The one you allowed to get away or the invisible one that you think is out there? The facts of the case, as I understand them, doesn't allow for the existence of another shooter. That idea is nothing more than conjecture. Do you have any proof, and I mean physical evidence, that this other shooter even exists? Anything?"

"No, sir," Katt replied with her head hanging.

"Keep one more thing in mind, Agent Katt. If I'm not mistaken, I specifically stated that I wanted this man captured alive. I did not want him to be brought in dead. He won't help with the other things if he's dead. And yet, without any consideration for my orders, you have sent this…this…civilian out there for the explicit purpose of killing the man you believe to be responsible. If there is another shooter, and I'm not saying there is, how do you justify these actions?"

Katt thought about what the director said and replied. "I make no excuses for my actions, sir. There's a lot going on here that does not comply with the norm. I cannot think of any other situation where I would even *consider* allowing a man like Brandenburg to get involved with a case…any case."

"And yet in this case you did."

"That is correct, sir. I believe that the circumstance of this case warrant the assistance of someone who can think like and understand how Homer, that's the shooter's name, sir, thinks. Brandenburg is such a man. I think he can stop Homer before he kills again."

"You have until midnight tonight to prove that he can, Agent Katt. Because as of then, I will be there to personally oversee this fiasco. That gives you less than six hours."

"As you wish, sir."

"And Agent Katt?"

"Yes, sir?"

"If you're wrong…you will no longer represent this agency. As much as we've grown to know each other over the years and care about each other, I'm responsible for a lot of other agents. I cannot allow your gut feelings and infatuations place even one of them in jeopardy."

Blythe did not wait for a reply.

After hanging up the phone, the deputy director placed his elbows on his desk and his head in his hands. How did he ever allow this to happen, he wondered?

Darkness had already settled over the city. A cold wind was blowing from the north. The leaves of autumn were flying on the wind because that's what they do. Homer paid no attention to the darkness, the wind or the leaves because he was focused on the caravan that was slowly driving up the street.

The judge was located in the second of the three SUVs and the guards would do everything in their power to see to it that no harm would come to one of Ohio's most influential arbiters.

Why the police would have chosen such a site for protection, Homer couldn't understand. However, such trivialities were something he spent little time contemplating. His job was to figure out a way to move to the target's area, eliminate the target and leave from the site before being captured—or worse.

The problem with this particular target was the timing. He understood that once the cars had stopped, the judge would be removed from the vehicle and quickly rushed into the building in order to minimize the window for anyone to cause harm. That window would be less than five seconds of exposure and the guards would be moving their principal at a blinding pace.

Homer knew all of this and understood that in order to assure that he was successful he would need to make sure that the time it took for the bullet to leave the barrel of his rifle and reach its objective would be measured in fractions of a second.

That meant he had to be close.

In terms of long shots, he was less than a hundred and fifty yards from the target; too close for comfort if the cops had any idea of what they were doing.

When the cars stopped, the officers of the lead and trail cars quickly stepped out and surrounded the one in the middle. As the judge stepped from the car, the cops foolishly took the path of least resistance and followed the sidewalk. It left a straight path for the bullet to travel.

The next mistake made by the security force was not accounting for one additional detail; an angle that came from an elevated position.

Two seconds from the point of extraction was all the time that went by before the sound of a rifle shot rang through the evening air. Two seconds and a fraction was the time it took for the judge to feel the pressure of the bullet as it entered her back, severing her aorta and causing blood to start filling her chest.

It took an additional minute for Judge Beatrice Ross's body to finally expire. However, she had already lost consciousness long before the time expired.

Chapter 45

Katt and James were arriving at the safe house where Judge Anderson had been taken when the call came. Judge Ross had been shot by a sniper's bullet and was dead. Katt had been given the address and reached the scene within a matter of minutes.

"How could this happen?" Katt asked one of agents. "I thought this area had been cleared and that you would be seeing to her safety."

The agent was about to speak and then thought better of doing so. He merely shook his head.

"Where did the shot come from? Who's taking point? Do we know anything?" Katt rattled off questions and yet heard no answers. "Somebody speak to me!"

"I'm afraid you've been ordered to stand down, Agent Katt," Agent Walker said as he approached Katt from behind. "I got a call from Deputy Director Blythe earlier who told me that I was to keep an eye on the situation here and report directly to him if there were any incidents. When this happened, I called him about it. He told me to tell you that you are to step down until he arrived. I'm sorry, but as of now…you are no longer a part of this team."

"So why didn't he tell me this personally?" Katt wanted to know. "Why go through you?"

"He didn't tell me why, Agent Katt," Walker replied and then hung his head. "I didn't ask."

Katt had expected more time. She figured that when Blythe arrived in Dayton that she would be able to explain what was going on in such a way that would make him understand the difficulties they were facing. She hadn't really expected to get another call about a shooting. Maybe she should have.

"He can't do this," James had taken in the scene and heard what agent Walker had told her. "It doesn't make sense that Blythe would bench his best player."

"Well if you're going to be using a sport metaphor, then you of all people should know that the coach or manager or owner, anyone higher up the ladder than a player, can put whomever he wants in the game."

"I love it when you talk all sporty to me," James smiled at Katt.

At first Katt just stared at James. Eventually, she returned the smile.

"He thinks Brandenburg did this and we just let him free to do it. That's why I'm done here. Frankly, I'm not positive that he's wrong."

"I know he's wrong, Katt, and so do you. Brandenburg isn't our shooter and we'll prove it, no matter what that pompous ass of a boss of yours says."

"Look, Mickey," Katt said, "I have a couple of hours before Blythe gets here. You want to come over and keep me company? I'm not sure I want to just sit around by myself."

James was watching the chaos going on around them; amazed at the efficiency that was working its way through the pandemonium. When he heard the offer Katt presented, everything stopped.

James turned and looked into the most beautiful eyes he had ever seen and froze for a moment as he thought that maybe he had heard her wrong.

"Well?" Katt asked again.

"Yeah. Sure," James replied. He wasn't sure what was going to happen, but wasn't about to let the opportunity to spend time with her get away. "I would like that a lot. But don't you think we should stay here and help?"

"There're already too many people standing around. If they haven't caught the shooter by now, then he's already long gone."

"We missed him, didn't we?" Detective Hershey said as he walked up to the two. "He came in here and did what he was planning to do and…we missed him." The detective's voice trailed away.

"It looks like it," Katt replied. "I can't see him sticking around for anything else. I wasn't positive that he would do another hit as it was. But to do three in one city and then stick around for more…I don't see it."

"Four, Agent Katt," the detective said. "Remember he also killed one of ours."

"I'm sorry," Katt apologized. "I didn't forget about him. I was referring to the hits he had planned. I don't think your friend was part of the original plan. Rather it was a kill of opportunity in order to frame Brandenburg."

"So you really don't think Brandenburg is our shooter?" Hershey asked.

"At this point, I don't see how he could be," Katt replied and then told Hershey about James' cousin—Melissa. "He couldn't have been with us and shot this judge at the same time. He simply couldn't have gotten here and done this in the amount of time he would have needed."

"I guess we need to get together and try to figure this out then," Hershey said.

"No, Detective Hershey, we won't. You see the agent over there? Well that's Agent Wesley Walker, and you'll be working with him from now on. I've been removed from the case as of immediately."

"That's bullshit," Hershey spat.

"Yes it is, Detective. However, that was what I was told. And until further notice, Walker is your man. Good day, sir. And good luck."

Katt turned around and started walking away. James looked at the detective and shrugged; Hershey did likewise. There wasn't anything that could be done on either of their parts, so they might as well leave and see what would happen later.

Homer left the hide immediately after taking the shot. But instead of running like the cops would figure him to do, he drove less than four blocks and pulled into the parking lot of a local convenience store.

With nerves of steel, the shooter considered to be on the FBI's most wanted list, walked casually into the market in order to buy a cup of coffee. As a rule, he never drank coffee before taking a shot. The caffeine would cause him to be jittery and destroy any chance of a quality long distance shot. However, he found the elixir to be almost soothing after the job was done.

Of course to Homer, running was never a part of the plan. What he had done up to this point was for money. The kind of money he would need to disappear after the next part of his plan was complete.

Three cop cars raced by as he was in the process of paying for his coffee and Homer smiled.

"Looks like it's a busy evening out there," he said to the clerk.

"Yeah," the clerk grunted in reply. "I guess even the wealthy have to look out for trouble."

"They certainly do," Homer said and then dropped his change into a receptacle for a charity.

They certainly do.

Chapter 46

Deputy Director Blythe stared out the window of the FBI jet and watched the flickering lights quickly pass by beneath him. He would be arriving in Dayton shortly and knew that he had to tell Katt something. He had effectively pulled the rug out from under her, and he couldn't tell her why.

He remembered the first time he had met the small and fragile girl all those years ago and knew then that he would do everything in his power to take care of her. The thing was...years before he had met her, he had made virtually the same promise to another child; a promise that he had broken so very long ago. The thought of betraying another was almost too much to bear.

When the jet landed, Blythe made a call and was surprised the man actually answered the call.

"You have to stop now," Blythe said. "You can't keep doing this."

"Where are you?" the voice on the other end asked.

"Dayton. I just arrived. I've come to see if I can do anything to stop this madness."

"It'll be over soon," the voice said. "I've only got one more thing to do and then you'll never have to worry about me again."

"I'll always worry about you. You know that."

"Maybe if you would have worried about me back in Detroit; maybe if you would have worried about my brother instead of your precious job, we wouldn't be having this conversation now."

"I've made my mistakes," Blythe said. "But I've never killed an innocent."

"Yes you did," the voice said. "When you allowed my mother—your wife—to die needlessly. Now it's time for you to pay for your sins…Dad."

Homer disconnected and immediately started focusing on the job at hand. The idea that his father, the great Jonathan Blythe, would be a part of the destruction put a smile on his face. *This was just getting better and better.*

Katt dropped James off at his hotel to pick up his own car. By her way of thinking, there was no telling how the rest of her evening was going to go. With Blythe coming to town, she expected that she would be raked over the coals for a while and then shipped to some remote location where she would eventually grow old and wither away to nothing before she would ever get out of his doghouse. After the case in California, her work with the bureau and assignments had gotten better. It didn't necessarily surprise her that things could also go bad. She just wished that the good would have stuck around a little longer.

Upon further contemplation, Katt decided that she didn't care about her future. She wanted more than anything to repair the damage between her and James. If her boss wanted to give her trouble, she was ready for whatever he might throw her way.

They decided to stay where they were and spend the next hour or so in the attempt to bridge a very large gap.

As James opened the door to his room, he turned to Katt and held out his hand for her to take it and follow him inside. As she reached out to touch him…his phone rang.

"Son…of…a…bitch!" James exclaimed. "We can't catch a break." He looked at his phone and his face softened a bit. "Hello?"

"Hey, cuz," Melissa said. She seemed happy. "I hope I'm not bothering you. I heard about Judge Ross."

"No, Melissa," James replied. He looked at Katt and mouthed an apology. "We're just standing around for a little while until something pops."

"Oh, good. I was wondering if you might be able to come by the house. I just got back, and I think we need to talk. Something's come up and I think you need to help us go over it."

"What's going on, Melissa?"

"I can't explain it over the phone. Can you come over?"

"What about Agent Katt? Is it okay if she comes with me?"

"Sure. I'll see you in a little while."

Melissa hung up the phone before James could get any more information. Turning to Katt, he said, "If there's a God...He has one hell of a sense of humor."

Katt, not taking the time to answer, stepped close to James and placed her hands on either side of his face. She looked deep into his eyes and smiled. And then, without warning, she lifted up on tiptoes and kissed James tenderly. James wrapped his arms around her and pulled her tight. The kiss grew deeper.

When it was over, Katt regained her balance and composer, and said, "I didn't want you to think that I wasn't willing to try to make us work because I am." She placed a lot of emphasis on the word *us*.

James, acting like he was waking from the dream he thought he was having said, "Damn, woman. Just try and get rid of me now."

They both laughed and headed back to their cars.

Somehow, in completely different ways, they believed that the future looked bright.

Everybody has regrets, Blythe thought. As a young police officer, he knew that he would have to work like crazy in order to make enough money to feed his family. Overtime and rising up the ranks were a must for the young man.

As time passed, he discovered that not only was he good at his job, but he liked it. He liked the idea that criminals feared him and would actually move somewhere else so as not to get caught by the relentless policeman.

When his oldest son died, it tore his family apart. His wife ducked into a shell and pretended that everything was just fine—at least for a while. Later, her world collapsed and nobody would be there to catch her.

His youngest son couldn't understand why his father dove deeper and deeper into his work, instead of taking the time necessary to comfort the needs of the remaining boy. A boy who idolized his older brother.

What Blythe discovered over the years was that, a career like his, came at a price. And in this case the price was *very* high.

In time, his son stopped talking to him. He and his wife divorced and eventually she committed suicide; another thing his son blamed him for. And he was probably right, Blythe mused. If I had been the husband and father I should have been, maybe…just maybe…there would have been a lot less death hanging around his shoulders.

Having moved from the Detroit Police Department, and as a young FBI agent, Blythe met a young girl who had lost everything. Her parents had been murdered. The killers had even made her pull the trigger. She was a mess, but not of her own making.

Blythe decided then and there that he would do everything in his power to protect that girl and save her. He had failed with his own family, but maybe the young and vulnerable Katherine Katt would give him a chance at redemption.

It never dawned on him that these two worlds would somehow collide.

As he thought about it, Blythe considered the two people, Katt and his son, to be like characters in an old comic book. There was the villain and the protagonist. Good versus evil. Then again, he could never imagine that the seeds of evil would spring from his own loins.

Now he had to face what was sure to come next. He was the deputy director of the FBI. He was a man of integrity. And now, he had to face the fact that his son was a killer.

Of course Blythe knew about his son's work with the military. He also knew that he left there under circumstances that were less than exemplary.

After that, Blythe had tried to keep tabs on his son, but like most things in his life, failed to do so with as much enthusiasm as he should.

Once again, his son fell through the cracks.

Over the years, there were hints about what his son might be doing. Unlike the CIA's ability to "disappear" someone, his son was never completely gone. A word here, a story there was all Blythe ever got, but it was enough to allow him to think—mistakenly—that he was doing his part as a father.

There were also the rumors about contract work. Blythe knew that his son had those kinds of skills. It was his job to know such things, but never considered that his son would be the one the agency was tracking.

He only put that together in the last twenty-four hours.

The name Homer put it all together for Blythe. He remembered the name from when his boys played together as children. He thought it amusing that instead of playing cops and robbers that they would play the game in an untraditional manner. To him it showed initiative and imagination. Those were the building blocks of an intelligent mind.

Blythe's concerns went beyond what to do about his son. If ignorance is bliss, then Blythe should be the most contented man on earth. He wasn't.

On one hand, he had a son who he now knew was being hunted as one of the FBI's most wanted.

On the other hand, he cared for and respected someone he considered as close as if she were his own daughter. And now that he knew who the killer was, a shudder spread through him just thinking about how close Katt had been to being killed by his son a couple of nights ago.

His career was over. Blythe knew that and understood why. It wasn't really a good thing for the FBI to have one of their top people fathering a wanted hit man—or a serial killer.

Katt would hate him too. He had already taken her off the case. She would think it was because she had messed up somehow. However, the truth was that he simply didn't want her anywhere around when the shit hit the fan. He wouldn't be able to live with himself if she were to get hurt. That option was not available. She would just have to be mad at him. Though difficult, he could live with that.

As Blythe made his way to the latest crime scene, he knew that this would be his last stand with the bureau. As such, he would make sure it went down the right way. Son or no son, he still believed in doing the job the way it needed to be done.

Chapter 47

Katt and James entered the general's house without knocking. James announced their arrival as they walked through the house and James stopped so abruptly that Katt walked straight into his back.

The surprise came as a result of him seeing Joseph Brandenburg sitting calmly at the kitchen table seemingly enjoying another bowl of the general's homemade soup. The smile on his face appeared forced as far as James was concerned. He imagined that behind the look was someone ready to pounce at the first indication of trouble.

"I didn't know you had company," James said with an even tone to his voice and an eye firmly fixed on the guest. Katt saw what the distraction was about and went for her gun. James halted her immediately.

The general was also sitting at the table and didn't look overly concerned about his guest, but didn't want to take any chances.

"He's here by invitation," the general said. "I would appreciate a little détente while Mr. Brandenburg is here. Is that something you two can agree on?"

"Well…considering that I've been relieved of duty for this case," Katt said, matter-of-factly, "I don't see why not."

"Care to share?" the general asked.

"Maybe later," Katt replied. "This is your rodeo. I figured that before my boss gets here and decides to ship me off to Timbuktu I would see what he could offer might keep me around." She paused for a moment then added, "That's if you don't mind." She said that while looking directly at Brandenburg.

"I don't mind at all," Brandenburg replied. The retired sniper took a few last bites of his soup and congratulated the general on another fine job. "I made a mistake," he said. "Maybe it's because I don't know the man as well as I thought. Or maybe it's because I don't have enough intel on what's going on to make intelligent decisions. Either way, someone else is dead and I'm sure you would prefer that no one else was added to that ever-expanding list."

"What I want," Katt said, "is to put the son of a bitch in the ground; or, at the very least, in a cell where he never again sees the light of day."

"If I get a vote," James said, "I vote for the former." He said it as something of a joke, but nobody laughed.

"I doubt if it makes any difference now, anyway," Katt stated dejectedly. "He might already be out of the state."

"I doubt it," Brandenburg said.

"Why?" the general asked. "Just how many people does he have on his list?"

"I can't give you a number," Brandenburg replied. "But I believe that he's here for something much bigger than what he's already done."

"Does this sort of thing happen often? James asked. "I was under the impression that guys like this Homer dude comes in, takes his shot and then gets the hell out of Dodge."

"That's what we normally do. There's seldom a situation where more than one target is assigned for a shooter. As a matter of fact, I've never once been involved in a situation where I was needed for more than two targets; and they were always right next to each other. No, this goes outside the scope of what we consider normal."

"Then why do you think this judge wasn't the last on his list?" Katt asked.

"Because of something I found out," Brandenburg replied. There was a long pause and the man looked around the room.

"Well," Katt said anxiously. "What did you find out?"

"In order for it to make sense," Brandenburg said, "I have to go back a while; back to when we were all pretty new to the job."

Everyone waited without interruption.

"Like I said, I never met Homer, either in the military or afterward. Frankly, I was a little busy with my own work to pay him any attention. At least I never watched his activities any more than the rest of the people I studied.

"We are a relatively small bunch—us snipers. We sort of keep an eye out to what the other is doing and to a degree we'd help one another if the situation came up. Anyway, about six years ago I was asked to help get one of our own out of a tight jam. I can't give you the details because the information is classified. However, I was able to pull one of my protégés out of the mess he found himself in and brought him back safely. He was new, and that was only his third solo assignment.

"When we got back, talking over a couple of beers, he told me that he was sure that I came in there to kill him. The comment struck me as odd, so I asked him why. He told me about a friend of his that was in a similar situation. The company sent in someone for him as well; someone not me. It didn't work out.

"He said that when the guy got back he was told that everything went to hell. That the friend was guarded heavier than what was reported and that he was being tortured. He said he had no choice but to save his friend the pain of the torture and finished him off."

"Jesus," Katt mumbled.

"So where is this going?" James wanted to know.

"This guy I saved," Brandenburg continued, "had no choice but to accept what he was told. He didn't like it, but there was nothing else he could do. Maybe a year later, he gets called up to do a job in the same area as his friend—same town, damn near the same building. Anyway, he decided to go off-script and track down the people responsible for his buddy's death.

"The long and short of it; the man responsible for killing his friend was this guy Homer. He was told that his friend had been captured and was being interrogated, but there was no torture involved. Oh there was a beat-down and stuff like that, but nothing that would qualify as actual torture."

"His informant could have been lying," James said.

"He didn't think so," Brandenburg replied. "Anyway, the point being that over the years, I've stayed in touch with my friend. He's always been a straight shooter. No pun intended. He's always been reliable. So I called him when I figured out who I thought it was that was doing all the killing around here. He just got back to me."

They were all leaning forward in their respective chairs not wanting to disrupt the man.

"Here's the thing, after my friend's buddy was killed, Homer decided to sorta take an interest in what my friend was doing; his jobs and things like that. We can't discuss most of the stuff we do with others. It's almost always classified. We can't even discuss it among ourselves. We've all done jobs that are questionable and you would think that it would be okay, but it's not. There's no pressure valve for any of us.

"While Homer was asking my friend about the things he had done, in order to loosen up the conversation, he told my friend a few secrets of his own."

"Is it too much to ask what those secrets were?" Katt asked.

"Only a couple of them make a difference to this operation," Brandenburg said.

"Which are?"

"That he hated his father."

"I don't see how this helps," James said. "All psychopaths hate somebody. They hate their mothers because they weren't breastfed enough. They hate their fathers because they were spanked too much, or not enough. They hate their teachers. Hell...the list goes on and on. But Katt, you would know that more than I do. Am I right?"

"To a certain extent I would agree, but that's way too generalized for my comfort. However, I think Mister Brandenburg has more to say on the matter."

"You're right. I do. As we continued our discussion, he told me another important tidbit. He said that all of the training he did, all of the effort he put in to his work was for the expressed purpose of getting even with his old man."

"You know, that would be really helpful if we knew who his father was," James was getting impatient. "So do you know who is father is?"

"I do not," Brandenburg said. Everyone groaned. "What I do know is that his father is an FBI agent."

Katt sat stunned at the revelation and James wasn't sure how to react.

"There are thousands of agents in the bureau," Katt exclaimed. "If you don't know the agent's name, can't you get your friends with the CIA or whatever-the-hell government agency you worked for to help us out a little? Can't they tell us who is out there shooting the hell out of this town?"

"No…I can't," Brandenburg the replied. "I made that call. I even called the Secretary of Defense…."

"You know the Secretary of Defense?" James blustered. "Hell, I barely know the secretary of my office."

"What did he tell you?" Katt implored.

"He said that they wouldn't give my name out either. That we were all protected to the highest level, good or bad. He told me that we would have to find him some other way."

"What good are friends in high places if you can't get the occasional favor?" James mumbled.

"Is there anything else you can tell us?" Katt asked. "Anything from your friend about Homer?"

"The only other thing he could remember was that back then, everyone called the guy, Johnny.

. And he didn't know the guy's last name. Anyway...I thought you all should know."

Katt was about to ask another question when her phone rang. As she looked at the screen, she automatically took a deep breath and sighed.

Chapter 48

Jonathan Blythe wasn't the only person doing reconnaissance. Homer had decided to do a little checking in on his father. It seemed, from his well-placed source, that his father had not only abandoned his family, he had managed to find their collective replacement.

Once he discovered that his father would be around for the festivities, Homer thought it might be prudent to see if the man had any weaknesses to exploit. It took the killer less than ten minutes to figure out that the weakness his father possessed had been here all along. Had he known that, he might not have been so forgiving with the lovely, Agent Katt.

That information changed everything. Not only could he make a name for himself. He now had a way to make his father suffer for years to come; if the old man lived long enough.

The time was earlier than Katt had expected. It was only eleven-thirty, and the deputy director had wanted to meet immediately. James had suggested that they go in together, but Katt would have none of that. She had to face her boss alone. She expected that things between her and Blythe might never be the same. He had placed faith in her and she had let him down.

As she drove to the police station, her usually sharp mind was clouded with concern about her future. In the short period it had taken her to go less than five miles, she had pretty much figured that if he decided to punish her for her lack of success or for pushing to get James in on the case, she would leave the agency. Her growth there had already been curtailed because of her past. She wasn't about to let it go farther downhill. It wasn't worth the hassle anymore.

The distraction was a detriment in another way. Without her knowledge, another vehicle was rapidly approaching to her rear. As she braked for a stoplight, the trailing SUV had not slowed quite so much. When Katt's vehicle came to a completed stop, the one behind her rammed her vehicle from behind.

Homer was thrilled that he'd had the foresight to track Agent Katt. Though his reasoning was for a completely different reason originally, those matters were no longer a motivation.

Katt's head whipped back from the impact and then forward quickly giving her a severe case of whiplash. It injury would not be anything permanent, but it certainly made her sluggish. She wasn't sure if she was alright, but her first concern was whether the people behind her were okay.

Slowly, Katt unlocked her door and managed to get out of her car. Dizzy, she placed her hand on the roof of her car for balance. The man driving the SUV got out of his car as well and staggered toward the shaken agent asking the whole time if she was alright.

Katt replied that she was okay and wanted to know if he was doing okay as well.

"I'm alright," Katt slurred her words, still feeling groggy. "What happened?"

"I had to stop you," the man said. "You have become very important to me."

"I don't under…," Katt started to reply when she was hit with something that caused her mouth to stop working and her body to start convulsing.

The stun gun Homer used would knock her out for quite a while. But given the last time they had met and with the fierceness that she fought, he was not about to take any chances. Right there in the middle of the street, Homer flipped the woman on her stomach and cuffed her hands behind her back and her feet together.

It only took thirty seconds to accomplish. In the long run, he knew it could make things immeasurably better.

After depositing his new captive in the back seat, Homer looked over his shoulder and wondered if it was thirty seconds too long.

If there was one thing about James that would make him stand out, it would be the fierce loyalty he had the people he cared about. He would risk everything to protect the people he loved. And beyond that, he would be willing to piss off the Pope if it meant he could keep a friend from getting in trouble when it wasn't her fault.

After Katt left, it took James less than a minute to realize that he was as much to blame for Katt's problem as her. Kissing his cousin on the cheek and telling the general he would see them later, James tore out after Katt. He wasn't about to let her take the blame—at least not alone.

Turning a corner and looking down a long straight stretch of road, James spotted Katt's car stopped at a traffic light. She was getting out of her car and walking back toward the vehicle behind her. He didn't know what she was doing and was surprised that she seemed unsteady as she walked.

The street was quiet and James watched from the distance of several blocks while sitting at a traffic light. It wasn't until he saw her spasm that he realized that Katt was in danger.

James didn't recognize the SUV or the man that was rushing toward her. He did know that he didn't have much time before it was too late.

James floored the gas pedal and almost hit a car that was legally entering the intersection. The car stopped directly in front of James and the driver started shouting obscenities. James needed to get to Katt, and he wasn't about to worry about hurting some driver's feelings.

It took only a few seconds to get past the car in front of him. However, James was still three blocks away and he noticed that the man was carrying Katt back to his car. At two blocks away the man was already putting the unconscious agent in the back seat. From a block away, James saw that the man was stuffing Katt's feet into the car and would be taking off if he didn't do something quick.

James slid to a stop and jumped out of his car. The man didn't appear to be troubled about what was going on or worried that he was doing something illegal. He seemed composed and even smiled at James.

James reached for his weapon. Regardless of what the man seemed, he knew that there was no way that Katt's spastic motions were normal. She was being taken without consent and James wasn't about to let that happen.

James was good; better than most, but Homer was better. It the blink of an eye, the killer had gone from empty-handed to armed and ready to fire. James had never seen anything like it. Had he not been fully alert, he had no doubt that he would have died.

As it was, just like his cousin less than a week earlier, James dropped.

Not soon enough.

The shot grazed James just above the temple and tore a large gash along the side of his head. The bullet did not penetrate the bone, but the percussion and the slight angle of the ricochet off bone was enough to finish James' descent.

Fighting to stay conscious, the California cop held onto his weapon and returned fire. In less than five seconds, James had spent ten rounds. He didn't know whether he hit his target because a few seconds later, the world around Mickey James went black.

It was after two in the morning when Blythe stormed into the emergency room demanding to locate Mickey James. He was angry and loud and had it not been for the badge he held high, the security guard would have escorted the man right back out the door.

"What the hell have you done?" Blythe yelled at James.

James would have been inclined to punch the deputy director in the mouth had he not been attached to the needle and thread the doctor was using to stich James' head back together. As such, James said nothing because he realized that if the circumstances had been reversed, he would have likely been doing the same thing.

"How could you have let this bastard take her?" Blythe asked.

"How could you have put her in a situation where she had to go chasing you down at that hour?" James countered quietly. "I tried to get to her and received this little token for my efforts. What have you done?"

James could see the wind flowing out of the man's sails and felt sorry for him. In the span of just a few seconds, the senior FBI man seemed to age by decades.

Against everything he held true, Blythe said, "I need you, James. I need you to do whatever it is you do and find Agent Katt...find Katherine."

The ache in his head and the nausea in his stomach from the injury had cleared up, mostly, and James had every intention of doing that very thing. However, he wasn't about to let the opportunity pass.

"Why the hell should I care what you want? You pulled her off the case like she was some rookie. You were as disrespectful a leader as anyone I've ever seen. Now you want me to just jump in and save your ass?"

Blythe looked defeated. It had nothing to do with what James was saying. It was because of the terrible secret he was hiding inside.

"I'm beyond saving, James," Blythe spoke barely above a whisper. "But, Katherine isn't. You know this case. You know this Brandenburg character. You've got to do something…please."

"I have every intention of doing that," James replied. "But just so we're clear…I'm doing it for her, not you."

"I don't care if you're doing it to spite me. Just find her and bring her back alive."

"I'm going to need some help," James said.

Chapter 49

Homer was more than a sniper. Throughout his military career, he had learned to be highly proficient in several methods in addition to being a sniper. Shooting from a distant was what he was known for, but on occasion, he would use his more obscure talents to get a job done.

Now that he had finished the work he had been hired for, he could now focus his energies and do what he really desired.

The FBI agent had awakened once and asked him the same questions all victims ask—why are you doing this? Followed by the old standby—why me? Homer didn't care what they asked and it would take too long for him to explain it to them. Instead, he dosed her with more sedative and went about his work.

Tomorrow would be a new day; a day of freedom. Tomorrow he would eliminate a large contingent of agents, and if he were fortunate, his father would be one of the first to die.

Brandenburg wasn't used to being the person doing the research for his assignments. Truth be told, he felt completely out of his element when he first decided to review the information that the general and James had put together.

It wasn't until several hours after Katt and James left before the family, and Brandenburg had heard what happened. Brandenburg knew that if they were going to stop whatever else might be coming, it would be up to him to do it. The general and Melissa wanted to go to the hospital, but James wouldn't allow it. He told them that his injuries were minor and that he would be home soon.

At a quarter past six in the morning, James managed to sneak out of the hospital against medical advice. There was too much to do, and Katt's life was at stake. With his head mostly covered with white gauze, he exited the ER and headed home.

Twenty minutes later, he entered the house and found Melissa sleeping on the couch and the general snoozing in his recliner. What he didn't expect was seeing Brandenburg at the kitchen table finishing his second go-around with the data.

"You look like shit," Brandenburg stated after the short glance. "Is that what you call a minor injury?"

"I've had worse," James replied. "What are you still doing here?"

"After you and the lady left, I asked if I could take a look at the files you folks had put together. Nobody thought you would be gone so long so the general figured it wouldn't do any harm. Later, they got word about you and the agent and thought it might be best if I hung around a while. I think they passed out a couple hours ago."

James looked at the ex-soldier and wondered what kept the man going. He wasn't sure how long it had been since he slept, but James was sure Brandenburg could still run twenty miles if need be.

"Have you found out anything?" James asked.

"Yeah," Brandenburg replied. "I figured out that the FBI isn't going to catch this guy. He's too mobile. He's too well informed. And he knows what he going to do, we don't. He has all of the advantages."

"Then how do we catch him? We can't let him get away with this. We can't let him kill Katt."

"I don't mean to be the bad guy here…but, your agent friend could very well already be dead."

"She's not. I can't think that way."

"It's not a matter of how you think. It's just one of the possibilities."

"If she's dead," James sighed, "then it'll all be for nothing. I have to believe that she's being used as a pawn for something."

"Like what?"

"I don't know. I just don't think from everything I read about this guy or what I've seen so far that he does anything without a reason. We just have to figure out the reason."

"Okay," Brandenburg said. "I'll play along. You're the investigator. If you were going to do this, if you were the shooter, what would you do next? Why would you need Agent Katt?"

"I would need her to either be a decoy or a drawing card. I would use her to get my opponent's attention for some reason and either send them on some wild-goose chase or I would use her to bring people to her location."

"I get the first part. We used distractions all the time. Not usually people, but I get the concept. Why would you want to bring people to her if the plan was to take her in the first place?"

"It's an old trick used by terrorist. They would set off some small explosion or do something that would draw a lot of attention by the police, fire department or medical personnel, and then when the rescue teams showed up, they would have a large number of people that they could target congregating in a confined area."

"That would make sense," Brandenburg said, "if he was a terrorist. But there isn't anything that suggests that as far as I know."

James was about to answer when the home phone rang. He answered and turned to get the general when his uncle surprised him.

"It's for you," James said and handed over the phone.

Though the sun was not yet visible, the sky was shedding all traces of the night before. Melissa had also heard the phone and got up to make a fresh batch of coffee. She heard her father talking quietly in the other room, and she walked over and gave James a hug. "I'm sorry about your friend," she said. "I know you must be going crazy."

"Some people would say that's normal for me," James replied.

"Don't hide behind humor, Mickey. I'm just saying...."

"I think we know who the son of a bitch is," the general said interrupting Melissa.

"Who was that?" Melissa asked.

"I may be retired, but I still have some friends in high places," Pound replied. "That was a friend of mine in Intelligence. After Joseph, here, told us about his conversation with his buddy, I put the dates together and called in a favor. Generally, they don't take to giving out information like this, and I had to use up a considerable amount of leverage to get him to talk, but given the circumstances, I thought it was worth it.

"Anyway, it took him a little while, and a few favors of his own, but he figured out who this Homer guy is. He used to do special ops—this Homer guy— several years back, he's from Detroit and was a hell of a player for a while. Then all of a sudden, he decided to go rouge and do some jobs that were unsanctioned.

"They gave him a chance to stop, but when he refused to do it, they gave him the boot. Actually, they tried to take him out and failed. He killed two of theirs getting away.

"So how do they know it's the same guy?" James asked.

"They just know, Mick. You remember the friend of your buddy's?" He looked at Brandenburg. "He said it was necessary in order to prevent information from getting in the wrong hands. The truth is, they discover later, that the reasons were quite different. My friend wouldn't tell me what, but…they know.

"And I'll tell you something else…this son of a bitch is connected somehow. There were times, back then, that he should have been discharged long before he was. Yet somehow he managed to stick around."

"So how good is he?" James asked.

"He was just about as good as they've ever had. His best recorded shot was close to two thousand yards. That's over a mile away."

"Then I know who Johnny-boy is," Brandenburg said. "I had it narrowed down to three shooters. Two of them have never hit anything over fifteen hundred yards. That only leaves it to one shooter…Johnny Blythe."

"What did you say his name is?" James asked.

"John, Johnny, Jonathan, whatever, Blythe," Brandenburg replied. "Why?"

"Son of a bitch!" James shouted as he headed out the door.

"I take it that whatever's going on isn't a good thing," Brandenburg said.

"I'd hate to be on the receiving end of where he's going and who he's going to be talking to," Melissa said.

"I don't know the man very well," Brandenburg said, "but even I wouldn't want to match up with him right now."

"Amen, my friend," the general patted the young new friend on the shoulder. "Amen."

Chapter 50

James had been a cop long enough to know that it usually takes one or two small pieces of information to break a case wide open. He also knew that whenever you deal with murder and high risk situations, people lie. And now he knew who the liar was.

When the door burst in the conference room at the police station, James looked around and didn't see the man he was looking for. His face was red with anger, and at that moment, he wasn't looking to make friends.

"Where is he?" James asked no one in particular.

"Who?" Bill Stetson, the Dayton chief, asked.

"Blythe," James stated in what could only be considered a sneering, growling voice. "I need to speak to that son of a bitch."

"He's not here," Agent Wesley Walker said and then stood to face James. "And I don't appreciate your tone. He's the Deputy Director of the FBI, and I won't have you being disrespectful to him."

"Really?" James replied, stepping face to face with the younger, shorter, agent. "Did the son of a bitch tell you that he's the person responsible for

Agent Katt's kidnapping? Did he tell you that if it wasn't for him, this city wouldn't be shot to hell? Did he…"

The agent went to grab for James. In his mind he knew that the Sacramento cop was bigger, but honestly believed that with his youth and the advantage of surprise that he would be able to stop James before he did anyone harm. He thought that James had come unglued. He thought that James was a threat.

He thought correctly about the latter. He thought wrong about the former.

James picked up the agent's move before he actually saw the act of aggression. As the agent's arm lifted to grab James by the collar, James reached over the agent's arm, pinning it and then stepped back. The motion stretched the agent's arm until it was completely straight and then, using his other hand, push Walker's arm in the wrong direction until it was hyperextended.

With the advantage completely in his favor, James swung the agent into a full circle and then let him fly across the table before landing harshly against the opposite wall.

The entire scene took less time than it took the rest of the members in the room get out of their chairs.

Stetson and Agent Williamson from the Ohio Bureau of Criminal Investigation grabbed James before he could do any more damage to the young FBI agent.

"Stop it damn it," Stetson yelled.

"I want that son of a bitch arrested!" Walker yelled.

"For what?" Williamson asked. "You started it and we all saw it."

"He was threatening me. I had a right to defend myself."

"You got your panties in a wad because he spoke harshly about your boss. Get over yourself."

"If you don't arrest him...I will," Walker said.

"And if you try to do that, I will arrest you for assault," Williamson replied. "You may win, but you'll have a lot of explaining to do. It just might hurt your meteoric rise with the agency. I suggest you think long and hard before you say anything else."

Walker stood up and dusted himself off, but kept quiet.

"Now, James," Williamson released James then turned to face him. "You mind telling us what the hell is going on?"

"I need to talk to Blythe first," James replied. "The SOB is no friend of mine, but I owe him that much. Agent Katt loves him like a father, and before I destroy his career, I need to give him a chance to explain himself. After that, I'll let him tell you what I'm sure he already knows." James turned to face the young agent, Walker. "Sorry, kid. I didn't mean to rough you up. However, next time you need to follow the FBI's guidelines before you get your dander up. Shit like this can get your ass killed. Now where's Blythe?"

"I'm right here," Blythe said as he walked into the room behind James.

"You've got some explaining to do, mister," James turned to face the FBI director. "We can either do it here, or we can do it private. I don't really care. But you will have a 'Come to Jesus' moment before we're finished."

"I don't have anything to discuss unless you know where Agent Katt is being held."

James looked at the man with disgust. On the surface, James got no sense that his opponent was anything but sincere. Then again, you didn't get to his position without having the ability to play a mean game of poker.

"Okay," James continued, "Then let's talk about your son."

The color quickly drained from the man's face as he realized that he could no longer keep the secret he had been holding for so long. He had hoped beyond hope that he could somehow control the situation without losing his integrity…and his career. Somehow, James had put the pieces together and that meant that his dream of taking over the top spot with the agency was now over. His only hope was that he hadn't gotten Katt killed by his silence.

"What about him?" Blythe asked.

James stared at the deputy director. Out of respect for Katt, he wasn't sure if he should address the issue in front of the rest of the people in the room. Seconds later, he decided that it didn't matter what happened to Blythe. All that mattered was getting Katt back alive and safe. He would worry about the fallout later.

"He's Homer," James stated. "Your son is our killer, and you know it!"

"That's bullshit," Agent Walker spouted. "You can get yourself in a lot of trouble by making libelous comments like that."

"Not if they're the truth," James said not taking his eyes off Blythe. "How long have you known?" James was testing a theory and wanted to see if Blythe would blink.

"Not until I arrived," Blythe replied, shocking the room. "I had an idea, a nagging suspicion a couple of days ago that it was him, but I wasn't sure."

"Director Blythe…" Walker started.

"Be quiet, Agent Walker," Blythe said. "There's no sense in skirting the issue. My son is a killer, and there's nothing I can do about it. We still have a job to do."

"You have a hell of a lot of explaining to do," James stated flatly. "But right now, we need to know how to stop him and get Katt back."

"I'm not sure I know how I can help," Blythe said. "I haven't exactly been the best father and I'm sure he feels the same about me. I just don't know how that'll help."

"Why did you suspect him to begin with," Stetson spoke up. "You had to have something that lead you that direction."

"First…tell me how you figured it out," Blythe said, looking at James. "The kid is a ghost in his world."

"Brandenburg," James said. "Brandenburg got us going in the right direction because of the people he knows in that world. He called in some favors. Then, the general…my uncle, made some calls of his own. It seems that retired generals know a lot of people in secret places.

"They still didn't put it all together even after they came up with the name because they didn't know you. You may be a big-wig in your circles, but most people don't know who the deputy director of the FBI is in this country.

"When they told me the kid's name, I just about shit bricks. That's how it came together. Now…can we get to the part where you help us stop the little bastard? Son or not, if he's hurt Katt, I will kill him."

"Son or not…I'll hold him for you when you do."

Chapter 51

Katt was finally able to get her head to clear and knew that she was in trouble. The room where she was being held consisted of four plank walls and an old mattress; though she couldn't see it. There was no light to give her any idea of the time. She knew that she had been out for some time, but didn't know if it was day or night. The only thing she could identify was that there was a crack beneath the door and that there was light coming from the adjacent room. On occasion she could see a shadow walk past the door—her captor she presumed.

When the door opened, Katt could see that the man standing before her looked to be the man she had met before at the B and B. When he spoke, she knew it for sure.

"Don't think for a moment that you can escape from here, Agent Katt," Homer said. "I have taken precautions to insure that even if you were to get past me that you will not leave this place."

Katt just looked at the man trying to assess her best approach. She didn't know if he was telling the truth, but wasn't willing, yet, to do anything that might get her killed. On the other hand, she wasn't about to die without a fight.

"I've no intention of trying to escape…yet," Katt replied, more calm than she felt. "For now, I would just like to know your intentions."

Homer laughed at the remark.

"That sounds like we're going steady and would be something your father would ask."

"My father is dead."

"I didn't know that. How did he die?"

Katt hadn't talked about her family to anyone except a psychiatrist with the bureau in many years. However, since it seemed to be something she could use to get a conversation going, she decided that she would go with it…for a little while anyway.

"He died when I was a child."

"I didn't ask that, Agent Katt. I asked how he died."

"He was shot…in a home invasion."

"Interesting. Is that why you became an agent?"

"It was one of many reasons. Maybe it was the biggest reason."

"And your mother? Did she die to? Or was she spared?"

"She was killed as well."

Katt was starting to get uncomfortable with the conversation and decided to try and change subjects.

"So are you going to answer my question?"

"I'm thinking about it," Homer said and then turned on a high-powered flashlight and shined it directly into Katt's eyes. "Maybe we can play a little game. We have some time before the grand finally. You answer one of my questions and then I will answer one of yours. Whoever, refuses to answer the other's question loses and the game will be over. How does that sound?"

Homer had nothing to lose with the game and everything to gain. He now knew that Katt had been his father's pet project. His informant had seen to it that he had a lot of information that he hadn't cared to know in the past. He even knew about Kat's parents before asking the question. It was his way to determine if she was lying.

Now that he had her, he was going to get as much information from her as possible. The expectation being that the more she told him the more he could make his father hurt before he died. Best case, she would slip up and give him something that he could use to finish his trap.

"I can live with that," Katt replied. "So you first…what are you intentions?"

Homer thought a long moment before answering the question.

"I intend to seek revenge on a long overdue wrong. I intend to kill several people for a crime that was perpetrated against me a long time ago. And now it's your turn. Did they ever catch your parent's killer or killers?"

"They know who killed them," Katt replied. "They've always known."

"You did not answer the question again, Agent Katt. I want to know if they were ever caught. Is that such a difficult thing to answer? Or is it too painful to discuss?"

"They never caught the people who invaded our home. They did catch the killer."

"And now you are hedging your answers again. What aren't you telling me? Or have you decided to stop playing the game already? If so...I will just leave now." Homer turned off the flashlight and turned to leave.

"I killed them," Katt cried out. "I killed my parents."

Homer stopped his departure and slowly turned back to face the now sobbing agent.

"Why?" Homer asked.

There was something honest about the way he asked and Katt was about to answer when she said, "It's your turn you son of a bitch. Who are you planning to kill?"

Homer turned on the flashlight. Though he was smiling, Katt couldn't see it.

"I intend to kill several agents from the FBI; including the Deputy Director, Jonathan Blythe.

See…isn't this a fun game?" Homer said looking at the shocked expression on Katt's face. "I take it you know the man?"

"Is that your question?" Katt asked.

Homer laughed. "You are good at this, Agent Katt. You leave me wanting to know so much more about everything. No…my question is…how close are you to that cop from California? James is his name, I believe."

"Detective James has nothing to do with you," Katt hissed at the man. "You shot his cousin. That's why he's here. He's just trying to protect his family." She was trying to protect James from unwanted attention from someone she was sure could get to James. She didn't want that.

"Come. Come, Agent Katt. Me thinks thou protests too much. He's more than that. You slept with the man just last night."

Katt was stunned by the man's knowledge. She was also stunned that she felt the heat rise in her cheeks. She had wanted very much to do just that— sleep with James. She wondered now if she would ever get the chance to show him how she felt.

Instead of denying the accusation, she felt compelled to get the information straight. "I stayed the night because he was helping me try to figure out how to find you. Sleep was all that happened." She had no idea why she had to explain that to the killer.

"So tell me," Katt continued. "Why Director Blythe? What's he to you?"

Katt knew that the man was trying to get some insight to the people she worked with. There was no other reason for him to question her. Maybe he figured that because he planned to kill her anyway, there was no reason to hold back from her. She could only hope that she wouldn't die and could get the information to James.

"He's the whole reason I am what I am," Homer replied. "Had it not been for him, the man before you wouldn't exist. And for that, he has to pay."

"Now who's playing word games?" Katt smiled at the man in hopes that it would disarm him. It worked.

Homer immediately turned off the light and slammed the door. Once again, Katt was enveloped into darkness. Her smile lingered for several long seconds.

"So why is he doing this?" James asked Blythe. "What's his end game?"

"I have no idea," Blythe responded. "I haven't seen my son in too many years to remember."

"You've got to have some idea," Williamson interjected. "You mean to tell me you've never tried to track his whereabouts?"

"I've tried," Blythe responded with a hanging head. "I discovered several years ago that he had left the military."

"You mean, kicked out," James corrected.

"Yes. I discovered later that he had been hired to do some private consulting."

"What kind?" James asked.

"I never found out. As time went on, I started reading about this corporate guy or that political person from various countries that had been killed by a sniper and wondered if it had anything to do with Johnny. I started putting the pieces together that there were just too many coincidences for him to be at all those places at the same time the shootings took place."

"So why didn't you say something to someone?" Stetson asked.

"Because I had no proof," Blythe said, raising his voice. "He was my son…He is my son, and I wasn't about to put a label on him without proof."

"Was that the reason," James asked. "Or were you simply worried how it would affect your status in the bureau?"

Blythe didn't answer. James took his suggestion as the real truth.

"So what does he want?" Williamson asked. "Why is he here?"

"All I could share would be guesses," Blythe responded. "Haven't you already done enough guessing?"

"The guessing we did happened because you kept some very important information away from us and Agent Katt. Your silence could have stopped him before others were killed. Your silence may have already gotten her killed, you *son of a bitch*," James stared directly into Blythe's eyes. "As God is my witness, if she gets killed because of this, I will see to it that what you suffer will be far greater than you could possibly imagine."

"Just a damn minute, Detective," Walker said. He had been in something of a shock hearing that his mentor had fallen from grace. He just wasn't about to let someone traipse over the man. "If you continue to threaten…"

"It's okay," Blythe interrupted Walker. "Detective James has every right to say what's on his mind. I've messed up, and someone I care for…we care for…has been placed in danger because of my error. Give the man his dues. If it wasn't for him, I may have let Agent Katt get killed trying to protect my ungrateful son. It may already be too late. I can only pray it isn't."

"That's very noble of you," James spat. "But you still haven't told us anything we can use to catch him."

"Fair enough," Blythe said. "You want my opinion? I'll give it to you."

Chapter 52

James and the other members of law enforcement that had been privy to the discussion argued long and hard about what the deputy director had said. Many of the group couldn't deny that the shooter's rationale had been correct. They just couldn't agree on the solution to fix the problem.

James on the other hand, felt no compunction regarding the resolution that the director had proposed.

At three o'clock, it didn't matter whether anyone else liked it or not.

When the telephone rang in the conference room, the Dayton police captain, Stetson, yelled, "I told you not to bother us for any reason!"

The receptionist replied, "I thought this call would be your one exception, Chief. It's a guy who calls himself Homer. He said that you all would know who it is and that if you didn't take his call, Agent Katt would be killed."

The room went quiet.

"I'll take the call," Stetson said as he pushed the only line that was lit. "This is Captain William Stetson of the Dayton Police Department, to whom am I speaking?"

"I believe you already know whom you are speaking to," Homer replied. "I suspect that by now, you know quite a lot about me."

"Okay," Stetson continued. "Then let me ask something different. What is it I can do you?"

"That is a much better question," Homer said. "You can put my Daddy Dearest on the line for me. I suspect he's around there somewhere."

"I'm here, Junior," Blythe said.

"I hate when you call me that, Daddy," he spoke the words as if he had just taken a large bite of animal excrement.

"Okay," Blythe said. "You called me. What is it that you want?"

"There are a lot of things I want, father. I want world peace. I want a cure for all fatal diseases. I want all mosquitoes to die and never return. Certainly God took a day off when he invented those." The room stayed quiet. "Mostly, I want you to suffer the way you made your family suffer. I want my mother to still be alive. Can you give me any of those things…father?"

"I'm working very hard…I've worked very hard at making the world a better place, son. Unfortunately, there's not a lot I can do about those other things; though I do kinda agree with you about the mosquitoes."

"Then maybe there's hope," Homer said. "It seems I have something you want."

"What's that?"

"Don't try being too funny, Mister Deputy Director. You just might find that it could backfire on you."

"Very well," Blythe said. "Yes. You have something…somebody, I want—Agent Katt."

"Very good. I do have Agent Katt. I have her safely hidden from you folks and assure you that she is both alive and well. However, the state of her health could deteriorate rather quickly if you don't agree with what I am about to ask for."

"I figured you had something in mind," the director said.

"I want you to come get her. It's been my intention to have a little one on one time with my old man. If you come alone, I will take you and let her go. It's a simple straight up exchange. What do you say?"

"I say yes," Blythe said. "My only problem is trusting that you will keep your word. I have a little problem trusting the word of a killer."

"There is that," Homer said. "But then, how do I know that you won't have a dozen of your agents swarming whatever location I give you? Trust is a two way street."

"You have my word as the director of the FBI."

"Well…you need to remember that I know better than anyone how little your word means, father."

"So we are at an impasse."

"Not necessarily," Homer said. "Is Detective Mickey James present in your little group of wise men?"

"I'm here," James said. "Whadoyouwant?"

"I want to give you your very special agent back," Homer said. "I understand that you and Agent Katt have a special bond."

Everyone in the room was looked at James for confirmation.

"Agent Katt is someone I care about a lot."

"That's good. Now she told me something about the two of you sleeping together two nights ago. Want to elaborate?"

"I want to know what the hell you want to know," James said loudly. "If you are interested in someone's sex life, get one of your own."

"I want to know what she told me about the two of you sleeping together. I need to know if I can trust what you tell me."

"I don't know what she told you," James replied. "I have no idea what kind of duress she was under when you asked the question. The best I can offer is the truth."

"Well, then there you have it. Tell me the truth. If you do that, I will tell you how to get her back...alive."

"We were working on the cold-blooded, useless murders of several important people here in town. Instead of leaving to go to her own place, she stayed at mine. She spent the night, but we didn't do anything...sexual."

"What? You didn't even kiss the beautiful agent?"

"No...I didn't," James replied.

"But you wanted to...right?"

"I'm not a monk," James thought about the night and what his desires had wanted. "But no, nothing happened."

"Very good, detective," Homer said. "Now the next question is my most important one. Afterwards, I will tell you want to know."

"You said that after the other question," James said. "You're acting more like a telephone solicitor than a kidnapper." James paused and wanted to tell the man off, but knew that Katt's life was at stake. "Go ahead. What's the question?"

"I want to know if you trust my father."

James head turned quickly at the director and knew that the answer was the one Homer really wanted the answer to. On the surface, it seemed that the best answer would be to give the killer a reason to trust the director. But then again, he already knew that there was no love lost between them. The director nodded in a way that he expected James to offer the former. James had other ideas.

"That's a complicated question," James finally replied after much thought.

"I only want the truth. If you can't give me that much then maybe you aren't as good a cop as Agent Katt led me to believe."

"You want the truth…okay. Here's the truth.

"Agent Katt respects and believes in Director Blythe. She would trust him with just about anything the man says. I trust Katt. However, as far as I'm concerned, I don't trust the man. He withheld information vital to this investigation to protect a lowlife prick like you." James took a short breath and then continued.

"And since we're talking about the truth, understand this. "I know who you are…Johnny. I know that you are amoral and seem to have a hard on for your old man. I get that. I really do. But if you do anything to hurt Agent Katt, I will use everything in my power to hunt you down and kill you. Do you get the truth in that, mister?"

"Indeed I do, detective. Agent Katt is very fortunate to have a friend like you. But seriously, you should really consider shacking up with her. She is one fine…"

"Watch your mouth!"

"Lady," Homer said, smiling at the passion James felt for the lady agent. "I was going to say, lady. Anyway, you've passed the test, Detective James. I will contact you later and let you know when we can make the exchange."

"What exchange?" James asked. "Do you want me? Or do you still want the director?"

"I never wanted you, detective. I just wanted to make sure that you understand that telling me the truth will keep your woman alive. As for the threat, though I can appreciate the emotional display, I have no tolerance for threats from amateurs such as yourself. The agent's life will be spared only if you cooperate."

He hung up the phone.

Chapter 53

There was no way for them to trace the encrypted phone that Homer was using. Blythe knew that, but waited to hear the official verdict from the tech people. Blythe decided that his career was over and wanted to keep that piece of information all to himself if needed later.

"Deputy Director Blythe," Agent Walker said, "you cannot possibly consider exchanging yourself for Agent Katt."

"Why not?" James asked before the director could speak. "It's his mess. Let him fix it."

"It's not your call, Agent Walker," Blythe said. "We will do whatever we have to in order to get her back alive."

"So what are we going to do?" Stetson wanted to know. "This has become a clusterfuck between a federal case and a domestic. It's not something in any of our manuals."

"This isn't in anybody's manual," Williamson replied. "As things stand, the best we can do is offer support. It's the FBI's call."

"I'm going to go see my uncle," James said. "Maybe there's something we can do from that angle."

"You're going to go see Brandenburg, aren't you?" Blythe said, looking directly at James. "You'll kill my son, right?"

"In a heartbeat," James replied. "But I don't know if I can get in touch with Brandenburg. He just sorta shows up whenever he thinks things are safe. So keep the hell away from me. I don't need anybody trailing me that'll scare him away."

"Do what you have to do, Detective," Blythe said. "But if you can avoid it, I would rather Johnny be captured instead of killed."

"Well…that's up to him."

James left and didn't look back.

In less than twenty minutes, James had updated the general and Melissa. Having been a cop for so many years, James hadn't been completely surprised by the deputy director's willingness to protect his son. Nor was he surprised by the man's contrition once he was caught. He would have a lot of explaining to do back in Washington, but right now all he cared about was getting Katt back safely.

Katt. She would be devastated when she found out what her friend and mentor had done. At least she would if she made it through this alive.

James wanted more than anything to save her, yet knew that the odds were very much against him— her. What he needed more than anything at that moment was a plan that could get her back safely. He needed Brandenburg to do or say something that would make this right.

"So what are you going to do?" Melissa asked. "You know that Homer—or Johnny—won't wait very long."

"I know that!" James replied more harshly than he meant. Melissa knew James well enough not to ask for an apology. James had no idea that he needed to offer one. "I don't know what to do. I've never taken on someone like this guy."

"I have," Brandenburg said, standing behind James; startling the three others.

"You have got to learn to give people some warning when you enter a room," James said, trying to calm his nerves.

"Sorry," Brandenburg replied. "Force of habit."

"How?" James asked without preamble. "How do you beat someone like this guy?"

"Figure out where he's going and then get there first," the sniper replied. "That's the problem, but I think it's a solvable one." Brandenburg paused to insure that everyone was listening. "He's done with his work here. He had a job to do and it's done."

"What job?" Melissa asked.

"You guys…the judges…that's why he came here. But it's not why he's staying. If we can figure out who hired him to begin with, then maybe we can get some idea where he's been hiding out."

"Do you think the money man would actually know his hideout?" the general asked. "That would be a prescription for disaster for a hit man."

"He won't know his address, but he will have a way to make contact. That information should be enough to get us a location."

"How do we find out about the person who hired him?" Melissa asked.

"I already think I know the answer to that," James said. "And if our new friend here is willing to help me, I think I can get to the truth quicker than if I were to do it alone."

James looked at Brandenburg for confirmation and the only thing the sniper offered in reply was a smile.

"Don't wait up for us," James said. "This may take a while."

"It's time," Homer said entering the dank space. "If you're lucky, you may live to see the morning sunrise. If not…well, let's just say that seeing a sunrise may be low on your list of priorities."

Katt was having difficulty adjusting to the bright light shining in her eyes again.

"Where are we going?" Katt asked. "And before we leave, is it possible for me to pee? I wouldn't want to make a mess on these fine accommodations."

"I would be happy to watch you pee, Agent Katt. Just don't think for a second that you will be left alone. I would hate for you to get hurt trying to make your daring escape attempt."

Katt stood and walked slowly towards the man holding the Taser. She knew that without that, she might have a chance getting past him. However, she had already felt the jolt the gun released and knew that she had no chance if he were to shoot her with it again. Without offering any resistance, Katt led the way. Her bladder was turning flip flops.

After finishing her business—it was her first with an audience—she had been instructed to place her hands behind her back. Plastic cuffs were slipped over her wrists and she was then instructed to get in the car. A bag was placed over her head. He attached a seatbelt and the two of them headed for her, maybe final, destination.

"You never said where we are going," Katt said.

"That's because where we are going will take us a little while, and I wanted us to have something to talk about while we were driving. I felt it would be fun reminiscing about the people we have in common."

"What people?" Katt asked, surprised.

"Well there's Deputy Director, Blythe and there's Detective Mickey James. Oh, by the way, he wanted me to tell you hi and that he was coming to get you."

Katt was surprised. "You spoke to Mickey? When?"

"A few hours ago. He is most fond of you, you know? I think you two should spend more time together."

"Is that ever going to be an option?" Katt doubted it very much.

"I guess it depends on a few things. You see, he wasn't exactly happy to be talking to me. As a matter of fact, he was downright rude, if I'm to be honest."

"Don't take that personal," Katt said in an attempt to defuse whatever James might have said. "He's an ass to everybody. As a matter of fact, the first time I met him he pissed me off too."

"Really?" Homer laughed. "And here I thought he was like that just with me."

"Not that you aren't special," Katt said. "James pisses off just about everyone he meets. I think it's some kind of man thing. If you can't take him at his worst, you'll never get a chance to know his best."

"Is his best worth getting to know? I mean...I know he really digs you and everything, but if he's that way all the time, I might have to take back what I said about spending more time with him."

"He's not that way all the time," Katt back peddled. "He's just that way when you first meet him. After a very short time, he can be a very caring person."

"Are you too sleeping together?"

"No," Katt answered, but remembered that he'd asked the same question earlier. "Why is that so important to you?"

Homer waited for a while before answering.

"I just don't like the idea of killing an unfulfilled woman; especially someone as beautiful as you." After another moment, Homer asked, "Is he gay? Is that why you guys haven't slept together?"

Katt almost spit into the mask that hid her face.

Once she recovered, Katt said, "No. To the best of my knowledge, he's not gay."

"It's okay if he is, you know. I know that the military is a don't ask, don't tell place, but I've never been one to judge a person's sexual preferences."

"Things just haven't worked out that way," Katt answered. "If I manage to live through this…" Katt pondered a moment and thought about what might have been. "Who knows?"

Chapter 54

James and Brandenburg knocked on the door to the one person James believed could help. The question was; would he?

"What do you want?" Blythe asked when he saw the large man standing at the door to his hotel room. When he saw the man behind James, he said, "What the hell...?" And then the last thing he saw was the fist of a very angry cop from Sacramento rapidly heading toward his face.

James knew that he didn't have the time to wait for the FBI man to wake up from his induced nap. To expedite the matter, he sloshed a coffeepot of cold water on the director's face. It worked perfectly.

After spitting out the water and coughing for almost a full minute, Blythe looked up from the floor at the two men he wanted more than anything to arrest.

"What the hell do think you're doing coming in here and..."

"Shut up," James said over the other man's voice.

"You've made a big mistake, James," Blythe said. "A very big mistake."

"You're right," James agreed. "I made the mistake of trusting you with Katt's welfare. I made the mistake of believing that you had the best interest of the country at heart when the only thing you ever cared for was yourself and your rise to the top. The difference between us is that I recognize my mistakes and learn from them. I'm not so sure that you do."

"What do you want?" Blythe asked.

"I want answers," James replied. "I want you to tell the truth, and then I want to see you rot in prison for you part in this mess."

"I have no part in it. It's my son who's doing this."

"A son that you suspected all along as being a serial killer or hit man or whatever the hell he is. The bottom line…you knew and kept quiet. That ends here."

"What are you going to do, torture me? You don't have the balls to do that."

James smiled at the arrogant man for a moment, and then said, "You really don't know me, Mister Deputy Director. When it comes to Katt, I would cut out your guts and hold them in my hands just so you could see them. However, the problem is that I don't have a lot of experience doing that sort of thing. That's why I brought along a friend; someone with more experience. Have you met Joseph Brandenburg?"

Blythe had forgot about the second man at the door and turned around surprised by the huge man who walked up from behind him.

"Joseph," James said, "I would like for you to meet the Deputy Director of the FBI, Jonathan Blythe. He's the man who can help us find agent Katt and his son; the man who is trying to frame you for murder. Deputy Director Blythe, I would like you to meet Joseph Brandenburg, the man who is going to show you the kind of pain that will come this close," James stated, putting his finger and thumb a mere quarter inch apart, "to making your heart stop. And for the record, Mister Deputy Director, you can't scare him. He's already wanted for murder. The only thing worse for him is not getting the answers he needs. So...do you understand the position you're in now?"

Brandenburg didn't say a word. He just stared at the scared man who was quickly coming to a conclusion that his time was about to run out. Finally, Blythe nodded his head.

"I take it you know who I am," Brandenburg stated more than asked.

"You are Joseph Brandenburg. James just told me."

Without out bothering to explain why, Brandenburg smacked Blythe across the face hard enough to knock him back to the floor.

"You seem to miss the point of my question," Brandenburg said. "So I will go over some rules with you."

James and Brandenburg picked up the deputy director and sat him on a chair. James placed handcuffs on his wrists and followed that with a gag of duct tape to keep the man from making too much noise.

"As you can see, Mister Deputy Director," Brandenburg continued, "my detective friend and I are not in a playful mood. We are not here to joke with you, tell war stories or even drink a beer. We are here to get you to do something that's completely foreign to you; to tell the truth. Your son is a worthless piece of shit that is planning to kill Detective James' friend and he's trying to put me in prison and then electrocuted for what he did. So when I ask you something you are going to answer my questions. You are going to answer them truthfully and if you fail, you are going to feel very severe pain.

"Now we're going to start by asking you some very basic questions. You are going to nod for yes and shake your head for no. Do you get the gist so far?"

There was a nod.

"Great!" Brandenburg said. "Now…when I asked you if you knew who I was, did you really think I was asking about my name?"

A reluctant shake of the head.

"That's right. You thought that maybe you could dick around with me and buy yourself some time or something like that…right?"

A nod.

"Are you expecting company?" James asked. Another nod.

"This will be tricky," Brandenburg whispered in Blythe's ear. "Using your feet—either foot—and using ten minute increments, tell us how long it will be until your company arrives."

Blythe tapped twice.

"So you are saying twenty minutes?"

Blythe nodded.

"Okay," Brandenburg smiled at Blythe. "But here's the thing...sir. I still don't believe you are quite convinced yet just how precarious of a situation you've managed to get yourself into here. So here's the deal. Friends being what they are, I will give your friend twenty minutes to show up. If he—or she—happens to show up by then, I will only knock, whoever it is, out. At that time we will continue our discussion. However, if that person doesn't show up in...nineteen minutes now...I will take this very sharp knife I carry and cut off one of your fingers. So...would you like to stick with that timeline? Or would you like a chance to reconsider and start over? Oh wait...you can't answer two conflicting questions with your mouth taped up like that. Can you?"

Brandenburg ripped the tape from the director's mouth.

"Are you starting to get a clue here, Mister Blythe?" Brandenburg asked. "Now how long?"

"An hour!" Blythe yelled. "He's supposed to come get me in an hour."

"See how easy it is?" Brandenburg said.

"Hurting you like this would never have been an option, Blythe," James said, "had you not turned your back on Katt. You knew how I felt about her. You also knew me. Did you think for a minute that I wouldn't throw everything away to protect her?"

"I was counting on it," Blythe surprised them both.

"What's that supposed to mean?" James replied.

"He's my son, damn it. Do you have any idea how much it hurts to betray family? I wasn't sure I could do it and it looks like I was right."

"You aren't making any sense, Blythe. Talk to me in English!"

"I love Katt like family. I would trust her with my life. I never once suspected that she would get taken like this. Damn it...I would never have put her in that situation."

"But you did," James said.

"I know that, damn it! I know I screwed up. He has her, and there's nothing I can do to stop him from whatever the hell he's planning to do. I needed an out. I needed someone to force me to do the right thing. I know that you're a wild card, James. Frankly, I pretty much expected this. I didn't expect you to team up with Rambo here."

"Rambo's a pussy," Brandenburg hissed.

"Anyway, I figured you would do something to force me to make the kind of choices I needed to make to protect Katt. You should have done it sooner."

"So what? You're blaming me now?"

"That's not what I meant. I mean...if you would have pushed me sooner, I might have been able to help. Now...I don't know what I can do."

"You can tell us how to find him," James yelled. "You bet on the wrong horse, mister. You thought that your psychopathic son would somehow come around because daddy was here? What bullshit!"

James was livid and wanted to kill the man before him, but knew that he couldn't. Brandenburg, on the other hand, had a more liberal moral compass.

Chapter 55

Katt felt the vehicle she was riding in come to a halt. Homer was whistling a tune that Katt didn't recognize and wondered where he had taken her. The only thing she knew for a fact was that they hadn't been on a paved road for quite some time.

Homer assisted Katt to her feet and was glad that she hadn't worn heels. The rocky terrain beneath her feet would not be conducive to formal wear.

Homer stopped, removed her mask and said, "Welcome home, Agent Katt. From this moment forward, the clock on your life is ticking. If you're lucky, only some of the other FBI agent will be sacrificed—sacrificed in their attempt to save you. Should they fail, then you will all die. Should any of them succeed, you will only have to live knowing that those men and women gave their all because you weren't smart enough to save yourself.

The anger Katt felt was beyond anything she had ever before felt. She started to turn from the man and even though her hands were tied, she extended a back kick that landed squarely in Homer's gut. For whatever reason, the killer had dropped his guard, and the kick knocked the wind out of him. Katt seized the moment and stomped down on Homer's chest, furthering her advantage. As she went to kick him in the head, Homer managed to deflect the kick and it barely missed.

Homer rolled away from Katt in hopes of giving himself a moment to catch his breath and get to his feet. Katt was relentless and charged after Homer with everything she had in her limited arsenal.

The problem for Katt was that the man she wanted more than anything to kill, also had extensive training and was able to deflect everything being sent his way. Now that he knew that he was in a fight, there was less than a small hope that Katt would succeed.

Katt managed to get in a few additional blows that hurt Homer, but nothing life threatening or even enough to cripple the man. Eventually, the tide turned and Homer toyed with frustrated opponent. He even started to smile at her as she tired.

She had nothing left to give.

Katt finally—exhausted—sat down on a small boulder.

"Why don't you just kill me?" she said. "You already have what you want. Why destroy the lives of good, innocent people?"

"Those good, innocent people, as you call them, took my father away. Because of their greed, my father ignored his family and one by one we all died. They have to pay for that. And they will."

"I get that. I actually do. But why kill the agents? They had nothing to do with your father's career. Why not just go after your father and leave the rest alone?"

"You don't get it. I don't want him to just die. I want him to die a disgrace to the bureau. I want the world to know that he was a deserter to his family and incompetent as an agent. I want the world to turn its back on him as he did us."

"And then what?" Katt asked. She was trying to find a crack in his armor. He had to have a weakness, but so far she couldn't find it. "Do you think that somehow after this is over that you will somehow feel better about yourself?"

"Feel better? I don't get you, Agent Katt. You're supposed to be some kind of psych genius. You should know that I don't expect that. As a matter of fact, you should know by now that I don't feel much of anything. So, no...I don't expect to feel better. I expect to finish this and then after one more job...retire."

"So it's all about the money for you? Then I *am* confused. Why risk everything for an outcome that doesn't matter? If you're telling me the truth, then your father's death and disparaging his name isn't worth the risk. So why do it?"

"Revenge," Homer smiled. "Not everything a person does has to be about money. I will know that this one thing that has driven me my entire life will never have to be dealt with again. The old man will be gone; just like the rest of my family. I can move forward, and that's all there is to it. Now get up. I have work to do."

"What are doing?" Blythe asked Brandenburg who had slipped a long black knife from its sheath.

"I'm going to get answers," Brandenburg said. "Detective James, you might want to leave the room."

"Wait! Wait!" Blythe yelled. After that he could only squirm because James had once again placed strips of duct tape across the director's mouth.

"In for a penny. In for a pound," James replied.

With a lot less effort than James had expected, Brandenburg had Blythe's hand lying flat on the room's only table. The deputy director balled his hand into a fist because he knew what Brandenburg was planning. Without conversation, Brandenburg slammed the point of the knife into the table a mere quarter inch from Blythe's fist.

"Here's the deal, Blythe," Brandenburg said. "You open your hand, and I will only cut off a finger. If you keep it as a fist, I will cut off your whole hand. Either way, it's going to hurt like a mother. You have a count to three to decide which way this is going to go. One!"

He didn't have to count further. Blythe opened his hand.

Brandenburg pulled the knife and placed the tip of the blade between the man's pinky and ring fingers. The technique wasn't anything difficult. All he had to do was use the tip and table as leverage and then bring the handle down. As sharp as the blade was, it would sever skin and bone without much effort at all.

"There is another alternative," James said, stopping the cut when it first drew blood. "We could give the guy one more chance to tell us how to contact his son. Who knows, maybe he even knows who it was that hired him in the first place. What do you think?"

"I'm tired of playing games, Detective," Brandenburg spat with words that brought a chill to both Blythe and James. There was no doubt in anyone's mind just how serious the situation had gotten. "He talks now…period. I won't give him any more chances."

"Do you understand what Mister Brandenburg is saying, Blythe?" James whispered in Blythe's ear. "If you don't start talking right now, I'm going to leave this room. What happens after that will be between you and the man with the knife. Understand?"

The whole time James was talking Blythe's eyes were focused on the blade as it pressed into

Blythe's finger. The entire time, Blythe was shaking his head in agreement.

James ripped the tape from Blythe's mouth pulling skin and hair. He didn't make a sound.

Blythe waited for Brandenburg to release his hand. He hoped that by agreeing to talk the threat would be lifted. He was wrong.

"The time to talk is expiring," James said. Brandenburg resumed the downward arc of the blade. Blythe started talking.

"I have a satphone number for Jon, Junior. I use it every once in a while to contact him. I called him right after I got into town and talked to him a few minutes."

"About what?" James asked.

"I wanted to know if he was the one doing all the killings. I knew that he had been trained to do that kind of work. Over the years, I've kept track of where he goes. Until last night, I never had confirmation of what he had become. He did everything but laugh about it. I was too shocked to know what to do."

"Do you think you should have told someone of your suspicions?" James said. "Hell...at the very least, you should have told Katt."

"I couldn't. I didn't know how."

"Go on. Tell us the rest."

"In order to track him, I've had to keep tabs on his phone. Over the last couple of months, I've noticed an increase in calls coming from one number; someone from right here in Dayton. I don't know if that person is the one behind the killings, but I would bet he knows a lot more than I do about how to track Jon down."

Brandenburg eased the pressure a bit from the man's finger. They needed that name and they needed it fast. Easing the fear would hopefully help.

"Who is it?" James asked.

The deputy director gave them the name and James wasn't nearly as surprised as he thought he should be.

Brandenburg told James to place the tape back over Blythe's mouth.

"We don't want him to draw attention before we have a chance to get away."

James did as he was asked and Brandenburg, without hesitation, cut off the end of the deputy director's finger.

"You could have saved a lot of good people by doing the right thing," Brandenburg said. "As far as I'm concerned, you got off easy."

Blythe finished screaming and tears flowed from his eyes. After the men wrapped the finger and left, Blythe had no reason to reject what the killer had said. He had gotten off easy. The problem, however, was that the evening wasn't yet over.

An hour later, Blythe had been found and taken to the hospital. Walker was the agent scheduled to meet the deputy director in order that Blythe could meet everyone at the police station and prepare for what his son might throw their way.

Though no one believed him, Blythe upheld the notion that he had no idea who had attacked or why they had cut off his finger. All the while, James had no idea that the deputy director had saved his career. He figured that when the night was over, he would, at the least, be facing suspension. More than likely, he figured, he would be facing jail time for what he and Brandenburg did to the deputy director.

Chapter 56

Throughout much of Ohio, caverns had been discovered and utilized by the Native American tribes of the area. The Ohio Caverns were by far the most recognized; however, there were many smaller places that had never gained the same notoriety.

These caves were no less fruitful regarding the historical aspects of the history of the area. There were simply too many for them all to get recognition.

Homer had had been shown such a place years before when he had visited a military friend from the area. It was a small cavern located on a government tract of land that only the most daring hikers and spelunkers knew about.

The mouth of the cavern was less than three feet wide, but after traversing less than thirty feet into the fissure, it opened into an enormous room cluttered with both stalactites and stalagmites.

There were no trails to follow or walkways to help negotiate the seeping waterways. The ground was potted in places, slick everywhere and treacherous for those who had never had the experience of walking on the slimy terrain.

Katt had no experience whatsoever and after her second fall uttered a word that even she was surprised came out of her mouth.

"You are slowing us down, Agent Katt," Home said as he bent down to assist her to her feet. "If you keep falling, we may never get to enjoy our grand finally."

"Then maybe I should slow down even more," Katt replied. "I'm not going to do anything that will assist you. You know that don't you?"

Homer smiled.

"You misinterpreted my comment. Or maybe it was me who misspoke. *We* won't get to enjoy it together. I have no intention of missing it myself. You simply won't be alive to see it. So…if you wish to enjoy your life a little longer, I suggest that you don't continue being a distraction."

"It's difficult to negotiate this floor with my hands tied behind my back. And these shoes weren't exactly made for cave walking."

"Weren't you a girl scout, Agent Katt? Didn't anyone ever teach you the value of always being prepared?"

"Yes," Katt replied. "Your father."

The light inside the cave was given by a single lantern. Had there been more, Katt would have seen the anger that instantly flared across the killer's face.

"Then he taught you more than he ever taught me," Homer replied.

Katt didn't have to see the man's face. By the timbre of his voice and the shaking of his head, she knew that she had finally found that crevice she needed into the man's psyche.

Katt smile as they walked further into the mountain.

Time was running out and James knew that if they didn't get where they needed to go quickly, they might never be able to save Katt.

Brandenburg wasn't motivated by Katt's disappearance. He was certain that if Homer had the woman, she was more than likely dead. Her only hope was that the killer had a plan that would include her being alive until the last minute. His only goal was to kill the killer; no matter what.

The two men entered the two-story brick home with the minimal of difficulty. The alarm system had been turned off. Apparently the occupant didn't consider himself to be a target. Maybe he should have thought the issue thru a little more carefully.

As he entered the kitchen to refill his coffee cup, the District Attorney, Jules Habersham, was startled to see Joseph Brandenburg facing him. He dropped the cup and turned to run only to have his exit cut off by James. The blow to his stomach doubled him over and greatly reduced the DA's desire to run further.

"Did you really think you would get away with it?" James asked as he pulled the man's face up by the hair. "We need to talk. Correction…you need to talk."

James half carried, half dragged the scared man into the dining room and placed him not-to gently into the king's chair because the arms could be used effectively to tie down his arms. He expected Habersham to raise a ruckus and threaten them both with an assortment of legal consequences. Instead, the man started to cry.

"I don't know where he is," Habersham offered without being prompted. "He's out of control, and I had no way to stop him."

"Why did you start him," James asked. "It seems to me that when you hire a psychopath to do your bidding, you would have at least considered that he may not exactly follow your wishes to the letter."

"I know that now," Habersham replied. "I just didn't think that a professional would go off the rails like this."

"So, in other words, you thought it was okay to sic him on the people you hired him to kill, but somehow think it's wrong for him to do it on his own. Is that about right?"

"You're putting words in my mouth," the DA said. "That's not what I meant."

"I don't give a crap about what you think," Brandenburg said. "I want you to tell us how to find him."

"I already told you, I don't know where he is. He stopped communicating with me."

"Then you are going to be in a lot of trouble before this night is done. You will be sorry if you can't come up with a good way to help us find him and Agent Katt."

"Tell me what I can do," Habersham pleaded. "I will tell you everything. Just don't hurt me."

"Where was he staying?" James asked.

"I don't know. He never told me. I tried to figure it out, but it was useless."

"How did he communicate with you when you had a job to do?"

"I sent him an encrypted message. He would call me within a couple of hours."

"We know about his satphone, but we can't trace it or triangulate where he is. What else do you know that could help us?"

Habersham realized that he did have something to bargain with. Apparently they didn't know about his other number and figured he could use that in order to maybe get a head start to run.

"I asked you a question," James repeated.

"I know he has another number that he started using after we made initial contact. I don't think it's a satphone."

"Why do you say that?"

"Because when he talked to me at first, there was a hesitation between when I asked questions and when he responded. I figured it was because of the time lag for the signal to bounce off the satellite. The other number didn't have the same lag time."

"So what's this other number? Maybe we can use it to track him. Right now that's all we have."

"I don't think it's in my best interest to give it to you until we make a deal."

"I see," Brandenburg said. "What kind of a deal do you expect to get for the information?"

"I give you the number and you let me go. If the authorities catch me, then so be it. If I get away, then good for me."

"I see," James said. "Maybe before we decide, you could tell us one thing; why did you have those people killed? Were they enemies? Had they somehow done you wrong? What?"

Habersham looked to the two men before him and smiled. "It was nothing like that. They were in my way. I wanted to get on the Ohio Supreme Court. If I waited for those fools that are there to retire, I would have been too old to enjoy the position. With them out of the way, I would have been a shoo-in for the post."

"I'm not following," James replied. "Abernathy was that kind of judge, but Salazar wasn't even a judge and Judge wasn't on the Supreme Court."

"Abernathy was my ticket. With him gone, Ross was the most likely candidate. With her out of the way, I could make a move up the ladder so much faster; especially after winning the Boyd gun case."

"What about Salazar? You were already his boss. That doesn't make any sense."

"He's the one who brought in the witness against Boyd. I couldn't just take it away from him. People would think I was greedy. However, with him out of the way, I could take it over and get the credit as well as the attention necessary to jump over any of the other contenders. It was a win/win for me."

"So…it was about you getting a job?" James said in disgust.

"Not just a job," Habersham said. "The Ohio Supreme Court is one of the most coveted in the nation. It would have given me a shot at the United States Supreme Court. There is no higher honor."

"It's still just a damn job," Brandenburg said. He then grabbed the DA's hand and twisted it with such torque that the sound of the breaking wrist sounded like a gun shot. "That's what I think of your deal."

Habersham never heard the remark because he was howling from the pain.

Chapter 57

A hundred yards inside the cavern, a small crevasse appeared on the far side of the large room and Homer instructed Katt to follow it. Another thirty yards further, a second, larger room opened and Katt could tell that this would be the end of the journey. What she didn't know then was whether it would be the end of her life, as well.

Katt saw that the room had already been prepped for whatever it was that Homer had planned. A crate had been placed against the wall by the entrance containing who knew what. Several feet further, the same wall held an old metal ring and chains that looked to be something from the turn of the century—just not this century.

Katt looked back and realized that Homer was pointing his gun at her face. The look in his eyes told volumes of the intentions.

"So is this where you plan to kill me?" Katt asked.

The psychopathic looked held in place for several seconds longer and then the harshness seemed to disappear. Had Katt not seen it with her own eyes, she would have discounted any attempt of someone trying to explain it to her as irrational.

After a moment, Homer smiled and said, "Whether you live or die here tonight will be largely up to you and those expecting to save you. If they follow my directions, there's a better than average chance that you will survive. On the other hand, I have a strong suspicion that they will try to kill me. If I have to go, then so will they—and you."

"I have an idea that might improve your odds," Katt said. "I know that you are hell bent on doing this your way, but would you consider an outsider's opinion? I mean, seriously, what do you have to lose? If you don't like it, then you lost nothing except a few minutes of time. On the other hand, it may actually work out for you."

Homer smiled at Katt again. He knew what she was trying to do. On the other hand, he liked the way she looked. He liked her. Why not enjoy her company a few minutes longer.

"Alright, Agent Katt. You have the floor. Let's hear your plan."

The room was filled with every dignitary of the Dayton Police Department and surrounding county. Doug Martin and Bill Stetson covered everything local while Mike Williamson handled the state. Even the FBI was present. Jonathan Blythe refused to step down. To everyone in the room it was an act of heroism. Only he knew better. *The heroes would have to be found elsewhere,"* he thought.

The only person missing was the district attorney, Jules Habersham. No one had seen him since the group broke up earlier, and he wasn't at his home. His car was there, but the man simply disappeared.

"So who is in charge now?" Williamson asked.

"I am," said Melissa Pound as she walked tentatively into the room. "Until we hear from DA Habersham, I will be covering the negotiations."

Everyone in the room knew who she was and respected her as a tough prosecutor. And given what she had already been through, not one of the men there would argue with her.

"I'm surprised to see you up and around," the Dayton police chief said. "I figured you would be out of commission for a while."

"They grow 'em tough in my family," Pound said. "Has the shooter called back yet?"

"Not yet," Williamson replied. "He's due to call soon. Then maybe we can figure out a way to nail the bastard."

"Our number one priority is the safety of Agent Katt," Blythe said. "We need to get her back alive."

"We don't even know if she's still alive right now," Martin spoke up."

"I understand that," Blythe said. "But we have to assume that she is until we find otherwise."

"Where's your cousin," Williamson asked. "I figured he wouldn't miss this for the world."

"Right now, he's trying to run down some military leads. He said he would catch up on everything later."

Her answer was slightly evasive and a whole lot deceptive. Melissa knew exactly where James was. She also knew where Brandenburg was as well as the DA. They were all at her father's house, and Habersham was tied and gagged and being held at gunpoint until the evening was over. Afterwards, she would deal with the fallout of holding a man hostage. Until then, James and Brandenburg was working diligently at trying to track down the killer known as Homer.

It was at that moment that the phone rang. The room got completely quiet.

Technology, during the last couple of decades, has improved the average person's life. Computers, cell phones, and a myriad of other components have evolved at such a pace as to be mind boggling.

One area that it has also improved is the technology used by law enforcement to track and capture criminals.

As soon as the phone rang, a trace was initiated with the hope of isolating the location where it was coming from.

Of course, there is also a counter culture in the electronic world that works just as hard to prevent the successful tracking. Over ninety percent of the cases, law enforcement won out. The average criminal was not nearly as smart or as sophisticated as the men and women that were tracking them down.

Homer was a part of the less than ten percent group.

Through elaborate technology and no small degree of intelligence on his part, Homer knew that the government would not be able to narrow his location and would have no choice but to follow his instructions to the letter.

"Good evening," a jovial voice stated immediately. "I suspect there is a large contingent listening in."

The group that had gathered was quiet until Blythe spoke up.

"What do you want?" Blythe asked.

"Well that's just plain rude," Homer said, though he didn't seem at all upset. "I would have thought you would've been a little more…gentle when you spoke to me. After all, I am the one holding the cards here."

"My apologies," Blythe said. "As you may know, we are concerned about Agent Katt. So what exactly can we do for you...son?"

"Ahhh! Isn't that sweet...Dad? You have no idea how much I've wanted to hear those words. Maybe, when this is over, we could go on a family outing and say...bond a little. How does that sound?"

Blythe's face was turning crimson as his son mocked him in front of the contingent.

"I think we could do something like that," Blythe said. "Maybe on the weekends I could come for a visit. How would that sound?"

"It sounds like you're prepared to place me someplace where visitation would be at your discretion. How about instead, I come visit you...and place flowers on your tombstone. I will miss you very much."

"Now that we've done our version of the family holiday visit, why don't you tell us how we can resolve this without anyone else getting hurt?"

"It's interesting that you brought that up," Homer said. "You see...I've been having a long conversation with your special agent Katt and she seems to want very little bloodshed as well. You see, I was prepared to have you go to the location where she is and then when you and the rest of the cops and agents went in to get her, I was going to blow you all up.

"However, she figured something out about me that I hadn't figured out on my own. I don't want to kill all of you, Dad. I just want to kill you. I want to see your flesh rotting. The rest of you don't really matter. You were all just a bonus."

"Agent Katt is a very smart woman," Blythe said. "I take it that you have informed her of our relationship."

"As a matter of fact I have. She seems a little put out about the whole father deserting his family thing. I guess it has to do with her parents dying at such an early age and all that."

"I'm surprised she told you. She's pretty careful about that piece of her history."

"Well, Dad, Agent Katt and I have been having a very spirited discussion about a lot of things; like how you wanted to tap that when she was just a little girl."

"Bullshit!" Blythe exploded. "She would never tell you something like that."

"Ha. Ha. Ha," Homer laughed. "Where's you sense of humor, Dad. Of course she wouldn't say that. I just wanted to get a rise out of you. But I can tell that you feel quite strongly about her...in a fatherly sort of way. I guess I'm a little jealous about that part. Maybe I'll have to do something about that too."

"Look, son...leave Agent Katt out of this. I know I've been a lousy father. I know that I've done things that give you every right to be angry with me. But you don't have to hurt anyone else. It's me you want. Tell me where to go and I will meet with you…alone."

"Really? Alone? You won't have any of your other very special agents hanging around somewhere just to take me out?"

"I promise you, there won't be anyone else. I will come alone."

"It's really tempting," Homer said. "Agent Katt told me that I could trust you to do what you said, if it was necessary to save someone else's life. The question is…can I trust her?"

"If there is anyone around here that you can trust, it would be Agent Katt. Now tell me where you want me to go and I will be there…alone. Then we can figure this out together."

"Okay," Homer stated as if just making up his mind. "I'll give you a chance—one last chance to do the right thing. If you fail, if you lie, I will kill you and Katt and then rain destruction on your agency like nothing ever before. You are going down, Dad. The question is…how many more of your people will you lose as well?"

Information was given and then the line went dead. Everyone in the room sat stunned. There was no way they would let one of the top men in the bureau go into the lion's den alone. The only question was; how were they going to save Agent Katt?

Chapter 58

Technology is almost always a good thing. The problem for the police revolved around the fact that they were trying to trace the call by going backwards in hopes of finding its place of origin. The conversation was certainly long enough. Unfortunately, it would not have mattered how long they were on. There was no way the call could be traced.

James and Brandenburg, on the other hand, had a distinct advantage; they knew where the call originated. All they needed was to wait until a call from that number was made. If you know the number, you can trace pretty much anything.

It took the two hunters less than thirty seconds to get a hit on the location and took off immediately. Ten minutes after they left, James' phone rang.

"So where is he sending you guys?" James asked his cousin without preamble.

"He said that Director was to go to Brandenburg's cabin and wait for further instructions. He told us that if anyone other than the director shows up, he will kill the director and Agent Katt and then would later come after various FBI agents just for the sport of it."

James had put the call on speaker and Brandenburg heard the whole story. He didn't respond.

"So what are they going to do?" James asked as they were already heading in that direction.

"The director said that he had no choice, and he was going to do as his son told him. On the other hand, there will be a large contingent of officers and agents flooding the area. They'll be holding back, but they won't let this guy get away."

"Yes they will," Brandenburg stated flatly. "They'll let him get away because he won't be there. He'll kill Blythe and then he'll kill Agent Katt and slip right through their net."

"Well aren't you just a bastion of hope, Mister Brandenburg. Care to tell us how he's going to do that?" Melissa asked.

"Sure," Brandenburg replied. "He's going to do that because he won't be there in the first place…and neither will Agent Katt. Somehow, he's already set things up so that when the director gets to the location, he'll know about it. He'll know about the backup group and he'll use that as an excuse to finish what he's already set out to do. Once the director is dead, he'll go back to Agent Katt and do whatever he has in mind with her and then leave town. He won't follow the plan because he already knows that the FBI won't follow the plan either."

"Then how do we stop him?" Melissa asked. "How do we keep him from killing anyone else?"

"You don't," Brandenburg stated without remorse. "You sacrifice the director. It will keep the body count down to an acceptable number."

"They can't do that, Mister Brandenburg. That would go against everything the bureau believes in."

"It's the only way to keep the number of casualties to an acceptable level. Otherwise, you'll have a bloodbath."

"Can you stop him?" Melissa asked hopefully. "Can you keep him from killing anyone else?"

"Not without time," Brandenburg shrugged to no one. "I *will* kill him. I just don't see how it can be done with the allotted time."

"Can you save Agent Katt?"

"That's where we're going now," James jumped in. "She isn't where Junior said she would be. Hopefully we can get to her while the psycho is busy with Blythe. It's the best we can do."

"So what do you want me to tell the director?" Melissa asked.

"Tell him to keep everyone else out of that building and not to get anyone else killed. It's the least he can do."

The line was quiet for several seconds, then Melissa said, "Be careful, Mickey. Don't get dead."

James smiled and told Melissa to stay as far away as possible. The night had the makings of a very bad time for them all.

Rocky Knob and Mount Ives are located north and west of Ross Lake just off Lick Run Road. If you drive a few miles from the lake, you will enter The Great Seal State Park towards Bunker Hill where the trails to multiple unnamed caverns dotted the local hillsides.

Katt was close to a quarter of a mile deep inside one of those cold dark holes.

Chained to the side of a cave and colder than she ever remembered being, Katt could see nothing except the black confines of her natural prison. She was hungry, tired and had no concept of how long she had been there. But the thing that bothered her most was the sound of things unidentifiable.

She could hear the constant drip, drip, dripping of the water as it continued to build on the already will-formed stalagmites. She could feel a slight breeze and heard a whistling at times when the breeze blew harder than normal. But the other sound—the sound of high pitched squeals—bothered her like nothing she ever feared before.

At first she thought mice were moving about and then decided it would mostly likely be rats. She had been around rats before, and though she didn't like them, she had dealt with them. It was when she heard them moving about above her that she realized that the sound wasn't coming from rats at all.

The sound was being made by bats—and there were a lot of them.

Two hours later, Jonathan Blythe was driving up to the front of Brandenburg's home. The night was as black as any the man had ever seen. Cloud cover blocked all traces of moonlight and stars. However, Blythe was sure that it had more to do with the guilt he felt for allowing his son to take Katt. He was also sure that it had something to do with being, what he believed to be, his last night ever. He was going to die, he presumed, and there was nothing he could do about it.

As he parked the black SUV, Blythe got out and walked cautiously toward the dilapidated porch. The two chairs were still there as always, and the place looked deserted. On the chair closest to the door, a walkie-talkie sat, leaning against the back of the chair. As he reached for it, Blythe heard his son one more time.

"Did you think I wouldn't know about the rest of your team?" Homer asked over the speaker. "Did you think I wouldn't know that they would be watching from a distance?"

"I tried to get them to stand down," Blythe replied into the microphone. "For some reason they think I'm too valuable to risk without a protection detail. They said they would stay as far back as necessary. I told them you would know."

"You've done more than lie to me, father."

"I know, son. I've been a fool and a lousy father. I've regretted my actions for a long time. Unfortunately, by the time I figured it out, it was too late. You were already lost to me."

"That isn't what I'm talking about," Homer said.

"Then what?"

"You've killed Agent Katt."

"No!" Blythe screamed. "Leave her alone. Let her live and kill me instead."

"What makes you think I won't kill you both? What makes you think I haven't already killed her?"

A few seconds later, a shot rang out, and a bullet slammed into Blythe's chest. It hit the man hard enough to throw him back to where his body slammed against the wall of Brandenburg's house. For a few moments, the fallen FBI man saw only the headlight of his SUV. Shortly after that, he saw nothing.

"How well do you know this place?" James asked Brandenburg,

"I know most of the caves around here," Brandenburg replied. I don't think there's a cave within a hundred miles of here that I haven't been in at least three or four times."

"How many are there—cave around here?"

"Dozens. That's why I think he chose this area. Even if the cops had a general idea where to look, I don't think they would find her unless they were just plain lucky."

"So how many of them are we going to have to look in?" James asked. Brandenburg knew by the expression on James' face that the unstated concern was that he didn't want Katt to be dead before *they* were lucky.

"There are two caverns around this GPS location that Katt might be in," Brandenburg said with an air of confidence. "The first one we are going to enter is the one I think she's in."

"Why? How can you be so sure?"

"Back in the mid 1800's, just before the Civil War, some of the slave owners in the North weren't completely in tune with the Union's beliefs as the majority espoused. As a matter of principle, some of the more crafty owners decided to straddle the fence and wait out the results before completely giving up the money makers of the era—their slaves.

"What they did around these parts was to find places, like these caves, and chain the slaves inside them so that they could brag to their friends about their own personal enlightenment while secretly waiting out the war.

"This particular cavern, at one point, housed over fifty slaves at a time. Some of the gear they used back then was discovered as recently as thirty years ago. Chains, old skeletal remains, and other things were found and sent to museums."

"So how does that help us?" James asked. "If it was all removed, it would seem that this place would be left as bare as all the rest."

"You might think so," Brandenburg smiled a knowing smile. "But they never get everything. My guess is that Homer knows what's left and considered it a viable place to hide someone for a long time. Just like those fools way back then."

Chapter 59

It was too dark for Homer to see the blood that must have spurted from the "old man's" chest. A smile crossed his face as he realized that he was finally free at last from the horror that he called his youth.

However, time for reminiscing was over. He had places to go and things to do. Another FBI agent was about to figure out just what it was like to be on the wrong side of Homer's vengeance.

"So exactly what are we going to do here?" James asked as he followed Brandenburg up the incline.

"It's pretty basic," Brandenburg replied. "We go in, we rescue the damsel in distress, I tell her how it was all your idea, and you get to be the hero. She falls madly in love with you and you live happily ever after."

"That's a pretty good plan," James mused for a moment. "Inaccurate, but pretty good."

"Look," Brandenburg said. "I'm not looking for glory or anything like that. Your FBI lady seems like an okay person, and I just want to get her out safe. After that, I plan on going back to my little hole in the wall and have everyone leave me alone."

"Not going to happen," James said and Brandenburg turned to square off. There was a look of expectancy on his face, so James continued. "You're going to have to explain yourself to the locals about what you did to their two deputies you manhandled. As far as they're concerned, you assaulted them and need to pay for that. And even though Homer was the one who's done all the killing around here, they could say that you were a co-conspirator or some bullshit like that in order to make those other things stick pretty hard on you. I don't think they'll let you just ride off into the sunset."

Brandenburg studied the California cop for a moment and then asked, "Why does Agent Katt call you 'Mouse'? I heard her do that, and it seemed sort of weird."

James wasn't expecting the conversation to turn in that direction and Brandenburg didn't wait for an answer. He turned and started climbing the rest of the way to the entrance of the cave.

"When I first met her," James said rushing to catch up, "we…I didn't exactly put my best foot forward," he smiled at the memory. "To be more accurate, I was an ass. I told her that my father named me after Mickey Mantle and went so far as to insult her by telling her that she probably didn't even know who he was." James heard the snort emitted from the man in front. "She decided that she didn't care for my 'attitude' and proceeded to educate me on things about Mantle I didn't even know. She then proceeded to tell me that my father was more than likely a closet Disney fan and started calling me Mouse to emphasize the point. She still does every once in a while. I think she does it just to piss me off."

"Seems to me, we better rescue her before she gets pissed off that we're taking too long. I would hate to have her angry with me."

"You have no idea how difficult she can be," James said.

"I have no intention of finding out."

They reached the entrance and entered without hesitation.

It was the wrong thing to do.

Homer watched the two men enter the small opening and smiled. He hadn't expected them to be able to locate the place so soon and was disappointed that he hadn't had the chance to spend some quality time with Agent Katt.

On the other hand, this particular job was about results and there were a thousand Agent Katt lookalikes where he was heading. One less would not be that much of a disappointment.

He pulled the small electronic device from his pocket and waited. He would at least give James a few minutes to say his goodbyes. Brandenburg, on the other hand, was someone he would miss. People like him were rare and Homer would have loved the opportunity to face off with him one on one.

Katt never liked bats. She wasn't sure if it was because of some childhood trauma, or maybe it was because of an old movie. Whatever it was, she knew they were spawns of the devil—metaphorically—and wanted nothing to do with them.

At first, she thought she was mistaken when she heard the voices. After listening intently for several seconds, she heard them again.

They seemed to be arguing about something, but she couldn't make out the words.

Neither voice sounded like Homer's, but that didn't mean they were friendlies. All it meant was that neither voice belonged to Homer and would be the best chance she had of getting away from the chain that held her captive.

"Hello!" Katt yelled. "I'm back here!"

The voices stopped.

"Hello!" Katt yelled again. "I need help!"

The voices continued to remain muted, and Katt couldn't figure out why. Then she heard the wings of a thousand bats—maybe ten thousand—flying around the room. They were everywhere and coming so close that Katt could feel the wind from their wings.

"Help!" Katt yelled again. The noise from the bats became so loud that she was afraid that the people exploring would never hear her.

"Shut up!" a voice yelled in return.

Katt recognized it immediately. It was Mickey James. She didn't know how he found her, but was grateful he did.

The bats were so close now that Katt felt them clawing at her face as they flew by. She didn't know if they were attacking or not. All she knew for sure was that they seemed to be pissed off.

Katt was too busy covering her face to see the lights James and Brandenburg were carrying. The squeals and flapping wings kept her busy. She turned to face the wall so that only her back would be exposed. Soon the noise receded and then finally disappeared. The place was quiet as a tomb.

James tapped Katt on her back, and Katt jumped as if she had been struck by a charge of electricity.

"Are you out of your frigging mind?" Katt screamed when she turned around to see James. She then threw her arms around his neck.

"I thought you were some kind of hotshot tough FBI agent," James said and then smiled. "You're not looking too proper right now."

"Just shut up, Mouse," Katt said, still trying to get past the bat scare. "I thought those things were going to devour me."

"Not likely," Brandenburg said. Katt hadn't realized that James wasn't alone. "They're Lasiurus cinereus, also known as hoary bats. You should feel special. Not many people actually get to see those magnificent creatures. They're one of the largest bats in North America and don't spend a lot of time around civilization. You're very lucky."

"I don't mean to break up this educational moment," James said. But if we're going to have that happy ending you promised, then we need to get the hell out of here."

It was at that moment that the explosion shook everything around them. Stalactites started falling and crashed near them. James grabbed and started to pull Katt toward the door only to be thwarted by the chain that was still hanging around her ankle. Then the dust and debris poured through the gap that used to be their escape route.

Homer watched the mass exodus of the bats and knew that the couple had finally met. He had been in the cave a number of times and was surprised when he looked at the walls and ceiling as the creatures started to move. There were thousands of them and the killer thought about how it might be if they were the thing that finally killed the agent.

He had hoped that they would be inside when he finally blew the entrance. That way they would have something to feast upon—for a while anyway.

When they left, that dream went away, and Homer decided that it didn't really matter. Agent Katt wasn't going to go anywhere, and that was the whole purpose of the exercise. Kill dear old dad and Katt—the tramp that took the place of his family.

Without preamble or remorse, Homer pushed the button and the cave entrance disappeared.

Chapter 60

James managed to get the antique manacle off of Katt while Brandenburg went to see how bad their situation had gotten. When he returned, his face told the whole story. They were trapped.

"How's that whole fairytale ending coming along?" James asked sarcastically.

"Not as well as I had hoped," Brandenburg replied. "It seems we're going to have to improvise a little if you plan to get back home in one piece."

"I can improvise as well as the next guy," James said. "But, I'm no MacGyver."

"Who?" Brandenburg asked.

"MacGyver," James repeated. "He's the king of repurposing crap. MacGyver for God's sake! Everybody knows who that is."

"Sorry," Brandenburg shrugged his shoulders. "Must've been before my time."

James looked at Katt for support.

"Must have been before my time too," Katt said. She then looked at Brandenburg. "So what do you have in mind?"

"Not much," Brandenburg said. "We walk out. It'll just take a while."

"How do we do that?" James asked.

"There's another entrance to this very cavern about eight miles from here," Brandenburg said casually. "It's the other cave I mentioned earlier. I've never told anyone that they connect. I've sorta kept that to myself."

"How did you figure it out?"

"Thomas Jefferson Dunbar," Brandenburg smiled. "He's an ancestor of the Shawnee chief, Tecumseh who tried to organize the tribes of Ohio in order to war against the settlers who came to overrun the state. He was killed during the War of 1812. The Shawnee were the last of the tribes in Ohio back then.

"Anyway, we've had some fun times exploring these old caverns. Correction...I was exploring. He was just going walkabout. I'm the only person he's ever told the secret to."

"Then I guess we should go for a walk," Katt said and headed toward the far side of the large room.

"Um, Agent Katt," Brandenburg said. "It's this way." He pointed toward the wall she had been chained to and headed that way. We better kill one of the lights to conserve batteries. This is not the place you want to be with dead batteries."

James killed his light, and he and Katt fell into step. It was going to be a long walk.

"Crap!" Katt said louder than necessary.

"Are you alright?" James asked. "Did you hurt yourself?" He was watching the bedraggled agent before him as she limped and hobbled about.

"No, damn it," Katt replied. "I just stepped in a pile of bat crap! I think my shoes are ruined."

Joseph Brandenburg turned to look at the two cops he was leading through the nearly black labyrinth and could not help but wonder how it was that they managed to stay alive as long as they had.

Then again, he also believed that they were the most entertaining couple he had ever met.

"So tell me," Brandenburg said, "why you two haven't been a couple? As much as you yell at each other and finish each other's sentences, you act like an old married couple."

"Bite your tongue," they responded in unison.

"Our relationship issues are none of your business," Katt said alone.

"I don't know," James said. "I think it's a legitimate question. "Why is it that we aren't a real couple?"

"I'm not about to answer that," Katt replied. "It's not the time or the place."

"Hey, I can put my hands over my ears," Brandenburg said. "You two seem to have issues that need to be worked out."

"Let it go," Katt replied gruffly. The truth of the matter was that Katt could see her and James in a relationship. She had even dreamed about that very subject. She just preferred handling personal issues in her own time and manner.

"No," James said. "I think we should have it out right here. Joe, how much further do you think we have to go to get out of here?"

"At least another four or five miles," Brandenburg replied. "At the pace we're going, it'll take the better part of three hours just to get out of the cave, and another hour or two to get back to the car. I'd say the timing couldn't be better."

"There you go," James said. "We have time. We have relative seclusion. What more could you need?"

"What I need is for you to just shut up. Maybe less talking will get us back sooner."

"Nope," Brandenburg said. "Talking won't keep your feet from moving. The trip will be the same."

"You're not helping," Katt said to the smiling marksman.

"So talk to me, Katt," James pleaded. "I, personally, would like to know why you've been ignoring me lately. Just be honest, okay? I'm a big boy. We had something pretty good and then for some reason, you stepped back. If I've done something to upset you or hurt you or anything…just tell me."

The darkness surrounded them as they kept walking over the rough terrain. Katt didn't answer and James wasn't about to plead. The better part of an hour elapsed before anyone said anything else.

"I'm scared," Katt finally said to the darkness.

"Look," James said. "We're perfectly safe here. Our friend up ahead knows where he's going and how to get us out of this place. We'll…"

"No, dummy," Brandenburg jumped in before James could say anything else. "That's not what she means. Damn…it's no wonder you're single. You don't know women for crap."

"Oh," James said. "Sorry. Go on. Please," he said to Katt.

"You know my history," Katt began again. "You know that things have always been me against the world. Throughout my life, the only meaningful relationship I've had is with Jonathan. Now I have a feeling that with what's just gone down, even that's questionable."

"Blythe isn't the problem, Katt," James started.

"You need to learn to shut up, man," Brandenburg said. "Let the lady talk."

Katt smiled at the perceptive man.

"I know Jonathan isn't the problem," Katt continued. "I'm the problem. I've always wanted to have a normal life. I wanted to find the right guy and settle down and do all the things that a couple would do. That's what I wanted.

"But as I grew older, I came to finally understand that the fairytale wasn't in the cards. I'm a federal agent for God's sake. I hunt killers for a living. What man in his right mind would want to be a part of that?"

James started to say something, but decided instead to heed Brandenburg's advice.

"I pretty much gave up on the idea. I created goals for myself. I decided to get into the BAU—Behavior Analysis Unit—and focus all of my energies there. It seemed the right thing to do. Now I can't even get that.

"Anyway, when you came along, I got a glimmer of what could happen. You understood the rigors of my work. You understood that there were times when we would have to be apart, but that would only make the times together that much better. At least that's what I thought."

"So what happened?" James asked. "None of that's changed. I would never put a restriction on your dreams."

"I know that," Katt said after a moment. "That's not it. The problem—my problem—is that I'm afraid that if I love someone, they'll leave me."

"I would…," James started.

"That's not what I mean, damn it! I'm afraid I'll get you killed. Okay? Are you happy? Everybody

I've ever cared for has ended up dead. My parents. I killed my parents! How can anyone ever love a person who killed her parents?"

Brandenburg stopped when he heard what Katt said and waited for Katt and James to work through whatever was going on. He had never heard the story and knew that whatever happened at that moment would mean everything to Katt.

"That's your reason for pulling away?" James asked incredulously. "I knew about that before I started having feelings for you. Damn it…don't you understand? You were a child when that happened. Those assholes put that gun in your hand and forced you to pull the trigger. You've hung on to that for too long, Katt. It wasn't your fault. What happened back then didn't define you. It defined them."

"It defined me too," Katt whispered.

James was about to challenge Katt and try and get her to understand that it didn't matter to him, but he knew that it wouldn't make any difference. Maybe, for the first time, Katt had finally managed to say the words out loud that had been haunting her for her entire life. She needed to work through this problem, James finally realized. For better or worse, He knew that he could not help her.

James decided that maybe he was doing the same thing Katt had done. There, in the darkness, he would tell her his fears.

"Several years ago, I was in love with someone," James started. "At the time, I thought she was the most beautiful woman alive. My whole world revolved around her. Then one morning I was called out to a scene—her scene. She was the victim and I found out in that alley that the future—my future—would never again be the same."

"I'm sorry," Katt said. "I didn't know."

"That's not why I'm telling you," James started, then took a moment to regroup. "I sort of fell after that. I became belligerent and antisocial...for lack of words I became the prick everyone still thinks I am.

"As far as I was concerned, life no longer had any appeal to me. I dove into my work and didn't care if the people around me liked me or not. As a matter of fact, I preferred it if they didn't like me. It relieved me of doing anything nice.

"Anyway, when I met you, I was still, very much, running on the same hatred that I'd had for such a long time. You changed me, Katt. Somehow, you got through all of the crap I was carrying around and showed me that there was still a reason to live—to go on."

"Why are you telling me this, Mouse?" Katt asked.

"I'm telling you because you were just giving me all the reasons we couldn't be together and I'm not going to let you off that easily. I don't know what the future holds for us out there. What I do know is that if you think for a minute that I'm going to just walk away because you think you're damaged goods…then forget it.

"I get it, you're damaged goods. Hell…we all are. But don't you see? People don't love each other for who they are. They love because of the future they perceive…together."

There was a long silence when Brandenburg spoke up.

"Good God…kiss so we can get going."

James and Katt laughed. They didn't kiss, but even with the low light from the flashlight, they looked in each other's eyes with the knowing that maybe someday soon it would happen.

They walked on.

Chapter 61

One month later:

The city of Dayton had managed to get back to normal. It was always the same. Whether tragedy came in the form of a natural disaster or the killings at the hand of a serial killer, once the devastation was over, time healed everything and those that remained among the living were resilient enough to get their lives back in order.

The FBI had given up the search for the long shot specialist known as Homer—Jonathan Blythe, Junior; at least in the Dayton area. They still looked for him in other parts of the world.

A large and nationally publicized wake had been held for Dayton Salazar and the judges who had been killed. Melissa Pound presented the benediction at the funeral. And before he left town, Mickey James, in full dress uniform, walked side by side with his cousin; staying close and grateful that she was still alive and able to do her job. Hundreds of dignitaries and thousands of ordinary citizens attended the ceremonies.

James left soon after to go back to California. He had work to do, and didn't need to stay any longer. Melissa was safe, he promised the general.

However, the real reason for his departure, which fooled no one, was that Katt had been called back to testify against her now departed boss, Jonathan Blythe.

What Homer hadn't known at the time when he shot his father with the intent to kill, was that Blythe had taken the precaution of wearing three vests when he showed up at Brandenburg's rusted out home. One vest could never stop a rifle round, and sometimes two weren't able to either. The risk was huge. If Homer had been close, the Deputy Director, more than likely, would have been shot in the head. Blythe had no protection there.

Blythe was willing to take the risk that Homer wouldn't expose himself by being too close. The assumption was that he would stand back to an almost record level to take that shot. At that distance, and knowing how important killing his father was to the shooter, there would be a better than average chance that he would go for the body. It was his only hope for bringing Katt back alive, and he was willing to exchange his life for hers.

Blythe wanted to resign in grace. He couldn't allow his failings to reflect on the bureau. He also couldn't put Katt through the kind of anguish she would feel if he tried to stay. He had lost everything. His son had taken everything that mattered. He could only pray that, someday, she could forgive him.

Jules Habersham had managed to escape after James and Brandenburg had left him behind to go find Katt. With all of the confusion going on at the general's house, he was given an opportunity and he took it. He managed to stay free for exactly eight days before he was caught trying to cross the Mexican border.

Melissa Pound was appointed the new District Attorney for the city of Dayton. Her first case was to take over the Boyd Manufacturing trial. With the old DA being hunted down and captured for his part in the slayings, she had no choice but to ask for and received a new trial at a much later date. The second case she took on was the trial of her former boss. He had begged for a deal and offered evidence to help his cause. He said that he had information to take down several criminal enterprises. Melissa decided that if her new policy of being tough on crime was going to be of any value or taken seriously, she would need to refuse the extended hand. Doing so was one of the easiest decisions she had ever made.

Secretly, she hoped the bastard would fry for what he tried to do.

Her father agreed.

Two days after he left the country, Homer heard the news that his father had somehow managed to survive. It took him the better part of a week to decide what he wanted to do. His first option was the easiest; do nothing. Let the bastard live. Somehow, the old man had outsmarted him, outfoxed the fox and that should have earned him the right to a reprieve.

Then again, there were other options. He could wait to hear what the bureau was going to do about his father's silence. He could see if the old man was going to get the big boot or maybe even a prison sentence for participating, albeit through omission, in a criminal enterprise.

Then there was another option; the one Homer decided was the only real option he had.

That's why he was resting on a cliff high above the cabin nestled in the woods just off just off Jimeson View Road in Colorado. Approximately halfway between Route 67 and the Mount Deception Peak, Jimeson View Road made a steady climb only to end abruptly in a canyon with no name.

Jonathan Blythe had found the spot almost thirty years earlier and purchased a fifty acre tract of land west of the road. It was his little slice of paradise.

Over the years, Blythe had built a small cabin on the land and then later extended the place to include indoor plumbing, two extra bedrooms and modern utilities. Included in the upgrade were satellite, Wi-Fi and other electronic toys that a former FBI deputy director could use.

However, there were disadvantages to so much seclusion.

First, the area of protection available to the occupant extended out from the structure only about one hundred yards; not nearly far enough for someone like Homer.

Another disadvantage was that a man like Blythe was used to being around people. As much as he enjoyed his solitude, he missed being able to spend time with the people he had come to enjoy and respect.

That was why his daily walks were important. He needed the time to reflect on the man he was and the one he hoped to one day become.

For three days, Homer had watched his father parade like a peacock up and down the trails. It was time for the charade to end.

A quarter of a mile from the cabin, Homer watched as Blythe stomped past the boulder and knew that he would soon be coming back. It was there he waited.

For three days, Homer had been patient. He knew that his father was a man of habit and because of that would die. Homer knew that he could never be free until his father was dead. He heard the steps before actually seeing the man, so he waited.

The time was now.

Homer jump out and smiled as Blythe came around the boulder. The old man's head was covered with a large hood that hid his face to the elements. It didn't matter. Soon Homer would see the shock on his father's face. And then he would gut the man like a fish.

Blythe stopped about fifteen feet in front of his son and looked up. He saw the man before him and smiled.

Homer saw the teeth before he saw the man under the hood, but Joseph Brandenburg didn't make him wait long to see the rest. The tall muscular man knew his opponent and knew that the fight was going to end. One of them would walk away. The other would be lost to the world forever.

"You took your time," Brandenburg said. "I was about tell your daddy that you were too scared to come out and play with the big boys."

"You seem to think we have something to discuss," Homer replied. "I've got no fight with you. I'm here on other business—personal business."

"Well, I disagree," Brandenburg replied. "You killed a cop and left me to take the blame. That's a coward's way. I don't appreciate going to jail for something someone else does."

"No offense, my friend, but that was business. Nothing personal."

"It was all kinds of personal to that man's family. I can't just walk away without telling them that the asshole that killed their husband and father was punished."

"You don't want to do this," Homer said. "You're out of the game. I don't want to kill you, but I really don't mind if I do."

"That's good to know, because right now killing me is the only way you're going to walk away from here."

The two men knew that the time for talking was through. They didn't need anyone to say "go." And they didn't need a bell to ring. One of them was about to die. It was that simple.

Homer lifted his right hand as if to charge with the knife he was holding, but then his left hand raised and exposed a small caliber derringer. With no remorse, Homer fired both shots, striking Brandenburg in the chest.

Brandenburg fell back and hit the ground with a thud. He hadn't been expecting Homer to move so quickly, and the shots surprised him.

Homer wouldn't waste time on such a pathetic opponent. He had work to do and the sooner he completed the job, the sooner he could go back to his comfortable little cottage on the beach.

Homer drew back the knife as if to cut Brandenburg's throat when he felt a powerful fist hit him like nothing before knocking him off the supine man.

Brandenburg moved like lightning and swung around to his feet before Homer could stop him. Now they were even as far as Brandenburg was concerned. The first bullet hit him square in the chest, but it was stopped by the Kevlar he was wearing. The second deflected off of the edge of the vest and hit him in the shoulder. Because of the loss off energy, the bullet didn't go through, but it still hurt like hell.

Homer attacked with a vengeance. He had come too far and for too long to let a *nobody* stop him from getting the revenge he so desperately needed. He would kill the ex-SEAL and then finish what he started with his father. Now was the time.

Brandenburg, however, wasn't like the targets Homer had faced before. There was an intensity about the man that differed from the rest. He was faster and more potent as an adversary than anyone the killer ever knew. It was indeed a battle to the death.

For several minutes, neither man could gain the upper hand. Brandenburg would move and Homer would counter. Then the other would do likewise with similar results.

It wasn't until Homer struck his opponent in the shoulder before he realized that his enemy could be beaten. The pain shot through Brandenburg's shoulder and caused him to pull back. Another hit and Brandenburg went to his knees. The arm attached to that shoulder hung useless by his side.

"You were a fool to think you could beat me," Homer said, smiling. "I've beaten better men than you a dozen times. Oh, you were good in your day, but I was better. I'm still better."

Homer leaped at the defeated Brandenburg and was surprised when the ex-SEAL moved with such a grace that it seemed as if he had never been hurt at all.

In less than a second, Homer went from being the aggressor to being trapped in a choke hold that stopped his ability to breath. He tried kicking and using every move he could think of, but nothing worked. Brandenburg had him and there was no getting loose.

"You were never better than me," Brandenburg whispered in Homer's ear. "They let you go because you were a parasite. You never had anything that would make you what we needed. You thought you were special. Who knows, maybe you could have been. But the truth was, you were only successful because you never had to fight a worthy opponent.

"You killed innocent people, and now you need to know that you're not as good as you thought."

"Don't kill me," Homer pleaded. "I'll stop. You have my word."

"Your word doesn't mean anything. I just wanted to make sure you knew the kind of fear you caused before you died."

"I have money. I can make you a rich man."

Brandenburg pulled from a hidden scabbard a three inch knife and slowly ran the blade across Homer's neck. The blood shot several feet from them and covered the ground. Brandenburg knew that he could have simply broken the man's neck. It just didn't seem like enough.

No one could come back from what he had suffered. No one would miss him either. Even his father knew the outcome and approved. Homer was dead.

It was over.

Epilogue

The night was warm, and the stars were bright as James sat looking out over the American River. His thoughts often drifted to what might have been had things turned out different between him and Katt. There was a longing and a hope of what could happen, but there was also the reality that they were on two different paths. It just wasn't to be.

"Hey, Mickey," James's partner, Lenny Duncan yelled. "Answer your damn phone."

Lenny had finally figured out that the best way to treat James was to be tough and straight. Anything less than that and James would consider you weak.

"Hello," James answered the call. "This is James."

"I know who it is, Mouse," Katt said. "I'm the one who called the number…remember?"

James smiled at the voice. The day was already looking better."

"I didn't think you would be calling," James said. "I hadn't heard from you in a couple of weeks."

"I know," Katt said. "There was a lot going on around here. I also had to finish a case I was working on before I went to Dayton."

"I hope everything worked out okay."

"Everything worked out fine. I got the hearings out of the way. I caught a really bad guy who was doing some really bad things. What more could a girl ask for?"

"I could think of a couple of things," James smiled. His thoughts were elevated to somewhere around the level of the gutter.

"I'm sure you could," Katt laughed. "So tell me Mouse, what're your plans tonight?"

"I don't know; maybe rent a movie or head over to a strip joint. A guy has needs you know?"

"I see," Katt said. "What movie?"

"I don't know. Truthfully, I'll probably just grab a pizza and go home."

"Too bad," Katt said. "I was thinking about a movie myself."

James thought he heard an echo in the phone.

"What movie did you have in mind," James asked. "And please don't say some stupid chick flick."

"Oh, I know you would never go for a chick flick," the echo continued. "Maybe something with Bruce Willis or one of those macho men I'm sure you like."

James turned around and saw the tall blond coming up from behind. Katt continued to speak to the phone.

"If the company's right, I would watch anything."

"Is the company right?" Katt lowered his phone.

"I don't know," James replied, hanging up his own.

James touched Katt's face tenderly. For several long seconds, all he could do was check to make sure it wasn't a dream. He then pulled Katt to him and kissed her full on the mouth. There was no way he would ever let her go again without tasting her and holding the woman he loved.

"The company's perfect," James whispered, and then kissed her again.

Monterey Madness – Mr. One Pocket

I did not guess the "who dun it" until it was revealed by the author.

Castle Grey – A Katt and Mouse Mystery

Not just a book I could not put down but a world that I became involved with. The plot was large in a natural way and much better than anything you could see on T.V.

About the Author

L.C. Wright lives in Carmel Valley, CA with his wife Melissa and their Black Lab, Barney. Born in Ohio, this book was an effort to go home for a long visit and get reacquainted with the region.

The other published work of the author is Monterey Madness – Mr. One Pocket and Castle Grey – A Katt and Mouse Mystery. He has two more books coming out soon: Through the Eyes of Death and Connections – The Devil's Door.

Keep an eye out for their release soon.

Made in the USA
Charleston, SC
23 April 2014